THE MIDNIGHT GROUND

Eric Dontigney

Rampant Loon Press edition published 2019
First Printing: January 2019

Rampant Loon Media LLC
P.O. Box 111
Lake Elmo, MN 55042
USA

This book is a work of fiction. Names, characters, places, and
incidents are products of the author's imagination and are used
fictitiously. Any resemblance to actual events, locales, or persons
living, dead, or undead is entirely coincidental.

ISBN: 978-1-938834-18-9 (ebook edition)
ISBN: 978-1-938834-19-6 (print edition)

Rampant Loon Press and the Rampant Loon colophon are
trademarks of Rampant Loon Media LLC.

To my brother, Troy, for listening to me ramble about my ideas when they're still half-formed.

Chapter 1

IT ALWAYS STARTED WITH SOMETHING STUPID, some seemingly innocuous action that set a ball rolling that I couldn't stop. No, that's not true. I usually could stop the ball, but never soon enough. This time, it was taking up a woman on her offer to dance. I'm one of those rare men who figured out early that, bizarre as it seems to most Y-chromosome bearing members of the species, women like dancing. Ergo, if I wanted women to like me, knowing how to dance was probably a good start. I was right about that, as far as it went.

I was in a tiny, hole-in-the-wall bar that made its home in a flyspeck town. The flyspeck town made its home in a blink-and-you-miss-it county in Tennessee. It was the kind of place where older men tipped their John Deere hats to women and young men drove girls out to the river with a six-pack of beer and a crotch full of hope. It was also the kind of place where the bars were well-stocked with three domestic brands on tap and every kind of country music your sanity could barely tolerate. In other words, it wasn't my kind of place.

Still, I'd been driving for a while, fleeing a disaster I had—depending on who was telling the tale—either created or stopped in Miami. The police seemed to be of the former opinion. There wasn't going to be any evidence, but I hadn't been in a mood to sit around in a jail cell for days while they figured it out. After I almost ran myself off the road for the fourth time, I decided the next town I came to was where I'd call it a night.

I checked into the first motel I saw, which was situated next to the bar. There were any number of conclusions one might draw from that setup, but I chose not to draw them. I dumped my bag in my room and headed for the bar. It was dark and dingy, but with an open section for people to dance. I opened with the universal signal of bartender friendship. I held up a twenty. I found myself immediately served by a thirty-something brunette who was desperately trying to pass herself off as a twenty-something blonde. That probably worked out for her by closing on most nights.

I took a couple of long pulls off the bottle in front of me and did my best not to make eye contact with anyone but the bartender. Eye contact invites conversation and, worse, questions. I wasn't interested in either. The thing I forgot is that a new face at the local watering hole is going to attract attention, whether you want it or not.

"Hey mister, you want to dance?"

I turned on my bar stool and reassessed my prior position on conversation. She was a cute redhead, mostly sober and even age-appropriate for a guy pushing forty. I shrugged, took a sip of beer, and smiled.

"I'm game," I said and hopped off the stool.

Line dancing was the thing there. I had to dig deep and rely on some basic observations to pull it off, but I didn't embarrass myself too badly. My rumpled suit probably looked out of place, but no one seemed to mind. Well, almost no one. The fast dances gave way to slower dances and people coupled off. To my credit, I did try to go back to the bar. The cute redhead wasn't having any of it.

"Where you running off to, cowboy," she said, grabbing my arm and swinging me against her.

"Didn't want to assume anything," I said.

"You're a long way from home, judging by that accent."

I nodded, but didn't answer the implicit question. "Just passing through."

"Too bad. You're a good dancer."

She pressed herself against me in a way that wasn't strictly necessary for slow dancing. That, it seemed, was the straw that broke the camel's back. I felt it, that change in the energy, the way people seemed to move back on instinct, before it happened.

"Get away from my wife!"

He grabbed me by the suit jacket and jerked me away from her. He was strong enough that my feet came off the ground and I found myself rolling away on the floor when he let go. I looked up. He was a big guy, nothing special to look at, but he had an honest face. He'd positioned himself between me and her. The ex, I thought.

The cute redhead started yelling. "Gary! Stop it!"

"Stay out of this, Liz."

I stood up and gave him a level look. "We were just dancing."

"You had your hand on my wife's ass."

I knew it was stupid, but I said it anyway. "I'm pretty sure you meant to say ex-wife."

Something very like physical pain crossed his face and was quickly supplanted by anger. Everyone had backed away and watched with voyeuristic interest. He rushed me and threw a crushing haymaker. I ducked out of the way and sidestepped. He crashed to the floor with an audible thud.

The bartender yelled at us both. "Take it outside!"

Gary lurched to his feet, face red with fury and embarrassment. "You heard the lady."

I rolled my eyes at him. "Spare me. If you've got unfinished business with your ex, leave me out of it. I just came in here for a beer."

"You're going outside to finish this, one way or the other."

Liz put herself between me and him. It was a gutsy move.

"Gary, you have to stop doing this. I'm not your property."

He got a look on his face I recognized. It was the expression my stepfather had gotten right before he knocked my mother around the living room. Gary was going to take his anger out on someone. I stepped up behind Liz.

"I changed my mind, Gary. You want to take this outside? Let's go."

I turned on my heel and made a beeline for the door. I walked fast because I didn't want him on my heels when I hit the night air. I'd seen how that turned out too many times before. He came out the door and a couple of his buddies came out the door with him. It was painfully predictable. I made a big show of taking off my suit coat. Then I took off my tie and my watch. I watched Gary and his buddies working themselves up mentally to hand me the ass-kicking of a lifetime. I regarded them from five feet away as I unbuttoned my shirt and slid it off. I noticed a handful of looky-loos clustered at the bar's door.

I let them take a good, long look. Then I folded my shirt and set it on the ground. "Any time you're ready, boys."

Gary hadn't learned his lesson. He came at me the same way, a brutish charge and a wild swing. I didn't sidestep it this time. I turned into the swing, grabbed his arm and used his own momentum to swing him through the air over my shoulder. I didn't let go of his arm. There was a sickening crunch as his shoulder dislocated and Gary screamed. I danced back a few steps and looked at the other two. One decided to cut his losses and vanished back inside, the watchers parting seamlessly to let him pass. Gary's other friend pulled a wicked-looking hunting knife from a sheath on his belt. Someone in the crowd whipped out a phone and started dialing.

I eyed the knife and gave him a little smile. "You sure about this?"

He closed on me slowly, waving the knife back and forth. I circled around him, staying out of reach. That was the big problem with a knife. If you wanted to use it, you had to get close. Impatience won out and he darted at me. He swung the knife in a wide arc. I leaned out of the way and then kicked him in the stomach. A kick like that hurts, no question, but it also knocks the wind out of you. It's hard to concentrate on a fight when you can't breathe.

He stabbed in my general direction. I slid past the blade and slammed my elbow into his nose. I felt the cartilage give way and blood spurted from his nostrils. His expression went slack for a stunned half-second. Then he dropped the knife and grabbed at his face with both hands. I moved back from him.

I thought about it for a moment. "You can stop now. I didn't want this fight in the first place."

I saw the decision on his face. I was in motion before he took his first step. I doubt he even saw the foot that connected with the side of his head. He probably felt it, though, right before he lost consciousness. By the time I got my shirt, tie, jacket and watch back on, the local cops arrived. Surprise, surprise, they took me into custody.

What did surprise me was when they didn't book me for anything. The sheriff, a heavyset guy with a bushy mustache, invited me into his office. The brass nameplate on his desk read, Jeremy Barnes. Despite looking a bit like a living, breathing cliché, there was a shine of intelligence in his eyes. Or maybe it was experience. The older I get, the less sure I become that there is any difference between those two things.

"Sorry to drag you down here like this, Mr. Hartworth," said Barnes. "I know you didn't start that fight."

"That's true. I didn't."

"Sure seems like you finished it, though."

"Couple of guys come after you in a parking lot, one of them with a hunting knife, you take it seriously. Or you get dead. I took it seriously."

"Can't argue that. Really, I just wanted to get you out of there until everyone went home. Gary has a short fuse. Plus, the ink's barely dry on the divorce papers and he's got a lot of friends. I bring you in here, everybody figures justice gets served. Nobody goes looking for it by themselves."

"That's smart. I'll sleep in one of the cells if it'll help you sell it."

"That's probably a good idea. Idle curiosity, you planning on staying long?"

I weighed the words, trying to decide if he was asking a real question or quietly suggesting I get the hell out of his town. I decided he was just asking. "No. I was just planning on the one night. I imagine I'll stick with that, barring something unexpected."

The sheriff's eyes narrowed, as if he'd read more in my words than I meant to communicate. His mustache moved up and down a few times. "The unexpected happen to you a lot?"

I shrugged. "No more than anyone else. I just notice it more, I think."

He leaned back in his chair, which squeaked quietly, and folded his hands across his stomach. "I expect you do. Mind if I ask what you do for a living?"

That was a deceptively complicated question. "I'm kind of a jack of all trades. I take the work I can get."

It was true, as far as it went. I did my best to avoid outright lies. Vague truths lend themselves to whatever specifics you want to give later. Outright lies, you have to remember verbatim. Who has the memory for that? Barnes regarded me impassively. I couldn't shake the feeling that I was, in some inexplicable way, telling him a lot more than I intended. It was possible that he just made everyone feel that way. It'd be a useful trait in law enforcement.

"You're pretty cagey, Mr. Hartworth. If I ran you through the system, would I find something interesting?"

"Probably."

There was no point lying. Either he'd already run my name and knew the answer, or he'd gotten a bead on me. I didn't see the point in aggravating the man after he did me a good turn by not booking me.

"Care to share?"

I hemmed and hawed for a minute. "Not really. Chalk it up to unexpected things. Sometimes those unexpected things got a little more exciting than I would have cared for."

"Exciting. Exciting enough for the police to take an interest?"

"I can't control what the police take an interest in. I don't go looking for trouble, though, if that's what you're worried about."

Barnes idly scratched his chin. "You remind me of a guy I knew a long time ago. He was a real quiet guy. Always tried to mind his own business. Couldn't seem to go outside without falling sideways into some kind of strangeness or another."

"That's a hard kind of luck to have."

"It was a hard kind of luck for him. He never talked much about it. It was all in his eyes, though. He'd seen some things. You've got that look in your eyes."

I half-nodded. "Yeah, I've seen some things."

"Hope it works out better for you than it did for him."

I took the bait. "How did it work out for him?"

"He ate a bullet. "

I moved my head a little to acknowledge the words. "I'm sorry for your loss."

"Mr. Hartworth," the sheriff started, before the words seemed to die on his lips.

"Yes?"

"Look, this isn't a big city and I'm not looking for things to get exciting in my town. If you get the feeling things are headed that way, I'd take it as a kindness if you'd move on."

I nodded. "Like I said, I'm just planning on the one night."

The sheriff got up from behind his desk and gave me a half-smile. "Let me show you to your room."

I followed him out and he swung open a cell door. I stepped in, half-expecting him to close it behind me, but he didn't. He pulled open a file cabinet drawer and tossed me a pillow. It was thick and soft. I raised an eyebrow at him.

"I end up sleeping here sometimes," he said with a shrug.

I stretched out on the cot in the cell. As jail cots went, it wasn't even that uncomfortable. I fell asleep in seconds.

Chapter 2

I WAS STRETCHED OUT ON A BEACH, with an arm tossed over my eyes. I listened to waves crashing on the shoreline and tried to decide if I needed a beer or a mixed drink. Both seemed like a lot of effort, so I just continued to lie there. A minute or two later, I felt someone watching me. I slid my arm away and looked up. Marcy stood there in a very tiny bikini, her dark, wavy hair blowing in the ocean breeze. She gave me a bemused look.

"The beach, again?" I asked.

She grinned. "I like the beach, and *you* like the bikini."

"I can't argue that."

"You do realize you're checking out a dead woman's tits, right?"

I shrugged, as much as one can shrug while lying on a beach, and said, "You look alive enough to me."

Marcy sat down next to me and looked out over the water. I wondered how much of the beach scene was her construction and how much of it was mine. I decided it must have been mostly hers. I'd have picked a nude beach.

"How have you been?" I asked.

"The same. Still dead, for now anyways."

"It's been a long time. Shouldn't you have reincarnated or something?"

"Has it been a long time?"

"Fifteen years, give or take," I said.

"Strange. You don't notice time the same way when you're dead. I guess you do look older. I'm sure I'll reincarnate or turn into a real angel or something, sooner or later. Are you saying you're bored with me?"

"Not at all. Just curious."

She turned and gave me concerned look. "You should leave first thing in the morning. Don't even stop for gas. Just go."

"Why?"

She struggled for a moment, as if she couldn't quite formulate the idea, and then she shook her head. "It's one of *those* things. Just trust me, okay."

Those things, things the dead knew but couldn't communicate, had saved my life more than once. I'd learned the hard way to trust Marcy about them.

"Okay," I said.

She smiled, reached over and pushed my hair back off my forehead. I knew without any apparent sign that the dream would end soon.

Marcy gave me a look and then rolled her eyes. "You want to cop a feel, don't you?"

"Since you're here…"

"Adrian Hartworth, show some respect for the dead!"

I put on my serious face, "I will totally respect you in the morning."

She snickered and then pulled off the bikini top. I took advantage of the moment. As the dream lost cohesion, the last thing I remembered was her hand landing in my lap.

"Fair is fair," she said.

"Hey, sunshine, time to get up," someone said.

I cracked my eyes and turned toward the voice. I blinked a few times and the room came into focus. There was a split-second when I couldn't remember where I was, or why, and then it came back to me. The cell door was still open and a uniformed woman stood there. I sat up and rubbed my eyes, trying to clear the cobwebs away.

"Morning," I mumbled.

"You hungry?"

I stood and walked toward the open cell door. The woman stepped aside and her eyes followed me with curiosity, but no ill intent. She was tall, almost as tall as I was. Her hair was straight, brown and cropped short, with some gray creeping in here and there. She was thickset, but not fat, just solid. Crow's feet created complicated webbing around her eyes.

"I could eat," I said. "Bathroom?"

She pointed at an unmarked door. I went in, splashed a little cold water on my face, and took a long piss. Images of the fight intruded on me. I felt a moment or two of guilt. I'd been tired and angry. I'd hurt that Gary guy more than I needed to hurt him. Then again, on balance, I'd hurt the guy who pulled the knife less than he deserved. I dubbed it a moral wash and went back out into the station.

The thickset deputy was sitting behind a desk, flipping through some paperwork. She pointed to a table and I saw bagels and a pot of coffee.

"Coffee, thank God," I said.

She gave me the knowing smile of someone who found a morning without coffee a sure recipe for a crappy day. I filled a Styrofoam cup and dumped half a dozen tiny packets of sugar into it. I spotted a mug by the pot labeled "Deputy." I picked it up and waved it in the woman's general direction. She gave me a little nod.

"I take it black," she said.

I filled the mug and took it over to her. She accepted it and gave me the once over.

"Sheriff said you had a little dust up last night. Heard Tucker Smith pulled a knife on you?"

"Yeah," I said. "It happens. Deputy?"

"Deputy Michelson. You can just call me Patty, everyone does."

I sincerely doubted that *everyone* called her that, but I rolled with it. "Okay, Patty."

"You want to file charges? Technically, it's assault with a deadly weapon, even if you did give him a much-deserved kick in the head."

"It was a bar fight. People do dumb shit during bar fights. If I press charges, I have to stick around or come back. I'm just passing through."

Patty looked disappointed, but she nodded. "Fair enough. I still need a formal statement from you, just so we have it."

"Understood."

I polished off my coffee, had a second cup, and then Patty took my statement. She looked it over, compared it with some other statements, and then nodded.

"It jives with what the witnesses said. I don't know what the hell Gary was thinking. Sure sounds like you knew what you were doing. You an ex-soldier?"

"I grew up in a rough neighborhood. I learned how to take care of myself."

It was true-ish. The neighborhood wasn't really that rough, but the people I ran with back in the day were very damn rough, and very dark, and very stupid. It had cost them everything. It hadn't cost me the way it cost them, but it cost me enough. Little things, like my identity, and my family, and any hope of a normal life. I went back, every once in a while, and drove past my childhood home. It was still tidy, with the fence scrupulously repainted every spring, and my father still drove an old Ford pickup, though not the one I remembered.

My three sisters were scattered across the country. My older sister, Kelly, was married and living in Seattle with a couple kids of her own. My younger sister, Emma, was running her own graphic design firm in Austin. My youngest sister, Laura, was off the grid somewhere. At least, she thought she was. I knew where she was and who she was with. I also knew that one day, in the not too distant future, I'd bring that dysfunctional situation to an abrupt end. I frowned at the thought of Laura and then pushed it aside. The time wasn't right, not yet.

"Penny for your thoughts," said Patty.

"I was just wondering if there's a cab company around here I can call? You know, take me back to the motel. I figured I'd get while the getting is good."

"I can give you a ride," she said. "If anything really bad happens, people know to call my cell phone directly."

"Appreciated."

We went outside and Patty locked the door behind her. I looked around. The sheriff's office was on the main drag through town, by all appearances. There wasn't a lot to be seen, really, just a handful of small shops that would have been put out of business if any big box stores were closer. Still, it looked like they took care of things. There was none of the casual litter you see in cities and larger towns. There were plenty of trucks and well-worn SUVs. It struck me as the kind of place that, come February or so, people actually needed those kinds of vehicles.

Patty walked me over to a white and brown sedan with a light strip on the roof and the word "Sheriff" airbrushed across the doors. She thought for a second and then cleared off the passenger seat in the front. I raised an eyebrow at her.

"Far as I can tell, you were the victim. No need to make you ride in back."

"Works for me."

Patty drove slowly through the town. It was probably the same speed she used on patrol. She pointed out a large, surprisingly ornate, brick building.

"Believe it or not, that's the high school. Used to be a church of some kind, back around the turn of the last century, but it didn't last. They donated it to the city when the church closed up shop for good."

"You go to school there?"

"Me? No, I moved here for the job. Sheriff did, though. Says the place creeps him out."

I eyed the building again and wondered what kind of church it had been. It wasn't Catholic. The architecture was all wrong, more Byzantine than Gothic, with lots of arches and a dome.

"Guess it is a bit foreboding, at that."

Patty gave me a sharp look and said, "Foreboding?"

"A feeling of impending doom."

"I know, just surprised you said it. Not a word you hear much anymore."

"Ah. I read a lot of old books."

Patty nodded and we passed the rest of the drive in amiable silence. I knew something was wrong as soon as we pulled into the motel parking lot. It was subtle things, like every window in my car being broken out and all four tires being flat. I sighed. Patty parked and we got out. I didn't get too close. If there was evidence, I didn't want to disturb it. The deputy did a wide circuit around the vehicle and then gave me a pinched expression.

"Seems you're a bit late for getting while the getting was good."

"Yeah," I muttered, "seems like."

Chapter 3

IT TOOK A MINUTE, but the shock of seeing my car's undrivable state wore off. Tension bloomed in my shoulders as the frustration took hold, building slowly to genuine anger. It wasn't the car itself, I had no attachment to it, but goal-blocking pissed me off. Best case scenario, I was stuck for a lot longer than I wanted to be stuck somewhere. I forced myself to stop grinding my teeth and spoke as rationally as I could to the deputy.

"I don't suppose there's a bus coming through this morning or an airport nearby?"

Patty gave me a look of bland sympathy. "Bus only comes through once a week, a few days from now. Nearest airport is fifty miles away."

"Used car dealership?"

Patty looked away, almost sheepish. "Yeah, we've got one of those, but I don't think you want to go there."

"Why's that?"

"You sent the owner to the hospital last night with a dislocated shoulder."

"Fucking hell. I don't suppose you know someone who's looking to get rid of a car cheap?"

"There's probably someone in town looking to sell, but I can't think of anyone with a car I'd trust to get you more than ten miles."

The pressure was building behind my eyes in preparation for the enormous headache I knew was coming. "I'm in hell."

Marcy's warning to get out was fresh in my head. I wanted to get gone. "Patty, if you can find me a car that will get me as far as that airport, there's a hundred bucks in it for you."

Patty adopted what I thought of as standard-issue police suspicion. "You seem to be in an awful big hurry to get out of here. You running from something?"

I pointed at the car. "You're damn skippy! I'm running from whoever was short-sighted enough to do that to a car in a public parking lot. I don't want to be here if they decide to do an encore on my body."

The suspicion faded. "That's fair. I need to take a report, but then I'll see about tracking you down a car."

"I appreciate it."

Patty pulled a camera out of the cruiser and took lots of pictures. Then she popped the trunk with a gloved hand and let me retrieve a few odds and ends I'd left in there. I retrieved my belongings from my room, mostly an overnight bag and a long, hard case. If I'd been in a real hurry, I'd have left the overnight bag. I checked out and dumped my stuff in the back seat of the cruiser. Patty eyed the hard case, but didn't ask any questions. I'd been on the receiving end of two crimes in less than twenty-four hours in her little town. Odds were good that she'd decided too much curiosity about my belongings meant more trouble than it was worth. She'd have won that bet.

We drove back to the Sherriff's office and I drank slightly burned coffee while Patty filled out a report. It was short, since I'd been sleeping in the sheriff's office all night. I certainly hadn't heard anything. She spared me the normal questions police might ask in that scenario. The suspects were obvious, but unlikely. Unless that tool, Tucker Smith, got released from the hospital and paid a visit to my car before sense kicked in. I didn't really care who did it, as long as I could leave and do so quickly.

Patty looked up from the paperwork. "What about your car?"

"Sell it. Junk it. See if a mechanic can fix it," I offered with shrug. "I'll leave a contact number and sort the details out later."

"Are you rich, Mr. Hartworth?"

"Not particularly."

"You really want to get out of this town, don't you?"

"Very much so."

"I'll make some calls. See about getting you that car. How much can you afford on short notice?"

I had a few grand, but I didn't want to advertise that fact. "Let's say eight hundred."

I waited while Patty called around, waking some people, cajoling others, and then negotiating down one recalcitrant soul. I tuned out the details and watched the street below coming to life. A little diner slowly filled with the early morning crowd of senior citizens and the working class. I checked the clock and was surprised to find it was only a little after seven in the morning. How early had Patty woken me? Lights flickered on inside the shops as people got ready for what I expected were probably fairly slow days. A couple school buses rumbled by, no doubt to fetch farm kids and the poverty stricken out on the edges of the township. At least, that was how it always seemed to work in small towns.

"Okay," said Patty. "I think I found you one that the owner will part with for seven hundred, if you bring it in cash, inside the next twenty minutes."

"Not a problem."

The car's owner was a pear-shaped man named Eddie Brubaker. He wore black, horn-rimmed glasses and an unfortunate goatee. By the look on his face, he was still half-asleep when Patty and I showed up on his doorstep. He had managed to put on slacks and a pair of beat up tennis shoes, but apparently lost concentration at that point. A maroon bathrobe hung open to reveal a t-shirt that read "Join the nerd side. We have Pi!" He blinked at us blearily and then stepped out onto the porch. He made it down the steps before turning around, walking back up the steps, and closing the door.

"Sorry," he grunted. "Early."

He led us to a cramped, two-car garage and opened it up. Inside there was a new Taurus to the right. To the left was a much-abused, or possibly well-loved, mid-nineties Neon. The unkind shade of green paint was mottled and chipped on the hood and the tires looked well beyond their expiration date. Eddie jangled a set of keys at me. I took the keys, unlocked the car and climbed in. It smelled like ancient fast food and cheap pine air freshener. Still, it started on the first try. I rolled down the window.

"Mind if I take it down the block?"

Eddie waved a hand at me and went back to looking half asleep. I took the car on a brief test drive. I could tell it had problems, but none of them were catastrophic. More importantly, none of them were things that needed the immediate attention of a mechanic. It was good enough to get me to an airport or train station, which was all I needed. I drove back up the driveway. Eddie gave me a semi-expectant look before issuing forth with a jaw-creaking yawn.

He gave a second small yawn and then looked at me again. "What do you think?"

"I'll take it."

I took some money out of my pocket, counted it out onto the hood and then handed him the bundle.

He stared at the cold, hard cash in my hand without comprehension, and then jerked back to reality. "I'll get you the title."

"Hey Eddie, this thing still insured?"

"Yeah. Why?"

"There's an extra hundred in it for you if you leave the insurance on it for another week. I'd like to leave now, but…"

"But the insurance people won't insure it until you get the paperwork settled. Hell, for a hundred bucks, I'll leave it on for another two weeks."

I handed him the extra money and he vanished into the house.

"You know," said Patty, "that isn't strictly legal."

"I know, but it's not like I'm planning on doing anything stupid with it. Hell, I'm probably only going to drive it fifty miles."

Patty raised an eyebrow, but let that one hang in the air. While he was inside, I unloaded my stuff from the police cruiser and dumped it into the back seat of the Neon. I walked back over to Patty and forked over a hundred.

She pocketed the cash and then shook her head. "I didn't think you were serious."

"I said I would," I offered with a shrug.

"People say lots of things."

"True."

Eddie came back with the title and signed the car over. He gave the vehicle a wistful look and then shook his head. "Had a lot of fun in that car. I drove clear to the Pacific Ocean and back in her. The lock sticks on the passenger door. You'll have to jiggle the key a little when you turn it."

"Good to know. I appreciate you getting up to sell it to me."

Eddie rolled his eyes. "When Deputy Michelson says jump, you jump."

"Good lord, Eddie, you can call me Patty."

The words seemed to pass straight through the consciousness of Eddie Brubaker. "I need to get ready for work, so I'll leave you to it. Mr. Hartworth, nice doing business with you. You'll need to mail me the plates when you get where you're going. Deputy Michelson, tell the sheriff I said hello."

"Patty," muttered the deputy, as if she could make the name stick through sheer repetition.

I gave her a wry smile. "As much fun as my stay here has been, I think I'm about ready to take my leave of small town America. You can leave me a message at that number once things calm down. I'll get things sorted out with that car."

That car, I mused. Not my car anymore, just that car. I thought there must be an object lesson in it about the impermanence of all things or the futility of concepts of ownership, but mostly it just made me realize that I didn't care that much about stuff. It also made me realize that, given the opportunity, I'd cheerfully punch whoever did it in the face because they made my exit so much more difficult. Stuff was just stuff. Time was irreplaceable.

The deputy nodded. "I'll do that. You remember how to get out of here?"

"I think I'll be okay. I've got a pretty good sense of direction."

"It's been, well, interesting to meet you, Mr. Hartworth. I hope your next stop is less trouble than this one has been."

"Me too."

I climbed into the Neon and headed back to Main Street. I followed the road west toward the edge of town. I stopped for gas on pure reflex.

Chapter 4

THE SMALL CONCENTRATION OF CIVILIZATION soon gave way to open countryside spotted with occasional houses. I blew past a white, two-story place that teetered between nice and unkempt, but something in my subconscious registered the thing that didn't fit. I glanced into the rearview mirror, then pulled to the side of the road and looked back over my shoulder.

I slammed my hand against the steering wheel. "Damn it. Damn it. Damn it!"

I seriously considered pulling back onto the road and going my way. It wasn't my problem. Someone else was bound to drive by before long. I rationalized my intentions for a good twenty seconds before I noticed that I'd already turned the car around and was racing back toward the house. I'd seen smoke pouring off the back of the building. The old station wagon parked out front told me that someone was probably inside. The absence of anything like sirens, fire trucks, and panicking people in the front yard suggested the person inside either didn't know or was already incapacitated. I pulled into the driveway way too fast and had to slam on the brakes to avoid rear-ending the station wagon.

The yard needed a good lawn-mowing, so the faded green hose that sent me sprawling wasn't obvious to the unobservant eye. I stood back up, ignored the pain in my hands and knees, and took the porch steps two at a time. I slammed my fist against the door.

"Hello! Is anyone home?"

I waited a full second before I repeated the process. Then I waited a full two seconds, possibly even three, before I tried to peer through the porch window. There were gauzy curtains, but I could see that smoke was already building up on the ground floor. I also saw a staircase with an old man sprawled on it, as if he'd been trying to make his way up to the second floor. I went back to the door, drew my leg back and then thought better of it. I reached out and gingerly touched the knob. It wasn't hot. I turned it and the door swung open. Small towns, I thought.

Smoke rolled out the door and the sheer noise of the fire buffeted me. I dragged my shirt up over my mouth and nose before I pushed through the smoke. Even while I focused on getting to the old man, my brain made of note of useless details. Antique chair, Arts & Crafts era. Reproduction Federal game table. Shaker cabinet, possibly original. I wondered if the guy was an antiques dealer, but I shoved the idea aside in favor of trying to get him on his feet. He was barely conscious, which made it a lot harder.

He was taller than I was and even a thin, tall man weighs a lot when he can't help you move that mass. I all but dragged him out of the house and was wheezing by the time we got into the clean air outside. I pulled him a good twenty feet away, almost to the road, before I nearly toppled us both under a big oak. I hacked and choked for a while before I felt his hand on my arm. I looked at the old man. He was out of focus and the sounds he made were more garble than words.

I leaned in closer. "What?"

"Abby," he gasped.

I looked back at the house in horror. Someone was still in there.

"Where?" I demanded.

He lifted a trembling hand and pointed at the second floor. Of course, I thought. I stood back up, swayed on my feet briefly, and then started back toward the house. I wished I hadn't left my cell phone in Miami. Or that I'd gotten another one along the way. I'd have called for help. I stopped short of the porch. I could feel the heat pouring off the building. I'd be no good to anyone if I passed out in there. I briefly considered using the hose to douse myself in water, until sanity kicked in and told me I'd be steamed to death. There was no good solution. I'd just have to make do. I took a half-dozen deep breaths and pulled my shirt over my face again.

I had another moment of hesitation. I'd already saved the old man. It was more than most people would have done in that situation. I looked back at the prone figure of the old man. *Abby better not be your cat*, I thought at him. I bolted back into the house and went up the stairs as fast as sanity and my legs would let me. On the ground floor, the smoke had been an irritant. On the second floor, it was all but impenetrable. It was also hot enough that it was going to get dangerous to breathe before long.

I guessed and went right, feeling for doors and knobs. I'd guessed wrong. By the time I'd gone five feet, it was clear that the room was on fire behind the closed door. I turned and went back, fighting the overwhelming urge to cough and an equally overwhelming urge to flee. Only someone suicidal or paid for it willingly goes into a burning building. I squinted through the burning and tears in my eyes. I knew I hadn't been in the building more than a couple minutes, but that smoky darkness made it feel like an eternity before I found a door off to the left.

I crouched down to where the smoke was theoretically less dense and opened the door. I shuffled into the room and tried to ignore the crackling and popping behind me. I felt along the floor, looking for a bed, or a body, and my hand landed in something wet and a little tacky. I went still, then moved my hand forward. I felt a tangle of hair and a cheek. It was all I could do not to just grab the hair and yank.

My shirt wasn't offering much protection from the super-heated air and smoke. I couldn't shake the feeling that if I started to cough, I wouldn't be able to stop. If that happened, the building would come down around me in burning chunks while I hacked and coughed and wheezed my way into a searing, agonizing oblivion. I forced myself to slow down, to feel around for a neck, and then for a pulse. It was there, weak, irregular, but there. Something was off, though. The head and neck were at a strange angle.

I reached out blindly and felt a thin leg suspended in the air. I traced it back to a sheet. I coughed and felt another building. I couldn't fight the panic anymore. I grabbed the sheet and hauled on it with terror-fueled strength. It offered fractional resistance and then came free from whatever held it in place. I hated to do it, but I turned over the body I assumed was Abby. I had a feeling she'd fallen out of bed and banged her head because of that sheet. Her neck could be broken for all I knew, but we'd both die for sure if I didn't get us out.

I took off my suit jacket and draped it over her face and chest. It was the only protection I could give her. I picked her up and stumbled back toward what I thought was the door. I felt around with my foot at each step, while a big part of my mind was screaming for me to run. Each second lost was one second closer to death. I lost more precious seconds when I started coughing again—deep, painful coughs that threatened to send me to the floor.

Something crashed to the floor behind me. A second later, the generalized heat transitioned into a wailing, stabbing spot of pure agony in my lower back. I sucked in a breath without any conscious decision and after that, everything became a nightmarish blur of heat, blindness, coughing and stumbling confusion. When the world started to make sense again, I was outside. I was beyond tired and the thing in my arms weighed a thousand pounds. A tiny spark of rationality screamed at me. *Don't drop it!* I staggered the last few feet toward a prone figure I could barely make out with my stinging, tear-filled eyes. I sank to my knees and the thing in my arms slid to the ground. I started crawling away. My smoke and heat-baked lungs made me cough until I stopped to vomit. Then, I crawled some more.

My hand landed against something rough and solid. I turned my back toward it and let it support my weight. I thought I might puke again, but that was when I passed out.

I dreamed in blurry, disconnected patches. I was back in Miami. Tony Damelus, the city's self-styled high priest of dark Vodou, was chanting a spell to kill me. I was in Seattle, and trying to convince Marcy not to go to work that day. I'd had a premonition. I was hiding from my life in the mountains of New Mexico, and accidentally getting an education in Pueblo religion. They invited me into a kiva for a ceremony and swore me to secrecy. I crossed into Canada under false pretenses and a false name. Friends of mine believed there was a wendigo.

"Jesus Christ!" someone yelled.

I opened my eyes and squinted. A fireman stood a few feet away with an oxygen mask in his hand. I reached up to rub at my eyes.

"Hey mister," said the fireman. "Mind calming your cat down? I need to give you some oxygen."

I wondered if oxygen deprivation gave me brain damage. Cat?

"Wha," I murmured and then I felt something moving on my legs.

I looked down and saw a cat standing on my thighs. Its ears were laid back against its head and it was crouched, as if it might attack. At motion and noise from me, it looked back and its ears popped up. The cat was dark gray and, even through my bleary vision, I could see it was missing part of an ear. It made a noise at me that sounded questioning. I reached a hand out and rubbed the cat behind its ears. It started to purr and then curled up on my lap. The fireman stepped toward me. The cat gave him a dark look, but didn't get up.

He gave me a thumbs up. "Thanks. Never seen a cat do that before. Must really like you."

"Not mine," I wheezed.

"Weird," said the fireman.

He put the oxygen mask over my mouth and nose and instructed me to take slow, deep breaths. I closed my eyes and leaned my head, which hurt in nine different ways, against the tree. I did as I was told and took slow, deep breaths. This, I discovered, led to a series of nasty coughing fits. One of them was bad enough that the cat looked up at me and, once again, made a noise at me.

"Mrow?"

I reached out and stroked the cat's head some more, which seemed to satisfy my feline protector. On the periphery of my consciousness, I was aware of people moving around. Vehicles came and went like extras on a movie set. I ignored them. I was so damned tired. The oxygen started to clear my head after a few minutes. I pushed aside the nightmare of the fire. There had been an old man and a woman. I opened my eyes and flagged down the first uniformed person whose attention I could get. It was a burly guy in his late twenties who looked like he could bench press a bus.

"You okay, mister?"

"Yeah," I croaked. "The old man, the woman. They make it?"

He squatted down next to me and gave me a serious look that I didn't much care for. "They're pretty sure Old Man Simmons will make it. His granddaughter was touch and go when they took her out of here."

"Granddaughter?"

"You didn't know? Who'd you think she was?"

I shook my head and shrugged my shoulders. I took a few more deep breaths and pulled the mask away. "Old man said Abby. Thought it was," deep breath, "his wife. Couldn't see."

"Mr. Hartworth, I thought you were leaving town this morning," said a voice I recognized.

I looked up at Patty with eyes I was certain were bloodshot. Then I rolled them. I pulled the mask away from my face. "Tried."

She shook her head and looked down at my legs. "I'll be damned. That cat hates everyone."

The cat demonstrated its interest in the goings on with an enormous yawn. Then it put its head down and went to sleep. I had a quiet few minutes while I soaked up oxygen. I wondered if the cat was depositing fleas all over me. Patty and a paramedic came over.

"Okay, Mr. Hartworth, time to clear you out of here," said the paramedic.

I nodded and tried to set the cat on the ground. The cat gave me the death glare of a lifetime and stepped, with a somewhat unnerving amount of purpose, right back up onto my legs. The cat sat down and all but dared me to try that stunt again. I frowned and settled on picking the cat up and setting it in the crook of one arm. That seemed to pass muster, so I held a hand out to the paramedic, who pulled me to my feet. I took a sharp breath as the pain in my back sent signal flares to my brain.

I heard a muffled curse behind me. "Dammit, Hartworth. Bill, he's burned too."

If I'd just had me to worry about, I might have passed out again. I was worried I might crush the cat beneath me, so I settled for slumping to my knees and swaying. I heard some yelling in the background and the word ambulance. After that, things got hazy again.

Chapter 5

THERE IS NOTHING GOOD ABOUT WAKING UP IN A HOSPITAL BED. To start with, there is almost always a TV turned on somewhere in the room. By itself, that annoys me. In a hospital, though, that TV is inevitably tuned either to a rerun of a show you didn't like the first time or a cable news channel you despise. Apparently, the wheel of pain came up News Channel that time and I was regaled to a paranoid screed about the socialist agenda of everyone more liberal than Cotton Mather. I started looking for something heavy to throw at the TV after ninety seconds. I came up empty.

I gave the cloth divider that separated me from my roommate a baleful stare. "Could you at least mute that television, please?"

There was a rustle and something that might have been a word, or a bodily function, but the TV went silent.

"Thanks," I said.

There was an unpleasant pressure on the side of my face and I reached up to figure out what it was. My hand met a mask that I could only assume I'd displaced with some movement in my sleep. I put it back over my mouth and nose. The high purity oxygen made me groggy and I drifted off. When I came around again, I'd been pushed over onto my side and someone was doing something painful to my back.

"Christ," I muttered.

"You're awake," said a woman.

I looked over my shoulder at the nurse. She looked at me over a pair of half-rimmed glasses. There was an air of crisp efficiency to her, from her hair in a bun to her motions.

I pulled the mask away from my face. "Stabbing pain has that effect."

She tutted at me in annoyance. "It's not the worst you've had, judging by your back."

"I'm clumsy."

"You're a liar. I worked in Detroit for fifteen years before I moved here. I know what bullet and knife scars look like. You in law enforcement? Some kind of private security? Career criminal?"

"Just unlucky."

"No kidding. Put that mask back on. I'll be done here shortly."

I did as I was told. In medical care, you ignored nurses at your own peril. She did some more painful things to my back for a minute and then put a fresh bandage over what, I finally remembered, was a burn. That would probably leave another interesting scar for some nurse to wonder about some day, I thought.

"Alright, Mr. Hartworth, you can roll onto your back if you can stand it. Really, though, you should lay on your stomach."

I rolled onto my back and gave her a defiant look. It wasn't the worst I'd been through. I risked her ire and pulled the mask away from my face again.

"What's the prognosis?"

"Doctor Sumner will be in to talk to you about that shortly, but barring complications from smoke inhalation or an infection of the burn, I expect you'll live."

"Awesome," I said.

She frowned down at me. "They think that Paul and Abby are both going to make it. They were lucky you were there."

"I'm glad they'll be okay."

"Put your mask back on," she said without conviction. "I think that girl is cursed sometimes. Both parents dead. Grandmother died a few years later. Then she turns up with cancer and now this. It's not right."

I didn't say anything. She wasn't really talking to me. She was unburdening herself on a stranger she expected would be gone soon. It happened to me more often than I cared to think about. What she told me was still food for thought. Some families were just unlucky with no outside interference, but it always made me curious. Maybe she really was cursed. Back in the day, old country witches, warlocks, and gypsies didn't screw around. They knew how to lay down absolutely vicious curses that carried for centuries.

"I suppose it's not right," I agreed, after she went silent but didn't leave.

"I'm sorry. Thinking out loud. Old age is getting me, I think."

I snorted and put my mask back on before she told me to do it, again. The corner of her mouth quirked up a little and she left the room with purposeful, efficient steps. I dozed for a bit before the doctor came in to talk to me. The visit mostly consisted of him telling me they were keeping me for a few days of observation. Smoke inhalation was tricky business and they didn't want to take chances with such a hero. I did my best not to gag. Hero, my scarred white ass. I'd figured out early on that most heroism was stupidity that you didn't recognize until after the fact. Running into a burning building qualified.

The rest of that day was a long crawl interrupted only by nurses doing painful things to my burn and a series of various kinds of imaging of my chest. The doctor had made it clear that until they were sure that my respiratory system wasn't going to suddenly go critical, a very real possibility when smoke inhalation was involved, I should settle into my new sedentary life. I tried to apply whatever good humor I could to it. It turned out that my good humor was in short supply.

Marcy's warning rubbed against my inactivity like sandpaper. The longer I stayed, the worse it would get. I couldn't say how I knew that, just that the intuition was undeniable. On the other hand, it did me no good to check out against doctor's orders, since that could mean my untimely death someplace where medical help wasn't nearby. Given my penchant for lonely highways and byways, that was most of the time.

I dreamed of smoke and fire that night. Hot, blistering fire and blinding smoke that hid the danger until it leapt out at you and seared skin and flesh. I stumbled through it in search of escape. Sparks landed on my skin and burrowed into my veins, carrying the searing pain into my heart. Or maybe, it just reminded me that the pain was always there, waiting, watching, biding its time until I wasn't paying attention. I crashed through a door and stumbled into the night. I fell to the ground and landed in grass made cool by condensation. Dewdrops reflected flickering orange.

I looked back and the Byzantine church-turned-high-school was in flames. Fire roared in the doorway like an open gate into hell or the mouth of a dragon. A figure stood next to me. He was a small man, with a tweed jacket and polished shoes. He looked down at some index cards in his hand, cleared his throat, and began speaking as though he was giving a lecture.

"It is important to note that most mystery school traditions started their lives as minor cults, typically beginning with specific families that embraced unorthodox beliefs, rather than as schisms in mainstream religions. The majority of mystery school traditions do have certain commonalities, such as a fixation on the death-rebirth cycle common to numerous religions and exemplified in figures such as Ishtar, Osiris, and of course, Christ.

"However, some mystery schools seemed to have developed with specific goals in mind beyond mere acts of faith, although the goals themselves remain obscured by a regrettable paucity of known records. These schools, perhaps the most mysterious of the mystery schools, may still be with us today, operating in the shadows and working toward their unknown goals."

"Professor, you don't actually believe that do you?"

I turned my head and found myself sitting on a stage and looking out over an auditorium of eager young minds. A young man stood six rows back and waited on the professor's response.

"I have my doubts, of course," said the professor, "but the absence of evidence is not evidence of absence. Intellectual rigor demands we at least entertain the possibility until a definitive answer presents itself."

A young woman in the front row stood and said, "We cannot let the liberal agenda derail the lives of good, honest Christians. We need to make a stand."

My eyes snapped open. I registered that the television was tuned, once again, to cable news of the least reliable sort. I wondered if mental self-defense would stand up as a legal argument if I murdered the person in the next bed.

"Mr. Hartworth," said a low, slow voice.

I turned my head. The sheriff sat next to my bed. I pulled the oxygen mask off my face. "Sheriff."

"Thought you were planning on leaving my fair city."

"You know how it is. These kids and their parties, just a bit too much for an old guy like me."

Sheriff Barnes gave me half a smile. Then, he turned serious. "Brave thing you did. Stupid as the day is long, but brave."

"Just stupid. I didn't think it through."

"Any reason you didn't just call the fire department?"

"No cell phone."

"Lose yours in Miami?"

I felt my jaw tighten. He had looked into me. I nodded. "Yeah, it got lost in the shuffle."

Sheriff Barnes' forehead bunched up and deep creases appeared. I had thought he was around fifty, but those deep creases made me wonder if he was older. The burn on my back sent a deep throb of pain up my spine and I winced. Burns weren't the worst kind of pain a person could suffer, but they made my top five list.

"Had a chat with a detective down in Miami. Interesting man named Costello."

The Sheriff waited a beat to see if I'd recognize the name. I didn't, but that didn't mean much. I'd bumped into a lot of cops over the years. A regrettably small handful of them recognized when they were out of their depth.

When it became obvious I wasn't going to react to the name, the sheriff continued. "According to him, the police down there would like to talk with you."

"Good talk or bad talk?"

"A couple days ago, it was a bad talk. Now, they think you're a witness or possibly a victim of gang violence."

I nodded. That was as close to the truth as they were ever going to get, at least in an official capacity. "So no BOLOs or arrest warrants? No extradition in my immediate future?"

"Doesn't seem that way."

"Small favors."

Barnes stood and gave me a pensive look. "You still planning on leaving?"

"As soon as the doc okays me to go."

Barnes nodded. "Good. Not interested in seeing any," he threw up some finger quotes, "'gang violence' here."

"Me either, believe it or not."

Chapter 6

THE DOCTOR TOLD ME THAT THEY PLANNED ON RELEASING ME later that day, which was a relief. My roomie, who I never actually saw, but who made his or her presence known with the relentless extreme right-wing "news" channel, was not someone I would miss. They took me off the constant oxygen and I was surprised by how even simple tasks left me a little short of breath. They'd warned me it would be that way for a while, but I was used to my body working well most of the time. They also warned me not to fly for a few weeks, since the pressurized cabin conditions would exacerbate my breathing trouble. I shrugged and said I wouldn't. I'm a ground traveler by nature.

Around noon, a nurse pushed an old man in a wheelchair into my room. She parked him next to my bed and said she'd be back shortly to collect him. The old man regarded me with rheumy, gray eyes. His face was deeply lined, with dark pouches under his eyes, and reminded me of a Burgkmair woodcut I'd once seen of Jacob Fugger. He didn't say anything right at first, just peered at me, as if trying to remember something important.

"Hello," I said, when the silence started to bother me.

"Hello," he replied.

His voice was still strong, with only a hint of the quavering that afflicts the voices of the elderly. He held out a hand toward me and I took it. He pumped my hand a few times and let go.

"I wanted to meet you," he said. "I wanted to thank you for you what you did." He paused, and took a few labored breaths. "As much as you can thank a man who saves the lives of your entire family."

The old man was no longer just "the old man," but Paul, the old man I'd dragged out of a fire. I'd hoped to avoid meeting him and his granddaughter, but I smiled and shook my head.

"No thanks are necessary. Just glad I could help."

"If you need something," he persisted, "money…"

I held up a hand. "Really, it's not necessary. I've got insurance for this kind of thing."

I was grateful that I'd been traveling as Adrian Hartworth. Of the various identities I had, Hartworth was the closest to being real. He had a social security number—someone's social security number, anyway—bank accounts, health insurance and a permanent address. Most of my dozen or so identities were throwaways. I could use them briefly, a few days if I needed to, but then they needed to die. I'd paid a lot of money for Hartworth to cover exactly these kinds of situations.

Paul looked at me, unsatisfied. I supposed he was old enough to feel beholden to a sense of honor that had gone out of style around the time bellbottoms came into style. I needed to mollify him somehow. Let him do something for me or, at the least, let him feel like he might be able to do something for me someday to balance the scales.

"If I do wind up needing something," I offered, "you'll be my first call."

The resistance faded out of his expression and he nodded. "Seems fair."

I wanted him off that track, so I asked the obvious question. "How's your granddaughter?"

"Alive. Thanks to you."

"She going to be alright?"

"Docs say she's past the worst of it. They want to keep her a while yet."

"Better safe than sorry."

"She wants to meet you," said Paul.

I pushed away a mental groan. I didn't want to meet the girl. I hadn't wanted to meet her grandfather. I just wanted to get out of the miserable little town that had caused me nothing but trouble and pain. The old man wouldn't understand it, though. Normal people never did, and I couldn't explain it.

If I said, "Hey, I want to blow off you and your grandkid because my dead girlfriend gave me a cryptic warning," I'd find myself on an involuntary 72-hour psych hold. It'd be even longer if I wasn't extra-nice and super-cooperative. I knew. I'd been through it before, when I was younger and less aggressively cynical about the narrowness of people's minds. I did my best to smile for the man and nodded.

"I'll swing by her room before I leave."

"She'll be thrilled," said Paul.

"Oh, I doubt that. I'm not terribly interesting or dashing."

Paul fixed me with his rheumy eyes and frowned. "You're a piss-poor liar."

I raised a bemused eyebrow. "No one's said that to me in a very long time."

"I'm old now, son. Means I get to say those impolite things most people keep inside. Fringe benefit."

"Good to know. When's that kick in? Sixty-five?"

Paul barked out a coughing laugh. "Seventy these days, I think."

"I'll mark the calendar."

"You're an odd duck, Mr. Hartworth."

"How so?"

Paul took a few more of those labored breaths. "Call most men liars and they blow their tops. Not you."

I shrugged. "We're all liars about something. Not much advantage to getting all bent out of shape when someone says so."

The old man blinked at me and then nodded. "Guess that's true."

The nurse came in to collect Paul.

I took a stab at the social niceties. "It was nice to meet you, Paul."

"It was nice to meet you, Mr. Hartworth. Like I said, you need anything..."

"You're my first call."

A couple hours later, Patty came by with my overnight bag. I was grateful. I doubted there was any salvaging the suit I'd been wearing during my little fire-and-rescue impersonation. The hospital had returned my belt, wallet and shoes, which still smelled charred. Patty stepped out of the room, while I pulled on a pair of slacks and a blue button-down from the bag. I was careful not to brush the burn on my back more than necessary, but the motion aggravated the injury. It sent low, throbbing pulses of unhappiness to my brain. I wondered how bad it would hurt without painkillers.

I made a mental note to stop by the pharmacy and get my painkiller and antibiotic prescriptions filled. I had no interest in testing the upper limits of my pain threshold or chancing an infection. The drone of cable news filled the air again. I gritted my teeth and decided to get a look at my roomie, so I could put a face to the aggravation. I walked around the cloth divider and stopped short, icy spikes lodging in my stomach. The other bed in the room was empty.

I ran the memory back in my head. For a bare breath, the bed hadn't been empty. There had been something in that bed. Maybe a someone, maybe not, but it was occupied. I didn't like the feeling that phantom presence gave off. It was both coldly alien and, beneath the overt alien feeling, I sensed an acidic anger. Marcy's warning to leave rose unbidden in my mind and I had to work hard not to turn on my heel, leave the hospital, and never look back. I forced myself to walk over to the stand next to the empty bed, pick up the remote, and turn off the talking head on the TV. The television snapped off and a wave of that acidic anger poured over me. I looked around the room, certain that I wasn't alone, even if I couldn't pinpoint the location of my invisible companion. This wasn't my first rodeo with the unseen, and I issued forth with an ostentatious sniff of derision.

"Go fuck yourself," I told the unseen presence.

I felt shock emanate from everywhere and nowhere, right before a box of tissues launched itself from the stand. The tissue box missile raced toward my face and I caught it, at a price. The dull throb in my back became a sharp stab and I couldn't breathe for a second. *God*, I wondered, *how bad was that burn?* The sense of shock and alien anger faded from the room, leaving behind a vague smell of burnt leather. Or maybe that was just my shoes.

I put the tissues and remote back on the stand and snagged my overnight bag, more certain than ever that leaving was the right move or, all things being equal, the smart move. I didn't owe the people in that town anything. Whatever was going on there, angry poltergeists of dead patients most likely, it wasn't my problem. I stepped out of the room and didn't look back, despite the feeling of being watched. Patty gave me a tight-eyed look.

"You all right? You look pale," she said.

"Moved wrong. That burn made itself known," I said.

She nodded. "Yeah, pain will do that to you. You ready to go?"

Christ in Heaven, yes! Please, please Deputy Patty, take me the hell away from here. Take me to my car and let me leave you all behind to deal with your own problems in your own way. At least, that's what I wanted to say. I didn't, though, as Paul's rheumy eyes floated in my memory like elderly accusation.

"She'll be thrilled," he had said.

That girl had almost died, would have certainly died if I hadn't happened to be driving by. Did I just "happen" to be driving by? Marcy had known something, maybe not the details, but known enough to warn me not to stop for gas. If I'd been driving by just a few minutes earlier, the fire wouldn't have been big enough to alert my subconscious. I'd have long-since arrived in Seattle to make my periodic, covert check-in on my sister. If I could make the time to check in on my family, I could take the five minutes to check in on that possibly cursed teenager.

"I promised to stop in and say hello to Abby," I conceded to the air.

"That's a nice thing to do. I bet she'll be thrilled."

My head whipped toward Patty, who took a full step back from me.

"What?" She demanded, sounding equal parts disconcerted and angry at being disconcerted.

"Nothing," I said, turning my face away. "Just odd. Paul said the same thing."

"Well, sure, why wouldn't she be thrilled? How often do you get to meet your own personal hero?"

I felt myself tense up as she used that word: hero. I could tell her that there weren't any heroes, just disappointments waiting to happen, but I didn't. She wouldn't understand or, maybe, she would understand all too well. I decided that was knowledge about Patty I didn't need.

"Do you know which room she's in?"

"Yeah, I'll go up with you. I've been meaning to stop by and say hi to her. Poor kid can't seem to catch a break. I thought it might do her some good to see a friendly face, even if it is mine."

I couldn't resist. "Who wouldn't be happy to see you, Deputy Michelson?"

I thought Patty might cry or punch me. I smiled to soften to the joke.

"Lead the way, Patty."

Chapter 7

PATTY TOOK ME UP TWO FLOORS to what, I discovered, was the ICU. I hesitated in the elevator. The last time I'd been in an ICU as a visitor, rather than a patient, was the night Marcy died. She'd been the victim of a car accident, just one of the faceless masses reported in the cold statistics issued by the National Highway Traffic Safety Administration that year. I'd sat next to her bed for eight hours, hoping she would open her eyes in spite of the surgeon's warning that she wouldn't.

The trauma was extensive. That was the word the surgeon used, extensive, rather than something more telling and accurate, like apocalyptic, cataclysmic, or unholy. Only extraordinary good health and relative youth accounted for her surviving the initial accident, caused by an SUV recklessly entering the highway and sideswiping her little two-door coupe. The impact pushed her into another lane, where a Volvo, the world's safest car, clipped her and spun Marcy's car sideways back into her own lane.

If there had been less traffic or more room to maneuver, she might have survived even that, but a pickup with nowhere to go T-boned Marcy. Her car popped loose from the truck's fender as the driver slammed on his brakes. The coupe skidded and then rolled down the highway, bouncing Marcy around like a rag doll, snapping bones and slamming her brain against the interior of her skull. It was anyone's guess how much soft tissue damage was done.

By the time emergency services arrived on the scene, the SUV was, of course, long gone. According to the driver of the pickup, who had almost gotten run over in a mad dash to try to help Marcy, the SUV never even stopped. The police did a cursory search, but highway traffic cams weren't as common then. The cops had nothing to go on. I was less hampered by pesky things like due process. Even then, I'd had some skills and contacts available to me that no self-respecting police department would employ, even if they believed in magic. I found the SUV. I found the driver. We had a very long, private, discussion.

After that discussion, my life as Jason Anderson ceased to exist. Six months later, with the assistance of a shadowy woman and most of Jason Anderson's liquid assets, a man named Adrian Hartworth appeared. He had a name, bank accounts, even a credit and tax history, no doubt the result of some high-order hacking about which I asked no questions. Adrian Hartworth had never been to Seattle. He had never sat by the bedside of a dying woman named Marcy. He had most certainly never met a man named Jack Reed, who owned a big, black SUV with long scrapes down one side.

"Mr. Hartworth?" Patty asked, her hand holding open the elevator door.

I shook my head. "Sorry. Damn elevator music hypnotized me."

I stepped off the elevator and followed Patty down the hall. She opened a door and stepped inside. I took a breath, tried my best to put on a smile, and followed her into the room. The girl lay on the bed with her right arm over the covers. Bandages wrapped that arm from mid-bicep most of the way to her wrist. Had she gotten burned? I couldn't remember. It might have happened before I found her, though I doubted it. She was painfully thin. I wondered if she was being underfed, then I remembered the cancer. Unless her short, dark, hair was a stylistic choice, her chemo treatments weren't long over. She looked like she was asleep, or very close to it.

Patty walked over and stood next to the bed, her expression grim and sad. I watched the deputy very consciously force that expression to change to a smile. I felt for her. It's hard to see anyone in pain. Seeing someone that young in pain brutalized you in a special, not-soon-to-be-forgotten way. You anticipate pain and illness as an adult, as the cost of being an adult. You expected kids and teenagers to be exempt from that shit. When it doesn't go down that way, it fills me with impotent anger.

"Abby," said Patty in a quiet voice.

The girl opened her eyes and I saw painkiller incomprehension in them. She fought it off, forced her eyes to focus on the deputy. Abby gave the deputy a brave smile.

"Hi, Deputy Michelson," said the girl with more cheer than she should have been able to muster.

"Hi Abby. How are you feeling?"

"I'm okay," said Abby, getting the thousand yard stare of someone asked the same question so many times it had become a form of personal torture. "It's better than chemo."

"I'm sure it is. There's someone here to see you, if you're up for it."

Abby's eyes flickered over to me, cautious at first, and then she seemed to realize who I had to be. She gave me a million-watt smile.

"You're him, aren't you?" she asked.

I walked over and smiled back at her. "I guess I must be."

She pulled her left arm out from under the blanket and held her hand out to me. I took it in my own left hand, thinking she wanted to shake it. Instead, she squeezed my hand and then held it.

"Abby," said Patty, "this is Adrian Hartworth."

I'm not a natural psychic, but we're all born with a little bit of it. The kind of low-level, hair standing up on the back of your neck stuff that alerts you to being observed, or intuiting that something you're holding is bad news. It's the kind of thing you can develop a little, with practice, and through repeated exposure to magical oddness and danger. I'd had plenty of both over the years and I bent all of my accumulated sixth sense on that girl. I didn't know exactly what I was looking for, save that the nurse's observation that Abby was somehow cursed stuck with me.

I think, maybe, I wanted to reassure myself that the girl was plain, normal unlucky. If she was just unlucky, with crap landing on her through unkind, cosmic coin-tosses that never went her way, my conscience would be clear when I drove away, never to look back. If she was cursed, it didn't mean I couldn't walk away, just that I would also do so knowingly. More often than not, there wasn't anything you could do for the cursed. They often inherited those curses. The person who did the cursing was often long-dead and the conflict long-since passed out of family memory.

What my intuition gave me was confusing and contradictory. It simultaneously told me that there was absolutely nothing un-natural happening with the girl and that something dark was working on her. It reminded me of heating up mashed potatoes in a microwave, then taking a bite to find that the potatoes were both hot and cold, depending on what part of the plate your potatoes came from. Words drifted into my mind from some far plane of existence.

"It's nice to meet you, Mr. Hartworth."

I blinked away the intuition and met the girl's eyes. "It's nice to meet you too, Abby."

"I'll give you two a minute," said Patty, before she retreated to the hallway.

Abby peered up at me, a tiny bit shy with Patty out of the room. I tried to imagine her at a normal weight, without the sickly gauntness that gave her face a somewhat skeletal quality. I decided that she probably wasn't a beauty queen. Her nose was a bit too big and her jaw a little too square for traditional conceptions of beauty. If someone was working black magic on her, it probably wasn't some other girl who was jealous of Abby's looks. I supposed it was a long shot, but it happened more often than most people would have credited.

I realized that I was doing that analysis of her features as a way to avoid an actual conversation. I had no idea what a grown man was supposed to say to a girl of, maybe, fifteen. I didn't think I'd spoken to a girl that age who wasn't a waitress since *I'd* been a teenager. I resisted the urge to ask her how she was feeling. She was still gripping my hand, with no obvious intention of letting go. I gave her bandaged arm a pointed look.

"Your arm get burned?" I asked.

"Yeah. I don't remember that happening. I wondered if you remembered."

I shook my head. "I remember getting your grandfather out pretty clearly. After that, it all gets hazy. I think you must have fallen out of bed. I have a dim recollection of yanking on a sheet to get your leg free. After that, it's a blur."

I decided not to tell her that it was a terrifying, smoky, fiery blur. I also neglected to tell her that it was only stupid luck that I hadn't dropped her inside the burning building while I tried to get out. I doubted it would make her feel better.

"I guess it doesn't really matter. It's just weird to be hurt without remembering anything about how it happened."

"I know what you mean."

"Really?" She asked without any conviction in her voice that I understood at all.

"Sure," I said and waved my right hand at the left side of my chest. "I've got a bunch of scars and some tattoos all through here. I know some of what happened, because people told me the bits they knew, but I have no memory of it."

It wasn't precisely true. I had one image with no context from that night. I remembered a raven-haired woman with cold eyes and a warm smile, but the rest was just emptiness. Abby was right. It was weird to know that something happened to you, but not remember it. It was more than weird, it was scary, because you didn't know what else might have happened. That blank spot in my memory kept me up at night.

"Can I," Abby appeared to second-guess herself and then decided. "Can I see?"

I thought for a second and wondered if I was about to cross some adult-child ethical boundary. I decided that I probably wasn't. I gently shook my hand free from hers and undid a couple buttons on my shirt. I pulled the shirt over enough that some of the scars and part of one tattoo were visible. Her eyes went a little white around the edges. I redid the buttons on my shirt.

"You really don't remember how that happened?"

"Not a bit," I said.

"I have a lot of scars. Do you ever worry that," she paused, not looking at me, "people will think you're ugly because of your scars?"

I guessed that she had a very particular boy or girl in mind when she said people. I couldn't even remember what it was like to worry that much about what anyone would think of my appearance, but I could see it meant a lot to her. What perplexed me was why she asked me that question. After a second, the answer was so obvious as to be painful. I had scars, at least as bad as hers, so I could understand. I doubted she knew many people with bad, ugly scars. I was sorely tempted to lie to her, to reassure her no one would think less of her, but that would just make it worse when she discovered the lie.

"Some people will think that," I admitted.

"Why?"

I tried to gather my thoughts. Why were people assholes? Talk about one of those existential questions without a good answer.

"A lot of reasons, I guess," I answered with the kind of lameness befitting someone who was dodging a question.

Come on, man, bellowed some part of my mind that felt like I should at least *try* to answer Abby's question with something useful.

I tried again. "Mostly, I think it's because they've never suffered. They can't understand what kind of pain goes with scars. I guess, most of the time, they don't even want to try. It's too much like work."

"You mean they don't care," she said in small, pained voice.

"Yeah," I said, and felt like crap. "I'd like to say it won't hurt, because those people are shallow and not worth your time. I think you know it does hurt, though."

She nodded, still looking away from me. I thought hard and fast, trying to find a way to salvage something positive from the death spiral the conversation was taking. Inspiration struck.

"Still," I said, "not everyone in the world is a hopeless asshat."

The girl giggled and then covered her mouth as red blossomed in her cheeks. "Oh my god, I can't believe you just said that. Grandpa would freak."

I gave her a little shrug. "I just call it how it see it. You have to look pretty hard to find those people who are worth a damn, but they are out there."

I saw the gear switch before she spoke. "Thank you for saving us. For saving grandpa. He's..."

She faltered then, coming across an idea that was probably too painful and abstract to cope with in her state or maybe at her age. That was something I could help her avoid.

"He's a good man," I said. "I found him on the stairs of your house. He was trying to get to you before the fire did."

She blinked a few times at that idea. I suppose she had never considered the lengths the old man would go to in order to protect her. Once the idea filtered down through the painkillers, she smiled another one of those million-watt smiles. Even as I stood in the reflected glow of that smile, I felt that disconcerting sensation that she was both under some kind of magical attack and that she wasn't. It unnerved me, because I'd never felt such a thing before. It was always an either-or, never a yes-*and*-no. I forced a smile back onto my face.

"And, you're welcome. I'm glad I could be there to help. Still, you should get some rest or they'll never release you."

Her smile vanished. "I'm never getting out of here. Stupid chemo wrecked my immune system. They won't let me go until they're sure *this*," she waggled her bandaged arm, "won't get infected."

The intensity of her pessimism caught me off guard. Then again, I didn't spend God knew how many weeks or months having doctors poison me in the name of curing me. It was a miserable enough experience to make most people pessimistic.

"All the more reason to let you get your rest," I said.

I reached out and took her left hand in mine. I gave it a little squeeze.

"You're going to be alright, kid."

She looked up at me, pessimism and youthful hope at war in her eyes. "You really think so?"

I squeezed her hand again. "I do."

I turned and walked toward the door. My hand was on the knob when she called after me.

"Will you come back and see me?"

I was gone already. I knew it. The road was calling to me. Marcy's warning was pushing me. That freaky yes-and-no vibe around the teen was enough to tell me that I wanted no part of whatever was happening to her. It was best to be honest and give her short-term disappointment, rather than big, ugly disappointment later. I glanced over my shoulder at Abby and steeled myself to deliver the bad news.

"You bet," said my mouth, in direct contradiction to all reason. "I'll come see you tomorrow."

Chapter 8

THE PROCLAMATION OF MY INTENTION to visit Abby the next day left me in a state of bleary disbelief. By the time normalcy and something akin to abject horror at my decision reasserted itself, I was in Patty's cruiser. I looked over at her and wondered if my disbelieving state was obvious to her. She glanced over at me and smirked.

"Well now, sunshine, I see you've rejoined us."

"Looks like."

"You ready to flee the state?"

I wanted to slap the back of my own head, but I controlled the impulse. "I thought I was. Looks like I'll be sticking around for a day."

"Oh?"

I sighed, loudly. "Apparently, I told Abby I'd visit her tomorrow."

"Apparently?"

"My mouth agreed before checking in with my brain."

Patty nodded. "Kids have a way of doing that to you."

"You have any kids?"

"Not me. Got a brood of nieces and nephews, though. I figured that was close enough. You?"

I wondered what it would be like to actually talk to my sister's kids. They all seemed like they were smart and happy.

"No," I said, remembering to stay in character, "no family to speak of. Is there another hotel around here? Not that my former accommodations weren't just lovely, but I'd like to keep a little under the radar."

"There isn't another hotel, per se, but there are some cabins you can rent by the night. Out near where Paul and Abby's house is," Patty jerked a little. "Well, where it was, I guess."

That didn't sound good. "House beyond repair?"

Patty shook her head. "Guess that's up to the insurance company, but it looked pretty bad from where I stood."

"They wrap up the arson investigation yet?"

Patty gave me a knowing look. "You seem to know an awful lot about how crime gets dealt with Mr. Hartworth. Anything you'd care to share?"

"You should call me Adrian. Where are we going anyway?"

"Figured you'd want your car. It's still up at Paul's place."

I nodded. I was going to have to go back there anyways. That thought shocked me a little. I'd already been planning a strategy, even though I wasn't sure there was anything to do.

"You didn't answer the question, Adrian," said Patty.

I snuck a peek and I saw the twitching at the corners of her mouth. "Tell you what, Patty. I'll show you mine, if you show me yours."

"Careful Adrian. I'm told these bosoms can stun a man into submission at thirty paces."

"Did you just say bosoms?"

"I most certainly did."

"You're a treasure, you know that?"

"I do," said Patty. "In answer to your question, yes, the arson investigation is done. As far as they're concerned, it was an accident. No signs of accelerants or tampering anywhere. Just one of those freak things."

"Awful lot of accidents and freak things happening to that family," I muttered.

"I noticed that myself. Okay, Sonny Jim, your turn."

"I worked for an insurance investigator on and off for a couple years. It was in a strictly unofficial capacity, of course, but I picked some things up."

"Seriously?"

"Seriously. I'll give you her name. If you call in a strictly off-the-record and unofficial capacity, she'll confirm it."

"That where you picked up those tattoos and scars? Unofficial insurance investigating?"

I kept my face neutral. "Nope."

"You play it awful close to the chest," said Patty.

"Some things are best left unvisited."

"True enough."

"You see them? The scars, I mean."

"No. Heard the nurses talking about it."

Patty pulled into the driveway and parked behind my newly acquired Neon. We got out and she tossed me the keys to the car. I caught them and slipped them into my pocket.

"Where are those cabins?"

Patty pointed west up the road. "You go about a mile up that way. You'll see a blue building on the right with Alan's Cabins painted on the side in big white letters. Tell them Patty sent you."

"Will that get me a discount?"

"No, but it will get you a cabin with working water and electricity."

"That's important, too," I said. "So, officially speaking, the house isn't a crime scene?"

"That's right," said Patty, curiosity writ large across her face. "Why?"

"I thought I might take a look around. Scratch an itch, so to speak."

"Mind if I tag along? See how unofficial insurance investigators do it?"

I did mind. Not so much because I believed that she thought I was up to no good, but because I was pretty sure she was too firmly grounded in the practical. Patty's world, I was quite sure, was populated by ordinary evils carried out by ordinary people with bad intentions. I wasn't really in a mood to shatter her expectations and then try to explain the way things really worked. Then again, it was her town. I had a feeling that the sheriff had been phoning it in for a while and that Patty was going to be the law around those parts before many more moons came and went. I shrugged at her.

"If you like," I said.

I opened my trunk and spun the little combination lock built into the latch on the hard case to the right sequence. I flipped the case open and pulled out what I figured I'd need. I pocketed those items and then closed the case, latching it firmly. I reached up and closed the trunk. The realization of my mistake hit about the same time as the pain. I stood there taking shallow breaths as nausea competed with pain for supremacy. To her credit, Patty didn't comment beyond offering a sympathetic look.

"Can you show me where the fire started?" I asked when the pain and nausea receded.

"Sure."

Patty led me around to the back of the house. The whole building stank of wet, charred wood and incinerated chemicals. There were huge pieces missing from the back wall of the house, exposing blackened pipes and something that used to be a kitchen. Linoleum squares had peeled and cracked unevenly, some browned and some blackened. I tried not to notice the wreckage of something I was pretty sure was another antique table. Patty pointed to a spot just beneath one of the holes that exposed the interior of burned kitchen cabinets and melted pots.

"That's where they think it started, though no one is sure exactly why or how."

"You might want to stand back a little," I suggested.

Patty gave me a dubious look, but she backed off about five feet, fire-roasted grass crackling and snapping under her feet. I took one of the test tubes out of my pocket and pulled out the rubber stopper. I took an extra step back and then flung the contents of the test tube at the spot Patty pointed out. The liquid landed with a quiet splash.

"The fire's already out," said Patty with a grin.

I waited, counting in my head. *Five. Four. Three. Two. One.* Nothing happened. I felt a surge of relief and an undercurrent of disappointment.

"I guess that settles—" I started.

Light the color and intensity of burning magnesium ignited where the liquid in the test tube had landed. I shielded my eyes and turned my head away, worried that the light might actually damage my vision. In the background, I heard Patty give off a brief scream of fright, before she descended briefly into some of the most inventive cursing I'd heard in years. The light burned out after a few seconds and a slight sulfur smell wafted over me.

"Damn it, Hartworth! What in the hell did you throw on there?"

I was still mostly blinded from the light, but I turned my face in the general direction of Patty's yelling.

"It was just water," I said.

"Water does not do that!"

"Holy water does. Sometimes."

The silence that followed that statement went on for long enough that my vision was mostly cleared by the time Patty spoke again.

"Holy water," she said.

"Yes."

"That was holy water you tossed at the house?"

"It was."

"You just happened to be carrying around holy water in your trunk?"

"More or less."

"Just in case you needed to do what, exactly?"

"Throw it at a house?"

Up until then, Patty was responding on instinct and leftover fright. The simple absurdity of my answer snapped her back to reality. All the usual excuses for the inexplicable took hold of her. I saw it on her face, the frantic rationalizations, the self-deception, and the assumption that I had pulled a fast one or, more likely, some kind of poor taste joke. It always shocked me how fast the desire for normalcy reasserted itself. It took Patty about three seconds.

"I get it," she said, as she forced a smile. "You played a little joke on local law enforcement. Spin a yarn to spook the rube cop. Well, it worked. You tricked me."

I didn't smile back at her. I didn't laugh. I didn't move. She eyed me, seeming to weigh whether I was carrying the joke too far.

"Seriously, Hartworth, what was that stuff? Something you picked up in a magic shop?"

"It was exactly what I said it was. It was holy water."

I walked over to the house and wiped my hand across the wet wall. I held it up for her to see. It looked like grimy water on my hand. She kept the smile in place, but it looked painful. I shook my head and held the test tube out to her. She looked at it like it might hold nitro glycerin or the Ebola virus. She didn't meet my eyes when she took the test tube from my hand. Patty lifted it to her nose, not too close, in case this was some kind of gag, and sniffed at it. She looked up at me in surprise and sniffed again. She gave me an angry look and shoved the test tube in my direction.

"Doesn't prove anything," she almost yelled.

I lifted the test tube to my lips, poured the little bit of holy water that remained into my mouth and swallowed it. Patty went three shades of white and took a step back. I doubted she realized it, but her hand was on the grip of her service weapon.

"No tricks, Patty. No jokes or games. You just saw what happens when holy water comes in contact with the remnants of black magic. Pretty potent black magic," I said, and then a thought struck me.

"What?" Patty asked, in spite of her better judgment, by the expression on her face.

"Potent black magic, or minor black magic carried out by something very potent and very, very evil."

"Come on! There is no such thing as black magic. You know that as well as I do, so cut the crap."

"One. Parents are dead in a so-called car accident. Two. Grandmother is dead, probably unexpectedly and from a previously undocumented condition, unless I miss my guess. Three. Girl gets cancer. I bet there isn't an obvious cause. Is there a family history of childhood cancer? I'd bet no. Four. House burns down with no explanation. Moreover, it happens when the family would be here, but there would be minimal traffic to alert the fire department. Five. Holy water at the site goes supernova. Even if you aren't comfortable with the idea of black magic, can you really tell me that all that strung together doesn't strike you as outlandishly improbable?"

Patty watched me with suspicious eyes and a clenched jaw. When she spoke, the words came through clenched teeth.

"Even if I did buy this conspiracy theory, which I don't, I'm not buying your black magic theory."

"Why not?"

"Because I like my job, dammit! I'll like it even better when I'm sheriff. Nobody is going to vote for someone who goes around spouting off about black magic!"

Chapter 9

IN SPITE OF MYSELF, I was a little disillusioned by that answer. I knew she was right. One whiff of a rumor that she thought black magic was anything more than a convenient plot device used by over-imaginative writers and her career was over. On the other hand, someone or something was targeting Abby. If it was a person, he or she had summoned darkness way beyond a run-of-the-mill demon. That teenage girl, who was worried that a crush might think she was ugly because of some scars, who had probably never done anything worse than shoplift some candy when she was five, who had suffered more than anyone that age deserved and still managed to find reasons to smile, was in very real danger.

I didn't doubt that Patty was a decent person. I also suspected that if I could point to a human culprit who was killing Abby by inches, Patty would come down on that person like one hundred and fifty pounds of holy vengeance. She might even give me five minutes alone in a room with that person, if I asked for it. Yet, I wasn't giving her anything she could work with inside the confines of the law. Asking her to willingly, knowingly, jeopardize the world she was trying to build for herself was asking too much. She would put her life on the line, because that was her job, but she wouldn't help me if I couldn't do better than fairy tales. More to the point, she couldn't help Abby. But someone had to help that girl.

I suppose that was when I admitted the decision to myself. The decision was actually made long before that, probably around the time I turned the car around and went back to the burning house. It was a bad decision. I wasn't at my best, not even close. My back ached and sent sharp stabs through my nervous system constantly. It wouldn't take much for that burn to get infected. I doubted I could run more than twenty feet without getting winded. If I pushed myself beyond that, I'd probably pass out. How much help could a man in my condition be?

I could walk away. I'd done it before. There were terrible powers at work in the world. Huge, awesome powers that could literally rip a man to pieces, and they operated on both sides of the good and evil divide. I'd met a few of those powers along the way. I wasn't one of them. I'd stumbled into a few of their conflicts and they played for stakes that made me want to wet myself. I'd walked. I had walked and not looked back. I was a middling practitioner with occasional flashes of brilliance and real power. I knew things, studied arcane lore and traditions, and that was usually enough to help me make up the shortcomings in my raw ability. At least, that was, if the people I was squaring off against were also mortals and the things they summoned weren't too close to relative omnipotence.

I didn't know the stakes at play around Abby. I had no clue. The smart plan was to leave, before I found myself dragged under by forces I underestimated. Whatever was at work around Abby was playing a long game. Most black magic happens on impulse in the pursuit of short-term goals. Love is patient, evil is not. Impulsive evil leaves mind-boggling amounts of human wreckage in its wake. *Patient* evil scared me right down to the bone. I literally couldn't imagine what patient evil might deliver when it played out its endgame.

I don't know how much of what I was thinking played on my face, but I think Patty read my disappointment in her. There was a telltale red across her cheeks that might have been embarrassment, but it might have been anger.

"Look," she said, trying to sound reasonable, "I think you're trying to watch out for that girl. If you want official police involvement here, you've got to give me evidence I can work with. I can't flip an alarm based on a flash of light and a lot of bad luck."

"Alarm," I repeated, as if the word was something I'd never heard before.

The word tickled something in my memory of the fire. There was something about the fire that hadn't been right. It was something about antiques. I remembered dashing through the high grass in the front yard and the vague sense of neglect about the house. That seemed out of character, but maybe not. Paint and the lawn were cosmetic and they were hot work. Paul was old, maybe waiting for better weather. Or maybe he was just more concerned about his cancer-ridden granddaughter. Who cares about the paint when your primary family member might be dying?

"You remembered something, didn't you?"

"Maybe," I said. "There was something off about the fire."

"Other than black magic," offered Patty, dry as sand.

"Patty, how long have you known Paul?"

"About eight years," she said, all caution. "Why?"

"He struck me as a conscientious, old-school guy. The kind of man who takes pride in his home."

"Yeah, that sounds like Paul."

"He's not the sort of man to let his granddaughter live in a house with subpar wiring or bad plumbing."

"No, he isn't. In fact, he had his electrical completely redone around the time I came to town. Where are you going with this, Hartworth?"

There had been so much noise when I opened the door to the house. God that fire had been loud, deafening really. There was something off about the memory. Something that I had expected that wasn't there. I'd been so focused on the old man, the girl and surviving, that I hadn't pieced it together. Still, something had been wrong. It was one of those essential things that you just expected during a fire. It clicked.

"He's definitely not the kind of man who lets every battery in every smoke detector go dead," I said.

Patty squinted at me. "Come again?"

"There weren't any smoke alarms going off when I went into the house. I had other things to worry about, so I didn't notice then. Still, not a single one going off? Should have sounded like a damn air raid in there with a fire like that. Plus, the house was full of antiques. Not millionaire expensive, but not chump change either. No way a guy invests all that money and doesn't invest five bucks for the batteries to protect it. Check the alarms. Maybe there isn't any evidence that someone set the fire, but if someone messed with the alarms that would be suggestive. Might even be attempted murder, right?"

Patty started nodding about halfway through my train of thought. She probably saw the angle before I did.

"Yes," she said. "That would be suggestive enough to warrant some official attention, I think. I might need you to make another statement to get the ball rolling."

I thought about the sheriff and frowned. I couldn't get a read on him. He wasn't outright hostile when we talked, but that didn't mean he wanted me kicking hornets' nests.

"See if you can avoid it for now. I suspect that the less involved people think I am, the better."

"Why's that."

"Call it an intuition. I don't understand what's happening here. I don't want to advertise until I do."

Patty slid her hands into her pockets and gave me an uncertain look. "I shouldn't trust you. I know I shouldn't, but you don't strike me as a crazy person."

"That's good, since I'm not."

"So you say, but you're serious about this black magic stuff, aren't you?"

I shrugged. "Let me worry about that. If it's black magic, it'll be my problem to deal with in the end."

"I can't have you taking the law into your own hands," said Patty with stern, quiet determination. "I won't tolerate a vigilante."

"You sound like a sheriff already," I said, avoiding the implied question.

The back of my neck prickled as a wave of cold washed over me. If Patty felt it, she gave no outward sign. It was possible that I was just being paranoid, but the sun was setting and I didn't want to take unnecessary chances. A lot of things came out to play at night and I was pretty sure we were being watched.

"I guess you were right," I said, loud enough that my voice would carry. "Your arson guy knows his business. You'll give him my apologies?"

Confusion crossed Patty's face before she masked it with an annoyed scowl. "You big city assholes always think you know better than we do. Yeah, I'll tell John you're sorry."

I headed back around the side of the house with Patty shadowing me. The sense of cold observation followed us until we got to the cars, then it evaporated. I let out a little puff of breath and fought off a dizzy spell. I made a mental note that holding my breath was off the approved activities list for a while.

"Thanks for playing along," I said under my breath.

Even if I couldn't feel an observer anymore, it didn't mean that there wasn't one out there in the descending darkness. One that might be exercising more caution with a stranger that seemed to be showing too much interest in Paul and Abby.

"You think we're being watched?" Patty asked in the same hushed whisper.

"Could be," I hedged. "Why chance it?"

I unlocked the Neon and slid into the driver's seat. Patty hovered by the door and I raised a questioning eyebrow.

"Was that really holy water?"

"Yeah," I said. "It really was."

"Christ. Black magic. Guys wandering around with holy water. Evil conspiracies. When did the world lose its mind?"

"The world was always insane," I said. "Always. We just started tricking ourselves into thinking it wasn't. Helps people sleep better, so it's not a totally useless lie."

"You're a real bundle of comfort."

"I hear that a lot."

"I bet you do," said Patty.

I waited as Patty pulled the cruiser out the driveway and headed back toward town. As the last remnants of sunlight vanished on the horizon, I watched the house. A few days before, it was a home. Maybe not a happy home, precisely, what with all the death and sickness and black magic that seemed bent on destroying a teenage girl, but a good home. A home where an old man was willing to die to save his granddaughter. All that was left was a burned out shell that would, in all likelihood, be torn down. Maybe Paul would rebuild, maybe he wouldn't, but it would never be the same home. A lifetime of memories etched into those walls, a psychic protection all their own, was gone.

I jerked forward in my seat. That made sense. The house shielded the girl to some extent, blunting whatever dark mojo was being hurled at her. Take the house out of the equation and it forced Abby into the open all the time. It made her more vulnerable. What I couldn't fathom was why anything or anyone would want to inflict such pain on her. She was a sweet kid that would, if she beat the cancer, probably grow up to be a kind adult. She wasn't powerful, though. I'd have sensed that, even if her power was nascent. She wasn't a threat to anything that crawled the outer darkness and the bowels of creation. Why the hell was she on the receiving end of so much evil attention?

"I guess that's what I'm supposed to figure out," I muttered to the steering wheel.

Then again, I thought, did I really need to know why it was happening? Knowing might make it marginally easier to stop, but that knowledge wasn't critical to derailing dark magic. Finding out might take more time than the girl had to live. The *why* of it could wait until after. What Abby needed was for the magical attacks to stop. I wasn't sure I could do that, but replacing the protective blunting influence the house had provided was in my reach. I could buy Abby some time while I worked out a permanent fix.

Chapter 10

PATTY HAD BEEN RIGHT that dropping her name would get me a cabin with both electricity and running water. I tossed and turned, though. Pain and worry gnawed at my limited peace of mind. In principle, giving Abby some protection was easy. The right combination of symbols, spells, and objects would go a long way toward warding off evil directed at her. The problem was that she was in a hospital, constantly surrounded by people, and more problematic, cleaning staff. I could get around some of those problems, but I wouldn't be able to perform a ritual purification of the room.

No matter how friendly Abby and Paul might be toward me, I was confident that lighting a bundle of sage in her hospital room would have three inevitable results. The fire alarms would go off with a possible bonus of triggering a sprinkler system. I would be banned from the hospital premises. I would spend a much less amicable night in one of Sheriff Barnes' cells, with the door closed. The cleansing wasn't an absolute necessity, but I was loath to do less than I was able to do. I decided that practicality was the greater part of valor and set my mind to developing a combination of protections that didn't end in any of those less-than-stellar results. I dropped off to sleep amid a mental swirl of runes, incantations and dead languages.

I woke up to blinding pain. My back was on fire again. Some rational part of me knew it wasn't literally on fire, but my body made no such distinctions. I managed to crawl across the bed in little spurts between explosions of agony that left me breathless and on the verge of tears. I clawed open the bottle of painkillers the doctor had prescribed. I had no memory of actually going to the pharmacy, but I must have done so. I dumped one of the pills into my shaking hand and almost popped it straight down my throat. A moment of clarity took hold then. I'd be performing magic later that day. High Magick, by most people's measure, and that kind of magic could backfire in horrifying ways if I did it wrong.

I closed my fist around the pill. The pain verged on unbearable, but I rode it out. I needed to know if I could endure it. It wasn't some machismo thing. I've got absolutely nothing against pharmaceutical solutions to that kind of pain. Hell, it was the exact reason pills like those existed. If I could endure it without the pill, though, it meant I didn't need to take the whole thing. I expected that the full dose would leave me in a more or less drug-induced stupor. Half a dose would probably cut the pain to a livable, if very uncomfortable, level. I lay there for a minute, as the pain cascaded across my body in great waves that made my muscles knot to the cusp of cramping up. I endured for two minutes and then for three.

I won't claim that the pain was less. It wasn't. What happened was that I started to get a little bit inured to it. It was a close call, but I forced myself to bite the pill in half and dry-swallow it. The idea of getting up to find water was almost enough to cause tears. I lay very still and breathed as steadily and deeply as my injured lungs would allow, meaning not very, for fifteen minutes. The drug started to kick in and the pain receded. It didn't recede as much as I would have liked, not even close, but enough that I was functional.

I went through the burn treatment routine. The burn's location on my back added challenges to applying the antibiotic cream and securing a fresh bandage, but I muddled through. I'd have given serious money to be able to take a shower. It wasn't practical, though, so I settled for a makeshift sponge bath in the cabin's tiny shower. I changed into the last of my clean clothes and made a mental note to find a laundry or dry cleaner in town. I sat on the edge of the bed. Twenty minutes drifted by without anything like a substantive thought crossing my mind. I snapped out of it with an effort. While some of my drifting was the medication, I thought the real culprit was the pain itself.

Pain exhausts your mental and physical resources. The act of experiencing pain was a trauma that, in many ways, was worse than the original injury. It was one of reasons why people who had experienced severe pain and trauma found action movies so implausible. People that have been shot know that you don't proceed to have a twenty-minute, running gun battle followed by hand-to-hand combat. You go into shock. If you don't get treatment very quickly, the shock will kill you before the bullet does. If you manage to survive the bullet and the surgery to remove it, then you experience the pain. Mind-numbing, body-debilitating pain that you believe, in your true heart, will never end.

You do not go out to settle scores. You don't even think about pulling out the IV that is delivering the pain medication that keeps you sane. You lie in bed and do everything possible to avoid feeling any more pain than you absolutely must. You move only when a doctor or nurse insists that you move. Afterwards, you collapse back into bed and embrace that pain stupor. My theory was that the stupor conferred an evolutionary advantage. It prevented you from going out and doing stressful and damned fool things like riding horses, hunting, or in my case, driving cars and engaging in higher order magic.

The problem with that evolutionary advantage was that it assumed your comfort and survival were the paramount concern. The real world didn't work like that most days. My comfort was all well and good, but it didn't account for Abby's survival. If I didn't get up and do something, I was sure that her life expectancy was going to drop into the days and hours category, rather than whatever the doctors had told her and Paul. I had to do it, because I seriously doubted anyone else in town had the necessary esoteric knowledge to act. My body voted to stretch out on the bed and sleep. My brain voted to do something. Those contradictory votes ended in a stalemate with me standing in the middle of the room and staring into space. I might have stood there for hours, if a confused bird hadn't flown against one of the windows. The noise startled me out of my near hypnotic state and sent my heart pounding.

"Easy, Adrian," I said out loud.

The sound of my own voice eased my panic. I knelt by the bed and slid the hard case out from underneath it. I set the case on the bed and opened it. I surveyed the contents. I picked out a piece of chalk that a bemused Buddhist monk blessed for me and a small pendant on a fine silver chain. Anyone who looked closely at the pendant would see that it didn't contain a stone or a picture, but a tiny mirror. I'd cast a mirror spell on the pendant, which ought to reflect back most minor harm spells. The chalk was for the heavy lifting. There were other things in the case, more dangerous things that I might need later, but I hoped not. I'd lifted most of them off the corpses of malicious entities or made them myself. Very few of them were meant to do nice things.

I pocketed the chalk and the pendant, along with the other half of the painkiller, and went outside. It was midmorning and the heat I expected later hadn't arrived. The sun filtered down through a healthy canopy of leaves, which left the cabin in a soft glow. A cool breeze wafted lazily by and I tried to imagine how such evil arrived at a place that seemed so peaceful. My burn throbbed then, as if to remind me that the evil was there and I had better remember that. I cast a hateful thought at the burn and locked the cabin behind me.

The Neon was not designed to be driven by someone with a burned back. I was grateful to climb out of it in the hospital's visitor lot. I glanced around and saw a lot of unhappiness. Hospitals weren't really joyous places, except maybe in the maternity ward. Most visitors arrived at hospitals because something that had been fine was suddenly going wrong. I did my best not to notice the woman crying hysterically into her husband's shirt, or his look of shellshock. I tried not to notice the grim acceptance on the face of the middle-aged man coming out the front door as I went inside. He had, no doubt, gotten the long face from his doctor.

I jumped into the first elevator I saw and made eye contact with no one. The potent antiseptic smell that marks all hospitals permeated that elevator. I hated that smell, because it made me think of Marcy in her awful, final hours. The doors slid open and a couple stepped off, looking apprehensive. Someone stood behind me, but I didn't look back. The doors slid shut again and a prickling feeling on the back of my neck took hold as cold washed over me. I turned to look behind me.

Doctor Sumner stood there. He looked fit for his age, save for a small potbelly that protruded over his belt. He had a hooked nose, large ears, and thin lips. He stared at me or, more accurately, something stared at me through him. I could feel its alien presence and its acidic anger. I knew that this thing, whatever it was, was here to threaten me. I also knew, through some basic intuition or simple experience, that it was not the real power at work. Underlings were sent to issue threats, while the boss did the important work.

"It's time for you to leave, conjurer," said the possessed Sumner.

"Oh, is it now?"

"Yes."

"Or what? Pain? Dismemberment? Endless cable news?"

Whatever it was, the underling seemed to have expected a bit more awe on my part. I guess no one told it that possession was a cheap trick and only frightened the uninitiated. The doctor's lips curled back to reveal age-yellowed teeth.

"You have been warned. Leave. *Now!*"

"Honestly, Toto, has that worked on anyone since the Enlightenment? I mean, seriously, anyone at all?"

Fury contorted Sumner's face. I think the underling might have taken a swing at me, but the elevator dinged. The alien presence melted away and the doctor gave me a confused look.

"I'm sorry," he said, blinking rapidly. "Guess I had a senior moment. Did you ask me something?"

"I asked if you have the time," I said, reaching out a hand to hold the doors.

The no-longer-possessed Sumner blinked a few more times. "Mr. Hartworth, how are you feeling?"

"Better than I was. It's just a waiting game."

"Not your first rodeo?"

"Nope."

Sumner shook his head and seemed to come back into focus. He checked his wrist. "You asked the time. Eleven o'clock."

"Thanks, doc. Guess I'm right on time, after all."

I stepped off the elevator and made my way down the hall. I'd made light of the underling to its face, but such a blatant appearance worried me. Demons generally trucked in secrecy and shadow. Open confrontation and warnings weren't really their speed. I stopped outside Abby's room and put on a friendly face. I reached into my pocket to grab the pendant and my hand brushed against the chalk. It was hot. Not the kind of ambient warmth that anything in a pocket picks up from your body, but almost too hot to touch.

I shoved my way into the room and felt the dark magic before I registered anything else. I looked around. Paul was unconscious, lurched sideways in a chair by Abby's bed. There was a moment when I thought he was dead, but I saw his chest move as he took in shallow breaths. I looked to Abby. She was rigid, her arms locked straight out down either side of her body, and her eyes were open as wide as they could go. Her skin was ghostly white and I couldn't see it if she was breathing.

As a rule, anger isn't a good place to start from when you work magic. Anger makes you volatile, reckless, and prone to mistakes. Anger also makes you commit to things you shouldn't and wouldn't commit to under rational conditions. Anger, more often than not, serves as a fuel for evil, rather than good. That is why, as a rule, magic is the domain of the calm, disciplined mind. Every once in a blue moon, though, you're compelled to chuck the rules. When some malevolent shit is using magic to murder an innocent teenager, I consider it blue moon time.

"The hell you will," I growled.

I grabbed the chalk, almost hot enough to burn my hand, and ripped it free from my pocket. Even in full daylight, it glowed bright enough to see. I dove for the floor beneath Abby's bed and then things got interesting.

Chapter 11

AS MY BODY FELL THROUGH THE OPEN SPACE, time slowed and twisted. Reality warped like overheated plastic and then splintered. My body continued to fall toward the floor. I stood in an empty white expanse and Marcy faced me, dressed for a funeral. I stood next to a younger version of Paul, who stared down at the graves of his son and daughter-in-law. Abby sat in a picture window and I had my feet propped up next to her. I sat at a park table and stared across a chessboard at myself. I needed to hurry. I had all the time in the world.

The other me yawned, took a sip of coffee, and moved a pawn. "Don't tell me you're surprised by this. Haven't you figured out by now that linear conceptions of time and mono-plane experiences of reality are cheap, convenient fictions?"

I blinked at myself as I tried to make sense of the multifaceted reality. I wondered if that was how it felt to be a fly, seeing everything like pieces of some fractured mosaic.

"What?" I asked.

"Come on," said the other me. "I'm you. Try to keep up."

I hit the floor hard and slid. I wrapped a hand around the railing on Abby's bed and dragged myself underneath it. I looked up at the underside of the bed, searching for a flat space large enough to do what I needed to do. I raised up the chalk, pressed it against the molded gray plastic, and drew a line.

Paul's eyes remained fixed on the graves as he spoke. "It isn't right. It's not right to stand over your child's grave."

I didn't understand his pain. I couldn't. I had no children and probably never would. It's a lifetime commitment. Over the last few years, my commitments rarely lasted more than a week or two. Every once in a while, they lasted a month. The notion of having another human life depending on me every waking minute of every single day frightened me, not because I didn't want it, but because I knew I would fail. I slipped my hands into my pockets and said nothing.

Beneath the bed, I shifted my hand and started to draw another line. I felt pressure building around me, pressing against my hand and my body. It felt like something ratcheted up the gravity to twice its normal pull. I started to sweat and my hand trembled a little. I gritted my teeth hard and forced my muscles to keep moving the chalk.

"You should have gone," said Marcy. "Why didn't you go?"

"Abby. She needed help. Who else was going to help her?"

Marcy looked down for a moment. She lifted her face to me again and shook her head.

"What?" I asked.

"I don't think you'll survive this. I don't think you can. I think we'll be together again, very soon."

A part of me rejoiced at those words and I felt a little stab of guilt. You're not supposed to want to die. If you want to die, it means you've given up on something essential to being a human being. Around the edges of the whiteness, I saw black, creeping tendrils.

I blinked the sweat out of my eyes and finished the line. My arm was trembling. I grabbed my right wrist with my left hand, steadying it. I shifted my hand again and began the third line to complete the triangle. In the periphery of my vision, I saw the room grow darker.

"I don't remember my parents," said Abby.

She looked healthy, as if the chemo had never happened. I thought that my original assessment had been right. She wasn't a beauty queen, but there was a wholesomeness to her that trumped those considerations. Her vibrancy, the sheer aliveness she exuded, was almost overwhelming.

"I'm sorry."

Abby shrugged. "It's hard to be sad. I know I missed something, am missing something, but it's fuzzy. I don't know what I'm supposed to be sad about."

"Family is hard," I said, not knowing what else to say.

"Do you have family?"

"Everyone has family somewhere."

I hated myself a little. I couldn't even give the kid a straight answer on another plane of existence that might not even be real.

It was everything I could do to keep the chalk against the bottom of the bed. Both of my arms were shaking. The gravity had intensified again to at least three or four or twenty times normal. I could barely breathe. Even so, I still found the air to be pissed.

"Fuck you," I gasped.

I dragged the chalk a few more centimeters.

"Come on," I got out through clenched teeth.

The chalk flared briefly and the pressure lifted enough for me to suck in a few quick breaths that gave me the spins. *Damn smoke inhalation*, I thought.

The other me moved a knight out onto the board, though I suspected he was as disinterested in the game as I was.

I frowned at the board. "Is this the whole linear versus circular argument again?"

"It's not that, not specifically. You're just a bit too fond of this idea of time as rigidly linear, even though you know better. Minimally speaking, time is more flexible than you credit. I have a notion that time is actually fractal and that your current condition is a nice demonstration of how you can unpack it."

I stopped frowning at the board and began frowning at the other me. "So, you're saying that *I* have the idea that time is fractal?"

Other me tapped the tip of his nose. "And that it unpacks across planes of existence."

I closed my eyes. "My head hurts."

"Price of multi-planar consciousness," said other me.

I finished the second line of the second triangle and the pressure overpowered me. The chalk dropped away from the underside of the bed an inch, then another. I tried not to think of Abby directly above me, unable to breathe, unable to move, watching death circle like a vulture. I tried not to think of Paul, maybe sensate, maybe not. I hoped not. What could be worse than helplessly watching someone you love die a mere two or three feet away? I tried not to think of them, but I did. I found anger deep beneath the pressure and muscle fatigue. I drove the chalk back up to bed, inch by trembling inch.

Paul turned away from the graves and started to walk. I kept pace with him.

"The Lord giveth and the Lord taketh away," muttered Paul, hate making his voice ragged. "He takes too much."

"Sometimes," I agreed and thought of Marcy.

"He's going to take Abby from me, too."

I stopped and reached out. I turned him to face me.

"No," I said. "He isn't."

"How do you know?"

I didn't know. No one ever really knows, but I also did know. I knew something that Paul didn't. Time is fractal. I had all the time I needed. I needed to hurry. I knew something else that Paul didn't know.

"I won't let him take her," I said.

It should have sounded arrogant beyond all reason. For all I knew, it did sound that way. It also sounded true. The younger version of Paul looked at me with eyes far less rheumy than they would be one day. He believed me. Then again, maybe he just wanted to believe me. Maybe there wasn't a difference.

The room was pitch black. The only light came from the chalk, which cast just enough to illuminate the symbol I was constructing through, I was confident, nothing but unadulterated hatred and willpower. I closed the second triangle, which left a passable Star of David etched in chalk. The completion of the star seemed to push the darkness back a little and the pressure lifted enough that my hand only shook violently, rather than spastically. I pressed the chalk hard against one of the points and started to draw a circle.

The empty whiteness that surrounded Marcy and me vanished in a howling explosion. We faced each other on a blasted desert plain. Craggy spires of obsidian speared into the amber sky like skeletal fingers. Marcy gave me a terrified look as a figure made of liquid shadow materialized behind her. I felt its hatred and fury like cloth against my body. It wrapped fingers of liquid shadow around Marcy's throat.

"You will withdraw your protection of the she-child, conjurer."

Its voice was like lava rolling over a home. It was like hail the size of softballs pummeling unprotected cattle in a field. It was like the primordial jungle in the heat of a killing frenzy. This was no half-pint messenger boy. That thing was the mind behind all the suffering of a teenage girl. I felt its power crashing around us. I was a flea screaming impotently at the descending foot of a woolly mammoth. I knew it and so did the demon; the demon that had wrapped its vile hand around Marcy's throat. Around. Her. Throat.

"You will withdraw or I will end this one forever."

The demon wasn't issuing idle threats. It had the power to do it. If it chose to, it could shred her living soul. For Marcy, there would be no afterlife or rebirth, just literal soul-rending pain and then nothing. She would cease to be and I'd have to watch it happen.

Five versions of me screamed the same thing at the same time. "No!"

"Help her, dammit!" Other Me bellowed.

"You can't let it do this," said Paul.

"You know how," said Abby.

I dropped my feet from the picture window and leaned toward the girl. "What do you mean?"

Abby looked at me then and her eyes were angelic fire. "Enochian."

I closed the circle around the star and completed the Seal of Solomon, one of the most potent protective symbols known to lay practitioners. The Seal ignited in silver light and I heard Abby start breathing frantically in the bed above me. The me under the bed sucked in a breath as the pressure vanished. The danger wasn't gone, though. The room was still pitch black.

On a blasted desert plane, a silver Seal of Solomon ignited in the sky above us, spinning like a pinwheel. The demon screeched in pain. It started to lose some substance. The light from the pinwheel symbol boiled away the liquid shadow bit by bit, but not enough. Marcy jerked in pain and let out a garbled cry of pain as the shadow thing's hand clamped down hard around her throat.

I had to act. The fire-eyed Abby was right. I did know how, but it was beyond dangerous. The Enochian alphabet granted the practitioner access to divine might. It was also approached with extreme caution by master sorcerers who were way beyond my skills. Angels possessed as little patience with dabbling mortals as demons. They were equally quick to punish the foolhardy. If I did nothing, though, the outcome was unthinkable. I prayed to whatever deity watched over fools and wayward warlocks and started scrawling on the underside of the bed again, left to right around the Seal of Solomon in angelic script. The script ignited in golden fire.

On the blasted plain, I heard a sound like wings the size of creation itself beating behind me. Great clouds of sand whirled past, each grain burning like a tiny ember. The blazing sand ripped through the liquid shadow. It screamed and the noise was something so obscene that my mind refused to register it, instead telling me that everything had gone silent. Something landed behind me with the force of a boulder falling from a clifftop. The blasted landscape fell away and once again I faced Marcy in white emptiness. A hand large enough to wrap itself around my head and glowing pure, divine white settled on my shoulder.

"You're insane," said Marcy, but with a little smile. "You need to call Helena."

"You know about," I started to say, more than a touch guilty, but she cut me off.

"You'll need her," insisted Marcy.

"Do I have to?"

"Go now," said a voice made of aching perfection.

Fractal time repacked itself and reality collapsed down to one plane. For a single moment, the room remained in darkness and then light pierced it. The darkness imploded and I heard dozens of car alarms screaming bloody murder in the parking lot outside. I couldn't swear to it, but I had the impression that the too-perfect-for-sanity voice said one more thing.

"Work on your grammar."

I let my head and arms drop to the floor. I started to laugh a quiet, wheezy laugh, and took a small comfort in the sound of Abby's labored breathing above me. Then I stopped laughing. I needed to call Helena.

"Well, shit," I wheezed.

Chapter 12

I CRAWLED OUT FROM BENEATH ABBY'S BED and stood next to her on rubbery legs that couldn't decide if they would support me or not. Abby was afraid. It was written across her face and hunched posture. Paul wasn't awake yet and probably wouldn't remember anything out of the ordinary. Abby, on the other hand, had been wide-awake through the whole thing. I didn't know if she remembered anything about alternate planes of reality, or if it had even really been her. That other Abby might have been nothing but a projection created by my own mind. I doubted that, but it was hard to know for sure.

What Abby did know was that something very wrong happened. If she was bright, and I thought she was, she knew that wrongness was aimed at her. She looked afraid. She didn't look afraid enough. She hadn't seen what I saw. She hadn't felt the enormous, oppressive power of that liquid shadow. She hadn't seen the Seal of Solomon, a symbol designed to compel the wills of demons, do nothing more than weaken it. The Seal should have sent that thing scurrying for cover. Instead, I'd been forced to hazard destruction and summon angelic powers.

I succeeded, but I doubted that had much to do with me. I think that whatever showed up and cast the demon back was looking for an opening, and I provided it. I couldn't count on the same cooperation, or leniency for third-rate summoning, the next time. I fished around in my pocket and pulled out the necklace. Abby didn't notice the necklace. She just looked at me, as if this were the first time she'd seen me. I guess, in the ways that matter, it was the first time she was seeing *me*. It wasn't the random guy who pulled her out of a burning building. She hadn't remembered any of that. She was seeing the man who got bloodied in the magical gladiator pits. That guy was a very different animal. He wasn't pretty, and he wasn't heroic.

"What's happening?" Abby asked in a tiny voice.

I pressed my lips together and shook my head. "I don't really know. Something that shouldn't be happening. Here, put this on."

I held out the necklace. She stared at it like it might bite her hand. I pushed it a little closer. She didn't reach for the necklace.

"What is it?"

I looked over at Paul. He was still out.

"Magic," I said. "It should help you avoid some of the bad things that keep happening to you."

"Magic," she said with some of the previous day's pessimism bleeding into her voice. "Whatever."

"You have a better explanation for what just happened?"

The color that had just started to come back to her cheeks drained away again. She grabbed the necklace and put it on. She held her breath, apparently waiting for something. She gave me a questioning look.

"Shouldn't it, I don't know, tingle or something?"

I smiled. "It's not doing something to you. It's doing something *for* you. It should reflect negative energy back to whatever sent it."

"Don't you mean whoever?"

I closed my eyes, unwilling to meet her gaze. "I wish I did, kid. I wish to God I did."

By the time the car alarms were deactivated, the hysteria induced by hospital-wide flickering lights waned, and a nurse came in to check on Abby, I'd cleaned myself up. The nurse gave me a second glance, as though she didn't quite like what she saw on my face. I was probably paler than I should have been, but I doubted I looked like I was in immediate danger. That would come later, when I made a call to Helena on orders from Marcy. After the nurse left, Abby looked to me.

"Why is this happening to me?"

There was still fear in her voice, but anger too. Something had picked her and made her life hell. Once she knew it, she had a target for all the anger that had never had a place to go. I thought, all things considered, she was remarkably calm.

"I honestly don't know. At this point, I wouldn't even want to guess."

"I didn't do anything to deserve this," her hands were bunched into fists.

"No, you didn't," I agreed. "Most people don't deserve the crap that drops on their heads."

I didn't believe that last one. Most of the time people actually *did* deserve exactly what they got. Maybe it was for the lies they told or the things they did, always rewritten in memory to make them look like the good guys, but most bad things happened because a person did something lousy first. The principle of action-and-reaction is as unforgiving as gravity, although rarely as immediate. Abby wasn't in that category. To draw down the attention of something as perfectly evil as that liquid shadow demanded a level of obscene, violent, inhuman behavior normally reserved to ethnic cleansing and the blackest magic.

"You did something, didn't you?" Abby asked.

"Yeah, I did something."

"What?"

"Magic."

I said it in the flattest, most serious voice at my disposal. I didn't want to give her the impression that there was room for doubt. Her belief wasn't a fixed necessity, but it might stave off questions later.

She fingered the little mirror pendant. "Like the necklace?"

"A little more complicated than that."

Several infinities more complicated than the necklace, I didn't add. She had enough on her mind.

"Is it over?"

"I'm afraid not."

"You stopped it," she said, confused and afraid again.

"No. I scared it off for now, but it's not gone for good. Not yet anyway."

I would have gone on, but Paul was stirring in his chair. No need to overcomplicate things by including him in the conversation. I gave Abby a significant look.

"You should keep the magic talk between us."

Abby gave a semi-hysterical giggle. "Like anyone would believe me."

"Someone might," I warned. "Someone who might not be inclined to help you."

That sobered her up. "Our secret."

I nodded.

"Are you going to stay?"

I lifted a shoulder. I'd tried to leave twice and been derailed twice. I was starting to think that something was keeping me in town. Like a giant angel with glowing hands, I wondered.

"Yeah, looks like I am. I need to go do a few things, but I'll be around."

Panic flickered across her eyes. "What are you going to do?"

"I need to make a call."

"Who are you calling?"

"Someone who can help," I said.

"Help you?"

I laughed. "No. She wouldn't help me, but she might help you."

"Why?"

"She'd help you because she's a good person."

Abby frowned up at me. "I meant why wouldn't she help you?"

"Oh. That," I fumbled. "It's a long story."

Paul stirred again and opened his eyes. He raised a hand and rubbed at one eye. "Guess I dozed off there. Mr. Hartworth, how are you?"

"I'm fine, sir. Yourself?"

"I'm fine. Odd dreams, though. Must be all the hospital noise."

"Must be," I said, with a warning glance at Abby. "I have to be going. Abby, Paul, it was good seeing you both again."

"Will we be seeing you again, Mr. Hartworth?" Paul asked.

"Oh, I'm like a bad penny. I always turn up, sooner or later."

"I look forward to it," said the old man with a guileless smile.

I nodded to them both and left the room. I spent a short hour driving around to find a place to buy some clothes and a laundromat. Then I stopped and bought a cheap, disposable cell phone. I sat in my car and stared at it for a few minutes before I went over to the diner. I hit one of those golden spells in food service between rushes. The handful of locals in the diner all cast suspicious looks my way. I wondered if any of them had been in the bar the other night. Those events seemed very old and distant to me, but were probably still considered fresh fodder in the local rumor mill.

The waitress came over and handed me a menu. She didn't seem enthused about it.

"Get you something to drink?"

"Coffee, please," I said.

I ordered one of their specials, which consisted of scrambled eggs, bacon, sausage, a biscuit, home fries, and a small orange juice. The waitress gave me a nonplussed look.

"You sure about that, hon? It's a lot of food."

My stomach rumbled loud enough for her to hear and she laughed.

"I'm sure," I said with a little smile.

After a short wait, the food arrived and I went to work. The locals eyed me and I ignored them. *I got ninety-nine problems and the hicks ain't one*, I thought. I ate the whole meal, though the last few bites were more about pride than hunger. I looked around and saw dim, but genuine, approval on the faces of the other patrons. I guessed that I'd succeeded in some rite of passage, The Cholesterol Binge, perhaps. I paid my bill and left a generous tip before I went back to my car.

The new phone sat on the passenger seat and looked shiny in its plastic packaging. I knew I was trying to procrastinate and avoid making the dreaded call to Helena. I chastised myself. I wasn't calling for me. Delaying only served to keep Abby in danger for longer than necessary. I drove back to my cabin and used the phone there to activate the new cell. I punched in a number. My thumb hovered over the send key as my will wavered. I expected unpleasantness. I depressed the key and put the phone up to my ear. The phone rang half a dozen times before a smoky voice rolled over the line.

"Yes. Hello?"

I took a breath. "Helena, don't hang up."

"I told you not to call me again," the smoke in Helena's voice was backed with fire.

"I was told to call you," I said, trying to placate her.

"By whom?"

"Marcy."

There was a sharp intake of breath on the other end of the line, followed by nothing. The silence dragged out for the better part of a minute. A minute of silence gave me a lot of time to think of all the ways the conversation could go bad. Still, she stayed on the line, which gave me a little fragment of hope. I needed Helena's help. There was too much going on that I didn't understand and Abby needed someone who could stay close at hand. I couldn't do that and deal with a demon that scared me on an epic scale.

Helena's smoky voice drifted over the line again. "Marcy. You mean to say…"

"Yes, I mean *that*. Marcy told me to call you."

"Jesus."

There was more silence over the line. It wasn't the dangerous silence it had been, just the silence of someone processing some things that they hadn't expected.

"What's happening?" Helena asked.

"Well," I started.

"Never mind, it must be God awful or you wouldn't be talking to me right now. Where are you?"

I told her where I was and where to find the motel. I did not tell her where to find my cabin. Telling her that piece of information seemed a bit like inviting disaster. She made noises at the right places and I heard the scritch-scritch of her writing. There was another long pause.

"Adrian," she said.

"Helena."

"You're a miserable bastard and I hope you rot in hell."

It was less venomous than I expected. "Thanks for helping."

The line went dead.

I looked around the little cabin and spoke to the empty space. "How could this possibly go wrong?"

In the back of my head, I started counting ways. The number was high enough to be depressing.

Chapter 13

THE NEXT DAY PASSED WITHOUT INCIDENT, as though everything had taken a breather to figure out what came next. Whatever was lobbing black magic at Abby was probably shocked by the divine intervention that I managed on her behalf. If it knew who I was, it wouldn't have expected me to be able to make that happen. I imagined it was reassessing and deciding how best to remove me. Before, I'd been a troubling but largely inconsequential obstacle to its goals. After that little stunt at the hospital, it probably thought I was a genuine threat. I added that to the list of things likely to keep me awake at night.

For my part, I dealt with practicalities. I did laundry. I visited Abby. I slept for a few hours. I worried like hell. I also tried to figure out what that thing had been. The ranks of evil are a lot more packed than most people realize. There are the big evil beings, like a lot of old, vicious gods, not to mention the Morning Star himself, but that is the tiny tip of a very big iceberg. Trying to put a name to a particular vessel of evil is easier than guessing the name of a human being randomly selected from somewhere on the face of the earth, but only just.

Even knowing the thing was potent only narrowed the field so much. It cut the list of potentials down into the thousands. The worst part is that human knowledge about literal figures of evil is limited. There is no way to be certain that anyone had ever encountered that presence, let alone put its name to paper along with a handy-dandy description of its weaknesses. Those who possess such knowledge guard it with great care, to keep the information out of the wrong hands—or just as often, out of the right hands. Long story short, I was flying mostly blind.

The combination of fretting and chronic pain from my back took its toll. By early evening, I wasn't good for much beyond lying on the cabin's little bed and semi-watching something on basic cable. The drone of the television acted like white noise and I drifted between sleeping and waking. Three sharp raps on the door snapped me out of the dreamlike haze I was enjoying. I picked up the knife I'd left on the nightstand and flipped it open with a flick of my wrist. The serrated blade would do a lot of hard-to-repair damage if I was forced to use it.

I stood at the door and wished the cabin had a peephole. At least then I'd know who was on the other side. I steeled myself for anything and opened the door. Apparently my mind's version of steeling myself for anything left some very obvious things off the list.

"Helena," I said.

She slapped me hard across the face and I took an involuntary step back. She slid by me into the cabin. I caught the scent of sandalwood as she passed me.

"Close the door, idiot," she snapped at me.

I shook my head, trying to clear the pain haze. I closed the door. I rubbed at my jaw and turned to face her. She looked thinner than I remembered. I checked that thought. She didn't look thinner. She looked leaner. She'd always had the willowy frame of a distance runner, but it looked like she might have taken up running as a serious pursuit. She'd cropped her hair short and dyed it blonde. Her eyes were sea-green and the contrast with her almond-colored skin shocked me, as it always did when I hadn't seen her in a while. No one seeing us side-by-side would have guessed that she was older than me. I guess she got better genes.

"There," I muttered. "The door is no longer ajar."

"Always the funny man, aren't you, Adrian?"

I chose not to rise to the jibe. "You could have called. How'd you find me anyway?"

She gave me the same expression you might give a malfunctioning toaster. I felt embarrassed.

She looked me up and down. "You're looking impoverished."

She shrugged out of a short, designer-label leather jacket and tossed it onto the bed. Then she looked around the cabin and sniffed.

"Very impoverished," she amended.

"Thanks. Always nice to be reminded of my shortcomings."

Her eyes flashed. "Would you like me to remind you of your shortcomings?"

I looked away fast. "No. No, I think that's probably something we can skip. Thanks for coming."

"Save your thanks. I didn't come here to please you."

I had expected her anger, but expecting something rarely made it any easier to experience. Knowing I had it coming didn't help matters either. I pressed forward, as best as I could.

"Fair enough. You may want to sit down. This will take a bit of explanation."

I thought she was going to snap at me again, but apparently she'd decided that I'd had enough abuse for the moment. She looked around the room again and sat on the bed. I dragged a small, uncomfortable wooden chair over from the corner and sat down facing her.

"Did you hear about Miami?"

Helena nodded and her expression softened a little. "Is Damelus really gone?"

"As good as. I didn't pull the trigger on his body. His soul is, well, it's somewhere else now. Not the kind of place souls come back from."

Helena whispered something under her breath. Her family had history with Damelus' family. From the little bit I knew, it was ugly history. Something occurred to her and concern replaced relief.

"I heard Daniel was traveling with you," she said. "Was he there?"

I shook my head. "No. I left him back in Vegas taking tourists for everything they had. We didn't leave off on good terms."

"Do you ever leave off on good terms?"

There was bitterness in her voice, but the undercurrent was pain. I rubbed my face with the palms of my hands. I didn't want to reopen old wounds.

"No," I said. "It doesn't seem like I ever do."

"Maybe you should work on that," said Helena, her voice a blade.

"Maybe I should," I said.

Maybe it was something in the tone of my voice, or the timbre, or maybe it was something in my expression. Whatever it was, Helena seemed to realize that she was pushing me too hard, too far and doing it too fast. I was moving into dangerous emotional territory, a kind of empty space that all too often preceded violence. She looked away first.

"Miami," she prompted.

"Yeah," I said. "Anyways, in the aftermath, I figured law enforcement would be looking hard at me because, well, that's pretty much how it always goes. I wasn't really interested in that, so I got out of town."

I filled her in on what had happened. I started with what happened at the bar, which was met with a flinty-eyed glare. I moved on, quickly, to the car fiasco and trying to get out of town. I told her about the fire and Abby. Helena perked up as I talked about the accidents and the cancer. Then I told her about what happened at the hospital. I did my best to describe my experience with splintered time. I still didn't have it entirely straight in my own head, so I had to go through that part several times before Helena was satisfied.

"Enochian! What were you thinking? Do you have any idea what could have happened if the thing that showed up wasn't in such a forgiving mood?"

"Nothing good, I'm sure. Mostly I was thinking that I had to do something. I wasn't overwhelmed by options at the time."

"No, I guess you weren't. Still, the risk you took. It wasn't just your life in the balance. And you wonder why people aren't happy to see you."

I snorted. "I don't wonder about that anymore."

Helena rubbed at her left temple. I supposed that tale would have given any sane person a headache. Her eyes took on an unfocused glaze and I could almost hear her shuffling through some mental filing system.

"Fractal time," she said, as if the idea was somehow familiar. Then she shook her head. "If I didn't know any better, I'd say you were cursed. What are the odds that you'd stop in a town where all of this was going on?"

"Pretty damn slim," I admitted. "I get the feeling that I didn't wind up here by accident, which fills me with all kinds of unhappiness. I don't like being manipulated that way. Any thoughts about what that shadow thing might be?"

She shrugged. "Sure, lots of thoughts, but none that I'd be confident enough to stand by. What I don't understand is what possible relevance this Abby girl can have to it. You said it yourself, she's not powerful. It doesn't even sound like she's got any native ability."

"None at all. At least, none that I picked up on, and I was looking."

I shifted in the chair and the burn on my back gently reminded me it was there with a lightning bolt of pain. I leaned forward and grabbed the seat of the chair with both hands. I was overdue for another dose of painkiller.

"What's wrong?" Helena asked, anger forgotten in her innate empathy.

"Back hurts," I said through clenched teeth.

"Getting old?"

"Got burned a little. At the house. Painkillers on the nightstand."

As I breathed through the pain, Helena got me a pill and filled up a little paper cup with water in the bathroom. She offered them to me and seemed taken aback when I bit the pill in half. I knocked it back with the water from the cup. She waited it out in silence until the medication took the worst edges off the pain.

"Alright, hero, let me see the burn."

"It's nothing," I said.

"Shirt. Off. It's not like I haven't seen it before."

I gave her a wan smile. "If you say so."

I stood, unbuttoned the shirt and took it off. She stared at the scars and tattoos. She hadn't seen those before. She reached out and prodded some of the puffed up scar tissue with her warm fingers.

"What the hell happened? Who did this to you, Adrian?"

I shrugged and shook my head. "I honestly have no idea."

The anger built to explosion levels behind her eyes.

"I swear to God, Helena. I have no memory of how this happened. There are stories, but you know how reliable those are."

"You're like a child. You need constant supervision. Turn around."

I did as I was told. She peeled the bandage off and there was a pronounced silence behind me.

"Got burned a little? Aren't we still the master of understatement."

It wasn't necessary, but Helena put another coat of antibiotic cream on the burn and a fresh bandage. Maybe it was her way of making amends for pushing so hard when she first showed up. Then again, maybe she would have done it for anyone. That was the thing about Helena, I never really knew her. I don't think anyone ever really had. She was a child of magic, raised in its mysteries from birth and practiced in its secrecy. Secrecy has a way of bleeding into everything.

She handed me my shirt. I felt her eyes on me as I buttoned the shirt and I looked up. There was a sense of expectancy around her, as if she was waiting for me to say something or do something. The moment passed before I had a chance to figure out what she expected. She picked her jacket up off the bed and slid into it. She looked thoughtful.

"I hope you realize how bad this all is," she said.

I grunted. "Yeah, I've got a pretty good idea."

She struggled with something inside her own head before she came out with it, all in a rush. "You might not be able to save her."

I'd have expected that kind of talk from Daniel, but not from Helena. Maybe I didn't know how bad things were, after all. My eyes wandered the barren walls of the cabin, looking for inspiration. I found none.

"Maybe not. Are you saying I should walk away, like I did in Charleston?"

She walked to the door and looked at me over her shoulder.

"No, not unless you think you should. I'm saying you should prepare yourself for the idea that she may die, despite anything you or me or anyone else might do to protect her. These are deeper waters than you're used to," she said. "Did you bring it?"

She was talking about the hard case.

"Yes," I said.

"Thank God for small favors. Try not to slip and kill yourself in the shower," she said, and then added, "idiot."

Chapter 14

AS PAINFUL AS I FOUND SEEING HELENA AGAIN, I woke up the next day feeling better than I had since my arrival. There was something iconic about the idea of the person who stood alone against extraordinary odds, but it was one hell of a scary thing to actually *be* that person. Support, however grudging and angst-ridden, provided me a relief valve. It also gave me someone to talk to about the situation. I didn't need to convince Helena about anything. I didn't need to slalom around legal obstacles. She understood the threat to Abby, probably better than I did.

In the realm of magical practitioners, I was the Johnny-come-lately journeyman to Helena's master craftswoman. The big difference between me and her, between me and most practitioners, was that I operated in the world. I got press in the underground lines of communication that served to keep us all informed of what was happening in our rarified community. I had the unsettling impression that all that press gave people the idea that I was much better at magic than I actually was. My continued survival no doubt contributed to that impression, but the facts remained the facts. She was better than me, plain and simple.

Having someone like that in my corner, or Abby's corner anyway, did a lot of good for my optimism. It also freed me up to do some digging. At least it would after I introduced Helena to Abby and Paul. Helena had called at the crack of too early for human compassion to set up a time to meet at the hospital. We walked into the lobby together and rode the elevator in silence. For my part, silence seemed safer. The elevator doors slid open and we started down the hall. I was becoming a regular enough presence that one of the nurses gave me a smile that bordered on flirty. I grinned at her and Helena elbowed me hard in the ribs. I gave her a dirty look and she stopped in her tracks.

"What?" I asked. The dirty look wasn't that bad.

"Good God, Adrian. Zero points for finesse, but full marks for amperage."

"Huh?"

"You weren't messing around. I mean, I knew what you did had to be strong, but you upped your game here," said Helena.

"Oh, yeah, I guess so."

Her unsolicited praise left me feeling a little unbalanced after the previous night's emotional bloodletting. I changed the subject.

"Any thoughts about how to approach this introduction?" I asked.

She rolled her eyes at me. "Just get me in the room."

I walked her into Abby's room and the teenager smiled at us. I was shocked at how much healthier she looked compared to the previous day. Paul was sitting next to her bed and he looked better as well, less beaten down, more like a vigorous sixty-year-old than a world-weary seventy-year-old.

"Paul, Abby, I'd like you to meet a friend of mine. This is Helena St. Clair."

That was the moment at which my participation in the conversation ended. When she wanted to, Helena blazed like a lighthouse in the darkness. She accomplished in three minutes of infectiously cheerful small talk what took me risking my life in a burning building to accomplish. She won their trust. After five minutes, I made some flimsy excuse no one really heard and slipped out of the room. I waited until I was sitting in my car before I punched in Patty's number. I toyed with her card while I waited. After a few rings, Patty picked up. She sounded groggy.

"Hello?"

"Hi, Patty. This is Adrian Hartworth. Did I wake you up?"

"Yes," she said around a yawn. "What do you need?"

"Do you know where Abby's parents are buried?"

There was a pregnant pause before Patty spoke again. "Why would you need to know that?"

"Black magic. Conspiracies. The usual."

"You're giving me an ulcer, Hartworth. Angel's Rest Cemetery."

I jotted down some sketchy directions and thanked Patty before I hung up. I pondered that name, Angel's Rest. Given everything I'd seen, I had my doubts about that one. I'd have been surprised if any of the dead were resting in that town. Or, if they were resting, I wondered how uneasy that rest proved. I pulled out of the hospital parking lot and, after a few wrong turns, found myself heading north. At first, I thought I was imagining it, but after a few miles I realized that a car was following me. I debated how to handle it and decided to do the easiest thing. I pulled over and parked on the side of the road.

I got out of the car to make sure I wasn't trapped in the vehicle if my follower planned me some ill. It also let me stare at the vehicle as it approached. I was surprised when the car pulled in behind mine and the sheriff got out. He was out of uniform, which made him look odd and incomplete to my mind. He wore jeans, heavy hiking boots, and a long-sleeved flannel shirt. His badge and gun were on his belt, though. I gave him a wary nod.

"Sheriff Barnes," I said.

"Mr. Hartworth," said Barnes as he leaned against my car.

He dropped an elbow on the roof and his right hand hung over the side. It was his gun hand. I relaxed a little. The sheriff noticed and chuckled a little.

"For a man who isn't in any trouble that I'm aware of, you're pretty twitchy."

"Being followed makes me nervous. It didn't work out so well for me once upon a time."

Barnes lifted an eyebrow, but didn't pursue my comment. "Most people don't even notice they're being followed. You seemed to pick up on it pretty fast."

"Couldn't comment on how normal it is," I dodged.

A pickup rolled by and the sheriff gave the driver a casual wave. I saw then how we must look, just a couple of guys shooting the breeze. What could look less comment-worthy than the sheriff out of uniform, leaning on a car and shooting friendly waves at passing drivers? They probably thought we were talking about the best place to hook a trout or something else I'd know even less about. Barnes wanted to talk about something, but he didn't want to do it officially.

"Patty tells me that old man Simmons and his granddaughter have taken quite a shine to you."

I shrugged and then nodded. "Yeah, seems like. I'm sure it'll wear off once she's feeling well enough to get out of the hospital. They'll have too much on their plate to be interested in me.

Didn't see any harm in sticking around. Good for Abby's morale and all that."

The sheriff nodded in all the right places to my bullshit answers, which I was pretty sure he knew were bullshit answers. There was nothing obvious to give it away, just a sense that he was going through the motions.

"She's a sweet kid," said the sheriff. "Had more than her fair share of misery. I only mention it so you'll understand my meaning when I say that I'd take it personal if more fell on her head."

I searched the sheriff's face and tried to tease out his meaning. I had no earthly idea what he was on about. What's more, he seemed to know that I was utterly lost. His face lost its guarded casualness and became unforgiving stone.

"There's a breed of so-called men in the world that look at someone like Abby and they don't see a child."

Once he spelled it out, my brain did the rest. Guy pushing into middle age takes an ongoing interest in a teenage girl. With the world the way it was, it would have been hard for a cop not to at least wonder about it a little. Hell, if I was just a casual observer, I would have wondered about it. I was still disgusted by the implication, however reasonable it looked on the outside. I opened my mouth to tell the sheriff where he could shove his innuendos, but he raised a hand.

"Don't bother telling me to go fuck myself. I didn't have you pegged that way, but I had to know. Christ, I hate this job some days."

"Why are you so sure now?"

"I practically had to draw you a picture, Hartworth. It's very damned hard to fake a total lack of understanding. No offense, but you're not much of an actor."

"True," I conceded.

"That's how I know you've got more than a passing curiosity. You didn't before, but you do now. There's oddness swirling. That stuff with the electricity at the hospital. Patty taking a second look at that fire. You're dangerously close to making things interesting here."

"It's not me making things that way. I think you know that. The same way I think you know I'm trying to help that girl."

The sheriff dropped his eyes to the ground and seemed to gather his thoughts. I'd have given a pretty penny to be able to peek into that thought process. I was confident he had a lot of information tucked away in that head that could have cleared things up for me. It was probably information he didn't under-stand without the necessary context. If I tried to give him that context, I expected I'd get a police escort to the county line. I kept my mouth shut. Barnes didn't look up when he spoke.

"Maybe you are, maybe you aren't, but she isn't the only person that lives here. I got three thousand souls in this town I'm responsible for and a damn sight more in the county. You stirring up whatever you're stirring up doesn't seem to be helping all of them very much."

That idea had never crossed my mind. I'd been entirely fo-cused on Abby's plight, but the sheriff had a point. Other people lived in that town who were probably just as innocent as Abby. I was meddling and, as Helena pointed out, the waters were much deeper than I normally hazarded. I nodded.

"I think I understand your position. I'll tell you what, sheriff, the minute I think things will be better if I leave, I will. I'm not looking to get anyone hurt."

Barnes looked up at me then. "I'll hold you to that, Mr. Hartworth."

I stayed quiet in case he wanted to add something, but he didn't. I got back into my car and started it up. Barnes knocked on the window. I rolled it down and looked up at him.

"Mind if I ask what you're looking for up at Angel's Rest?"

"How do you know that's where I'm going?"

He laughed. "That's the only thing out this way. That and some fallow fields. You don't strike me as much of an out-doorsman. That leaves the graveyard."

"Flawless deduction. I'm looking for…"

What was I looking for? I didn't even know. A trail, a bread-crumb, or a helpful spirit that would tell me exactly what I was up against? All of it seemed to start with Abby's parents, so I wanted to start with them. Maybe it was pointless to go up to the graveyard, but graveyards were a kind of way station, a starting line and a finish line all rolled up into one. It was the finish line for Abby's parents in this life, but I hoped it would be a starting line for saving hers.

"Mr. Hartworth?"

"I guess you could say I'm looking for insight."

"Insight into what?"

"I'm not sure yet. If you listen close enough, sometimes, the dead will surprise you with a secret or two."

I thought the sheriff might laugh or roll his eyes, but he looked thoughtful. "Yeah, I guess that sometimes they do surprise you that way."

I wished that I had a better read on the sheriff. There was something behind the slow drawl, country sheriff routine. Like maybe he'd seen something that belonged to my world rather than the orderly, explicable world of the everyday. He must have seen something of that question on my face.

"World's full of ghosts, Mr. Hartworth. You don't work in law enforcement as long as I have without picking up a few. Usually the victims of crimes you didn't solve. They haunt you."

I almost asked him, right then, if he was being figurative, but I lost my nerve. He turned to go to his own car and then stopped. He spoke without looking back.

"I hope you find your insight."

I thought he even meant it.

Chapter 15

ACCORDING TO THE BRASS PLAQUE NEXT TO THE GATE, Angel's Rest Cemetery was established in 1894 and maintained by an endowment from the estate of Everett Jeremiah Cavanaugh III. As I walked through the wrought iron gate and into the cemetery proper, I wondered about the lives of all the people buried there. Had they been good people or bad people, and did the cemetery care either way? Probably not, I decided. The ground gets us all in the long run and her embrace doesn't discriminate.

The headstones closest to the entrance were also the oldest. Most were made of limestone and it showed. More than a century's worth of weather and acidic rain created separation in the layers of rock. The surface layers peeled away slowly, but surely, and obscured the names and dates. Compared to older grave-yards, where that process left grave markers all but unreadable, the headstones in Angel's Rest only looked weathered. Still, the cemetery was clearly being cared-for on a regular basis. The grass was mowed and no weeds clustered around any of the graves, even the oldest ones.

I felt the presence of the restless dead. Every graveyard had a few, but they weren't showing me any particular interest. Their incorporeal gazes would slide over me and then away. I glanced to my right and slowed to a stop. A small mausoleum stood there and, although less grand in scale, it bore the same Byzantine ar-chitectural influences of the high school. I turned and walked over to it. Where the dead had been showing minimal interest in me before, I felt dozens of ethereal presences cluster around me as I approached the mausoleum.

The name carved into the granite wall over the sealed doors was E. J. Cavanaugh III. Beneath that, carved in small, careful, but otherwise unremarkable script, were the dates 1870—1931. Beneath the dates an inscription read: "God grant him angel's rest." Well, that explained the cemetery's name. I guessed that Cavanaugh must have been a big deal in his day. He probably built the odd church the town saw fit to use for educating its young.

I turned from the mausoleum and headed toward the back of the graveyard, where the more recently dead were laid to rest. The limestone and sandstone headstones gave way to more durable granite. My ghostly entourage lost interest the farther I got from Cavanaugh's tomb and it was a relief when their creepy presence faded into the background. I started to get a sense of déjà vu and flashed back to my conversation with the younger, other-plane Paul. I knew where I was going. A minute or two later, I stood over the graves of Randall and Mary Simmons.

I knew they must have been fairly young when they died, but I wasn't prepared for how young. Randall Simmons had been thirty-two. Mary Simmons had been twenty-nine. That was barely old enough to have lived at all. They'd had a little girl, maybe owned a house with twenty-five years of payments left to go on it. Then, in a blink, it was all gone. No more parenting, no more work or car payments, no more anything.

"The Lord taketh away," I muttered.

I stared down at their graves, wondering why I had gone there. What did I expect to find there that I couldn't find online or in some old newspapers? Mary and Randall Simmons were gone. They had nothing left to give to the world. Yet, I stayed, yielding to a subconscious certainty that there was insight to be found, if I was patient. A prickle at the base of my neck told me I was being watched. It wasn't the dead that time, but something alive and behind me. I whirled. A few feet away, looking up at me with green eyes, was a small, gray cat missing part of an ear.

Something swirled up from my memory in Patty's voice.

"That cat doesn't like anyone."

I remembered the cat now. It had perched on my legs and hissed at the paramedic. Something else had happened, but it was lost in the trenches of my brain. I walked toward the cat. It looked up at me without fear, craning its head back as I got closer. I reached down, slow and cautious, and the cat sniffed at my fingers. Then it rubbed its face and ears against my hand with the poised enthusiasm only cats can achieve.

"Nice to see you, too," I said.

The cat stopped rubbing its head against my hand long enough to issue a little, "Mrew." The cat went alert, eyes fixed on a point behind me. Its ears went back, and it hissed a sound that came out as both threat and warning. I looked back. The cat was fixated on Mary's grave. There was nothing that I could see to account for the cat's behavior. All that meant was that the cat, more divine spirit than animal at the best of times, was seeing into the hidden.

I could see what the cat was seeing. It wasn't difficult, with the right tools. I even had the right tool in my pocket. I'd grabbed it out of the hard case that morning when I decided to visit the graveyard. Only, I didn't reach into my pocket. I didn't do anything. Knowing I could do it wasn't the same as wanting to do it. The veil between the living and the dead, the seen and the unseen, existed for a reason. There were things on the other side of the veil not meant for us. Some of those things are beautiful beyond description. Some of them are horrifying enough to shatter sanity.

That idea of mad old witches cackling around a pot wasn't just inventive description. Nor was the idea of vengeful wizards closeted away in remote towers. They were my ilk, spiritual kinfolk, and they had seen beyond. They had seen beyond and found it more than they could bear. The cat let loose with another hiss. That did nothing to make me want to look. The cat wouldn't make those noises at something warm and friendly. Yet, I went to the graveyard looking for insight and knowledge. Those came with a price. I took a steadying breath and reached into my pocket.

What I pulled out of my pocket was small, made of copper, and inlaid with ivory and ebony. It was an Eye of Horus. I suspected it was lifted from a tomb or museum at some point. It had the weight of age that someone like me gets a sixth sense for detecting. I stared down at it. Where there would normally be an empty space denoting the eye, there was a semi-translucent crystal. I took a steadying breath and held the Eye of Horus in front of my own eye.

For a moment, all I saw was the hazy light coming through the crystal. Then the cloudiness cleared away and I saw what the cat had seen. Thick, black smoke billowed up from Mary's grave. It was the kind of smoke that roils like visible hatred over burning oil rigs. I took an involuntary step back from the grave. I started to lower the Eye of Horus, convinced I'd discovered what I came to the cemetery to discover, when I saw something moving in the smoke. I tried to bring whatever it was into focus with sheer concentration.

A woman's hand, and then arm, reached out of the smoke. A moment later a face emerged. I experienced a moment of pure terrified nausea when I thought the face was Abby's. I dropped the Eye of Horus and lunged at the grave, determined to pull Abby from that smoke. The phantom smoke and the woman vanished. My hand closed around thin air.

"Idiot," I muttered.

I scooped the Eye of Horus off the ground and slammed it back up to my own eye. The billowing smoke reappeared. I waited for what felt like forever before the woman's face pressed out of the smoke. It wasn't Abby's face, but it was close enough to account for the mistake. Abby took after her mother, but Mary Simmons' nose was less prominent and her chin rounder. She saw me, saw me seeing her, and she started screaming. I couldn't hear her. It's not called an eye for nothing. I could just see her mouth moving, but I understood well enough.

"Help her!" Mary screamed. "Help Abby!"

As if it had a will of its own, the smoke poured into Mary's mouth, up her nostrils, and seemed to physically drag her back inside its opaque depths. The pain and fear in her eyes as that black nightmare swallowed her up made me want to scream, to help her, but there was nothing I knew to do. Whatever she endured was beyond my experience. I pulled the amulet away from my eye. I didn't want to look at that smoke any longer than necessary. I was furious that, even in death, Mary Simmons couldn't find peace. Was that what Abby had to look forward to when she died, an eternity trapped in a cloud of darkness?

I turned, stumbled away, even as I felt the massed attention of the restless dead on me. I'd seen enough, too much, and I just wanted to get out of the cemetery. I pushed through the gate and leaned against the hood of my car. Something told me that I was starting to hyperventilate and that my unhealed lungs wouldn't stand for it. I forced myself to slow my breathing to something more controlled. A morbid idea lodged in my head. If I passed out in the parking lot, they'd just dump me in a grave and bury me.

Something brushed against my leg and I bit off a scream. I made myself look down and saw the cat rubbing its body against my calf. I reached down and ran my hand along its spine. The cat arched its back and purred at me.

"At least you're shrugging it off better than I am," I told the cat.

I looked down at the Eye of Horus still clutched in my other hand. I entertained the idea of hurling it with all my strength into the woods across the road. It had shown me nothing I wanted to see. I forced myself to push aside the anger thrashing in my chest. No, it had not shown me anything I wanted to see, but it might have shown me something I needed to see. Blaming the tool was pointless. I was the one who aimed it at Mary Simmons' cursed grave. I pushed the copper amulet into my pocket and tried not think about that smoke.

I walked over and opened the door of my car. The cat, maybe seeing an opportunity, jumped up into the driver seat. It looked around and then jumped into the passenger seat, where it curled up into a little gray ball. I looked at the cat in surprise and then bemusement.

"Why not? It's a long walk back to town. I'll give you a ride."

I climbed into the driver's seat and fired up the Neon. If the cat's presence bothered the car, it didn't show.

Chapter 16

I DEBATED STOPPING FOR SOMETHING TO EAT, but the image of that black smoke pouring into Mary's mouth made me feel ill. Instead, I went to the hospital to see how Helena was getting on with Paul and Abby. When the car stopped, the cat opened its eyes and looked around. I climbed out of the car and waited. The cat yawned and put its head back down. Not sure what else to do, short of picking the cat up and putting it on the pavement, I cracked a window and closed the door. I walked toward the hospital. As I approached the front entrance, I spotted Helena off to one side. She was talking on a smartphone and looked happy. She laughed. She spotted me about the time I got within earshot.

"Speak of the devil and he appears. One sec," she said and held the phone out toward me. "Someone wants to say hello."

I looked at the phone like it might explode. I doubted that I wanted to talk to anyone who actually asked to speak to me. I sighed and took the phone.

"Hello," I said.

"Adrian, it's Laurie."

I recognized the voice. "How's it going, Chicago?"

"Don't call me that!"

"Sorry."

"Yes, you are sorry. I just wanted to tell you what a world-class asshole you are for dragging Helena back into your bullshit."

"Laurie," I started to object, but she steamrolled over me.

"I also wanted to say that if she gets hurt, I'll gut you like a fish."

I counted backwards from five. "Always nice to catch up, Laurie."

"I hope you die."

I held the phone out to Helena, who looked exceedingly pleased with herself. She talked with Laurie, another founding member of my "fan club," for another minute or two.

"Okay," said Helena. "I love you too. I'll be home soon."

Helena hung up. She looked at me with defiance and a touch of fear in her eyes.

"So, you and Laurie?" I asked.

"Yes."

I felt a twinge of jealousy, but it was reflexive jealousy, ghost jealousy from another life. It lacked either bark or bite. I nodded and smiled at her.

"Good for both of you."

She looked relieved and, if I hadn't known better, a touch disappointed. Maybe I had failed to fully embody my asshole reputation and deprived her of an excuse to open up with both barrels. With her fun over, Helena gave me a long look.

"Are you alright?"

"Not really. I learned something, but I don't really know what it means."

"Tell me."

I looked around and spotted a bench that was away from casual foot traffic. I gestured to it and we walked over. I sat quietly for a minute and organized my thoughts. I walked Helena through the sequence of events. After I finished, it was her turn to sit quietly. The sun was out in full force that day and the temperature was already into the eighties. I felt sweat soaking through the back of my shirt. I'll have to do laundry again before too long, I thought, and then wondered at how the prosaic asserts itself at the oddest times.

"Where did you get a functional Eye of Horus?" Helena asked, breaking the silence.

I eyed her. "Do you really want to know?"

"Probably not. I'm sure it's a lurid tale filled with cheap, tawdry sex and violence."

"Half right. There was violence. Cheap, tawdry sex would have at least made it a little fun, so obviously that couldn't happen."

"I don't recall that you ever went without when you really wanted it."

"I'm not as pretty as I used to be," I said.

"You were never that pretty."

"Wound my pride a little more, why don't you?" I said, pressing my hand to my chest in faux-theatrical fashion.

Helena stood and I looked up at her. She reached out and patted my cheek. "It's the danger that gets us, silly boy. And, if there is one thing you excel at, it's being dangerous."

She got a faraway look on her face that lasted five or maybe ten seconds and then she shook it off.

"Thank God I'm not single."

I laughed. "Wouldn't I have some say in the matter?"

"Did you ever?"

"Fair point."

"Alright," said Helena, "I think I'd like to meet this cat of yours, Adrian."

I took a beat to process that one. "You want to meet the cat?"

"Yes, Adrian, the cat. You know, a small quadruped, goes meow, and looks like a tiny panther. The cat."

I rolled my eyes. "I am vaguely aware of what a cat is. I meant, why do you want to meet the cat?"

"Call it curiosity and, so help me, crack one joke about cats and curiosity and I will hurt more than your pride."

The joke died on my lips. "Noted. Let's go see the cat."

We walked over to my car. As predicted, I needed to jiggle the key in the lock to open the passenger door. Hot air whooshed out of the vehicle and I frowned. If the heat built up that fast, I couldn't leave the cat shut inside it for any length of time. Helena nudged me out of the way and leaned in to see the cat, who sat up and watched Helena with knowing eyes. Something passed between the two of them. I suspected some form of feline telepathy was at work. Helena was always ninety-percent cat in my estimation. She smiled at the cat and gave me a sympathetic look.

"Well, I guess it was inevitable," she said.

"What was inevitable?"

"Your friend there is now the proud owner of a slightly used human being."

"Sorry?"

"Apparently she thinks the mileage gives you character."

"What?"

"I told her you're more trouble than you're worth, but she won't hear a word of it. She's quite proud of her new biped."

The absurdity of Helena's words were spinning out of control and giving me nausea, a headache and a vague sense of lightheadedness. It reminded me of altitude sickness.

"Helena, what are you on about?"

"She claimed you," said Helena, nodding down to the cat. "It's not traditional. I mean, usually we pick our familiars, when we have them. Still, it's not unprecedented. She says you can call her Lil."

"Lil," I repeated, with absolutely no meaning attached to the syllable. "Helena, I think one of us has been in the sun too long."

Helena looked at the cat. "He's slow on the uptake sometimes, too."

"He's standing next to you," I grumbled.

"She's hungry, by the way."

"Mrowow," offered Lil.

"You're not messing with me, are you? I mean," I paused and tried to wrap my head around it. "I own a cat now?"

"Don't be ridiculous. No one owns a cat. That'd be like owning a thunderstorm. She owns you, though. I think this will be good for you, Adrian. There's nothing like a cat to keep you grounded."

Too many things I didn't understand were happening all at once, so I latched onto the one part I had understood.

"Do I seem ungrounded to you?"

"Painfully."

I shot Helena a look and she grinned at me in wicked glee.

"What am I supposed to do with a cat? I don't even have an apartment, let alone a house. I have a storage unit and a P.O. box."

"That certainly does sound like a problem," said Helena with all the sympathy of a dental pick.

"You're enjoying this entirely too much."

"You have to learn to take joy in the little things, Adrian."

"Like my suffering?"

"See, now you're catching on! One more thing you should probably know."

"Do tell," I said with unrepentant insincerity.

"I'm not sure she's actually a cat."

That got my attention. "She's not a cat?"

"Well, she is, I think, but I don't think she's entirely a cat."

"I don't suppose there's an explanation coming that I might understand?"

"I can't think of a better way to put it," said Helena.

She looked apologetic. Vague explanations were par for the course in the circles we ran in, but "not entirely a cat" was vague even by our standards. I looked from Helena to the cat, who observed the conversation with an opaque, kitty cat expression.

"So let me see if I've got this straight. I am now to be owned and operated by a not-cat cat, who has self-designated as my familiar, and goes by the name of Lil?"

The cat perked up at the sound of her name and gave off a soft purr.

"I guess you were paying attention," said Helena. "It seemed like you lost focus there for a while, but way to rally."

"Thanks."

Helena gave the cat's head a ferocious rubbing and Lil purred loudly. Apparently, Helena fell into the tiny category of people the cat did like. I rubbed a spot near the base of my skull and pretended I wasn't about to develop a blistering headache. I wasn't sure what to do about the cat-slash-familiar-slash-my-new-owner, so I changed the subject.

"How is it going with Abby and Paul?"

Helena gave Lil a little more petting and then turned her attention back to me. "Quite well, actually. Your little gamble is paying off in spades. Abby's improvement is exponential. One doctor came within a breath of calling it miraculous. They'll probably release Paul today or tomorrow. If Abby continues to improve at her present rate, they'll release her a few days after that."

I tried to decide what to do with that information. On the surface, it was good news. Of course, Oppenheimer confirming the feasibility of a fission bomb was probably also met as good news. I supposed it was all a question of context.

"Adrian," said Helena, "you seem less pleased by this than you should be."

"I'm just trying to see the angles. As long as she's in that hospital room, I think she's…"

Helena saw it. "She's protected. Once she leaves, she's fair game again."

"I could be wrong about that part, but," I thought of the smoke over Mary's grave, "I don't think I'd put money on it. Would you?"

"No, I wouldn't."

"No matter which way you cut it, the only way I can see to protect Abby is to keep her isolated to one location."

Helena looked pensive. "That's fine for now, but it's not a solution. You can't keep this up indefinitely, and that kind of isolation kills as surely as cancer."

"I know. This goes back to Abby's mother somehow. That horror at the cemetery proves as much. I'm going to have to ask Paul some questions."

"Like where Randall and Mary met? How long they lived here? Those kinds of questions?"

I nodded.

"I can handle that part. Still, what good will that do you?"

"No idea, but until we learn something we can act on, we're at a standstill here."

Helena offered me an uncertain look, and then pressed forward with her thought. "That business in the graveyard, with the smoke, you should dig into that."

"I already said I didn't know what it was."

She rolled her eyes. "Yes, *you* don't know what it is, but you know people who might."

I knew who she was talking about. I shook my head.

"Adrian," she pressed, "we need information. They don't do business with me, but they'll talk to you. You should call The Twins."

"There was this thing a while back. It went sour. It wasn't my fault, but they blame me for it. I doubt they'd even take the call."

"You won't know until you try."

I sighed. "I'll think about it."

Chapter 17

I DIDN'T KNOW WHAT ELSE TO DO, so I took Lil to the vet. As long as I was in the room, she endured the vet's poking and prodding with surly disdain. All freaking hell broke loose the minute I left the room. So it was that I found myself standing in an examination room, feeling very superfluous, and watching the vet do mysterious vet things. What I knew about small animals and their care could fit into a pixie's thimble. After what seemed like an inordinate amount of time and a couple of injections, the vet addressed me.

"Well, Mr. Hartworth, I have to give you credit. I never thought this cat would ever wind up in my office."

The vet was a genial man, with pale blue eyes and long, sandy hair that he needed to push out of his face every few minutes. His small badge identified him as Dr. Heath. He smiled a lot, even at the hijinks of "my" cat.

"Not sure I can take much credit. She sort of adopted me."

Dr. Heath nodded as though this made perfect sense. "Cats are funny like that. They pick people. It's the reason a lot of them wind up abandoned or in shelters."

That was news to me. "Really?"

"Sure. Maybe a kid picks out the cutest little kitten to be their very own, and the only person the cat likes is the dad. The dad isn't much for pets, the kid is angry, so the cat gets turned loose on some back road or taken to a shelter to keep the peace in the house."

I wondered if the vet was just pulling my leg. That sounded an awful lot like wanton cruelty. I said as much.

"It is," said Heath. "A lot of people think picking out a cat or dog should work like picking furniture. You get one that you like the look of and it should fit into the house."

Even my limited experience in dealing with Lil told me what an asinine notion that was. "No real consideration of personality?"

"A-plus for the new student."

Lil had settled on the table in a sphinx-like pose and her head tracked back and forth between me and Heath as we spoke. I reached out and scratched behind her ears. I hoped it would encourage continued docility. It also gave me a minute to figure out what to say.

"So, doc, I never really had pets as a kid. What do I need to know about taking care of Lil here?"

"Well, there are really two levels of care. Your essential care consists of making sure she gets food every day and has ready access to water. She'll also need a litter-box. I recommend clumping litter. It costs a little more, but it's easier to clean up."

"I'm all for easier. What kind of food?"

"Your basic adult cat dry food should be fine. You can mix in some wet food, occasionally, which I recommend. Helps to make sure she's getting the right combination of nutrients, vitamins and minerals. She's not a big cat, so half a cup, maybe three-quarters of a cup a day of dry food should do the trick. Cats will self-regulate their eating, all things being equal, so you can usually just throw the food down once a day."

"Okay, I think I can handle that. What's the other level of care?"

"Attention and affection. I can't help you out much there. Some cats seem to require a lot of love, pet me for hours and hours kind of love. Other cats only seem to need a little bit of intermittent affection to get by. I suspect Lil is in the latter category."

"Why's that?"

"She's been living more or less wild the last couple years. Wouldn't let anyone near her. If she needed sustained attention, she'd have found a place to call home by now."

"Speaking of living wild, do I need to worry about fleas or ticks? She's been riding around in my car all day."

Heath frowned at that. "You should have to, but you don't. There isn't one on her. I have no earthly idea how that can possibly be the case, but it is the case. I put a flea and tick repellant on her neck, just to be safe, so you should be pest free for the next month."

I picked Lil up and she settled in the crook of my arm. "I don't suppose there's a pet store in town?"

Dr. Heath shook his head. "Not to speak of, but you can get everything you need at Connor's."

"Connor's?"

"It's kind of a general store. Our version of a Walmart or Target."

The vet glanced down at Lil and then up at me. He chuckled a little.

"What?"

"It's just the damndest thing. That cat really does hate everybody."

I shook my head. "So everyone keeps telling me."

"You should get her a collar too, to put the rabies tag on."

"Collar, right."

I went out and settled up with the woman at the front desk to the tune of several hundred dollars. My supply of ready cash was dwindling faster than I liked. I wasn't exactly broke, and I had money stashed with other identities, but I was loathe to go down that road. If things continued as they had, it might come to that before too long. The woman at the front desk gave me directions to Connor's that were surprisingly succinct and specific. According to her, the store was located on the eastern edge of town.

I'd probably driven past it when I first arrived. Of course, I'd been all but sleep-driving, so it's no mystery why I didn't notice it. It wasn't until I was in the car, Lil curled up on the passenger seat again, and halfway there before I wondered why the go-to store wasn't more centrally located. When I pulled into the lot, that tiny mystery was solved. Connors was set back from the road to accommodate a sizeable parking lot and looked more like a medium-sized warehouse than a store.

I left Lil in the car again, because I was sure they wouldn't like me hauling an ill-tempered cat through the store. I left the windows cracked and resolved to make the trip as short as humanly possible. The interior of the store reminded me of a warehouse too. The floor was smooth concrete and everything was set out on plain metal shelves. A teen with bags under his eyes, the kind that teens get when they're working too hard, rather than when they're doing drugs, gave me a strained smile.

"Welcome to Connor's, sir. Can I help you find anything?"

I looked at his nametag. "Sure, Tim. Pet food and supplies?"

His eyes went blank and I watched the gears grind. Then I got it. He probably spent most evenings and weekends asking that question and being told, "No thanks," by people who shopped there all the time. Between that and apparent exhaustion, my request for assistance was a non sequitur. It took a second, but he got it together.

"Aisle seven," said Tim.

"Thanks," I said.

Tim smiled. "You're welcome."

I wandered past rows of dried goods and canned vegetables. I ignored the crap meant to encourage impulse buys that filled the shelves on the end of every aisle. I'd given up on rank-and-file junk food long ago, courtesy of Marcy's health obsession, and there was no room in my life for bric-a-brac. After a few years of that, you stop even thinking of chips and candy as food and you grow almost superstitiously wary of increasing your belongings. I turned down aisle seven and soon found myself frozen in indecision.

There were shelves and shelves of cat food in a dozen brands and each intended for a different kind of cat. There was food for outdoor cats, indoor cats, mature indoor cats, indoor kittens, outdoor kittens, food to prevent hairballs, food to improve the sheen of coats and so many more. There was wet food and dry food. There were soft treats that tasted like fish or turkey. There were dry, crunchy treats that tasted like beef. Part of me half expected to see a variety of food that tasted like New York strip steak and would sublimate into pure nutrition that entered directly into a cat's bloodstream from his or her mouth.

"Christ," I muttered. "How the hell do people decide about this crap?"

I shook my head and found a moderately priced bag of something calling itself "Kitty Yumtastic" that claimed to be for adult, indoor cats. I grabbed a few cans of wet cat food at random and went looking for non-edible things. The collar proved simple enough. By the time I had the litter box and the litter itself, I found myself fighting with gravity as things threatened to leap from my overfull hands and arms. I wondered why I hadn't gotten a cart.

Ignorance, I thought. It was simple ignorance. Until that moment, I had no sense of the size of things like litter boxes and bags of cat food and the enormous, twenty-pound tub of litter. I made my haphazard way toward the counter, stopping every five steps or so to readjust the things in my arm. That was why I didn't see him before he spoke.

"If it isn't the badass," said someone, trying to cover fear with anger.

I looked up and sighed. The man who blocked my path had two black eyes, a bandage across his nose, and a huge purple bruise across the side of his face. It was sort of impressive. I didn't usually hang around long enough to see the end result of my handiwork. I didn't feel any sympathy for him, though. Pull a hunting knife on a guy and you get what you get. I tried to remember what Patty had said his name was. I knew his name started with a T and it was more than one syllable. Tony? Tommy? Terrance? I couldn't pull it up. Too many other things were in play, much more important things than the waste of space in my path.

"I don't have time to deal with your bruised pride or machismo bullshit," I said in a tired voice.

"What the fuck did you say to me?" he demanded, taking a step closer.

"You heard me. We're done here. Stand aside."

"I decide when we're done here," he barked, jerking a thumb at himself and drawing stares.

I cocked my head a little to one side and just looked at him. I kept just looking at him, way beyond the point when silence grows uncomfortable and becomes oppressive. I saw him decide to break the silence, but I beat him to it. When I spoke, it was very soft and very gentle. I'm told that is disconcerting when someone wants to rile you up.

"Do you really believe that," his name came back to me, "Tucker Smith?"

He responded to his own name coming out of my mouth with the kind of jerking twitch you usually saw when someone cracked a whip. Maybe he thought that I didn't know his name and that anonymity would give him some kind of edge in a confrontation. It was ridiculous to think that the police wouldn't have told me his name, but Tucker didn't strike me as an especially sharp guy. The confrontation was futile and had next to nothing to do with me. He wanted to prove something to himself. I'd seen it before. He needed to convince himself he wasn't frightened of me.

The problem with that plan was that it hinged on legitimate lack of fear, and he was deeply afraid of me. Most of his fights probably ended when he pulled that hunting knife. Knives scared most people, as well they should. While not as overtly threatening as a gun, knives could kill you just as dead and it usually took a lot longer. His knife hadn't frightened me. It hadn't even slowed me down. I'd taken his power and we both knew it.

With a flash of self-hatred on his face, Smith stepped aside. I walked past him. I felt his eyes on my back, felt his hate and fear, and remembered why I stayed on the move. If I hung around too long, his wounded pride would force another fight and one of us would likely die. In all likelihood, the man bleeding out on the ground would be Tucker Smith.

Chapter 18

I DIDN'T KNOW WHAT, IF ANY, pet policy the cabin company maintained. So, I took discretion as the better part of valor and snuck Lil in after dark. I put down some dry food and water for her. She drank a lot of water and nibbled at the food. She batted a piece of the food around on the floor while I set up the litter box in a corner. She leapt, pounced, and generally treated the piece of Kitty Yumtastic like a tiny hockey puck. I wasn't sure if she was commenting on the quality of the food or just felt like play-killing something.

After she got bored with that, Lil came over and observed me with an unwholesome degree of solemnity as I tried to figure out how much litter should go in the box. I put in the inch the container suggested, but it looked woefully inadequate to me. I dumped some more in and pushed it around with the slotted shovel that came with the litter box. It reminded me of a Zen sand garden, except for the inevitable future poop. That idea took a lot of the romance out of the thought. I declared it good enough and walked away. Lil spent several minutes giving the litter box a thorough sniffing before she climbed in to do her business.

I averted my eyes out of some vague, hard-to-define sense of propriety. I wouldn't want an audience watching me poop, so it seemed appropriate to give her a little privacy. I settled onto the bed and turned the on TV for background noise. I set the volume so all I heard was a dull, inarticulate murmur. My back ached, throbbed, and did its level best to make sure I knew it was still hurt. Even so, I had the impression that I was starting to mend.

I'd switched over to the regular painkillers you can buy off the shelf anywhere. They didn't dull out the pain the same way the doctor's prescription pills had, but they made the injury livable without turning me into a drooling narcoleptic. The tradeoff was worth it. I prized being able to reason in straight lines more than I prized not hurting.

I dozed a little and then felt a telltale thump on the bed. A quick look showed Lil exploring the top of the bed with the same intense, almost zealous thoroughness she employed with the litter box. She regarded my sprawled body for a moment. Then she unceremoniously walked over my stomach to get to the other side. Once she'd decided that the bed was indeed safe and was not food, she sat down next to my hand.

"Mrew," she offered.

I lifted my hand, another random guess, and she rubbed her face and ears against my palm. It occurred to me that my participation in the process was minimal. So long as I held my hand there, she was content. I stroked her head and found myself surprised by the softness of her fur. She purred at me, kneaded at the blanket for a moment, and curled up against my side. I drifted off to the low murmur of a sitcom and Lil's almost imperceptible breathing.

I stood in a clearing, surrounded by forest for as far as I could see. It seemed like there was sufficient light for a moment, but it was the false light that comes immediately after sunset. A phantom light that concealed more than it revealed. There was unnatural silence. No birds chirped. No leaves rustled. It was as if the forest held its breath.

I'm dreaming, I thought.

Only, I didn't believe myself. It felt like a dream, where the edges of all things blurred and bled into one another like an impressionist painting, but it was a lie. It was a dream in form, but not in substance or function. There was an underlying reality to it, a solidity that did not belong to the world of dreams and fantasy. I also realized something else. I was an interloper. No, I was not an interloper precisely. I was an unexpected presence in a place that had gone unchanged for eons.

If I die here, I will not wake up, I thought. *If I die here, I simply die.*

I felt the weight of eyes on me. With that weight came the certain knowledge that I was no longer alone. I spun in a slow circle. I peered into the false light and sought my silent observer. Nothing gave away its presence. Just as surely, though, I felt it drawing closer. I didn't remember a decision, but I ran into the woods. The weight of observation grew closer and closer, like an anchor that slowed my movements. I ran harder.

The observer paced me for a time, sometimes off to the left, sometimes off to the right, sometimes behind me. Then, an explosion of speed and something huge, silent, and black slammed into me. I went down hard, tumbled and rolled in the underbrush. Old branches snapped beneath my weight with sounds like gunfire in that silent forest. I came to rest staring up into the sky. I saw constellations hurtle by at impossible speeds.

Something black beyond imagining blotted out the stars. It towered over me, even though I had the impression it was sitting. Eyes the color of blood rubies stared down at me and slitted, feline pupils bisected them. It made a noise that pressed me down against the ground with its sheer, undeniable force. That noise seemed to shatter me with its power and I shrank away. That noise was too much, too big, and it was, I realized, familiar. I stared up at the black shape over me and, without knowing why, I raised my hand.

Something that felt like a battering ram plowed into my hand and knocked it around. At first, I thought it was mauling my hand. Then, I realized, it was trying to rub its head and massive ears against my palm. I pressed my hand hard against the presence's head. It let out a purr that shook the ground, shook me, and seemed to shake the sky itself.

"Lil," I said.

My voice sounded loud and alien, an unwelcome thing in that place. The presence let out another low purr that merely made the ground, me, and the sky tremble a little. Then, as if to add emphasis, a shocking splash of pink the size of a turkey platter flicked out. It felt like a sheet of huge, wet sandpaper rubbed across my palm. I heaved a sigh of relief and pushed myself to my feet. Dream Lil rose to stand. The black shape loomed over me. If Lil had wanted to, she could have lowered her mouth and bitten my head off.

Is this what Helena sensed? I asked myself. I shook my head, negating the question. Whatever Helena had sensed, it must have been little more than an echo of the incredible predator that stood over me. I could feel the ancient strength and power that radiated off Dream Lil. If Helena had sensed anything like what I was sensing, she would not have played it so vague or so calm. She would have been worried, if not downright afraid, that a power like that had somehow claimed me.

"Why are we here, Lil?"

I expected the enormous cat to answer. Why draw me to a dream space, however grounded in some reality it might be, if not to communicate more directly? It didn't happen. The giant head lowered and nudged me with what, I imagined, was probably its gentlest motion. I staggered back a step or two. The giant shape moved toward me and then slipped past. It took a few silent steps and then waited. Ruby eyes looked back at me before she took another step or two.

"Oh," I said. "You want me to follow you."

Another purr rumbled the forest floor. I did try to follow, but it was easy to lose sight of a completely black creature in an ever darkening forest. After a while, Dream Lil settled for me placing my hand on her side and I moved as she did. In the dream, the journey lasted for days, for weeks, in never-ending darkness, in a never-ending forest. Finally, we broke through the edge of the forest. I stared in dumbfounded awe. My gaze tracked up, and up, and up even more.

There was a statue, if anything so far beyond human ability could be called a statue, which stood thousands of feet tall. I don't know how wide it was at the base. We must have been some unspeakable distance away from the statue, because it looked proportional. It was completely, perfectly white. Not white like marble, or paper, but white in its true meaning of the absence of any color. That perfect absence of color threw off a glow, a radiance that lit everything for miles.

I looked at the enormous Dream Lil and could, in the glow of that statue, make out vague features. Even here, in the odd dream space, part of one of her ears was missing. On regular Lil, it looked cute and endearing. On Dream Lil, it looked angry, violent, like the physical reminder of some long ago battle that would never go forgotten. She gave me a piercing look with her ruby eyes. She turned and pushed her head forward a little toward the statue.

That required no telepathy. *Hey jackass, look at the huge statue I dragged you all this way to see.* I turned and looked at the statue. It was a sexless, androgynous figure that otherwise looked human. Its hands were lifted in penitent supplication to some unseen master. It was beautiful and fundamentally awful. Its face was absent anything like personality as I understood it. It was consumed, utterly, in worship of whatever gods or monsters it served.

That emptiness of expression unnerved me. No human expression, no matter how purely devoted to a single emotion, was ever utterly that emotion. Human expressions are tempered by restraint, by self-knowledge, by knowledge of others, by the ten-thousand small things we do to protect ourselves and others. That statue's face showed none of it. It was open, unfettered, and I knew, to my core, that such openness was wrong.

I didn't notice at first, but the pure whiteness of the statue began to shift, to darken into gray and then into red. The open expression of supplication grew less open and then it grew angry. Hands raised in supplication became fists raised in unabashed fury. The white light gave way to red light and then all light vanished. I could feel the presence of the statue. Even at so great a distance, it was palpable and appalling. I wanted to flee the overwhelming anger and betrayal that rolled off that statue like an ocean tide. I could guess what had happened. Its master, whoever or whatever that master might have been, had abandoned the statue.

We stood in the shadow of that statue's emotions for what seemed to me like ten thousand years. I started to turn away, but Dream Lil put herself in my way.

"Lil, I've seen enough. My god, this is beyond awful. Let's go."

Dream Lil made a noise. It was a soft, low sound of warning that nonetheless almost knocked me from my feet.

"Alright, alright, I'll stay," I said, as if I had a real choice.

I turned and waited another eternity. I heard a sound like static crackling. Red-black lightning shot skyward from the statue's fists. The lightning lit the statue's face enough to see its pure hatred. Its mouth was open in a silent scream. It was, I assumed, trying to take its vengeance on whatever had gone away. The red-black lighting continued to lance into the night sky and I could smell ozone. I realized that, because of the distance, the lighting looked as proportional as the statue had. Up close, though, that lightning had to be monstrous, and each bolt hundreds of feet wide.

The statue's show of power went on so long that I lost track of even the most subjective notions of time. When the statue finished its—well, temper tantrum, I suppose—I lowered my eyes. Why was Lil so insistent I see this? A shaft of golden white light slammed down into the statue's face from somewhere in the heavens. The light passed straight through the titanic form. Cracks that must have been as deep as canyons, glowing with golden light, materialized over every inch of the statue. A final pulse of golden white light descended from on high and the statue exploded.

Most of the pieces flew off at trajectories that would take them thousands of miles, if not farther, but one piece landed comparatively close. It was glowing red and, as I watched, the stone liquefied and seeped into the ground. Then all was darkness.

Chapter 19

HELENA STARED AT ME OVER THE LID OF HER COFFEE. "Sounds like a fall from grace myth."

I suppressed an annoyed noise. "Yes, the symbolism was not lost on me. The fall from grace followed by divine retribution is common enough that even I couldn't miss it. What I don't understand is the relevance."

"Did you ask Lil?"

I could see the twinkle in Helena's eyes as she posed the question. Helena might have full access to feline telepathy, but I didn't. I knew, because I'd tried and tried harder at it than almost anything I'd done in twenty years. I met with abject failure. Lil emoted cheerful laziness during my efforts. She napped, stretched, and then napped some more.

"I did," I said. "Her answer went something like, 'merew,' unless I'm misremembering."

"Cats do have a knack for concision."

"Cute. Maybe you'd care to give it a try."

"Oh," said Helena. "I think I'll be giving that a pass. I'm very confident that I don't want to brush up against the mind of her other self, even accidentally. It was pure dumb luck she didn't liquefy my brain that first time."

"Terrific. So, one more piece of information I have no idea what to do with. Still, you should have seen it. That statue was just so damn big. It's probably a metaphor for something, but I'll be damned if I know what."

Helena swirled her coffee absently. "Is it always like this for you? Your life, I mean. Getting hurt, protecting cursed teens, trying to puzzle out meaning from dreams and glimpses into alternate planes of reality."

I leaned back in the uncomfortable chair. For reasons I couldn't fathom, hospital cafeteria chairs were always the least ergonomic things. A vertebra popped into place with an audible crack. Helena snickered at me.

I shook my head. "Not really. Maybe the getting hurt part, a little. Most days, things are pretty straightforward. I try to steer clear of obviously lethal situations."

"Except this time, for some reason."

"Yeah, except this time, for some reason."

"Why *are* you doing this, Adrian? You've never been squarely in the white hat camp."

"I'm a black hat, then?" I asked, but I smiled.

"You know that isn't what I mean," she chided. "Like you said, though, you usually steer clear of things like this."

"Oh hell, I've got no idea. I spend half my time thinking I should bolt. Just pack up and leave."

"But?"

There it was, the question that had nagged at me since the get-go. I'm not heartless or a sadist. I don't observe the suffering of others with ease, my knife-wielding friend notwithstanding. That might have explained why I stayed in the first place, and why I had acted with such rash abandon in Abby's hospital room. The costs weren't clear then and I reacted. I wasn't an idealist, though, nor driven by any particular moral code to intervene.

In my experience, most of the people who got slapped with the label of evil weren't particularly evil. Nor, for that matter, did they commit many actions that were objectively evil. I'd seen more evil carried out in the group homes I'd worked at for a while than I ever had in the dens of those practicing black magic. That wasn't to say there wasn't real, objective, scary evil in the world. I'd seen that too. I'd seen it in that graveyard and I watched it wrap an inky hand around Marcy's throat. Sometimes, you had to fight, because there was no other practical alternative.

That wasn't true in Abby's case. The practical alternative was obvious. Walk away. Whatever was going down, and whatever was making it happen, had no specific quarrel with me. If I left it to finish doing whatever it was doing, it would leave me be. That was the smart move. I wasn't a crusader. I had no agenda, beyond getting by as best I could. Yet, I stayed.

"Maybe I'm just stupid," I said.

"Ha! You're a lot of things, but stupid isn't one of them."

I shrugged. "Maybe, unconsciously, I'm looking for some kind of redemption."

"Redemption? For what?"

I gave her a look. "Take your pick. You hear the stories, right?"

"About you?"

I nodded.

"Sure," she said. "I assume most of it is bull or exaggerated."

"Some of it, without question, but there's plenty of truth drifting around too. I could probably use some redemption for what happened in Tijuana."

A cloud swept over Helena's face. Things had gone bad in Mexico. She'd lost friends. It was the kind of bad that a person never really gets clear of, no matter what. I'd cut out early, when I saw which way the wind was blowing. I'd told everyone to do the same, but they didn't listen.

"From what I heard from—" she paused, "from the survivors, you made the right decision. You told them to get out."

"I didn't try very hard. I damn sure knew that the whole thing was going sideways and that it was going to be a bloodbath. I got out and didn't look back."

"So, you should have what? Tried harder? Stayed yourself?"

"Maybe. If I'd stayed, it might have gone differently."

"Or you might be dead. Is this some kind of survivor's guilt?"

"No. I don't think so, anyways. You asked a question, and I'm trying to puzzle out an answer. The truth is that I don't know why I'm sticking around or even if I'll keep sticking around. Right now, I'm leaning strongly toward the stupid theory."

"Maybe some long-dormant hero gene is finally expressing itself."

"Add that to the list of things never to wager money on," I said and then switched gears. "You get a chance to talk to Paul about Abby's parents?"

Helena took a sip of coffee and nodded. "I did. I don't know if it's going to help you very much, though."

"Can't possibly hurt."

"Well, they met in California. Randall went out there to go to college on a tennis scholarship. He met Mary when he was a junior and she was sophomore. He brought her home to meet the family that Christmas. It was a whirlwind romance."

"Whirlwind romance?"

Helena grinned. "Paul's phrase, but I like it."

"Ah. Go on."

"I had to read between the lines a little, but I think Paul thought Mary might have been pregnant that Christmas. She and Randall were already talking about marriage, so it made a kind of sense."

I quirked an eyebrow. "Was she pregnant?"

"No. She was just young, eager, and certain. You know how it goes. At that age, it's all romance and love conquers all. Seems like they were making it work, though. After college they spent a couple years working in California before they decided to move here. To hear Paul tell it, Mary loved this place. She gave voice lessons and Randall opened up a small accounting business. I guess everything around here is small by comparison."

"You should check out Connor's," I said.

"Connor's? What's that?"

"Local version of a big box store. Big as a damn warehouse. It's not relevant."

"Ah. The rest you know. They had Abby about a year after they got back. Then the accident."

It didn't track. "Was there trouble at home? Domestic violence or, I don't know, something?"

"Not according to Paul. He wasn't evasive at all, so I'm inclined to believe him."

"What about her family? Did Paul say anything about them?"

Helena frowned. "No. She didn't have any family. Both her parents were long dead by the time the wedding rolled around. No siblings or none that she talked about."

"Something isn't adding up here. That thing didn't pick Abby at random. It sure as hell didn't do whatever it did to Mary's spirit for kicks. They have to intersect somewhere."

I shuffled the information in my head, reordering it and looking for some new angle. Evil that potent was never a casual affair. It'd be like a person singling out a lone ant and spending months systematically torturing it. If it was all clustered together, it might be random, but not when it was spread out over years. That suggested planning and purpose. If Mary didn't intersect with that evil while she was living in town, maybe it happened before she and Randall moved. Maybe it even happened before she and Randall met. That felt promising in my gut.

"Maybe it happened back in California."

"What?"

"The intersection between Mary and whatever is putting the bad juju on Abby."

"It's plausible."

"Did Paul say why they moved back here? Did something happen in California?"

Helena shook her head. "No. It wasn't a rush move. They planned for months before they came here. Paul did a lot of the legwork, finding them an affordable place to live and an office space for Randall. You do realize what that means, right?"

"What?"

"If Mary had some kind of contact with ye old evil monster, Randall probably didn't know about it."

"Not really surprising. Would you announce something like that?"

"Yes," said Helena.

"Okay, I know that you, you personally, would, but I mean basically normal people."

"I am normal."

I stared at her in shock. She had been vehement. She glowered at me for a good five seconds.

"Say you're sorry, Adrian," she demanded.

"Um, okay. I'm sorry."

"With sugar on top."

"What?"

"Say you're sorry with sugar on top."

"Okay, okay, I'm sorry with sugar on top."

She gave me a slow, disappointed shake of her head. "How do you survive in the world being such an easy mark?"

I groaned. "You haven't had enough of that yet? Still punishing me for sins past?"

"Oh, honey pie, I will never be done punishing you for sins past. You should get real comfy in that hot seat."

"Awesome."

"Yes," she said in self-satisfaction, "it is awesome. So very, very awesome for me."

"Not for me."

"It wouldn't be fun if it was awesome for you. How do you not understand this yet?"

"I refer you back to my stupid theory," I said.

"Yes, maybe you were onto something with that. Okay, enough fun, what next?"

"Now, I make a call to someone in California. See if he can dig up some more information about Mary."

"A friend of yours?"

I thought about it for absolutely no time at all. "No. Not even a little bit of a friend. He owes me a couple favors, though. Even if he would like to forget that I and those favors exist."

"How mysterious. Did you sleep with his wife?"

"What? No. Why would you even ask that?"

"I decided I wasn't really done having fun yet," said Helena, lifting her coffee in mock salute.

"He's a cop. Had a few run-ins with some less than run-of-the-mill problems. I helped him clear them up."

"In your usual charming and discreet ways?"

I nodded, a little put out. "Unfortunately, not every problem has a quiet solution. There might have been a little property damage," I said, before adding very softly, "to a city block."

"I swear. You really do need a keeper."

"Isn't that Lil's job now?"

Helena gave me a surprised smile. "Well played."

"Thanks."

"Go make your call, before your cop acquaintance decides he really doesn't know you at all."

"Come on. That only happens…" I considered for a moment. "Yeah, I better hurry."

Chapter 20

"MACINTYRE," SAID A GRUFF, ANNOYED VOICE.

"It's Adrian Hartworth. Don't hang up."

There was a long pause and I could almost see MacIntyre's bulldog face staring at the phone in his hand, trying to decide whether to slam the phone down hard, or really hard. I heard him heave an enormous sigh.

"What the hell do you want, Hartworth?"

"I need to call in a favor."

"A favor," said MacIntyre in something just shy of a bellow. "What in almighty Christ would I owe you a favor for?"

It was my turn to sigh. "Do you really want me to say it over an open line?"

MacIntyre coughed and went silent again. The gears were spinning in his head, doing the math, trying to decide if I was about to pull him into some career-ending disaster. When Mac-Intyre spoke again, he sounded very tired.

"Tell you what. Your name came up in a case a month or so back. Couldn't track you down. Apparently your address is a post office box. Changed your number too."

"I spend most of my time traveling," I said, flat, even, una-pologetic.

"Alright, alright. Don't get your thong in a twist. You help me clear that up, I'll see what I can do for you."

I hadn't been in California for close to six months. I hadn't been in Los Angeles for the better part of two years. I tried to imagine how I could be connected to something in LA in the last two months and came up empty. I got very wary, very fast.

"Ask your questions and I'll see if I can help you."

"Picked up a kid named Daniel Wilkes in connection to a murder. Local thug named Julio Rubio, if you can believe that. Anyways, Wilkes looked good for it, but he says he was with you at the time of the murder. You know him?"

I did my best to stay calm. Fucking Daniel never knew when to keep his mouth shut. Back talking to someone like Rubio sounded exactly like Daniel to me. I worked to keep my tone even.

"Yeah, I know Wilkes."

"How about Rubio?"

"Never heard the name until today."

MacIntyre let me hang on the end of the line for a good twenty seconds. He probably wanted to see if I'd start babbling about Wilkes or Rubio. For once, though, I had zero knowledge or connection with the dead person. That always made it easier to not talk.

"Circumstantial evidence puts Wilkes in Vegas at the time, but it's a pretty short drive to LA from there."

I said nothing. I knew it was a short drive. I'd just been thinking it was a short drive. You could make it in four hours, if the traffic wasn't bad. You could make it in less, if you ignored speed limits and didn't mind a ticket or two. I finally broke the silence.

"When did this happen. Date? Time?" I asked.

I heard some typing on the line before MacIntyre answered. "Looks like it happened around 10pm on April 15. Were you with him then?"

I thought back. When had I left Vegas? I started subtracting my time in reverse order. Miami, Atlanta, Baltimore before that.

"Hartworth?"

"Just a second. It's not like I've a got a day planner in front of me. I'm doing math in my head."

I thought it through. I was there, but was Daniel with me that day?

"I was in Vegas then," I answered.

"What about Wilkes? Was he with you?"

MacIntyre must have sensed my uncertainty, because he sounded focused and a little eager. I thought some more. I tried very hard to dredge up the details. There had been a running series of illegal poker games that blurred together, but April 15 rang a bell in my head. There was something attached to it, something about dancing. It came back to me.

"Yeah," I said. "He was there. He dragged me to a dance club."

There was total silence on the other end of the line and then MacIntyre let loose with huge, booming laughter. It annoyed me.

"What?"

"You," he wheezed, "in a dance club. Were you wearing a suit? One of those double breasted jobs you like?"

I rolled my eyes. I had worn a suit.

"Yes," I muttered.

More laughter.

"Probably wore a tie too, didn't you?"

"Yes," I said through clenched teeth.

He laughed even harder. I let it roll on for as long as I could stand. Entire seconds passed. "Yes, yes, you've had your fun."

"Tears, Hartworth," said MacIntyre. "Laughing so hard, I'm crying."

"Any time you want to get on with it."

MacIntyre snickered some more and then quieted down. "Can you tell me what you did there?"

"It was a dance club. So, mostly, I went deaf."

"Was anyone with you?"

"Some girls Daniel met. Can't remember their names. A blonde, a brunette, both lookers, neither was terribly smart. I guess I was supposed to be his wingman or something. We drank. They danced. I didn't. I think he took them both home with him."

"He didn't leave at any point?"

"Not for longer than you need to take a piss," I said.

"You remember what time you left the club?" he asked, barely suppressing his laughter.

"Pretty late. It wasn't last call, not that Vegas casinos have a last call, but it was definitely after one in the morning."

There was some more typing. "Well, shit. Guess he really didn't do it."

"You liked him for it?"

"Maybe, but it's hard to know for sure. He rubbed me the wrong way. I held him overnight for being a smartass."

"Yeah, Daniel has that effect on people," I said.

MacIntyre went silent for another long pause. "Alright, Hartworth, you held up your end. What do you need from me?"

"Information."

"Someone going to wind up dead if I give it to you?"

It was a fair question. Things had gone that way once, though not by my choice. Even MacIntyre admitted it was self-defense when it was all said and done. Still, the question irked me.

"No. The people in question are already dead. I'm trying to figure out if there was a reason for it beyond stupid bad luck."

"Jesus, you're a godawful liar."

"Sorry?"

"You damn well know there was some reason. I can hear it in your voice," MacIntyre said. "This is one of those things, one of those Hartworth things that don't make any God damn sense, isn't it?"

"Probably," I admitted.

"Fuck. Please tell me you're not in town."

"I'm not in town. Not even in the state."

"Why call me?"

"The couple that died lived in California for a while. Separately and then together. I just need to know if there was some kind of trouble, especially for the wife, while they were out there."

"You thinking some kind of domestic abuse?"

"First thing I asked, but the consensus seems to be no. Honestly, I'm not sure exactly what I'm looking for, or even if it exists."

MacIntyre heaved another enormous sigh. "Way to narrow it down for me."

"I would if I could."

"Give me whatever information you've got."

I rattled off the salient, non-mystical details to MacIntyre. He broke in a few times to clarify spellings and to try to pin down dates more specifically. MacIntyre was good at his job and, I suspect, would have made lieutenant if he didn't hate politics so much. He was the kind of guy who would slide into retirement using his detective shield as a sled. He liked the investigation, building the chain of logic, assembling the evidence and cuffing the suspect. It usually worked out that way, at least when I wasn't involved.

"Mind if I ask what your interest in all this is, Hartworth?"

"Got a nagging suspicion. I think that someone might be targeting their kid."

"Their kid? If they had a kid, couldn't be older than, what? Eighteen? Twenty?"

"Fifteen."

"Christ, Hartworth, you should have opened with that."

"I didn't want it to come off as emotional blackmail."

There was silence on the other end of the line and I had the intuition that MacIntyre wanted to say or ask something.

"You gonna help that kid?" he asked.

"I'm going to try," I said. "If I can."

There was another long pause. "This a good number to reach you?"

"It is, for now anyway."

"Okay, I'll get back to you tonight, tomorrow at the latest."

I was surprised. "That fast?"

"A fifteen-year-old kid, Hartworth. I don't much like you, but I won't drag my feet when a kid's life is at stake."

"I appreciate it, Kyle."

I heard a quick inhalation. I hadn't used MacIntyre's first name in a long time. It didn't seem right to me, given the angst between us.

"Don't go soft on me now. I'd still break your nose if you gave me an excuse," said MacIntyre. "Adrian."

Then he hung up on me. I smiled for a second. I didn't think for a minute that we'd broken through any kind of barrier there. He *would* break my nose, given the opportunity. He was going to help, though, or at least make good on a favor. That was enough. I just hoped it would give me something to work with, because Abby needed help. She was going to be getting out of the hospital before too long. She'd be in the open. She'd be vulnerable. It was a race against time and I was still in no condition to run.

I leaned my head back against the headrest and gave the hospital a baleful look through the Neon's windshield. I still hated hospitals and probably always would. That the hospital was Abby's only safe haven was an irony that wasn't lost on me. I got out of the car and went inside to say hello. I'd been more or less absent the last few days and figured I should make an appearance.

I found Paul in the lobby, wearing a pair of slacks and a button-down shirt, typing on a laptop. I made my way over to him. It took him a minute to realize I was standing there. He looked up, blinked at me, and then his face split into a smile.

"Adrian," he said. "Good to see you."

I returned the man's smile. "Paul. How are you feeling?"

He shrugged. "Not a hundred percent yet, but I guess they've decided I won't keel over without constant supervision. At least it gives me a little time to catch up on some work."

"Antique business keep you busy?"

He blinked up at me warily and answered slowly. "Yes. It does keep me busy. How did you know?"

"I saw some antiques in your house."

He stared hard at me. "When?"

"When I came in to pull you and Abby out. I notice things," I said, trying to wave off his look of consternation. "I didn't stop to look around. I just noticed them."

"You're either a very strange or very remarkable man, Adrian."

"Strange," I assured him. "Definitely strange."

He smiled a little at that. "I don't doubt that's true. Still, most people wouldn't recognize an antique if they had the time to look. You recognized antiques at a glance, while dragging an old man and a teenage girl out of a burning building? You in the business?"

I shook my head. "Not to speak of. I've worked a lot of different jobs over the years. I was a personal buyer for a while. My client had a taste for antiques. I picked up a lot of general information and never really got out of the habit of noticing them. I wouldn't think there would be a booming trade in antiques in a town this size."

Paul snorted. "There isn't. I've got a tiny little store, but mostly it's there so I've got a physical address. Most of my business happens online."

The old man picked up the laptop and turned it so I could the screen. It looked like he was in the administrative section of a hosting service. I was impressed.

"Didn't let the march of technology leave you behind?"

"Didn't seem prudent to me. I made a point to start getting savvy about computers back in the late Nineties and launched the website about ten years ago. Best thing I could have done for myself. Quadrupled my business in a year."

"Nice. So, they're letting you out?"

Paul nodded. "Good thing, too. I need to find Abby and me a place to stay. At least until they can decide if the house is salvageable."

He went quiet then, his eyes losing focus, and it didn't take a genius to realize he was thinking about all the years he'd lived in that house. Its loss would be a blow to him. I thought he'd recover from it, but it's a hell of a thing to lose a home, for any reason. I would know. He shook off the distraction.

"I'm going out this afternoon to look at some rental properties," said Paul.

I nodded and a thought occurred to me. "Mind if I tag along?"

Chapter 21

I DISCOVERED THAT LOOKING AT APARTMENTS was unbelievably, drive a pencil into your own eye, boring. For my part, I hovered in the background and engaged in covert psychological warfare. I raised my eyebrow at minor problems. I murmured disapproving noises. I eyed things askance. The realtor looked ready to crucify me after the first couple hours. As we drove to the next place, Paul gave me a bemused look.

"I get the impression that you don't approve of my temporary housing solutions."

I shrugged. "Apartments are fine for a single guy. I was thinking about Abby. She might like something, I don't know, a little homier."

Paul frowned at that idea. I was sure that he was engaged in straightforward man-think. Shelter must be provided. Therefore, find shelter that is not too offensive. If all they needed was something to keep the rain off their heads, I wouldn't have cared one way or the other. There were, however, practical considerations unrelated to mere physical shelter that Paul knew nothing about.

"You think so?" Paul asked.

"Well, I don't know much about teenage girls, but the women I've known all seemed fixated on having a homey place to live."

Thank God for convenient truths, I thought. The real reason was that a place where people had lived their lives, a place with memories in the walls, would afford Abby some of the same shelter that her home had provided. It wouldn't be as good, but it would be a damn sight better protection than an apartment.

Paul took that advice under consideration and asked the realtor if she had any small houses he could tour. She had been giving me dark looks, but brightened up considerably at the prospect of renting a house. We went to four before we found what I was looking for in a place. It wasn't a house so much as a big cottage. The kitchen and living room ate up the lion's share of the space, but there were two bedrooms and a full bath. Even better, it was furnished.

I ran my hand along one wall, reaching out with my mostly adequate sixth sense. It was there, the imprint of memory and emotion that only a permanent home acquired. From the feedback I got, it had been a mostly happy home for whoever lived there before it became a rental property. I smiled around at the place. In another life, I could see myself living in a little cottage like that one. Paul gave me a sidelong glance, saw my smile, and nodded to himself.

"I think I'll take this one. How soon can we get the paperwork dealt with?"

"We can take care of it today, if you have the time," said the realtor with a big, fake smile.

Okay, maybe her smile wasn't fake. It was possible that I projected my own cynicism onto the situation and assumed she had ignoble intentions. It was also possible that she was just as cynical as me and perfectly willing to give an old man a huge, fake smile in order to make some money. Sometimes, you just can't tell. Paul dropped me off at the hospital on his way to the realtor's office.

"I don't think she likes you very much," said Paul.

"I can't imagine why," I said. "I'm so charming and easy to please."

Paul shook his head and drove off to sign a lease. I pulled out my phone and looked at it for the twentieth time since I'd talked with MacIntyre. It was a useless exercise. MacIntyre would call when he knew something or discovered there was nothing to know. I turned the phone off, pushed it back into my pocket and went inside. I knocked on Abby's door and a voice called out a moment later.

"Come in."

I stepped in from the hallway. Abby and Helena were playing a card game I didn't recognize. Abby beamed at me. Helena was right that Abby looked better. She was less gaunt and had some color in her cheeks. Her arm was still wrapped in bandages from wrist to mid-bicep, but she seemed to be moving it without too much pain. Helena gave me a little nod.

"Hi, Mr. Hartworth," said Abby.

"Abby," I said and mentally drop-kicked the impulse to ask how she was feeling. "Are you winning?"

Abby frowned down at the cards on the table tray, then at the cards in her hand, then at over at Helena. She shook her head, shrugged and laughed. "I have no idea."

I grinned, infected with her good cheer. I dragged over the only other chair in the room and sat next to Helena. I watched the two of them set out cards, discard cards, and then play cards that seemed to create tidal shifts in the game. Face cards did something special, but I couldn't quite work out the rules.

"What are you playing?" I asked.

"Cuttle," said Helena.

"Cuttle?" I asked. "Never heard of it."

"I hadn't either until a year or two ago. It's good for two players," said Helena with a shrug. "I bet you'd have picked poker, wouldn't you?"

"Probably," I muttered. "I know how to play that."

They kept playing for another twenty minutes before Abby's eyes lit up. Her eyes moved over the cards she had set out in front of her. It looked like she was counting.

"Cuttle!" Abby screamed in delight.

Helena laughed and put her cards down. "You don't need to shout Cuttle."

Abby looked a little embarrassed. "Oh, I thought it was like rummy."

I blinked at the girl. "You play rummy?"

"Grandpa plays with some of his friends. They let me sit in when they need a fourth."

It made sense, but struck me as sad. How many games had she sat in on because cancer or chemo made her too sick to go outside, or to see a movie, or to hang out with her friends? How much living had Abby missed out on because her body betrayed her with out-of-control cells? I wondered why she wasn't a lot more bitter than she appeared to be. God knew that most people didn't deal with those kinds of experiences with smiles and cheer.

Come to think of it, I thought, *where the hell are her friends?* I'd seen no sign of cards or balloons, let alone live human beings, to indicate Abby had any close friends who were worried about her. In my experience, even frenemies tended to find their humanity when someone's house burned down. It's the sort of thing I wanted to ask about, because it might be relevant. I kept

120

my mouth shut, though. She didn't need the reminder if she was essentially friendless.

I let myself get roped into playing card games with them, most of which I didn't recognize. I'd have thrown the games, but it wasn't necessary. Helena and Abby flat-out kicked my ass, game after game, hand after hand, and I smiled through it. I could afford to be a good loser, and Abby seemed delighted to have both company and a distraction. I supposed there was only so much television a person could stand.

When it started to get dark out, I excused myself. I went down to the lobby and turned my phone back on. I had my doubts about cell phones interfering with hospital equipment, much as I doubted they would interfere with airplane electronics, but why risk it? After my phone finished its interminable startup process and found a network to connect to, it dinged at me. I had a voicemail. I punched in the number and listened.

"Hartworth, it's MacIntyre. I know it's been entire hours, but I'll assume this is still your number. Call me back."

I stepped outside to get a little more privacy and called MacIntyre.

After the second ring, a gruff voice came over the line. "MacIntyre."

"It's Hartworth."

"What's with the voicemail? I thought this was urgent."

"I was in a hospital. They get all tetchy about cell phones."

MacIntyre thought, loudly, for a moment. "You get hurt?"

"Feel free not to sound so cheerful about that prospect. No. I was just visiting someone."

"Visiting? Visiting who?"

"Mary and Randall's kid."

"Jesus. Did someone go after her?"

I frowned. "No. Not the way you mean."

"That's pretty fucking cryptic."

"If someone did, they did it in one of those Hartworth, doesn't make any sense, kind of ways you love."

"I'm so glad you're in someone else's jurisdiction. Every time you get cagey, everything goes straight to hell."

"Not every time," I objected.

"Every damn time, Hartworth."

I brushed it off and changed the subject. "You find anything?"

MacIntyre muttered and made noises without actually forming words.

"I didn't quite catch that," I said.

"I don't know. Maybe. It's all just—it's just weird."

"Weird? Weird how?"

MacIntyre hemmed and hawed for a few more seconds, heaved a tremendous, put-upon sigh, and started talking. "Near as I can tell, Randall was just a regular citizen. No real brushes with the law, except a couple of tickets and a fender bender."

"But Mary?"

"Yeah," said MacIntyre, "but Mary, indeed. She was never in trouble, per se, but a whole lot of stuff went wrong for her over the years. You know, the kind of stuff you expect a person to have happen maybe once in their lives."

"Like what?"

"Well, her parents died when she was fairly young. Around twelve or thirteen years old. Got chalked up as a boating accident and both parents died. Sad, but it happens sometimes. So, she ends up in foster care. Foster parents were getting set to adopt her, but they die in a mugging gone wrong."

I let that soak in. "Seems improbable."

"Yeah, it's rare, but it does happen. So, she winds up with another family. The kind foster kids pray they don't get. Angry, abusive people that only care about the money. Foster dad decides he likes the look of Mary one drunken afternoon."

"Fucking hell."

"Yeah. To her credit, she made a ruckus, yelling and screaming. Neighbor heard it. I guess that guy had his Good Samaritan badge on that day, because he busts in and puts a stop to it. According to the report, foster dad had nearly choked the life out of Mary before the neighbor got there."

"Lemme guess, nothing happened to the foster dad."

MacIntyre laugh was a cold, menacing sound that sent chills down my spine. "Depends on how you look at it. Neighbor was a Green Beret, fresh out of the service. Apparently, he beat the foster dad senseless and then threw him out a window. Last time anyone laid a hand on her, near as I can tell, but there's other stuff. Her car caught fire on the highway and the locks malfunctioned. She managed to break a window and get out. Nearly got crushed when some idiot cut down a tree the wrong way and it crashed into her house. It goes on and on like that, Hartworth. I mean, mother of God, nobody is that unlucky."

I looked back at the hospital. Yeah, nobody but Abby, I thought. Something cold settled around my stomach. "Any indication that Mary's parents' death wasn't an accident?"

"Not that I could see, but that accident was ages ago. Evidence is all long-gone. Why?"

"Just wondered," I said. "Seems to be a lot of accidents in that family."

"Noticed that. This is all very *you*. Anyways, hope it helps."

"It might. Thanks, MacIntyre."

"This was tame. I wish all your favors were so easy."

"I'm getting old. Like things a lot quieter than I used to."

"You're so full of shit, Hartworth."

"See ya, MacIntyre."

"Not if I'm lucky."

Abby's parents died in an accident. Mary's parents died in an accident. It was possible that Mary's parents' deaths really were just an accident, but my intuition didn't buy it. If it didn't start with Mary, where did it start? Did it start with her parents? Even further back? And why? Evil carrying a grudge for twenty or thirty years was hard enough to buy, but forty years? Fifty? What could possibly have been so egregious that a demonic being would spend that much time punishing mortals for it?

Chapter 22

I DON'T KNOW HOW LONG I STOOD OUTSIDE, trying to piece together some kind of coherent theory for what was happening. It was long enough that Helena came looking for me. I was deep in thought, almost completely unaware of my surroundings, when she touched my shoulder. Her touch shocked me so much that I took a swing at her. I pulled up short, but it was a close call. She stared up at me, her eyes very wide, like she was seeing me in an entirely new light.

"So, this is what you've become," she said after an awkward silence.

I gave her a hard look. "It's what I need to be to survive."

She winced. "There is more to life than survival, you know."

"Maybe, but you have to survive for any of that other stuff to be possible."

She tilted her head to one side. "I'd never thought of it like that. I guess most of us take day-to-day survival as a given."

"Most people can," I said. "I'm just not one of them."

"How's your back?"

"Hurts, when I think about it anyway. It's like background noise most of the time."

"Don't get lazy about changing your bandages. That burn gets infected and you'll be spending a lot more time in this hospital."

I shuddered. "That's a cheery thought."

"Did you speak with your acquaintance?"

"I did. Not sure it was much help."

I filled Helena in on what MacIntyre said. She listened without interrupting me. Afterwards, she stood in silence, her eyes unfocused and her head moving from time to time, as if she was trying to sort something out.

She shook her head. "I don't see how it answers anything. It certainly doesn't help with the immediate problem."

"No, it doesn't. At least, not that I can see. I know I'm missing something obvious, but this whole situation is counterintuitive. New information should make things clearer, but it feels like stumbling through a fog bank."

"Did you imagine this would be easy and straightforward?"

I frowned. "Well, yes. Okay, maybe not easy, exactly, but I thought it would be direct."

Helena stared out into the mostly empty parking lot. She shivered, but I didn't think it was because of the cooling night air. There was a tightness around her mouth and eyes that made the lines stand out a little more. She looked older, more tired, and fragile.

"Given your experiences, that assumption probably makes sense to you. It's a stupid assumption, though. Evil isn't always banal. If it were, we'd know it on sight. Evil can be subtle, Adrian. Old evil can be frighteningly intelligent and seductive."

"Seductive?"

"Lucifer convinced a full third of the angels to rebel, didn't he?"

"So the story goes," I said.

"How do you think he did that? It certainly wasn't by logical deduction. Logic dictated that it was an unwinnable fight. Yet, they fought. He didn't convince them. Lucifer seduced those angels with words and thoughts."

I stared at her. "You think we're fighting the literal devil here?"

She gave me a wan smile. "No. It's just an illustration, but the point stands. You're used to being smarter than the people who pick fights with you. You've brought that mindset into this situation. I think you're underestimating what we're up against here."

"I've seen what we're up against, Helena. I've felt its power. I'm not kidding myself."

"Power is just power. Having a lot of it doesn't make you unbeatable. A river has a lot of power until someone dams it. Whatever we're up against here, it's obscured its existence for a long time. It hasn't been sloppy or stupid. Think about it."

I rolled my head. She was right. Of course, she was right. That idea had been lurking behind my own thoughts for a while.

I just hadn't been savvy enough to see it. I'd been so fixated on how goddamn powerful that demon was, I hadn't given enough consideration to how it was operating.

"I have been thinking about it, in a roundabout way. If I thought he was the type, I'd tell Paul to get the hell out of Dodge and take Abby with him."

"Do you think that would work?"

I thought about Mary's many brushes with death. They were scary, but they had been intermittent. Whatever the demon was, it wasn't all-powerful. It was limited or constrained in some way. I'd felt the scope of its power, and if it wasn't constrained, it would have vaporized Mary. Abby wouldn't have fared any better.

"No," I admitted, "but I think it would slow things down enough to give Abby a fighting chance. Whatever is happening is tied to this place somehow. Unless I'm misreading things badly, which is possible, that demon needs to build up a lot of strength to reach out into the world. Even here, Abby isn't dead yet. It wants her dead, but she's survived this long. Get her away from here and I'd be surprised if her cancer didn't vanish outright."

"Seems like she's got a start on that already, thanks to you."

"It won't last. I wish it would, but it won't. I caught that thing off guard. Once she walks out of here," I hitched a thumb over my shoulder at the hospital, "she'll get very sick, very fast."

Helena nodded. "She wasn't that excited about going back to school. Brutal way to avoid it, though."

An intuition set my stomach lurching. "Wait. What did you say?"

"Cancer, it's a hell of a way to avoid school."

"No, not that. The other part about her not wanting to go back to school. What's that about?"

Helena shrugged and gave me a look that suggested that I was being entirely too serious. "She doesn't like it. Honestly, can you blame her? It's hard enough to be in high school when you're healthy."

"Did she say why she didn't want to go back?"

"She just said she didn't like it at the school."

That rang a bell. I scoured my memory. It was hard. There'd been so much pain and medication right at first that everything was blurry. Someone else had said something about not liking that school. Was it Patty? No, I thought. She'd told me who it was. It was the sheriff that didn't like the place. It creeped him out. The stomach lurching intensified. I turned and ran into the hospital. I heard Helena yelling behind me.

"Adrian! What's happening?"

I bypassed the elevator and went straight into the stairwell. I took the stairs two at a time. Somewhere between the second and third floors my lungs mutinied. A wave of dizziness rolled over me. I would have toppled down the stairs if my hand hadn't slapped down onto the railing. I grabbed it hard and tried to fight off the vertigo. I forced myself to take even breaths until the dizziness passed. It felt like it took twenty minutes. As it was, my arms and legs were weak and shaky, like I'd just run a half-mile flat out. It was oxygen deprivation, I realized. Standing, walking, those I could do without any trouble because they just didn't demand as much oxygen. Running, any running, was just more than my lungs could support.

I felt a surge of anger at my own body. It had never failed me like that before. Sure, the ravages of time had taken their toll. My knees ached more than they did when I was younger. I wouldn't be catching any teenagers in a foot chase. My endurance wasn't what it had been. Those things I expected and understood. That wave of dizziness, though, felt somehow like treason.

"Stop being an irrational tool, Hartworth," I wheezed to myself.

I turned and scrambled up the stairs in a lurching jog that I thought my body might support for the rest of the steps. By the time I got to the landing, I was starting to feel dizzy again, but not the deadly vertiginous spinning I'd felt lower on the stairs. I hurried to Abby's room and crashed through the door. I must have looked god awful because Abby stared at me in open concern.

"Mr. Hartworth, are you okay?"

"Helena said you didn't like the school."

She gave self-conscious roll of her shoulders. "Yeah, that's true."

"Why don't you like it?"

I watched something pass over Abby's face, a kind of calculation. "School sucks."

I stepped closer to her. "Abby, this is important. Even if you think it sounds crazy, I'll believe you. I swear to God, I will. Please tell me, why don't you like the school?"

She pulled her knees up to her chest and hugged them hard. She watched me like she expected me to call in the cops or the navy or, more likely, the men with the butterfly nets. She turned her head away and looked at me from the corner of her eye.

"It makes me feel sicker. Whenever I'm there, it's like I can feel the cancer getting worse. I hate that place."

I closed my eyes. So, it was centered there. The closer she got to the demon's epicenter of power, the more influence it could exert. It was nothing short of a damn miracle that she hadn't had an "accident" in the science lab or experienced an "unexpected fall" from a climbing rope in gym class. *Tell them to get out*, I thought. Paul can work from anywhere. They just needed to get the fuck out of this cursed town. Then I wondered how I would explain it to him. What excuse could I possibly use to justify that advice?

"You don't believe me, do you?" Abby asked.

I opened my eyes. Huddled in that bed, she looked small, afraid and very alone. I had the brief, paternal urge to give her a hug. I decided that would have crossed a boundary. Instead, I gave her the steadiest smile I could manage.

"I do believe you, Abby."

I'd all but known before I even asked the question. I didn't have to work hard to sell it.

She blinked at me in apparent disbelief. "You do?"

"I do. There are places in the world that are bad for some people. Sounds like that high school is one of them, for you anyways."

"I wish grandpa believed me. He thinks I just don't like school, but I *like* learning about things! Just—" she took a shaky breath, "just not there."

I felt a surge of protectiveness and fought down another impulse to hug the beleaguered girl. I had a moment of insight then. I understood why I had stayed, when everything told me to leave. It was so obvious, so stupidly obvious, I couldn't believe I hadn't realized it sooner. If Marcy and I had a child, the way we'd planned to, that child would be about Abby's age. If we'd had a daughter, and she'd been unlucky enough to favor me, she might have even looked a bit like Abby. *Later*, I told myself. *You'll have plenty of time to psychoanalyze yourself later, if you survive this mess.*

"He means well," I said. "Teenagers not liking school is sort of a time-honored tradition. He's seeing what he expects to see."

Helena burst through the door, casting wild looks at every corner. I felt the power she'd gathered around her like mist against my face. It was cool and refreshing, the kind of protective, healing magic that Helena specialized in wielding. My magic, when I used it, did not feel like that. Healing wasn't really my forte. I gave her the tiniest of head shakes. Helena glared at me and I felt her power drain away.

"Whoa," said Abby. "They must have given me some drugs when I wasn't looking."

Helena and I turned our heads in unison and eyed the girl.

"Why's that?" I asked.

"It was crazy. For a second there, it looked like Helena was glowing."

Well, son of a bitch, I thought.

Chapter 23

ABBY LOOKED BACK AND FORTH, from me to Helena. Her cheeks went very pink.

"What?" Abby demanded.

I glanced over at Helena. She looked dumbfounded. I realized that I must have had the same look on my face. *Dammit. Way to cover, Hartworth.* For people schooled in secrecy, Helena and I were doing a pretty piss poor job of covering what was, all things considered, a fairly minor revelation in a series of sobering, frightening revelations. I shot Abby a bemused smile.

"Yeah," I said, forcing a chuckle, "I had some of those drugs once. Saw some crazy shit."

Abby cast me a rightfully suspicious look and turned her gaze back to Helena. Helena had taken the opportunity to compose her face into gentle amusement. Score one for fast recovery. Abby wasn't dumb, and she knew we were covering something. Lucky for Helena and me, Abby wasn't an adult yet. She was probably used to challenging her grandfather about things. After all, what teenagers don't challenge the parental figures in their lives?

Other adults were something else entirely. She wasn't used to challenging them, let alone demanding answers from people who seemed intent on secrecy. I saw the mental tug-of-war on her face. She wanted to understand what had made Helena and I look at her that way. Hell, who wouldn't want to know what caused that? She also didn't want to start stepping on our toes. Some of her hesitation might have been out of fear that we'd withdraw our attention. That was probably a lot of it. There was an unpleasant dearth of people around who seemed to give a crap about her. Alienating the few people who were being kind must have sounded like a losing bet to her. Her curiosity lost out to either deference or self-interest. I resisted the urge to sag in relief.

I looked at Helena. "It's getting late. We should let Abby get her rest."

"Yes, we probably should," Helena agreed.

Abby still cast suspicious expressions at us. The certainty that we were lying our asses off was painted in her furrowed brow and on lips pressed into a line. Helena did what I hadn't. She went over and gave Abby a hug. The gesture seemed to soften Abby's suspicion, or at least her belief that we were deceiving her with malicious intent. The girl hugged Helena with a nigh-hideous expression of need on her face. Paul probably wasn't big on hugging.

In fact, I'd have bet money he stopped hugging her almost entirely right around the time she hit puberty. He wasn't a bad guy, just made from a mold that aspired to different ideals. I couldn't fault him for that. Truth be told, I was probably cast from a relatively similar mold. It might have been years since a maternal figure of any kind had given Abby a meaningful hug. It was difficult to watch the girl hug Helena. Abby was emotionally exposed in a way that would have horrified her, if she knew someone saw it. God, it was enough to break even my callous heart.

I couldn't help but wonder whether Abby represented some kind of a throwback to an earlier generation. She had, after all, been raised by a man who grew up in the wake of World War II. My own lack of experience with kids notwithstanding, I did occasionally stumble onto the Internet. I saw articles bemoaning something called Millennials and their sense of entitlement, their laziness, and their lack of work ethic. Like most generalizations, I assumed it grossly overstated things, but those kinds of generalizations don't come from nowhere, either.

If Abby belonged to the Millennials, it seemed as though it must have been a mere chronological happenstance, rather than evidence of a shared worldview. She struck me as someone who just wasn't jaded enough to have grown up in a post-Watergate, post-9-11, post-economic meltdown world. She was too innocent and too willing to let it go when adults clammed up. That didn't really jibe with the entitled thing. She also didn't strike me as lazy. The TV in her room was never on. If she was looking for a mental anesthetic or a way to avoid doing anything, TV would serve that function.

When we'd played games, she played well. She played to win. She focused on the game with all her attention. She wasn't a poor winner or a sore loser, which said a lot about her character to me. She was happy when she won, but didn't respond with the in-your-face ridicule that pervaded all modern competition. When she lost, she was far too busy analyzing the loss to engage in sulking or whining. She engaged with the world around her. People who engaged with the world rarely lacked a work ethic.

Of course, all that was overshadowed by her unintentional revelation. She had *seen* the power around Helena. In my experience, maybe thirty percent of people sensed it when someone was actively engaged in using magic or gathering the power to do so. Most of those people didn't know what they were sensing. They thought it was a draft, or an errant noise, or just their imaginations. In other words, they needed it to be explicable. Therefore, thought following need, and working from a host of false assumptions, it became explicable.

A slim fraction of one percent of those who sensed it *saw* gathered power. I'd been at the magic game for years and I didn't see it most of the time. Then again, I'd made exactly zero effort to learn how. Seeing was an advantage in some respects. It gave you an early alert. It was also a disadvantage. When you see gathered power, it's hard to ignore and harder not to react. In a subculture devoted to secrecy, noticing the wrong person with gathered power can reap unpleasant consequences, like your untimely death. That was especially true when you didn't have any magic to defend yourself, and I was certain, down to my damned DNA certain, that Abby didn't.

What that meant was that she was psychic, maybe very psychic. There were a lot of people who considered psychic ability to be magic. Maybe it was on some grand scale, cosmic metalevel, but not for practical purposes. I'd go so far as to say I believed they were inextricably entwined: like two species that evolved from the same parent species, which had manifested different traits over countless generations. Even so, it wouldn't do Abby any good to go running around willy-nilly noticing things that people didn't want noticed.

The timing also bothered me. If she was psychic, why had she chalked up her insight to drugs? It was as though she had no earthly idea of what she could do. Had Helena and I witnessed the first manifestations of that psychic ability? It seemed so improbable as to be insane. To have seen Helena's power the way she did suggested Abby was a first-order psychic. That kind of power didn't show up during adolescence. It showed up around conception and began torturing its possessor from the get-go. In my opinion, that was one of the universe's more malicious decisions. A benevolent universe, or a benevolent God, wouldn't saddle the most helpless members of humanity with direct access to the unvarnished truths of existence. A benevolent universe wouldn't ever do that to anyone.

The lucky psychics received guidance early on from knowledgeable family members and mentors. The unlucky ones got institutionalized and drugged to the gills. Apparently, psychiatrists found the exposure of their deepest, darkest, innermost secrets worthy of the moral equivalent of murder. After all, when you pharmaceutically lobotomize a person and then lock them away for life, you have murdered that person in all meaningful ways. Oh, they don't call it that. Murder is wrong, after all. They call it treatment, or protecting society, or some other euphemistic bullshit that lets them sleep at night. Make no mistake, though, it is medically-sanctioned murder. They just waited for time to kill the body. It was cleaner that way, and western medicine loved to keep things clean.

I only wished it was a paranoid fantasy. I'd thought it was for a long time, until I saw it happen to someone I knew. Only the exertion of old money, political connections, and I was fairly certain, the kind of threats only underworld types knew how to deliver, freed Peter from the situation. He learned his lesson. Secrecy. It all came down to secrecy. If you enjoyed freedom; if you enjoyed the ability to continue using your mind unfettered by chemical inhibitors; if you wanted to continue participating in the world, you kept your damn mouth shut.

Abby was innocent of that kind of knowledge. It was a dangerous innocence. I wouldn't see her locked away because of a quirk of birth. She had to be told. She had to be instructed. She had to be warned, but, my mind reminded me, she had to survive first. More to the point, none of us were prepared to have that conversation. It couldn't be broached lightly. Groundwork needed to put in place. Ideas needed to planted and watered. Once they'd had time to grow and mature, the conversation could take place.

It was easier with small children. They weren't as paralyzed by "knowledge" as someone Abby's age. They grew up accepting the actual facts about existence as facts. The world was complex on orders of magnitude that science just wasn't sophisticated enough to cope with yet. Some of the bleeding-edge physicists seemed to be nosing around the edges of it, getting the scent, and figuring it out through sheer brainpower and diligence, but it would be a long time before science caught up enough to join the conversation at the grown-up table. Abby didn't have that kind of time. I wanted to scream in frustration. As though things weren't complicated enough before her abrupt entrance into mine and Helena's world.

I found myself profoundly grateful that Helena was there. She was a velvet touch compared to me. It wasn't that I couldn't start the process or even see it through. I'd been through it myself. Subtleties weren't my strong suit, though. I knew enough to know that reordering the conceptual groundwork that held a teenage girl's mind together wasn't a smart move for a ham-fisted, journeyman practitioner like me. I could mess her up in all kinds of ways with the best of intentions. *Priorities*, I reminded myself. *Focus on the priorities. Keep her alive, now. The rest can happen after.*

I realized that I'd been lost in thought and refocused on the room. Helena and Abby were watching me with nearly identical expressions of blazing curiosity. I nearly took an involuntary step back under the weight of their combined gazes.

"Penny for your thoughts," said Helena.

Her voice sounded sweet and innocent, but I figured she'd guessed the line of my thinking. I could have strangled her. I waved a dismissive hand while I thought up a fast lie.

"Trying to remember if I left food out for Lil," I said.

"Who's Lil?" Abby asked.

"She's a cat," I said. "She kind of adopted me."

Abby's eyes lit up and she squealed in a way that made her seem very, painfully young. "I love cats! Can I meet your cat?"

I looked to Helena.

She mouthed, "How should I know?"

I shrugged at Abby, "Okay. I'm sure that'll be fine."

She gave a wordless cheer and I was blessed with another of her million-watt smiles. If I wasn't careful, I'd go snowblind in the glow. She surprised me then. She held out her arms in the universal sign of hug time. I flicked another glance at Helena. That time, she offered guidance. She jerked her head toward Abby hard enough that I got sympathetic whiplash. I walked over to the bed and leaned down. Abby threw her arms around my neck and squeezed me hard enough that it almost cut off my air flow. I didn't mind. I wrapped my arms around her. I was horrified and saddened by how frail she felt. *Fucking cancer*, I fumed. *Fucking demon*, I seethed. I wanted to lay a world of hurt on someone or something right then, preferably with my bare hands and teeth.

On another level, one that was tied to my memory and all my unlived dreams, I wondered if that was how it might have felt to hug my own daughter. A wrenching, awful pain that would have doubled me over if I wasn't already bent down tore through me. That pain had nothing to do with my burned back or even my body. It was all in the intangible spaces of my heart and my head. It also hurt a hell of a lot more than getting burned. If I could have done it without being seen, I'd have wept.

Chapter 24

WE STOOD NEXT TO MY CAR. The sky was clear overhead and the number of visible stars shocked me. I spent most of my time in places with awful light pollution. The town's light footprint was so small that the stars glittered overhead like a wash of diamonds spread across black velvet. I leaned against the Neon and did my best to exorcise thoughts of non-existent daughters and a life that never was.

Helena watched me obliquely. "Are you alright?"

I nodded. "Yeah, just some ghosts I thought I'd laid to rest a while back. Took me by surprise."

"They do that," said Helena. "Abby will need instruction. I assume you'd prefer I handle it."

"Probably for the best, all things considered. It's not like I'm really teacher material."

Helena sniffed. It sounded derisive.

"What?" I asked.

"You and your self-loathing. I forget how bad it gets. You would be a perfectly adequate teacher, if you ever managed to stay somewhere long enough to see it through."

She meant what she said, but old pain laced the words. She wasn't the first person I hadn't stuck around for, but I thought it had hurt her more than anyone else. She had loved me, actual, legitimate love, and I had left. I'd told myself that I wasn't made to stay. I'd lived most of my adult life by that credo, never settling down anywhere, not even bothering to establish anything like a home. My world consisted of hotel rooms and motel rooms and, from time to time, staying for a few days or weeks with the handful of people who still opened the door when I knocked.

Years of experience provided me with a bit of clarity. The truth proved more complicated than the catchphrase I fed myself, as the truth always does. I was a natural wanderer. That much was true, but it wasn't the whole truth. I also wandered because I was broken. I'd never gotten clear of Marcy and the things we had planned. Settling down somewhere, let alone with someone, would have been too much like burying Marcy a second time. I couldn't face that prospect. I couldn't make that choice without engaging in mental self-mutilation that would have crippled me even more than my inability to move on.

"Maybe," I hedged. "It'll probably be easier coming from you."

She sniffed again, somehow managing to cram even more derision into it. I was impressed. It took hard work to communicate that much with one, brief noise.

"Spare me. That girl has so much hero worship going on toward you right now that she'd crawl through a cobra pit filled with razor wire and burning tires to please you."

"All the more reason for me not to do it, don't you think?"

Helena stood there in silent thought for a moment. "Maybe so. Still, it might smooth things over if you participated from time to time."

"She'll be more pliable when I'm around, you mean?"

"Yes. You know how difficult the transition is coming at it as an adult," she paused, "or nearly an adult. It's painful enough when you're a willing participant. She won't be willing, but she has to learn."

"She does. Assuming she doesn't die in the next couple days."

"I have an intuition that a broody, wandering father-figure won't let that happen."

My head snapped back. Christ, had I been so obvious? Helena laughed, but not unkindly. If someone was going to be able to read me so easily, Helena would be that person. I just wasn't used to it happening.

"I forget how perceptive you are," I said.

"I have my moments, but it wasn't hard to figure out."

"No?"

"You are many things, Adrian Hartwell, but gentle is rarely one of them. You've been handling that girl like she's made of crystal. It's actually rather endearing, in a cognitive dissonance and migraine yielding sort of way."

I gave her a little bow. "I'll be here all week, providing the cure to your mental well-being."

"Speaking of curing mental well-being, do you have any thoughts about dealing with the current problem?"

I waggled my hand in a maybe-maybe-not gesture. "I know where to look now, even if it doesn't make any sense."

"The school?"

"Yeah."

"Why doesn't that make sense?"

I frowned at Helena. How could she find it anything but bizarre and perplexing? The damn place was a church not that long ago. A demon squatting there should have been impossible, or the next best thing to it. Was she testing me? Being intentionally obtuse to force me to work through my own reasoning? Then, I remembered. She didn't know. She hadn't seen the school, and I hadn't had a reason to mention it to her.

"It used to be a church," I said.

It was her head that rocked back that time. I took more than a little smug satisfaction in that. Pettiness wasn't becoming, but it could be satisfying. She sputtered for a few seconds before words finally took shape and shot out into the night air.

"A church!"

"You see my quandary. If anything, she should be safer there than anywhere else in the entire town. Instead, she gets sicker whenever she sets foot in the place. It's as incomprehensible as everything else in this shitty situation. It's like I slipped into some alternate universe where they scrap-heaped the rules of magic and basic reasoning."

Helena offered a sympathetic look. "So what's the move? Visit the school?"

"Are you out of your mind? I don't want to get near that place until I know more about it. What's happening here shouldn't be happening. That it is happening scares the shit out of me. If that place is evil central, just walking in might be a death sentence for me and anyone near me."

"So what's the plan?"

"I do things the old fashioned way."

"Which is?"

"Dollars to donuts, some industrious local wrote about that church. I just have to run the information down. So, I go to the library and see what they have on local history."

Helena threw her head back as peals of laughter flew from her lips. The laughter went on for so long that she was holding her stomach before she wheezed to a stop. I gave her a hard-eyed stare.

"Care to share what's so amusing?"

"Library," she said. "Unspeakable evil, curses, conspiracies and you're going," more laughter, "to go," harder laughter, "to the library!"

I felt offended on behalf of libraries everywhere. "What's so funny about that? Libraries have served us all pretty well over the centuries."

"I just suspect that," she said, catching her breath, "people would be less intimidated by you if they knew you went to libraries."

I lifted an eyebrow. "If they were smart, they'd be more intimidated."

Helena wiped at one eye. "True enough. You'll let me know if you find something?"

"Of course."

"Get some sleep, Hartworth," she said, a little giggle in her voice. "You've got a hard day of research at the library tomorrow."

"Har, har."

Helena turned away and started walking toward her car. Every few steps, I heard a little snort, tee-hee, or snicker. You'd have thought I'd just announced my plan to become a fan-dancer. I drove back to the cabin and found Lil sitting right inside the door. She glared at me, stepped out the door, peered around suspiciously, and went back inside. She walked to the far side of the cabin, glared at me some more, and issued forth with a discontented noise.

"Mrrrwwwww."

"What's wrong? Are you out of food?"

I walked over and found her dish still half full with food. I poured more water into the other side of the little dish from a bottle I'd left sitting on the nightstand. She eyed me, unimpressed.

"Not the problem, huh."

I checked the litter box and scooped out a few sandy clumps into a small plastic bag. I didn't bother looking at her. Even knowing almost nothing about cats, I was sure the litter box was too clean to account for her annoyance. I sat down on the bed and regarded Lil for a moment. I held out my hand near the floor. She watched my outstretched fingers for a long time before she—ever ever so casually—sauntered over and let me scratch behind her ears.

"You're out of sorts because I was gone for so long, aren't you?"

Lil sat back on her haunches and looked up at me. Her kitty face was locked into an opaque, alien expression that probably would have told another cat, or Helena, several million things. It told me nothing. I reached down again and she deigned to let me pet her head.

"I'm pretty new to this," I offered. "I'll do my best to figure it out, but you need to be patient and bear with me a little."

She tipped her head to one side, as if trying to pick up a transmission from a satellite, or possibly, the home world of the Cat Overlords. She held still like that for the better part of fifteen seconds before she seemed to decide that she was no longer aggravated. She leapt up onto the bed and started sniffing at things I couldn't smell. I went through my nightly routine of bandage changing. It was getting slightly less agonizing. No one would ever mistake it for a massage, but it didn't draw immediate tears.

All the day's activities caught up with me. I yawned several times and crawled into bed. I told myself to turn off the light by the bed. Myself agreed that that was an excellent idea, but made no move to perform the action. Myself isn't really a team player, I guess. Somewhere between telling my hand to turn the little knob on the side of the lamp and the signal reaching my arm, I fell asleep.

"You make an excellent point, young man," said a small man in a tweed jacket, standing behind a podium. "Orthodox religion has always been intolerant of mystery schools, typically under the guise of maintaining the purity of accepted practice. Of course, the reality was always about maintaining a grip on temporal power."

I stood in the aisle of an auditorium that was filled to capacity. If anyone had noticed me, or cared where I stood, they kept quiet. Someone asked a question and I was shocked to discover the speaker was me.

"Professor, in your opinion, was orthodox religion the primary threat to mystery schools?"

The professor squinted at me. "Yes, you there. What is your name?"

"Hartworth, Professor," I answered against my will.

"Hartworth, mmmm, yes. Who is your large friend, Mr. Hartworth?"

I turned my head left. Rows and rows of students looked at me in utter silence. It was creepy. I turned my head right and found Dream Lil towering next to me like doom's familiar. Even in the steady light of the auditorium, her features were difficult to make out, save for the savage scar on her damaged ear and her blood ruby eyes. I turned back to the professor and wondered what possible answer I could give that would sound sane.

"Lil," I answered automatically.

"Ah yes, Hartworth and Lil, glad to see you could make it," said the professor, scratching a note onto a piece of paper. "As to your question, no, in my opinion, orthodox religion was not the primary threat to mystery schools, nor was social pressure. Perhaps ironically, the primary threat to mystery schools was the most prosaic of all things: economics."

"Could you expand on that thought?" I asked.

"Certainly," said the Professor, warming to the topic. "By their very nature, mystery schools placed increasing demands on the time and energy of their members, especially at the upper levels. The longer the school existed, the more intense the demands. The elite of the mystery schools couldn't devote themselves fully to careers or financial management while also pursuing the goals of the school. Some mystery schools collapsed under the financial demands. Others maintained themselves by bringing in a steady stream of novitiates and collecting dues.

"That strategy, naturally, leads to a corrosion in purpose. Take the Masons, for example. When they began, I am confident they were a true mystery school, but time and an increasing membership led to a devolution into something more akin to a social club. Without a steady influx of wealth, mystery schools seemed doomed from the outset to collapse. With uncertain finances, the schools couldn't pursue their goals as readily. That in turn diminished membership, which served to exacerbate the financial problems. To survive, they have to allow more open membership, but at the cost of drifting from their initial purpose. It is a dilemma to which I have seen no obvious solution."

"Perhaps a wealthy founder," I offered.

"A plausible notion, on the surface, but ultimately unsustainable. Consider the realities of inflation. In 1901, a fortune of five million dollars was a staggering sum, worth the equivalent of one hundred to one hundred and fifty million dollars in today's market, give or take. Yet, the actual five million dollars loses value at a shocking rate as time passes, unless significant time and effort are put into managing it toward growth. Time and effort, Hartworth, the exact things the elite of mystery schools didn't have to give."

I started to ask another question, but resounding booms shook the auditorium. It felt like a giant was slamming a fist against the roof. I put a hand against Dream Lil's side to steady myself. There was a moment of disorientation, as though I moved some great distance, and my eyes snapped open.

Someone was knocking on the cabin door with hard, steady bangs.

Chapter 25

IN MY EXPERIENCE, hard banging on the door never bodes well. It's just an immutable truth. My first instinct, on coming-to, was to look for a back way out. I could have gone out a window. They were big enough, if I didn't mind some scrapes and cuts. I doubted I could get out one without making some noise. Lil was standing up and looking at the door, but her ears were forward and she didn't give off a fear vibe. I found that oddly reassuring and took a second to consider the implications. There were only a few people who knew where to find me. I was also on speaking terms with all of them at the moment. I hemmed, hawed, and listened to several more serious sounding thumps. Decision made, I heaved myself out of bed. I went to the door and opened it.

"Hartworth," said Patty, her eyes watching something off in the trees, "I wanted to talk…"

She looked back at me and her voice caught. Her eyes were fixed on my chest. I glanced down and winced. I wasn't wearing a shirt. Patty's eyes swiveled up to meet mine. There was anger in her eyes, but it wasn't aimed at me. She'd been a cop somewhere else before she moved into small-town policing. Apparently, it was the kind of place where bad shit happened to people regularly enough that she knew the signs. Someone had done that to me. If I was one of those sad souls that cut themselves, there would have been newer scars, some of them red with the more recent trauma. My scars were evenly faded-out to pale white.

"Sorry," I said. "Let me grab a shirt. Come on in."

Patty followed me into the cabin and shut the door behind her. I dug around until I came up with a package of white t-shirts I'd bought. I ripped it open and, after fumbling with some stickers and a hunk of cardboard, I pulled it on. I turned to face the deputy. She looked thoughtful.

"Piss off the wrong person?" she asked.

"It's possible," I said. "I rub a lot of people the wrong way."

"Nice of them not to cut up the tattoos."

"Since they gave them to me, it would have been counter-productive."

Patty blinked at that. "Somebody tortured you and took the time to give you tattoos?"

"Not sure it was torture. I don't actually remember any of it."

"That's probably a mercy," said Patty. "They mean anything?"

"Does what mean anything?"

"The tattoos."

"Oh, yeah, they do."

Patty made an exasperated noise. "What do they mean?"

"They're alchemical symbols," I said.

"Alchemical?"

"Um," I verbally stumbled as I searched for a simple explanation. "Alchemy is the transmutation of elements or material into something more perfect, broadly speaking."

Patty sighed.

I thought about it. "Alchemists tried to turn lead into precious metals and other things along those lines."

"Ah," Patty said. "Do you know what the ones on your chest mean?"

"Not specifically," I admitted.

"How can you not know? I mean, isn't that your thing?"

"A dermatologist might understand the anatomy and general processes involved with heart surgery. It doesn't mean you want one giving you a bypass. I'm not an expert on alchemy."

She gave me a perplexed look. "Given that someone tattooed those symbols onto you, seems like you might have looked into it."

I sighed. "I did. It's not as clear-cut as you might think. There's a lot of bleed-through between old schools of magic and mysticism. The symbols are alchemical designs, but it doesn't make them alchemical in intent."

"I don't understand," said Patty.

I frowned and looked around. I found a scrap of paper.

"Do you have a pen or pencil?" I asked.

She handed me a pen. I used it to draw on the paper and handed both items to her. She pocketed the pen and glanced at the paper.

"Okay?"

I smiled. "What do you see there?"

Patty didn't pause. "Crosshairs."

"Maybe. All you actually see on that paper is a circle with a vertical and horizontal line inside it. You're a cop, so you see crosshairs. Maybe I intended to convey a pie cut into quarters. Maybe I was trying to draw a Celtic cross, but I'm a shitty artist. Or, maybe I'm an X-Men fan who likes to doodle, and you're holding the paper wrong. That drawing *is* a symbol, but it only becomes meaningful after you understand my intent. Until you do, it could be a lot of things, and easily misinterpreted."

Patty nodded. "So, you understand the form, but not the substance. You don't want to guess because you don't have enough information to make an educated guess."

"Pretty much."

"Strange," said Patty.

"What's strange?"

"It just sounds a lot like police work, is all. You try not to jump to a conclusion until you've gathered all the evidence and information. It seems terribly rational."

"Why wouldn't it be?"

"You blather on about black magic, which is obviously irrational and not real. Then you apply a rational methodology to trying to understand it. Talk about counterproductive."

I snorted. "It's only counterproductive if magic actually is irrational and fake. I defy you to prove either assumption."

"Well, obviously it's irrational and fake because," she paused.

"Because someone told you so, once upon a time," I said.

"It's irrational and fake because it has never held up under any kind of scientific scrutiny."

I laughed. "You better believe it hasn't. We all go out of our way to make sure of it."

Patty shot me an annoyed look. "That's stupid. Why would anyone do that?"

"It's self-preservation. Can you imagine the mass panic if people realized that psychics really could pick thoughts out of their heads? Or that some wacko with a hotline into Hell could sic a demon on you, or your kid, at the drop of a hat?"

Patty frowned and I saw her thinking it through. "Okay, yes, I can see how that might cause some panic, but people would get over it."

"Sure they would," I said. "You know, because human beings have such a stellar track record dealing with things that are different. And you haven't thought about the politics of it. What do you imagine the government would do in the face of all that human chaos and terror?"

She chewed that one over for a lot longer. "Nothing good, I expect. They'd probably start rounding people up or quarantining them maybe."

"Shit, they'd shove them into internment camps faster than you could say civil rights violations. That's assuming the government didn't use them as lab rats or try to weaponize them. How about the law enforcement ramifications? How do you police a crime like thought theft? Or, I don't know, arson with no apparent cause. How do you even start to investigate that?"

Patty said nothing.

"Bear in mind, we're talking about a moderately civilized place here. This isn't some war-torn nightmare or dictatorship. It's America. Could you imagine what would happen in places where human rights, let alone civil rights, are considered an irrelevance? It'd be a fucking massacre."

Patty looked down and shoved her hands into her pockets. It finally hit me that she wasn't wearing her deputy's uniform. She wore jeans, a light sweatshirt, and beat-up cross-trainers. I was struck again by the simple solidity of the woman. The there-ness of her was profound. She was fully present in the moment. I was impressed by that. Most people, myself included, barely managed to stagger by being all of twenty-five percent present at any given moment. She shook her head firmly in the negative.

"It's all hypothetical anyway," she insisted.

"As you choose," I said. "Just think of it this way. The best defense most people have against psychics and magic and all that other supernatural mumbo jumbo is that people like me don't want to be noticed. Not getting noticed is our best defense against everyone else. As long as you think we're fakes no federal task forces or shiny new law enforcement agencies are hunting us. We can move in the world freely."

"Like regular people," said Patty.

"We are regular people. Stupid, flawed, petty, and generally speaking, boring people. At any rate, I'm pretty sure you didn't stop by to discuss alchemical tattoos and the political ramifications of magic being public knowledge."

Patty sniffed. "I should hope not. I'll probably try to pretend that conversation never happened at all. I stopped by to talk to you about that fire."

I took in the fact that she was out of uniform. I made a guess. "You want to talk off the record, don't you?"

"I do."

"Fair enough. Lay it on me."

"There were no batteries in the smoke detectors. Not one."

I nodded. "Sounds pretty suspect to me."

"It is, but I'm closing the investigation down."

"Why?"

"A couple of reasons, the biggest one being that if I call it arson, it could screw with Paul getting any insurance money. I'm pretty sure he didn't set that fire, so I won't punish him."

I closed my eyes. God, I'd been so out of it. Those damn pain pills had done a number on me. If I'd had my head screwed on straighter, I'd have realized that obvious truth about the investigation. I opened my eyes and knew that Patty saw the comprehension in my eyes.

"Right," I said. "I get it. I'm not interested in making Paul or Abby's lives any harder. Sounds like something you could have told me over the phone though."

"That part of it, sure, but there is still the matter of the missing batteries. Someone took them out. You don't do that unless you plan on hurting someone. Somebody took a shot at Paul and Abby. If you figure out who, I expect you to tell me."

"What if it wasn't a person? What if it was something you can't lock up in a cell and put on trial?"

"Don't give me that crap, Hartworth. Boogeymen don't set fires. People do. Just because some asshole figured out how to do it without leaving obvious evidence doesn't make it magical."

I wanted to scream in frustration. I damn well knew it was magical. I also knew that the "criminal" behind it was a demon. She was also wrong about boogeymen. They did set fires sometimes. Patty didn't want to hear it. Maybe she just couldn't hear it. People committed crimes, end of story. Anything else was just too far-fetched for Patty to latch onto. I gave her a resigned nod.

"If I find a *person* was responsible," I said, "I'll tell you."

She narrowed her eyes at me. "I'm not messing around with you. No vigilantes in my town. You find something out, you tell me. Then, I handle it the right way."

"If I wanted to go vigilante, I'd have done it by now. Tucker Smith tried to go all alpha male on me at Connor's the other day. I didn't even send him to the hospital."

"God, that man is a moron."

I laughed. Lil, maybe looking to join in, made a little noise. Patty's head jerked to one side to look past me. She eyed Lil and then me. "You kept that cat."

"She kept me, I think. She's good company."

Patty stepped around me and held out her hand toward Lil. She stayed far enough back that the gesture wasn't a threat, just an offer. Lil regarded Patty's hand with curiosity. The little gray cat stood, did one of those impossible arched stretches that cats do, and stepped over to sniff at Patty's hand. Patty slowly reached her hand up and scratched under Lil's chin. The cat let out a soft purr, rubbed the side of her head against Patty's palm, and then retreated to curl up again.

"Huh," said Patty. "Guess she doesn't hate everyone anymore."

"Maybe she just likes you," I said.

Patty raised an eyebrow at me, but didn't comment on it. "I wouldn't go mentioning you've got her in here to anyone. They don't allow pets."

"Heh," I chuckled. "Listen to you. Pet. Like I actually have any kind of control over her."

Patty went over to the door and threw me a serious look over her shoulder. "I mean it. You find something out, you tell me."

"Like I said, I find a person, I'll tell you."

Patty rolled her eyes, shook her head, and closed the door behind her.

Chapter 26

THE LIBRARY WAS A TINY BUILDING guarded by two elderly librarians. One was a surly, pinched-face man. The other was a soft-spoken woman who turned out to be his wife. The man eyed me with suspicion when I came through the door. I wondered if he looked at everyone like that or if it was just for me. I smiled and nodded at the man.

"Can I help you?" the librarian asked in high, nasal voice.

"I hope so. I'm looking for some information on local history. The school in particular. I understand it used to be a church."

The man wrinkled his nose in a manner that suggested he found me, the fact that my parents elected to procreate, that queries were part of the English language, my specific query, and possibly the existence of the school, distasteful. With an attitude like that, it was no wonder the library remained an afterthought in the town. Though, I admitted, the Internet had also probably played a role.

"Will you be taking anything out? If you plan to take anything out, you'll need to get a library card."

That was said in a tone that implied that the man would rather pour gasoline on his face and spark a match than give me a library card. I started losing patience, but I kept my cool.

"No, I won't need to take anything out," I said through only slightly clenched teeth. "Just indulging my curiosity."

"Hmph," said the man.

"Edgar," chided the man's wife, "stop being such a grump."

Edgar gave his wife an annoyed look. "You know how these kids are today. No real respect for the books. It's all Google this and Wikipedia that."

That took me off guard. It had been a very long time since anyone had lumped me into the category of "these kids." Then again, Edgar appeared close to eighty. Maybe, to someone that age, I really did look like a teenager. The woman appraised me with filmy, brown eyes. She shook her head and smiled.

"Edgar, this man has to be nearly forty years old. I doubt he's planning on vandalizing the library or the books. Are you a vandal, young man?"

"No, ma'am. I'm fairly confident that I'd recall sacking Rome."

Edgar gave me a calculated look. "I believe you're thinking of the Visigoths."

"They did it first, but the Vandals took their turn about 40 or 50 years later," I said, recognizing the ploy. "Although, if we're being technical, the Senones were the first to sack Rome."

"You know your history, son," said Edgar, his voice still high and nasal, but with an undercurrent of grudging respect.

"We can't know who we are without knowing where we come from, or avoid the mistakes of the past without studying them."

"I told you he wasn't a vandal," said the old woman.

"You were right, Mary Beth," said Edgar.

The admission sounded like an often-repeated ritual to me. The old man inclined his head to me.

"Mary Beth handles the local history. Why don't you show him around, dear?"

Mary Beth gave Edgar a pleased smile and patted his arm with her liver-spotted hand. "Come with me, young man."

The old woman came out from the behind the—I frowned at the piece of furniture. It was too small to be a counter, too solid to be a table, and too high to be a desk. I dubbed it the descountable. The old woman came out from behind the descountable. She moved quite well for someone her age. I fell into step beside her, consciously shortening my stride and slowing my pace. She noticed and gave me a little nod. She led me toward the back of the building, past shelves stuffed with fiction of every description, a rack with some new releases displayed face out, and the countless varieties of non-fiction.

"Don't think too badly of Edgar," said Mary Beth. "The last time a man in a suit came into the library, it was to say the library's budget was getting cut. We had a girl working here part-time. Edgar had to fire the poor dear. I don't know who was more upset, him or her."

"I'm sorry to hear that," I said.

"Seems as though everyone in government thinks libraries are just books. Most of the time, I think books are the least thing we offer here."

The old woman shook her head, as if to dislodge the thoughts. She led me through a door into a small room dominated by a large wooden table. Generations of careless pens and intentional teenage defacement scarred the tabletop. Bookshelves lined the walls, though only half the shelves contained actual books. The rest were filled by plastic bins, each labeled to indicate a year or years, which held a variety of files and papers. The labels were chronological and stretched back to what had to be the founding of the town.

"You said you were interested in the school, yes?"

I nodded my head. The old woman didn't hesitate before she went to one of the shelves and picked out a half-dozen books. Most of the books were slender little volumes that looked self-published. I guessed there was limited demand for such books beyond the county border. No big, or for that matter, regional publisher would show much interest, no matter how well-written they were. Mary Beth set the books on the table.

"All of these reference the old church. You know, it was still a church when I was a girl."

"Oh? Were you part of the congregation?"

"Me? Heavens no. I was inside the church lots of times, of course. It was the only building big enough for community events for years. The congregation was small, tiny even, for a little town like this. I never understood why they built such a large church. It must have been fearsome expensive. Though, I suppose only Mr. Cavanaugh knew for sure."

"E.J. Cavanaugh?"

She gave me a surprised look.

I shrugged. "Saw the name out at the graveyard."

"The graveyard? What an odd place to visit."

"Morbid curiosity, I suppose." The lie rolled off my tongue with an ease that shocked me. "The state of the local graveyard can tell you a lot about the people who live somewhere."

She mulled that notion for a moment. "I suppose it probably can tell you something, at that. As to your question, not E.J.

Cavanaugh. I suppose he must have known, since he paid for it, but he was dead before I came along. I was thinking of his son, James. He was a nice man, but sad. He moved away when I was, oh, seven or so."

"Anyone know what became of him?"

"There were rumors that he ran off to all sorts of places, Brazil, Morocco, and even post-war Germany, though why he'd have gone there was never clear. No one really knows, not for sure. I think he just went to live somewhere where no one knew him. Probably a place that didn't remind him so much of his father. Old E.J. was an institution here. But listen to me blathering on. I'll leave you to your books."

"Not at all. I appreciate you taking the time."

"If you're especially keen on the subject, there's information about the church in some of those plastic bins," said Mary Beth, gesturing to the plastic containers. "Old documents and the like, though it's an acre of work to find anything in them."

I eyed the bins with some doubt. "Hopefully, it won't come to that."

Mary Beth gave me a grandmotherly smile. "If you change your mind, I know someone who might be able to help you with the bins."

At that, Mary Beth turned and left the room. I had a suspicion that she was going to tell Edgar that I was a very nice young man and that he shouldn't think so poorly of people. That wasn't true, but who was I to try to dissuade her? I spread the small pile of books out in front of me. I started with the oldest two, since they were written closer to the time of the church's construction. I was less than impressed with the content. One had a single page that discussed, in the driest possible tones, how a church was constructed using a list of materials that I skipped entirely and completed sometime in early 1894.

The other book was slightly more helpful. It specified that the church was built "at the behest of one E.J. Cavanaugh." It said that the church was erected prior to the establishment of the town as a legal entity, which happened sometime around 1910. It also noted that Cavanaugh took a hand in the design of the church and singled out the oddity of the building compared with other churches found in the region. I sighed. I could have guessed all that without stopping by the library. I pushed the two older books aside and turned my attention to the handful of self-published tracts.

While none of the small books were devoted specifically to the church, they were all shockingly well-written. More important to me, they were all useful. I learned that E.J. Cavanaugh hadn't just built the church. He purchased miles of land in every direction, had a road built, and then had a couple dozen homes constructed. He sold most of those homes at negligible profit to a select group of families. The other homes, more like boarding houses, were used to house the crews of men hired to first build the houses and then the church. Two of the small books mentioned an unspecified tragedy that occurred late in the church's construction.

What caught my attention, though, was the subtext. I'd done enough reading over the years to fill in the gaps. There were hints everywhere at the oddness of Cavanaugh, his church, and the families he brought to the little community he built. The word *cult* never turned up in any of the little books, but it might as well have been written in giant neon letters. I leaned back in the chair, trying to imagine what the unspecified tragedy had been, when Mary Beth poked her head into the room.

"You've been in here a while. Thought I'd see if I could help you with anything."

I turned and blinked at the woman, as my brain tried to configure the jigsaw puzzle of information into a solution. I shook myself out of the thought haze and smiled at her.

"Oh, well that was very thoughtful of you," I said.

An idea occurred to me and I gave Mary Beth a considering look. She was the right age to have heard the stories from people who were there at the time. She also struck me as someone who liked to tell a tale or two. Not gossip, as she'd surely be offended by such an idea, but telling an old story from her childhood would just be good fun. My expression must have been a little too intense for Mary Beth's comfort, because she got a nervous look and started to shuffle a little. I cut her a break.

"You know," I said, "Maybe there is something you can help me with."

Chapter 27

IT TOOK A MOMENT for her brain to transition from "he's giving me a creepy look" to "oh, he was just thinking real hard." Once she made the transition, though, Mary Beth perked up and smiled. She came over to the table and sat down across from me.

She sighed in evident relief. "I hope you don't mind if I sit. Legs aren't what they used to be."

"Not at all, ma'am."

"Such a polite young man," she said, giving me an approving smile. "Now then, what can I help you with?"

I weighed the best way to frame the question. Whoever wrote those books went out of their way to avoid saying anything outright. That probably meant it was still considered a taboo topic. I decided there wasn't a good, innocuous way to maneuver the conversation that way. That only left the direct approach.

"These books all reference some kind of vague tragedy, but there aren't any details. I was hoping you might be able to fill in some of the gaps."

The grandmotherly friendliness was replaced with deep wariness as Mary Beth gave me a long, considering look. That wasn't a good sign.

"Do you mind if I ask why you're so interested in the old church?"

I shrugged. "Intellectual curiosity. It's weird architecture to see outside of Eastern Europe or a big city, especially given its vintage."

She didn't look like she believed me, but Mary Beth let it go without comment. She puffed out a troubled breath and fixed me with a stern glare.

"You aren't from a small town, are you?"

I shook my head.

"I thought not. You'd have the good sense not to ask about that, if you were."

"I don't understand," I said.

"Things hang on in small towns. Old rivalries, old tragedies, they never lose currency. There's one poor girl, people still talk about the scandal when she got pregnant in high school."

"Not that uncommon," I offered.

"That was twenty years ago."

"Seriously? Don't people have better things to do?"

"I told you, things hang on. Still, I don't see any real harm in telling you the truth."

Despite her words, she kept looking at the door as if she expected some kind of goose-stepping thought police to crash through it the second she opened her mouth. She studied her hands for the better part of a minute. "People died. Supposedly, it was an accident."

"Supposedly? You don't think so?"

"I know it wasn't. They were murdered."

My brain tried to follow the implications of her statement. *Murdered.* On the one hand, it might explain how a demon took up residence in a freaking church. Murder left a spiritual stain on the places it happened. The unwilling loss of life, the pain, the fear, the wrongness of it took a very long time to wash away. That was if it ever could be washed clean. More often than not, the stain drove away exactly the kind of people and behaviors that would rectify the wrongness. It's why houses and neighborhoods where awful things happened tended to decay and attract a bad element.

On the other hand, I was quite certain that the church had been used as a church. I wasn't sure why I held the certainty, but I believed it. The act of worship, the accumulation of prayer, and the community of belief were precisely the kinds of things that could heal the spiritual damage done by murder. If it had been a church, then the foul aftereffects of the murder should have been largely ameliorated and made the place inhospitable to a demon. It just didn't make any damn sense.

Mary Beth was giving me a concerned frown. I noticed my mouth was hanging open and shut it. I was still missing something.

"Why are you so sure it was murder?"

"Alex Burman, God rest him, investigated at the time."

"Alex Burman?"

"Sheriff in those days. I think he was the hardest man that ever lived. Lived to be over a hundred years old. Wore the badge until he was seventy."

"That's pretty hardcore," I said, impressed.

"Hardcore," repeated Mary Beth, who probably wasn't used to the slang. "Yes, I suppose he was pretty hardcore. Anyway, the whole awful business got covered up because E.J. Cavanaugh was richer than God."

"If it got covered up, then how do you know?"

"Burman kept a journal. The woman who wrote those books found it and showed it to me. He wrote about the investigation," she said in the absent way of someone who's lost in thought. "Hard to imagine a time when thirteen deaths could be swept under the rug."

I jerked forward in my chair. "Thirteen? You're sure it was thirteen?"

Mary Beth leaned back and gave me a disapproving look, but she nodded. "Yes. Thirteen people died that day. Based on Burman's description, it sounded like they were given some kind of drug and had their wrists cut."

I felt a chill go through me. I had an idea what had happened and it made me a little ill to think about it. Mary Beth and old Sheriff Burman had entirely the wrong picture of what those bodies represented. Their mistake was understandable, since they were processing the information with a complete ignorance of magic. If I was right, though, I was pretty sure that Abby was doomed. There wouldn't be anything that Helena, or me, or anyone else could do to help her in the long run.

"Are you all right, Mister..." Mary Beth paused. "I never caught your name."

"Adrian," I said automatically.

"Mr. Adrian?"

"What?" I asked, jarred by the incongruity of her words.

"Your name is Mr. Adrian?"

"Oh, no. Hartworth. Adrian Hartworth."

"Ah, that makes more sense. Are you all right, Mr. Hartworth?"

No, I was not all right. I was mortified by my intuition and what it might mean for Abby. What in the hell had E.J. Cavanaugh been mixed up in? If I was right, he'd engaged in nothing short of naked insanity. If I was right, the demon hadn't taken up residence in the church. The church itself had been built and thirteen people had sacrificed themselves to contain the damned thing. Someone must have screwed up somewhere along the line, though, because the containment had failed. No, I reconsidered. It hadn't failed entirely, but some portion of it had failed. It was the only explanation for why that inky black monstrosity could reach into the world.

"I'm fine. Just a little shocked by the whole thing. Like you said, hard to imagine."

It was harder still to imagine thirteen people willing to off themselves in the name of containing a demon. I'd done more than my fair share of exorcisms and spirit containment over the years, but I'd have never died to make it happen. Getting thirteen willing souls, thirteen people who believed in the cause enough, seemed almost ludicrously difficult. Something clicked in my head. I traced the logic. It held up.

"Will you excuse me," I said. "I just remembered that there's someplace I'm supposed to be."

Mary-Beth blinked at me in confusion, but she nodded. "Of course."

"Thanks," I said.

"For what?"

"Breaking the small town code of silence."

"Why do I get the feeling that you've just figured something out?"

I shrugged and stood. "Crossword this morning. Eight-letter word. Clue was 'striking revelation.' I just realized the answer. Epiphany."

I nodded to her and started to leave the room, then stopped. I looked back at Mary-Beth.

"Mr. Hartworth?"

"Did you ever meet a woman named Mary Simmons?"

"Of course I did. Everybody knows everybody in a small town. She was smart as a whip and such a pretty thing. Terrible for that family, her and Randall dying so young. Why do you ask?"

"I met Paul and Abby. They told me a little about themselves."

"Bless them, their house caught fire a few days ago. Awful, awful business. Word is that some stranger ran into the house to get them," said Mary-Beth. She gave me a long look. "It was you that pulled them out of that house, wasn't it?"

I shrugged. "I did what anyone would have."

"If you say so."

I tried to get back on topic. "Mary-Beth, was there anything unusual about Mary?"

Mary-Beth looked perplexed and shook her head. "Unusual? No. I don't think so. Except that she was from here."

I stared at the librarian, trying to understand her meaning.

She laughed. "Well, not her personally, but her people were from here. They'd all moved away ages ago, you understand, but there were a few folks who remembered her grandparents."

I kept myself from showing any exterior reaction, but there it was. The definitive link I hadn't been able to make was laid bare by a simple question. I thanked Mary-Beth and walked as quickly as basic courtesy would allow out of the library. I called Helena from the car and asked her to meet me at my little cabin that evening. First, I needed to check a couple things before I let my bowels turn to water. I called Patty and asked her if it would be possible for me to get a tour of the school. She muttered something about pain-in-the-ass tourists, but agreed to set it up. I thanked her and drove back to my cabin. I spent a few minutes petting Lil, who didn't purr, but stared up at me with knowing eyes.

"Yeah," I said. "I think I know what's happening. I think this is worse than I ever imagined it could be."

"Mrrrr," replied Lil.

It was a low, somber sound and struck me as infinitely sad and just a touch fearful. Then again, maybe I was just projecting my own feelings onto her. God, I hoped I was wrong. If I was wrong, at least Abby had a chance. I stroked Lil's head a few more times and then slid the hard case out from beneath the narrow bed. The burn on my back sent a spike of pain up my spine as I stretched the wound beyond its limits. My breath caught in my throat as the muscles along my spine did their best to contract me into a fetal position on the floor. I made myself take slow, controlled breaths for thirty seconds and the pain eased off.

It had gotten easier and easier to forget about the burn as the constant pain became mental background noise. It was just one more thing to tune out as time went by. The sharp reminder made me feel physically weak. The abrupt adrenaline spike made my legs shaky. The pain also made me feel, in a way that I'd never felt before, old. I tried to push that idea away, but it held tight. I wasn't a young buck anymore. I was slowing up. I couldn't shrug things off the way I did when I was twenty. I wasn't sure how many years I had left before I just wouldn't be up to the challenges of my own life.

That thought made me feel even older and exhausted. I wanted to sit on the floor. I wanted to rest. This had never been my fight. I'd stumbled into it by accident. My presence was little more than a quirk of travel. If I'd sucked it up for another fifty miles, I'd never have met Abby or Paul. I wouldn't have gotten into a nasty bar fight or bought a beat-up old Neon. I'd have long since finished my periodic check-in on my sister and her family in Seattle. I was so tired. I was tired of all of it. I was tired of the constant traveling. I was tired of being an outcast. I was tired of the violence. I was tired of all the terrible memories of the people who'd died and the unspeakable things that had done the killing. It all sat there, in my head, like the anchor of a great sea ship that was too massive to ignore and ready to drag me under.

My head lolled forward. I wanted to close my eyes and sleep. Just sleep and sleep until all of this was over. I didn't need these problems. Abby and Paul weren't blood, weren't even family of choice. They were just unlucky. It *wasn't* my problem. I didn't need to do anything to get out of harm's way. I only needed to do nothing. Send Helena home and do nothing. My body started to sway as I drifted closer and closer to sleep. Blessed sleep would be a relief. An escape from all the responsibilities I never wanted in the first place.

My equilibrium shifted in a way that my body didn't like very much. I put my hand against the side of the mattress as weariness threatened to drive me to the floor in earnest.

Red-hot pain flashed as Lil sank her claws into my hand.

"Jesus Christ!" My mind thrashed back to full awareness.

Lil calmly removed her claws.

I stared at the blood that beaded near my knuckles. My heart raced in my chest. Something had happened, was happening, and it was something wrong.

I'd been under attack. Some bastard had tried to put the mental whammy on me. No, I realized, they hadn't tried. They'd succeeded. If not for Lil, I'd have been unconscious on the floor. If my attacker was motivated enough, I might not have woken up. I tried to shake off the cobwebs. To do that to me, they'd have needed to be close. Really close. I lurched to my feet and stumbled toward the door. I flung it open and stepped outside.

I saw a flash of flannel disappear into the woods that surrounded the cabin. I took a few steps in pursuit before reason kicked into gear. I didn't know the woods. Whoever tried to put me out of play almost certainly did. Chasing them into their own territory was a good way to get dead. I stopped before I entered the woods proper. A deep anger almost made me reject the objections of reason and hurl myself into the trees. I fought it down. Even at my best, it would have been a stupid idea and the remnant throbs from my back reminded me just how not at my best I was at that moment. I gritted my teeth and went back into the cabin.

Lil sat on the bed and gave me another of her patented opaque expressions. I went over and scratched behind her ears. She purred up at me for a few seconds before she hopped down off the bed and went to her food dish. I watched her eat and wondered about what she was and why she had picked me. I'd probably never get a clear notion of either. I shook my head and crouched, with far greater care, to retrieve the Eye of Horus from the hard case. I checked to make sure Lil had enough food and water, topped both off, and then I set out to make my second drive to Angel's Rest Cemetery.

Chapter 28

LIKE ALL PRACTICAL PLANS that should be carried out immediately, the trip to the cemetery was doomed to failure. I hadn't even gotten into the car when my phone rang. I looked at the screen and saw Helena's number.

"Hi," I said, my hand still grasping the handle of the car door.

"I think you should come and pay Abby a visit," said Helena without preamble.

Fear squeezed my chest. "Did something happen?"

"No, no, nothing like that. She's just being," Helena waffled for a moment, "truculent is the word, I think."

"About?"

"What do you think she's being truculent about?"

I lifted my hand off the car door's handle to reach up and massage a spot between my eyes. I'd expected her to be resistant to the process, but not quite so soon. It usually took a few weeks before the mind started to rebel in earnest at having its assumptions deconstructed and reconstructed with an alternate worldview. I'd harbored some vague and obviously incorrect hope that Abby would prove more flexible about her introduction to the world of the supernatural. She wasn't that old. I'd been several years older than her when I first started. God knew *I* wasn't anyone's definition of tractable, but even I hadn't gotten stubborn until a week or two into the process.

Resistance was normal. In fact, a lack of resistance was generally considered a serious warning sign that someone was not temperamentally suited to operate in the shadowy world I occupied. Too much willingness to surrender one's own worldview in favor of another, especially one that flew in the face of the facts of everyday existence, almost always meant an unacceptable weakness of mind or will. Strength of mind, strength of will, were not mere necessities for controlling the often unpredictable ebbs and flows of magic, but were the bedrock of raw survival in the face of things that could construct illusions, warp perception, and offer all manner of temptations.

Too little willingness to entertain and eventually accept an alternate point of view was just as bad. In the case of someone with Abby's exceptional native talent, it could make an already difficult job impossible. It also left her without any protection from things she had no framework to understand. That could be lethal. In an equitable world, that might be an acceptable choice. Allowing someone the free will to choose who they wanted to be wasn't something to be taken lightly. If she wanted to reject mine and Helena's world, she ought to be allowed to do so.

We didn't live in an equitable world. Leaving her talents un-restrained didn't just threaten her. They posed a threat to anyone she might meet. Psychics as powerful as Abby could do un-speakable things to another person's mind. She could literally force someone to think they were in love with her. She could make someone step into traffic. Given the right impetus, she could probably create enough fear to stop someone's heart. She couldn't be allowed to wander the world without some internal checks and balances on that power. And she was fighting the process.

"Damn," I muttered. "I'll be right down."

I drove to the hospital, but, once I got there, I just stood in the parking lot and glowered up at the building. I'd been there so often in recent days that they should have reserved a space for me. As I stood there, I did my best to ignore the nagging sensa-tion that I had not performed a perfectly reasonable action. I supposed it was the parking lot itself that triggered that feeling. Helena had told me to call the Twins and I'd said I'd think about it. I hadn't called them. In fact, I had not thought about calling them for one second. If my intuition about what was happening was right, though, I needed to make that call. I'd just have to hope they'd take the call and, even less likely, tell me what I wanted to know.

I sat down on my hood and stared at my phone, not moving, and certainly not dialing. In the shadowy world of the supernatu-ral, there were a lot of gray people. Semyon and Dmitri Osinov, who everyone simply called The Twins, were the grayest of those gray people. That grayness extended well beyond their moral orientation. They lived and worked in a small, gray building they owned in Manhattan. They wore identical gray suits, gray shirts, and gray ties. The only way to tell them apart was by the color of the handkerchiefs the men kept tucked into their suit coat pockets. Semyon favored a cool blue handkerchief, while Dmitri favored pale green.

Their offices were carpeted in dark gray, painted in light gray, and even their business cards were custom-printed on gray paper. Officially speaking, for tax purposes, they were businessmen engaged in dozens of extremely boring but perfectly legitimate enterprises that ranged from commercial real estate to boutique stores and investing in a range of startups. Among the supernatural set, they were widely considered to be information brokers of the most valuable sort. They didn't judge. They simply quoted a price.

If you wanted to know how one might go about resurrecting a dead loved one, they could provide or acquire the information on how to perform such a ritual. If you were a little suicidal and wanted to spend the night in bed with a demon or demoness, they could provide you with the appropriate contact information. Have a burning need to set off a minor apocalypse, they knew which discarded deity had an axe to grind with humanity. They could get it all for you, if you had deep-enough pockets or could offer a sufficient favor in exchange.

Of course, nothing is ever as simple as it sounds on the surface. Members of the supernatural community are tribal both by nature and as a defense mechanism. You stick with the groups you know and trust because you can anticipate their behaviors. It also gives you a support system if something comes looking to start a fight with you. The tribe closes ranks around you. Information rarely crossed tribal walls, which was how I came into contact with The Twins.

For a variety of reasons, my wandering ways not least among them, I had contacts all over the place. I wasn't beholden to any particular tribe. Not that any of them would have accepted me anyways. I came with capital-b Baggage. Yet, there were always times when one tribe or another needed a go-between to arrange meetings or serve as a neutral arbiter. I was the perfect choice for such tasks. No one wanted me hanging around with their people too long, but that meant that I didn't have a lot of vested interest in helping or screwing anyone over.

The Twins had used me on a number of occasions to make arrangements for them to meet with third parties, collect objects of interest, or deliver payments that couldn't be handled through more traditional channels, like banks. They once had me oversee the delivery of a cow to something that was, I was pretty sure, some kind of mountain troll. Another time, they had me handle what they called "the third most important exchange of their career."

I flew to Denver and met with a tiny Japanese woman who did not speak English. She insisted, through a translator, that we spend the day experiencing the curiosity of life. It was a strange sort of day. She undertook a rather complex tea ceremony that, the translator informed me, was a great honor for me. I did my best to look appropriately humbled by the gesture. The next stop was a koi pond. The translator hovered behind us and related some kind of parable or legend about carp becoming dragons. The lesson, I was informed, was about the value of perseverance. I nodded as though the story made sense to me. It, of course, did not make sense to me, but I wasn't there to offend The Twins' business associate.

Then we went to a mall, sat at a food court, and people-watched for hours. Several times, wide-eyed men and women came over and spoke to her in hushed whispers I didn't understand. I asked the translator about it, but he shook his head and said it was unrelated to my business with her. Late in the afternoon, for two very memorable hours, she dismissed the translator. At the end of the day, I provided her with a single gold coin of a make I did not recognize. She offered me a box that contained a lone cherry blossom. Everyone acted as though they were getting the better end of the exchange. I never could figure out the exact nature of that deal.

It was a good gig for me while it lasted. My arrangement with The Twins came to an end when they asked me to arrange an exchange between them and a man named Ambrus. I advised them against it. Ambrus was a murky figure even in our murky community. His reputation was uneven. Sometimes he acted exactly as promised. Sometimes he murdered people for miniscule offences or no discernible reason at all. The guy made me look downright polite and housebroken. In the end, my job was to handle the arrangements. I did my job.

The Twins went to meet with him in person, so I only heard about what happened after the fact. Ambrus showed up and took whatever The Twins had offered in exchange at the point of several sub-machine guns. They blamed me. I thought blaming me was a bit ridiculous, since I had advised them against any kind of deal with Ambrus. I had suggested they take security, advice they ignored. I had even offered to go with them, or in their stead, which they had waved off as unnecessary. There was a shaky second when I thought Dmitri might shoot me, but Semyon muttered a few words in Russian, I think, and Dmitri backed off. I always liked Semyon better.

I hadn't spoken with either since, though I did see them once in San Francisco a few years later. I'd been in an antique shop, during my personal shopper days, and they came strolling into the place. Dmitri gave me a narrow-eyed glare for a moment. Then he sighed, waved his hand as if to dismiss an annoyance, and went to look at old clocks. Semyon just stared at me for a long moment. I think he was surprised, more than anything. Then he offered me a little smile, dipped his head in acknowledgement, and joined his brother. I think it was the nod of acknowledgement that convinced me that calling them wasn't a totally lost cause.

I dug through my wallet—I'd kept their card, just in case— and dialed their office. I knew their personal cell phone numbers, but that seemed like pushing things a bit more than necessary. Calling their office was a meager way to show respect for their privacy and add a patina of professionalism to the first moments of the call. I listened as the phone rang on the other end. There was a click, then a second click, and I heard a weird double voice, like two radios playing the same station a fraction of a second apart.

"Osinov's," said the double voice.

"It's Hartworth," I said. Then I added, trying to keep the resignation out of my voice, "Don't hang up."

There was a long pause before a voice wafted over the phone. "Hartworth? Hartworth? Oh yes, I recall. We employed a Hartworth years ago. Unreliable, as I remember."

Dmitri, I thought and bit back the sharp reply. I needed them. Decades in the States had mellowed his accent, rounded out the harshness. He still sounded foreign, but not recognizably Russian anymore. There was another, shorter pause before a second, nearly identical voice wafted over the line in a chiding tone.

"Dmitri," said Semyon. "I thought we agreed that there was no reasonable way that he could have foreseen Ambrus' behavior. Moreover, he did warn us."

Dmitri made a noise that could have meant anything.

"Adrian," said Semyon, "how are you?"

"Above ground," I said. "You?"

"In fortune's favor."

I waited a beat. "And how are you, Dmitri?"

There were more inarticulate noises of discontent before he said, "I am well."

"Adrian, let us spare my brother and draw to the point."

I weighed the best approach. No matter what, this would cost me. I decided just coming out with it was the easiest way. "I need information."

"You can't afford it," said Dmitri.

It was jarring. I'd expected something like that from him, but not the passionless way he said it. The second I made things business, his personal angst just vanished. He wasn't being spiteful or bitter. His tone was even, just reporting a fact to me. He was right. Even at my most flush, I would never have had even close to enough money to afford information from them. Of course, I'd never planned to offer them money.

"You're right," I acknowledged. "I can't offer you cold hard cash. If you help me out, I'll owe you a favor."

"Two favors," said Dmitri and Semyon simultaneously.

I blinked. That answer had come way too fast. I leaned my head back and thought it through. Why two favors? Why not six or twelve? Then I got it.

"One to make up for Ambrus and one for the information?" I asked.

"Of course," said Semyon. He sounded pleased, like I'd given him an unexpected and welcome surprise. "You should have made the offer years ago."

I felt like slapping myself in the back of the head. They were businessmen and, my perceived failure aside, I was a valuable resource. Cutting ties with me had undoubtedly cost them time, money, and made a number of potential deals impossible to complete over the years. Dmitri had been angry, furious with me, but I had the insight that it was the unclosed account that had kept him angry. If I'd been smart enough to balance the scales in his eyes, the matter would have been closed.

"Two favors, then," I agreed.

In an instant, Dmitri's attitude changed. "Very good, Adrian. God's blood, man, do you have any idea how trying it was to keep pretending to be angry with you? I almost forgot when we saw you in San Francisco."

"What? You weren't angry?"

"One of us needs to maintain a reputation for being volatile and vengeful," said Semyon. "Appearances, you understand."

"Of course," I said.

It made perfect sense. In their line of work, with the kinds of people they dealt with, it would have been stupid not to put on that front.

"We have a great deal of work for you, should you be interested," said Semyon.

"You can also pay off the favors over time. We hear you've been, how do they say it, cash flow restricted as of late. You aren't much use to us if you starve to death in the meantime," noted Dmitri.

I needed the money, assuming I survived the next day or three. "I'd be interested."

I could hear Dmitri beaming over the phone as he said, "How would you like to make some money today?"

"Uh," I said, "sure."

They gave me the details. It was an Adrian special. Someone wanted a particular kind of protective talisman that only three people in the world could make. All three of them resided on a Pueblo a bit north of Santa Fe. I'd spent some time there. I made some calls and, after promising that a visit would be forthcoming, the arrangements were set. It took half an hour. I called The Twins back and it netted me a cool ten grand, wired to an account I hadn't used in a long time.

"Now, what is it you'd like to know about?" Dmitri asked.

Chapter 29

"I SAW SOMETHING THE OTHER DAY that I didn't recognize. I need to know what it is, what could have done it, and how to undo it."

There was a very, very long pause on the other end of the line. It was understandable. I rarely ran across things I didn't recognize, in general or specific. The Twins were accustomed to me not needing a lot of explanations.

"Describe it," said Semyon.

I thought back and did my best to describe the smoke over the grave and the feeling of utter wrongness it elicited in me. My mind didn't want to play ball. It kept shying away from that memory, only willing to bring it into focus for a few seconds at a time. I've seen some godawful shit in my day, but that really raised the bar for me. The Twins spoke to each other in rapid fire Russian for a good three minutes.

"A smoke binding," said Semyon.

"Very interesting," said Dmitri.

"Very rare," they said together.

"How rare are we talking?"

"Profoundly rare," said Semyon. "It's not quite as rare as a Mona Lisa, but certainly rarer than an original Cartier Tank Cintrée."

"Cartier Tank Cintrée?" I asked.

"It's a watch," clarified Dmitri. "Approximately fifty of them were made."

I blew out a breath. That wasn't a good thing. It went a long way toward confirming my suspicions, though. At the rate I was going, The Twins might never get to collect on those favors.

"What could do something like that? Could a person do it?"

The Twins laughed.

"Not a person," said Dmitri in total confidence.

"It would take a third- or fourth-order demon…" started Se-myon.

"Or higher," amended Dmitri.

"…to accomplish such a thing."

"How many orders of demons are there?"

I knew that demons were categorized into orders, but most demon activity was done by small, weaker demons. They were easier to control. I'd never needed to know which order they were in before, so I never took the time to learn.

"Twenty-three," said Semyon.

"Seventeen," said Dmitri.

"Uh," I said.

"There is some disagreement about whether the last six orders are demons proper or simply potent nature spirits of some kind," explained Semyon. "I err on the side of inclusion."

"Ah," I said. "So, for my own reference, how much juice would a third- or fourth-order demon have?"

"This is a gross simplification, but first-order demons stand directly below Satan in terms of power. Second stand a rung below them and so on," explained Dmitri. "Each order has an internal hierarchy, based on our limited knowledge of their membership, but at those levels of power, the weakest second-order demon could probably obliterate a small continent, such as Europe."

I thought Dmitri sounded a bit too cheerful at the thought of an obliterated Europe, but I kept that opinion to myself. No need to poke the bear. Especially when I considered what a third- or fourth-order demon could conceivably do. They might not be able to crush a continent, but, sweet baby Jesus, they could crush me, and the town, and probably the state as a whole, without much effort.

"Let's say I wanted to dismantle the smoke binding. How would I do that?"

"You wouldn't," said Dmitri.

"But if I wanted to," I persisted.

"You misunderstand," said Semyon. "It's not that you would or wouldn't do it. Dmitri means that you can't. Such an action is beyond your knowledge, power, and spiritual purity. To a staggering degree. It's not that it would be difficult or painful for you. It is flatly impossible for *you* to unmake such a binding. The mere attempt would destroy you."

Holy shit. I'd known I was out of my league, but I hadn't comprehended just how far out of my league I was until that moment. It was the first time in my life that I'd been told, in no uncertain terms, that a magical action was utterly beyond my ability. Not dangerous, I'd heard that plenty of times and, as a rule, had avoided those actions, but impossible. I tried to imagine how much power would be involved to make it beyond my capacity to even survive. I was no nuclear power plant, magically speaking, but I wasn't a double-A battery either.

I found my hands trembling and a voice I'd been suppressing surged back into my active consciousness. *Get out*, it screamed. *Get out while you can! You can't win this thing. Just go. Take the girl, if it makes you feel better, but get your ass clear of this shit.* I beat the voice back down, but I still felt the insistence of it. At the end of the day, I wasn't equipped to do what needed to be done. It wasn't that I didn't want to help Abby. I still wanted to help her just as much, but I was starting to grasp just how ineffectual my help would actually be for her. The Twins, unaware of the gibbering in my head, continued on.

"The Pope might be able to do it, if he's sincere in his beliefs," mused Dmitri. "A saint could probably do it. Some of the Buddhist Llamas."

"Bodhisattvas and Arhats, assuming you could find one. A handful of shamans that are steeped in untainted traditions," offered Semyon.

I caged the panic, the fear, the knowledge of my own inadequacy, and focused. Information now, terror later, I promised my mind.

"Right, I get it. Holy people. Really, really holy people." Then a thought struck me. "What about someone like Helena St. Clair?"

There was another exchange of rapid-fire Russian.

"Well," hedged Semyon.

"St. Clair is an..." Dmitri hesitated, "uncertain quantity."

"It is possible, *possible*, that she could unmake such a binding. But the cost could be terrible for her," Semyon warned.

"Okay, so unmaking the binding is a desperation move. What about the demon itself? How would someone fight that?"

Both men let out nervous laughs.

"Seriously," I pressed.

"Summon an archangel," ventured Dmitri. "That might do it."

"There are a handful of old gods that could fight such a demon, not that you could bend them to your will," said Semyon.

"Run away, if you can," said Dmitri, his voice earnest and concerned. "You don't fight something like that. You flee."

"Is there a single mortal practitioner in the world who could fight something like that?"

"No," said Semyon.

"Yes," argued Dmitri.

"He said mortal," countered Semyon.

"They are mortal."

"By what measure, Dmitri?" Semyon demanded.

"They can die."

"Gods can die, too," said Semyon. "That doesn't make them mortal."

"Gentlemen," I interrupted. "Let me put this another way. Is there someone who could fight it that would be able and willing to help me?"

"No," they said together.

"Awesome. Any particular reason why not?"

"They aren't available at present," said Semyon. "One is incommunicado, whereabouts unknown. One is presently engaged in preventing the end of the world."

"What?"

"It's less terrifying than you might think," said Dmitri. "There's a fight like that going on most of the time. You get used to it."

"Okay," I said, not at all convinced that was true. "What about the others."

"Other," corrected Dmitri.

"You won't get help there," said Semyon.

Dmitri chimed in. "She doesn't like you very much."

My head jerked in shock. Somewhere along the line I'd bumped into a quasi-immortal being capable of taking on a demon so powerful it required an archangel to fight it? More chilling, I'd managed to aggravate said being? I needed to work on my people skills. I shook my head. Fine, there was no cavalry to call in on this particular problem. I drummed my fingers against the side of my car.

"Let's say that I could talk Helena into trying to take down the smoke binding. What would she need to do?"

The Twins explained it to me. Then they reiterated, several times, that there was no guarantee Helena could pull it off at all. Then they reiterated that it would be stupid and dangerous for her to try. Then they reiterated that I should run away, as fast as I could, just like a me-sized gingerbread man. I said I'd bear that all in mind and promised to be in touch. I rubbed the back of my neck and tried to think. There was a chance that I was wrong about everything. The Twins' information might be bad. Granted, that didn't happen often, but it could happen.

I needed to be sure about things. I needed to go back out to that cemetery and take another look. I glanced at the hospital and strangled a groan. I needed to go, but only after I went and browbeat a teenage girl into being more pliable. I expected that experience to be some real pleasant icing on my day. After all, what could possibly be more fun than scaring the shit out of a girl who'd had nearly universal bad luck since she'd been born? For kicks, maybe I could pour battery acid on my testicles afterward to experience something a bit less painful.

I seriously reconsidered the idea of trying to get Paul to take Abby away from town. I could tell him that she could get better care somewhere else. I could spin yarns about specialists at urban hospitals. Hell, it might have even been true for all I knew. I could play the emotional trump card. Abby didn't seem to have any friends in town. At a better hospital, one with a serious oncology department, she'd meet other kids who also had the misfortune of getting cancer. They'd have the kind of common ground people need to strike up friendships. It might work. I loathed the idea of launching that kind of emotional nuclear strike on the guy. Given the alternatives, though, I might have to do it.

I grimaced as I realized that I was procrastinating. I guess it said something about me that I preferred to stand in a parking lot in ninety degree weather rather than go into the hospital and participate in Abby's indoctrination into the world of the spooky. I hoped it said something good about me. At the least, I thought, it said that I wasn't such a wreck of a human being that I could shrug off the innate cruelty of that indoctrination. Understanding the necessity of it, especially in the long run, didn't alleviate my own misgivings.

That didn't exactly make me feel better about myself. Discomfort at the notion of being cruel to a sick teenage girl was probably automatic for decent people. More to the point, I was going to carry through with that cruelty. Perhaps that was what really separated the magical community from the rest of the humanity. Maybe practitioners were built with a capacity for a specific kind of cruelty that didn't fit into the everyday world. We shared a willingness to shatter beliefs and undo learning, albeit false learning, and impose a cold, terrible truth in its place. I didn't think for a minute that truth was somehow better than the falsehoods most people lived. In fact, I was pretty sure it wasn't better by any objective standard. It absolutely wasn't kinder. It was just true, which wasn't a redeeming feature in my estimation.

I started toward the hospital entrance and dragged my feet every step of the way. I pondered the idea of truth. It was always bound up with a strange, psychological golden glow, as though it were somehow a pristine, marble statue that needed to be defended and idolized at all costs. I didn't buy it, though. The cult of truth was as absurd as any other cult. Truth wasn't some kind of savior. It was a slavemaster with a tireless whip arm. An unpleasant thought struck me as I stepped inside the hospital. That day, the whip was in my hand.

Chapter 30

ABBY'S DOOR WAS PROPPED OPEN and I poked my head into the room. The tension was obvious, but not overwhelming. It seemed Helena decided not to press things too hard before she called me off the bench. Abby's face looked set in stubborn defiance. Helena was doing her best St. Francis of Assisi impression. I might have backed out of the room and let the chips fall where they may, but Abby caught sight of me. Her face split into that blinding smile.

"Hi, Mr. Hartworth!"

Damn, I thought. I was committed. I smiled at Abby, nodded to Helena, and stepped into the room. I already felt like shit and hadn't even done anything. Proactive guilt was a new one on me. My guilt usually appeared after the crap behavior. I pushed those thoughts and feelings aside as best I could and walked over to stand by the bed. I positioned myself opposite of Helena to avoid Abby's subconscious reading my choice of where to stand as implicit support for Helena. Even if that idea never reached the girl's conscious mind, it would inform her response to me.

"Hi, Abby," I said. "Where's Paul?"

"He said he needed to take care of things at the new place," said Abby.

She frowned at the mention of the new house. It had to be hard on her. She hadn't seen the little cottage in person. The place wouldn't be home any more than a pup tent was home on a camping trip. It was just a place to sleep. I hadn't asked about it, but it stood to reason that most of her belongings were smoke-damaged or burned beyond salvation. That would add to the strangeness of the place. There were a lot of things I couldn't do for Abby, but maybe I could ease that particular worry.

"It's a nice place," I said. "Smaller than what you're used to, but it's got good vibes."

"Yeah?" Abby asked.

Helena gave me a sharp look. I hadn't mentioned that to her.

"Yeah. If I was looking for a place, it's exactly the kind of place I'd pick. It feels like home, you know?"

Helena's jaw hung open a little as she stared at me. She might have looked less stunned if my head spun around while I vomited pea soup. I guess the idea of me considering what I wanted in a home, or wanting a home for that matter, never crossed her mind.

Abby considered my words for a moment. "It's a good place, sort of like the school is a bad place for me."

"Something like that," I agreed.

Helena blinked and gave me a speculative look. I blinked back. I got it after a second. The topic offered a natural inroad for the necessary conversation. If I could keep Abby on this track, introduce the ideas without making it obvious I was trying to teach her something, things might go a little smoother. It was a good plan with only one obvious flaw. I'm about as subtle as a fire truck with its lights on, sirens blaring, barreling through a red light on its way to a five-alarm building fire. Still, it beat the standard approach.

"My grandmother had a house like that," I said. "It just felt good to be there. You ever go somewhere and like it right off the bat?"

Helena gave a near-imperceptible head shake that I ignored. That was top-shelf subtlety for me. It probably wouldn't have worked on someone even a little older than Abby, but she didn't make the connection between what I was asking and the conversation Helena tried to have with her earlier. I took my win and was grateful for it. Abby thought hard for a minute before she started to nod.

"Yeah, I did. Grandpa took me to this horse farm last summer. I wasn't too sick then. I really liked it there," she said, then added, "but maybe it was just the horses."

I smiled at her. "Probably not. I've been to a few horse farms that I couldn't wait to leave."

Abby looked up at me with bright eyes. "You ride horses?"

I shrugged. "Ride might be a strong word for it. I know enough not to fall off, if the horse isn't too excitable and doesn't move too fast."

Helena snorted and Abby looked over at her. Helena gave the girl a conspiratorial wink. "I suspect Adrian is downplaying things a bit. He does that. Usually when he's very good at something."

"I'm not. Well, not this time anyways," I said.

Abby looked around the room and got a strange look on her face. "You know, I don't usually like hospitals. But I like this room the way I liked that farm. It's bright in here, like there's something glowing all the time. Makes me feel, well, safe."

Her hand drifted up to finger the mirror pendant around her neck. I did my best not to stare as I considered the implication. Her subconscious already made the correlation between the enchantment on the pendant and protective power I'd pulled up around the room. It made the correlation and then it drew the conclusion. At least, it might have. If it had, then we were trying to refight a victorious battle. The challenge wasn't to teach Abby anything or break down false mental constructs. All we needed to do was draw out what she, against all odds, already knew. The thought didn't track, though. If she already knew, on some level, why was she so ignorant of her own power? It didn't make sense.

The only possible reason she wouldn't know would be if... my mind reeled. Mother of God, it would only make sense if all of that power was being used for something else already. It snapped together for me. She didn't know because she was under attack in one form or another since she was born, and maybe even before she was born. Her psyche, undeveloped, but driven by the most primal need to survive, turned that power toward her defense. In all likelihood, she'd spent her entire life wrapped in a psychic shell. A psychic shell driven by the astounding power Abby possessed could have deflected an awful lot of negative energy being sent her way. Not all of it, obviously, not with such a powerful demon in play, but a whole lot.

Helena and I just happened to be in the room the first time, maybe the first time in Abby's life, that every ounce of those resources weren't crucial to keeping the girl alive. Helena did something dramatic, something that would have drawn the mental attention of a powerful psychic. Abby's abilities, finally free to take a breath and look around, showed her what Helena was up to in the most direct possible way. It let Abby see Helena's gathered power. It was one hell of an introduction to the world of magic, but it could have been so much worse. I looked at Helena, but her gaze was fixed on Abby. I looked down at Abby. She stared up at me in something akin to horror. I took a step back. What the hell was that look about?

"Who," Abby's voice cracked. "Who is Jack Reed?"

For a few awful seconds, my world tilted at crazy angles and my vision went dark around the edges. Hearing Abby say that name out loud disoriented me more than a serious blow to the head. There was no way for her to know that name. Even Helena didn't know that name. I'd never spoken about him to lovers, to friends, not to anyone. Ever. I started to fall, but Helena managed to get around the bed and grab my arm before that happened. I swayed in place for a moment, trying to reorder the world into something sensible.

I looked at Helena, whose eyes were huge, filled with questions, but mostly startled. I turned my head to look at Abby, but the girl was staring at Helena. Abby still looked horrified, but also more than a little awestruck. The girl's lips moved, but no words escaped, not at first. When sound issued forth, it sounded like a mantra, but in a language I didn't immediately recognize. Helena's face went slack. She and Abby stared at each other, as the mantra spilled forth from Abby, over and over. Abby's eyes were glassy, her pupils huge. The mantra cut off, like a stereo with a pulled plug.

Abby started to talk. "The pursuit of material gain and the dependence upon relationships are illusory attachments and cannot coexist with the pursuit of enlightenment. To achieve Buddha Nature, to achieve freedom, one must renounce attachment. Along the path of enlightenment, many transitory powers may manifest and become attachments themselves. The enlightened being acknowledges the appearance of such powers and releases them as merely another illusion."

Abby's pupils contracted and her mouth closed. I was certain that Abby had never thought about anything even remotely like Buddha Nature, let alone read a treatise on the Noble Eightfold Path. As I had listened to her talk about it, my creep-o-meter went to a hitherto unknown eleven.

"Abby," said Helena, her voice little more than a whisper, "are you alright?"

"Him," said Abby, pointing at me. "He is your attachment."

"What?" I asked.

Helena's face went perfectly blank. "No. He is not."

"You can't save him," continued Abby, her face ashen.

"I'm not trying to save him," insisted Helena, her face locked in that creepy blankness.

"You *cannot* save him. No living hand can save him," Abby looked at me again, "but he might yet be saved."

As the creep-o-meter moved up to the also unknown level twelve, I started to ask what that meant. I never got the chance. Abby shuddered. It was an ugly, violent thing. She squeezed her eyes shut and started to shake her head back and forth.

"Too much," she gasped, her voice edged in deep pain. "Too much noise. So loud. Oh my God, it's so loud!"

Helena made the connection first. She grabbed my arm in a vice-like grip.

"Veil your thoughts," she ordered.

It took a second to process. Why would I veil my thoughts? The hamster lurched into motion. Right. Abby. Powerful and inexperienced psychic. We were the closest. We'd be the loudest. I slammed a wall of total silence around my consciousness. I presumed Helena did the same, because Abby's gasping, shaking, violent head thrashing slowed considerably. Tears were running out the corners of her eyes.

"Why is it so loud?" said Abby in a tiny voice.

She sounded like a small child then, one in the middle of her first experience with bone-deep pain. I didn't really understand what she was going through. My own psychic abilities being only marginally better than your average tarot card reader, I had no experiential frame of reference. I had spoken to a few hard core psychics over the years, people who might have been on a level with Abby, and they had given me an idea of what it might be like. One man described it as like having ten symphony orchestras in your head, only every instrument was out of tune, out of time with every other instrument, and all ten orchestras were playing different music. In short, it was deafening, discordant and agonizing. It was also something Abby had no practice shutting out.

Helena went over and grabbed Abby's hand. "Abby, listen to me."

"So loud, so loud, so loud," said Abby, lost in the noise in her head.

Helena bowed her head. She reached out and placed her hand over Abby's eyes. Power gathered around Helena. The same impression of cool mist I'd felt before washed over me, only several orders of magnitude stronger.

"Abby," said Helena.

There was something different about her voice, a strange timbre, and a kind of authority I'd never heard there.

"Abby, listen to me. You need barriers, here, and here, and here. You need to build them. I know it hurts. I know. You can do this."

There was a long pause and I realized my hands were clenching and unclenching in helpless frustration.

"No, that's good," said Helena. "That's very good. You're most of the way there. You just need to focus a little longer. I know, child. I know it hurts. It will pass."

I stood there watching for the better part of a minute. Abby went still on the bed. Helena sagged. I let out a breath I'd been holding. Abby curled into a ball. I walked over to the bed and gave Abby a look. She was staring into the deep, deep distance. I helped Helena to a chair. She looked like she was in as much pain as Abby had been in moments before. I crouched next to Helena and took her hand.

"Helena? Are you alright?"

She looked at me and shuddered. "The noise. I can't even...I got it secondhand. It *hurt*." Helena took her hand back and wrapped her arms around herself. "I just need a minute. Check on Abby."

Helena closed her eyes and her body shifted between shivers and shudders. I frowned at her, but did as I was told. Abby was still curled into a ball. Her eyes were wide and she was breathing in fast, shallow breaths. Even without medical training, I figured hyperventilating after an episode like that was bad. I put my hand on Abby's arm. She jerked, but it came across like a reflex action. I made my voice as soothing as I could.

"Abby."

She didn't react.

"Abby, can you hear me?"

She blinked.

"Abby, can you look at me?"

I waited to see what would happen. It took the better part of ten seconds, but her eyes flickered up to me, then away. I nodded.

"Abby, you're breathing too fast. Can you take a couple deep breaths for me?"

Her eyes flickered to me again, but she kept breathing at that same hectic pace.

I tried again. "Abby, I need you to take a couple of deep breaths for me. Okay? I'll do it with you. In," I took a deep breath in, "and out," I breathed out.

I kept that up for a while and, by barely discernible increments, her breathing slowed to something a little less frightening. After five minutes of deep breathing, Abby looked exhausted, but she wasn't hyperventilating. She was even blinking again. I didn't really think about it at the time, I just reached out and smoothed her short hair.

"Jesus," I said. "You poor kid. You can't catch a break."

Abby closed her eyes and I felt her building up to something. I should have expected it, but I didn't.

Abby opened her eyes, gave me a blank stare and said, "Who's Jack Reed?"

Chapter 31

I CLOSED MY EYES. That question was the exact kind of thing that made people so afraid of real psychics, the exposure of secrets, hidden pain, of unvarnished truth. It also made me a little ashamed. I didn't regret what I did. I knew I didn't, because I'd do it again. I was ashamed because Abby had to confront and live with what I did. It wasn't something she ever needed to know or carry. I doubted she'd ever hated anyone enough to understand why I did what I did. How could she? I was tempted, for a second or two, to lie to her.

The uselessness of that hit me immediately. She might not know everything. It was anyone's guess how much she gleaned in the middle of all that psychic noise, but she gleaned enough to pluck that name out of thin air. It stuck with such force that she hung onto it though all of the pain. In all likelihood, she knew the general shape of what I did. I opened my eyes and met her gaze.

"Someone who caused me a great deal of pain. He killed someone I loved."

Abby didn't look away, but I saw how much her new, unwilling knowledge ate at her. "You did things to him. You," she stopped and did look away that time.

"Yes," I admitted to the girl. "I did things to him. I took vengeance."

It's tough to watch a hero fall. What most people didn't get was that it was even tougher to be that fallen hero. To stand there and watch the incomprehension, the pure disappointment, seep into someone's face was enough to kill you. At least, it sure felt that way. It didn't matter that I hadn't actually failed or that the reason for her disappointment was ancient history in my life. It didn't matter that I hadn't set out to be some kind of hero. All Abby knew was that she had believed in me, had thought me better than I was, and I proved her wrong.

"How could you do that?" she asked, not looking at me.

My hand was still stroking her hair, as steady and rhythmic as a metronome. Don't ask me how I pulled that off. By rights, my hands should have been shaking.

"I guess I could tell you that it's complicated. Someone else might tell you that you'll understand when you're older. But it isn't complicated and you don't need to be older to understand. I just," and then I paused.

I'd never put it into words before. Oh, sure, I'd thought about it a lot. Reed was never far from my thoughts, but thoughts have a liquid quality, taking shape without necessarily giving words to those shapes. I think that I never put words to the thoughts because it meant giving them a concrete reality. Maybe I knew that it would tell me things about myself I didn't know or, barring that, didn't want to admit to myself. I think that we're all cowards about self-knowledge. Plus, it's hard to be the hero of your own story when you know that you've been the villain in someone else's story.

"I just hated him, Abby. I hated him for what he did, what he took from me. I hated him more than I've ever hated anyone in my life."

She glanced at me. The disappointment didn't evaporate, but it looked like it went down a notch or two in intensity. She started to say something, but I held up a hand. It wasn't hard to guess the direction of her thoughts.

"I'm not saying it was the right thing to do. Acting on hatred is stupid. It's dangerous. But that kind of hate, it…" I fumbled for the right thing to say. "It blinds you. You may know in your head that something is wrong, but it doesn't mean anything. It doesn't feel wrong. All you feel is hate and all you think is that if you don't do something about it, that hate will kill you."

She blinked at me a few times, her eyelids sliding closed and open slowly. The physical toll of all that pain and fear were catching up to the girl. She wasn't quite done, though.

"But you aren't," she said, the confusion evident on her pale face, "I saw, you aren't a bad person."

A deep tide of pain, relief and gratitude threatened to swallow me whole. I'd spent a lot of time wondering what kind of man I was at my core. I'd more or less concluded that I wasn't a particularly good man. Everyone I met seemed inclined to believe the same thing. That sort of belief and reinforcement tended to warp a person's self-image. To be told I wasn't, by someone, anyone, sent a wave of hope through me.

"I don't understand," she said. "You aren't a bad person, but you..."

Her breath caught and she stared off into nothing. It looked like she was trying to push away a painful mental image. I felt a stab of guilt. Odds were good it was an ugly memory from my head.

"Yeah," I muttered. "Yeah, I did. Life isn't always, well, it's not always clean. I've done some bad things. Maybe I'm not a bad person, but I'm as flawed as anybody else. I make the wrong choices sometimes."

Abby's eyes closed then opened again, but only halfway. Fatigue was winning the war. I tried to smile at her. Maybe it looked like one.

"Get some sleep, kid," I said, my voice hushed. "You'll be okay."

She mumbled something and then her eyes slid shut and stayed that way. I stared down at her for a long time. My head was the last place I'd wish on anyone, and Abby got an economy-sized dose of it. I hoped I told the truth about her being okay. I turned and came up short. I'd been so focused on Abby that I'd forgotten Helena was there. She was staring at me. Helena wasn't stupid. She knew enough about me to draw the lines between the dots Abby made, but I couldn't tell what she had made from those revelations. I just knew she was staring at me with an expression I couldn't identify.

I jerked my head toward the door and walked out of the room. We rode the elevator down in awkward silence. It was awkward for me, at any rate. Helena just kept looking at me with eerie intensity. I bought myself a little time by feeding coins into a vending machine. In return, the machine spit out an obscenity masquerading as coffee. I handed the first cup off to Helena and got one for myself. She sipped at the liquid, winced at the taste, and powered-gulped the rest.

"How are you doing?" I asked.

Helena shook her head a little. "I'll be alright. I don't know how Abby did it. Putting up those walls. I couldn't have done what she did."

I raised an eyebrow at her.

"You don't understand. The sheer," Helena's voice trembled, "size of that noise. The potency of it. It was like a living thing. Psychic lava pouring into her head."

I gritted my teeth. "If there is someone in charge out there, they've got an ass backwards sense of justice."

She gave me a pained look. "You know it isn't like that."

"All I know is that what's happening to that girl is wrong."

Helena continued as if I hadn't spoken. "I think that all of this is something coming home to roost. A chain of choices and decisions that's been building for a long time."

"And that makes it okay? That makes it okay for Abby to suffer? What fucking choice did she ever make to deserve what's happening to her? Cancer," I dropped my voice. "So much psychic power that the second it's off the chain it all but blows a hole in the back of her head, and no training to deal with it. You know what kind of decisions she's going to spend the rest of her life dealing with, and you can't possibly tell me that's fair."

Helena continued staring at me with that same unidentifiable expression she'd been wearing almost continuously. "Without all that psychic power, she'd be dead already."

I glared at Helena. I just wanted to be angry. I didn't want to reason my way through it. I wanted to hit something, hard, in the face, over and over again. I tried to push those thoughts down, but my emotions were up. Abby bringing up Jack Reed had thrown me way off balance. I rubbed my face with my hands and made another attempt to put my emotions in check. I didn't get them locked down, but I penned them up in a corner.

"Maybe so," I conceded. "Doesn't make it right. Damn sure doesn't make it any less ugly."

Helena nodded and went back to staring at me. I looked away.

"Ask," I muttered.

"Reed," she said, very soft and gentle. "He killed Marcy?"

I didn't speak. I didn't dare open my mouth for fear that it would turn into a scream of pain or hysteria. I nodded my head.

"Was it mur—" she cut herself off. "Was it intentional?"

I shook my head and took a chance on speaking. My voice was rough. "Accident. Stupid, stupid, careless, unnecessary accident."

She frowned and studied me some more. "What did you do?"

I felt my expression go blank. "You know better than to ask a question like that, no matter what the answer might be. I did something. That's all that matters."

She seemed taken aback by the answer for a moment, but then she nodded. She couldn't answer a question she didn't know the answer to, if it came down to it. She closed the distance, slid her hand into mine, and squeezed. There was nothing romantic in the gesture. She was being kind to me. She was being Helena. I squeezed back, calmed by the warmth of human touch and empathy.

"I'm sorry, Adrian. I knew it was tragic. I just assumed it was some kind of illness. Something swift and painful enough to scar you the way it did. I never imagined that it was..." she trailed off. "I'm sorry."

I gave her an empty smile. "Yeah, me too."

Helena glanced up at the ceiling, though I had the impression she was really trying to look up several floors at Abby. She frowned and sighed. I couldn't blame her.

"This will complicate things with her."

"You think? I'd be surprised if she let me back into the room."

"Maybe, but I doubt it. What she saw in you frightened her. I don't think it frightened her as much as you think."

"Huh," I said.

"I mean that she saw things in both of us, things she wasn't ready to know about our world. Imagine it. If you had been exposed to everything you know now, right at the very beginning, what would you have done?"

"Run for the hills probably, but," I saw her point, "but Abby can't, even if she wanted to."

Helena nodded.

I shrugged. "Nothing to be done about it. Damage done."

"True," she said.

I gave her an oblique look. It was my turn to ask a personal question.

"Helena, what was that business about attachments and saving me?"

Helena stood there in silence, but she didn't let go of my hand. I let it ride. She'd answer, if I gave her long enough. It took about two minutes.

"She was mistaken," said Helena. "For the most part."

"She read me pretty well," I countered.

"You were," she sighed, "are, important to me."

That admission didn't come cheap for Helena. I saw the pain of acknowledging the truth on her face.

"When we were together, I thought, I believed it was so I could save you from yourself. Or maybe it was just from your pain. I don't know that I really knew which, at the time. I thought if I could save you from that, then we'd be happy, genuinely happy. When you left, I felt like a failure at saving you, at building a life, at relationships. It felt like that for a long time. I know I can't save you. You can never really save anyone."

"But?"

"But, knowing it doesn't automatically free you from the feelings that went with it. Believing I could save you was hubris and self-serving hubris at that. Feeling like a failure after was a bruised ego. You were damaged and still in love with Marcy. Expecting you to change, believing I could heal you, it was expecting too much from both of us. I still struggle with that hubris and frail ego. My attachment isn't you, but it's locked up with my memories of you. It isn't always easy to separate them."

"Especially for a frightened kid with limited life experience," I said.

"Yes," she said.

I gave her hand another gentle squeeze and then let it go. "I never really said it, but I am sorry. You weren't the only one expecting too much from both of us."

She let out a surprised little laugh. "Oh? What were you expecting?"

I'd asked myself that more than once. "A miracle."

Chapter 32

"I SPOKE TO THE TWINS," I said, before she could ask the inevitable follow-up question.

I never figured out more than that I'd expected some kind of miracle. The exact nature and timing of the miracle was anyone's guess. Helena spotted the dodge, but let it go. Drilling into one another's psyches was questionably wise. She knew that as well as I did.

"What did they say?"

"Nothing good. I need to go back out to that graveyard and take another look."

"Why?"

"I need to make sure I saw what I thought I saw and to, um, confirm a theory."

"What theory?"

I waved the question off. "Let me check it out first. I don't want to scare anyone without a reason. If I'm right, though, we need to get Paul and Abby out of here immediately."

"They may not want to go," said Helena.

"That's a perfectly reasonable assumption and it doesn't matter at all. They'll still need to go."

"Okay, now you're scaring me. What did The Twins tell you?"

Helena crossed her arms and lifted an eyebrow at me. We'd had—or rather, I'd lost—a number of arguments where that posture played a prominent role.

"In short, they told me that we'd be fighting a losing battle if we went head-to-head with whatever is causing all of this."

"How sure are they?"

"It's The Twins," I said, in my best that-should-say-it-all voice.

"I've never dealt with them directly," she reminded me.

"Oh, right. In my experience, you ignore their information and advice at your own peril."

She tapped her foot a few times. It wasn't impatience, just a nervous habit. She'd had it for as long as I'd known her.

"Let's say it comes to that. How do you propose we convince them?"

"I doubt Abby will need much convincing. She's seen into our heads. She knows this is all real now. Big, scary real."

"Granted, but she isn't the one calling the shots about where they are, is she?"

"I don't think Paul could handle the truth about all of this," I said. "Do you?'

Helena frowned and then shook her head. "No, probably not. I know it's happening and I can barely believe it. This is bizarre even by our standards."

"Then, all other things being equal, we'll probably have to resort to emotional blackmail."

Helena didn't look convinced. "He doesn't strike me as the sort to bend that easily."

"Maybe not for himself, but for Abby?"

"God, Adrian, that's cold."

"It's better than letting her die."

Helena closed her eyes and then nodded. "Alright, if we have to. So what now?"

"I go to the graveyard and try very hard to prove myself wrong."

I took my sweet time driving to the graveyard. I was looking forward to what I expected to see there about as much as I looked forward to being beaten with a baseball bat. I realized I was checking the rearview a lot more often than necessary. I snorted. I was looking for the sheriff, but I'd been staying comparatively low profile since our chat. I didn't think he had a reason to come looking for me. Even driving slowly, the entrance to the cemetery appeared all too quickly. I parked and reminded myself how important it was to do what I went there to do. Only, I didn't immediately open the door and step out.

I just sat in my car and looked at the wrought iron gate for several minutes. I usually liked wrought iron. It was decorative without being ostentatious. Staring at the gate, though, it didn't look decorative to me at all. It looked like prison bars. The living might be able to come and go easily enough, but not the dead. The dead were locked in there, in cells of smoke, and I doubted their jailor ever let anyone go.

"Damn it," I said. "Stop creeping yourself out."

I struggled to banish those kinds of thoughts. I hadn't known what I was in for the first time, but blissful ignorance was just a fond memory. I thought I knew what I was going to see, would have bet money on it, but I wasn't eager to confirm my beliefs. Like I said, the veil between the living and the dead exists for a reason. You look across it at your own risk. I told myself to quit stalling and got out of the car. I made the short walk to the gate and stepped into the graveyard. I glanced across the weathered faces of the closest graves. They all bore identical dates of death.

I wasn't much for prayer, but I looked up at the sky. "You know, Big Guy, I generally like being right about things. It's gratifying and all. Honestly, though, I'd much rather be wrong here. If there's anything You could do to help make sure I'm wrong, I'd appreciate it."

The sky remained blue and still. I was not encouraged by that. With nothing left but to do what I went there to do, I closed my eyes and tried to raise some kind of mental shield to protect myself. The effort was pointless. It would be terrible, because I was human and alive. No mental shield could blunt those facts. I hunched my shoulders a little and raised the Eye of Horus. I looked through it at the nearest grave. The milky crystal cleared and my stomach flip-flopped at the sight of the roiling, hellish smoke that poured from the grave. I lowered the Eye and tried to let the sudden nausea pass.

"So it isn't just Abby's mother," I said, trying to reassure myself with my own voice.

My hopes crumbled under the weight of what I'd seen. I was right. I knew I was. Still, there was no benefit in being sloppy. I raised the Eye again and turned to the next grave, and the next, and the next. Every single one was consumed by that unnatural, pitch-black smoke. I braced myself and lifted the Eye of Horus so I could take in the graveyard as a whole. Hundreds of graves were desecrated by the unholy smoke. The sight nauseated me, so it took a while to realize that the smoke was thickest at the front of the cemetery. The deeper into the cemetery I looked, the fewer graves I saw with the smoke bindings.

I understood why I hadn't been able to connect Abby's parents and the demonic presence. There hadn't been one, not a direct one. The connection was right in front of me. Thirteen lives sacrificed, but not entire families. The families had stayed, lived, and died in the town, for the most part. Decade after decade, generation after generation, the demon had taken its vengeance, thinning the bloodlines. Each death would have freed the demon's power a little more. Of course, not everyone stayed. Abby's mother, Mary, was raised in California. One of Mary's parents, or grandparents, must have left the town.

A random thought wandered through and I wondered if Abby was the last. If she wasn't, she had to be close to the last. If the bloodlines died out, the binding would fail utterly. I lowered the Eye of Horus. I'd seen enough. I'd seen more than I wanted to ever see of those smoke bindings. I turned to leave the graveyard and stopped as another thought occurred to me. I lifted the Eye one last time and pointed it at the tomb of E.J. Cavanaugh. The smoke was there as well. Where it billowed out of the other graves, though, the smoke lashed and battered the tomb, unable to find a point of entry into the small Byzantine structure. I frowned and shook my head.

"You son of a bitch. You knew what was happening and built yourself a post-mortem safe house. You've got a lot to answer for, Cavanaugh."

I turned my back on Cavanaugh's tomb and went back to my car, more certain than ever that I knew what was happening, and hoping against hope that I was wrong. I checked my phone. Patty had texted me at some point and told me to meet her at the school at four. I decided that, if I drove slowly, I'd get there right about on time. I fired up the car and headed for the school.

Events had raced well ahead of my ability to process them all. It was only during the comparative downtime of the drive to the school that my mind finally turned its attention to the question of who could have launched the psychic attack on me at the cabin. I couldn't even venture a guess. Someone local, obviously, but I hadn't met anyone aside from Abby who showed even telltale signs of supernatural ability. Even if they weren't using magic, the one place my intuition did serve me well was in spotting my ilk. I suspected it was years of exposure that let me do that, rather than any kind of natural talent at spotting a practitioner.

Even so, someone in town had some kind of mojo going on and was good enough to slip in under my radar. The attack had been smooth, subtle, and aimed at my weaknesses. Helena knew me well enough to come after me like that, but I couldn't see her taking that kind of action. It went against everything she believed. She held that we had a responsibility to use whatever power and skills we had to try to leave the world a better place than we found it. It was why she chose to be a healer and a teacher, even though she could have used her strength differently. There weren't a lot of people who could have done anything about it, either, if she'd taken the shadowed road.

I tested the idea that it was her, found it to be possible, but wholly improbable, and dismissed her from my suspect pool. That left me with several thousand people in the immediate vicinity who could have done it and no information to narrow the list down. That realization left me feeling all kinds of worried. There was no guarantee whoever it was wouldn't do the same thing when Lil wasn't around to bail my ass out. I felt a surge of something that was not quite panic. My heart started to beat a little faster.

There hadn't been time to be afraid or to process how close a call it was for me. Now that my mind was on the subject, fear reared up to collect its due with interest. Whoever it was could have killed me or, bare minimum, taken me out of play long enough to kill Abby. An image of Abby's pale, lifeless body sprawled across a floor rose unbidden in my head. I saw her locked into a smoke binding of her own. That image was all too easy to conjure, thanks to Abby's resemblance to her mother. The possibility that I could have found myself locked in a dream state nearly sent me into a panic attack.

My whole body started to shake at that idea. I saw myself trapped and motionless on a bed in some coma ward, unaware of my condition and living out a false life conjured by my imagination. A more chilling idea was that I would be completely aware of my condition, aware of the false life and its cause. That would be a prison as terrible and effective as the dead found those smoke bindings. I'd have been alive, but only in the most technical sense of the word. I'd be little more than a corpse, just waiting to happen.

My rational mind, the only real defense against unreasoning fear, reasserted itself. True, it conceded, someone could try the same thing again. However, now that I knew the threat existed, I could take steps. In hindsight, I should have put such protective measure in place from the start. I'd taken it for granted, just assumed, that Helena and I were the only real magical power players in town. My assumption was ludicrous, but also a forgivable mistake. I formed that assumption when I was in a lot of pain and on fairly potent painkillers. Statistically speaking, there would almost need to be at least one or two other people in town with *some* magical talent.

If someone came after me that way again, they'd find it a much trickier business. If all went well, it would also be a horrifyingly painful experience for them. Helena's idealism about how we should use magic to leave the world a better place was all well and good. It did not, however, leave much wiggle room to deal with assholes. That usually called for playing dirty, playing mean and not showing much squeamishness. Being that way was hard work for someone like Helena. It was about hard as starting a car for me. You know what they say, play to your strengths. That thought actually did more to dispel the low growling of fear than any of my cold reason.

I managed to get disoriented in town for a few minutes and drove up and down maddeningly familiar streets. It was sort of predictable. I'd only driven by the school twice and hadn't made much note of its position. My brief encounter with being geographically challenged meant I arrived about ten minutes late. Patty leaned against the side of her cruiser and tapped her watch as I pulled up. I got out of the car and gave her an apologetic look.

"Hartworth," she said.

"Patty."

"Do I want to know why you want a tour of the school?"

I gave it a moment of weighty consideration, or what I hoped looked like weighty consideration. "You absolutely don't want to know."

Chapter 33

SHE ROLLED HER EYES. "More of your conspiracy nonsense?"

I shrugged. She wasn't ever going to be a believer until she saw something a lot more impressive than my holy water light show at Paul and Abby's house. That caught her off guard, but the inextinguishable need for things to make sense had done its work. I'd tricked her with clever sleight of hand, or maybe she was misremembering, or maybe she'd seen light from Venus reflected through swamp gas. Whatever explanation she settled on didn't include black magic, holy water, or a conspiracy. At least, it didn't on the surface.

I figured there was a good chance that Patty, with recourse to some rational-sounding excuse, had started rechecking the locks on her doors at night. If she had a shred of faith, she'd probably started wearing some kind of religious symbol. I wondered what it would be. A crucifix, maybe? She did have something of the lapsed Catholic vibe, but so did a lot of people who'd simply walked away from organized religion. Right before she went to sleep, when the moon slipped behind a cloud and heavy darkness settled, I bet she wondered if I was for real.

That sliver of doubt, the niggling possibility that I might be telling her the absolute truth, and the DNA-level memory of when demons walked openly in the world, kept her from dismissing me. It gave her the latitude she needed to indulge my, all things considered, innocuous requests. On the conscious level, though, I think she just liked the fact that I'd beat the hell out of Tucker Smith. Whatever the reason, she was willing to help me. That was enough.

"Is this going to become a full-time occupation for you, Hartworth? Or is there a conclusion to this little project sometime in the near future?"

The question did a lot to dampen my moderately good mood. "Day or two, I think. Three on the outside."

She gave me a surprised look. "Why do you say that?"

"Abby's set to get out of the hospital."

"And?"

"If something's going to happen, it'll happen then."

"If it doesn't?"

"I thank God, Jesus, Buddha, all the My Little Ponies, and Santa Claus for good measure. Then, I move on."

"Really? Just like that?"

"Why Deputy Patty, I think you're saying you'll miss me."

"Pshhh," she said, but she flashed me a grin. "Well, maybe a little. You're weird, but that's fun sometimes."

"That's fair."

Patty face went serious. "What if something does happen?"

I didn't say anything. I didn't say it in a very loud voice.

"Damn it, I told you…"

"You won't tolerate a vigilante. You won't have to. It won't be that kind of thing."

A voice drawled behind me. "How do you know that?"

I resisted the impulse to spin into a kick. It took a second, but I recognized the sheriff's voice. I shot Patty a look, but she seemed as surprised to see him as I was to find him there. The sheriff stepped past me and regarded Patty with an inscrutable expression. She met his eyes without shame or embarrassment. Either she had titanium nerves or she really didn't think she'd crossed a line.

After I thought about it for a second, I realized she hadn't. I hadn't asked her to break any laws, and when you got right down to it, there was nothing all that sinister about asking for a tour of a high school. Hell, I'd asked law enforcement to make it happen. It only felt sleazy to me because I knew the ghastly stakes and kept the information to myself.

The sheriff turned his inscrutable expression to me. "Well, Mr. Hartworth. How do you know it won't be that kind of thing?"

I didn't jump into an answer. I cleared my mind and waited to see what came up first. After a few seconds, I knew what I needed to say.

"Insight, sheriff."

Barnes blinked at that and then frowned. "So you found what you were looking for?"

"Not exactly, but I learned enough."

Barnes never took his eyes off me when he spoke to Patty. "I'll take it from here, Deputy."

She looked at him and then me. I could see the confusion and the suspicion in her eyes. On the other hand, he hadn't exceeded his authority in taking over any more than she had exceeded hers in agreeing to take me on a tour. She hesitated. The sheriff narrowed his eyes in her direction. I caught her eye and shook my head.

"Yes, sir," she said.

The sheriff didn't say anything until after Patty was gone. "I went to school here."

"So I heard."

"Hate the place," he said in a hard voice.

"Heard that too."

"Looked into you, you know."

"I figured. If not right off the bat, then certainly after you caught wind of that Miami business."

"Yeah. Thing is, nobody knows what to make of you. Talked to one fellow out in Los Angeles."

"Christ," I muttered.

Barnes gave me knowing look. "He said you're the biggest pain in the ass alive. Said you're probably a liar and definitely a con man."

"We've had some issues."

"Gathered that. He told me something else."

"I'm sure it was very flattering."

The sheriff grunted something that might have been a laugh.

"He said if you're fixating," the sheriff blinked a few times. "That's a strange word. Anyway, he said if you're fixating, best thing to do is stay the hell out of your way until it's done. Now, why would he say a thing like that?"

I rolled a shoulder. "Experience."

"That's what he said, too. Wouldn't say another word about it. Just, 'Stay the hell out of Hartworth's way. It's less paperwork.'"

"He isn't wrong," I said.

"Talked to another fellow in Boston. He says you're some kind of exorcist or monster hunter. Used those very words, 'monster hunter,' like it made sense."

I stared at the sheriff. He stared up at the school with something just shy of blinding hatred. He'd barely glanced at me since Patty left. He'd talked to someone in Boston. I could only think of one person in Boston who might have called me a monster hunter.

"You talked to Father Ryan?"

"I did."

I was impressed. "That's no mean feat. He's been," I hedged, "in seclusion for a while."

Barnes raised an eyebrow at me. He'd talked to Father Ryan. He knew exactly where the man was and probably why he was there. Most people don't line up to get into mental institutes. Fewer still line up to get in voluntarily. Like I said, I have baggage. Father Ryan and his choice of where to live were part of it.

I felt defensive. "I didn't put him in there."

"I know that, boy. He told me that much. Not much else. Given how many people you seem to meet, awful lot of not talking about you going on."

"I'm a private sort of person. People respect that."

"Hell they do. You scare them."

I winced. It was true, but it wasn't true. Yeah, I was all tied up with what scared them, a lot like I was all tied up with Helena's attachment, but it didn't make them afraid of me.

"It's a little more complicated than that. It's not me that scares them."

"If you say so. Found out a few other things."

"Oh?"

"Stories about you go way back, fifteen years or so, all over the country. Near as I can figure, save for a year in Connecticut, you've never had a home for more than a few months. You literally live on the road."

"I like to travel."

Barnes sniffed at me. "No, you don't. Not the way you do it."

"Force of habit, then. Look, sheriff, not to be rude, but is this coming to a point?"

Barnes turned and faced me then. He seemed calm, disturbingly, unnaturally calm.

"Before I let you walk into that building, I want to know what you are. You a con man, a liar, an exorcist?"

"Probably."

Barnes narrowed his eyes. "Which?"

"All of them. I've been a lot of things and done a lot of things over the years."

The sheriff nodded, slowly, and then fixed me with a steady look. "I expect that's true. So tell me this. Who were you before you stole the name Adrian Hartworth?"

Bone-deep fear tried to claw its way out of my chest, but I kept it off my face. "I have no idea what you're talking about."

"I'm not stupid, Hartworth, or whoever you really are. Got my degree in Criminology. Been a cop for most of my life. Oh, your paperwork is solid, better than solid. I can't prove you aren't who you say you are. Doesn't mean I don't know you aren't Adrian Hartworth. You became him fifteen years ago."

I didn't flinch or avert my eyes. He could *know* all he wanted, but, like the man said, he couldn't prove any of it. I spread my hands in a 'what can you do?' sort of way.

"Even if that were true," I said, "and I'm not saying it is, what difference would it make today?"

"Maybe none, but maybe it makes a lot of difference. Depends on why you did it."

I did avert my eyes that time.

"If I changed my identity, it wasn't for a reason that would matter to you right now." I met his gaze again. "It was because of family."

I'd even told him the truth. The first time I changed my identity, it *was* because of family. I did it to protect them. The second time was about family, too, but in a very different way. Whatever the sheriff expected, that wasn't it. He believed me, though. I saw that much. I watched his eyes flicker back and forth. He was redoing all of the mental math that made him certain I was a criminal on the run and probably running some kind of long con on Paul and Abby. He'd expected me to lie and spin some convoluted tale, to say something he could use to catch me in the falsehood or ferret out my real identity as a crook.

"Why should I believe that?" He asked.

"You already do," I answered. "You aren't the only one who can read people."

Barnes grimaced. "Losing my touch."

"Nah, I'm just an observant guy."

"I just bet that you are."

I glanced up at the school. "So, I've answered your questions, more or less. Are you satisfied?"

"Enough, I suppose. Enough for now."

"Good. Then do you mind if I ask you a question?"

"Go ahead."

"Why do you hate this school so much?"

Barnes folded his arms across his chest and looked at the ground for a spell. I couldn't tell if he was gathering his thoughts or putting on some kind of passive-aggressive show. The older man turned his head and looked up at the old church. I saw tension gathering in his shoulders and back. Just being in proximity to the building stressed the man out. No, I realized, as the truth crystallized in my head. He didn't hate the place. It didn't stress him out. Barnes was afraid of the building.

"Couldn't rightly say," said Barnes. "Always hated it. Hated it when I was in school. Hate it now. Wish the town had torn the damn place down instead of making it a school."

I doubt that he would have much liked the result if the town had torn it down. I thought that, all things considered, it wasn't the building the man hated. What he hated was what he sensed in the building. The malevolence of a demon, any demon, was nothing to scoff at, let alone the malevolence of something as powerful as what the Twins had described to me. Tearing the building down might have been enough to free the demon, regardless of any other measures put in place to contain it.

Barnes face settled into grim determination. "Damn it, let's just get this over with."

With that, the sheriff turned and walked toward the front door. I followed after him, quite certain that I wasn't doing the smart thing. It might have been a necessary thing, but it wasn't the smart thing. I checked a laugh at my lips. It wasn't amusement, just a bit of hysteria. I'd been doing the stupid thing since word go. No point in worrying about doing the smart thing at that point.

Chapter 34

SOME PEOPLE SEEM ABLE TO RETAIN perfectly good, accurate memories that are immune to the influence of fear. Some seem able to do that even when faced with the near blind panic I experienced one second after stepping through the front door of the school. I am not one of those people. Generate sufficient fear and my memory started to develop big holes that, even in retrospect, were filled with something that could make me sweat. I don't have a single clear memory about my tour through that school. I have hazy, nightmarish recollections of halls and doors and Barnes telling me things about the school. I couldn't tell you what the things he told me were, but I remember his mouth moved and noises came out. I remember thinking that they probably strung together into coherent thoughts.

The fear that spent a full thirty minutes raking its way across my mind and heart didn't even allow me to experience satisfaction over being right. I guess my little plea to the Almighty got jammed up in the queue somewhere. I shouldn't have been surprised. I'm told he's a busy guy. That being said, I knew what we were up against. Somewhere in my truest heart, I'd wanted to think I was wrong. I'd wanted to think I'd misread the signs. Like everyone else, I wanted things that I wasn't going to get.

The absolute darkness of the place enveloped me the second I was inside. It felt the way dank, standing water smells, full of putrefaction and death. It pulsed and quivered against me, my mind, my senses, and I wanted to scream. I wanted to run away. I just wanted to get out. I tried to imagine how they got teenagers to come to the place at all, let alone for months and months every year. To spend most of your waking hours wrapped in that absolute, stomach-wrenching awfulness, that kind of spiritual blight, would be enough to drive some people mad. It would turn others, those inclined that way, to crime and outright evil.

If someone had told me that there were an unusually high percentage of serial killers spawned from those hallways, I wouldn't have batted an eye. In fact, I'd have probably said they were underestimating the number. Every step through that building was like wading, fully immersed, through the week-old discarded flesh of a slaughterhouse. Don't ask me how I managed not to sob. I don't know. Maybe I did and Barnes just did me the courtesy of not mentioning it. By the time we stepped back outside, I was shell-shocked into visceral, mental, and emotional numbness. You couldn't pay me enough to go back inside.

I stood there, shaking a little, not hearing or feeling anything. I just wanted to close down, huddle into a tiny ball and stay that way for a year. *They send their kids there*, I thought. *They sent their children into that cesspit. They did it on purpose. How could they do that? How could they not know? How could they be in that building for more than a second before boarding-up the doors and windows and declaring it a public hazard?* I'd have put up thirty-foot fences, topped with spikes and razor wire and fucking machine gun turrets, just to keep people out.

I thought that I'd never be clean again. I was stained, forever, just by having come into contact with that corruption. And they sent their kids there. They sent their kids there every day. *My God, what have they done?* I have no idea how long I stood there, insensate, or how many times Barnes said my name before he grabbed my arm and gave me a firm shake.

"Hartworth," he growled. "For God's sake man, snap out of it."

I shuddered and nodded. My legs felt weak, but I made them propel me, unsteady and listing from side to side, toward my car. The Neon looked like it was a thousand miles away, but I kept moving toward it. I heard Barnes moving behind me, asking me something, but I just needed to get away from that building. I made it as far as the front of my car before everything in my stomach raced up my throat. I stumbled and dropped to a knee, one hand against the car, the other on the ground, and I puked my guts out. I vomited for centuries. That's how my brain interpreted it, anyways. In the real world, it might have gone on for twenty or thirty seconds. Once my stomach realized there just wasn't anything left to send upwards, it subsided.

I stayed on the ground like that for a minute, trembling and certain that I might get sick again at any moment. *I'll never be clean again*, I thought for the second time. *I'll never get that stench, that wrongness, I'll never get it off me. There wasn't enough soap or acid in the whole world to get that evil off me. Oh God, how had Abby ever made herself go inside that building? How could anyone go in there more than once?*

"Hartworth?"

I looked up. The sheriff was looking down at me, all the cop suspicion gone. He just looked worried about me. It was regular human concern for another person that was in obvious distress. I looked down at the ground for a minute, saw my own vomit, and had to fight down an urge to be sick again. I pushed myself up from the ground and sat down on the hood of my car.

"I'll be alright," I mumbled.

"You sure?" Barnes sounded like he'd heard that one before and didn't believe it this time either.

"Yeah. Something I ate, I guess. Teach me for eating gas station food."

"Uh-huh."

I gave him a wan look and focused on steadying my nerves. *New plan*, I thought. *Take The Twins' advice. Run away.* Barnes didn't leave. He waved on a handful of kids who stopped to gawk. I caught sight of some soccer cleats. It took about ten minutes, but I got myself together. I found a bottle of water in the car and rinsed out my mouth. The sheriff watched me with a neutral expression. Once it became clear I wasn't about to die, the cop part of his brain started reasserting itself.

"Care to share what you learned from that?" Barnes asked.

I gave the man a level look. "Sure. I learned it's time for me to go."

Barnes tilted his head to one side, like he didn't quite understand. "Sorry?"

"Not complicated. I'm leaving. Nothing left for me to do here."

"You don't strike me as a man who leaves things unfinished."

"Sheriff, I told you the second I thought people would be better off if I left, I'd go. People will be better off. So, I'm going."

Granted, the people who would be better off were pretty much just me and Helena. Paul and Abby might be better off, if I could somehow convince Paul to take Abby and leave. People

underestimate the value of the strategic retreat. On very rare occasions some fool emerged victorious from a fight they had no
business winning. The infrequency of such victories accounted
for their celebration. Most of the time, when someone walked
into an unwinnable fight, they died. I had no intention of being
that guy. I checked-in with my conscience and discovered I could
live quite easily with my cowardice. Mostly, I'd be able to live
with it because I lived. Bravery was noble. Suicide by demon
was just stupid.

Barnes frowned at me, clearly suspicious about my motives.
Then he hit me with a bomb. "What is Midnight Ground?"

I had it together enough not to start screaming incoherently
at him, but not together enough to come up with a passable half-
truth. Instead, I opted for playing dumb.

"Sorry?" I asked.

"Midnight Ground," he repeated. "You were saying it over
and over again."

"No idea," I lied. "Must be something I heard in a movie
once."

His expression didn't change, but I somehow knew that I'd
said the wrong thing. My playing dumb act, an act that had
served me so well and often, pushed a button in Barnes. I felt the
change in him and watched his stance shift in a number of small,
subtle ways. He pulled his hands out of his pockets and they
hung loosely at his side. His center of gravity shifted downward
and one of his feet slid back a little. His eyes went slightly out of
focus, and he wasn't looking at my face anymore. His eyes took
in my whole body.

It was that last part that tipped my wariness into full-fledged
alarm. Even among people accustomed to physical violence,
there was a tendency to focus on the other person's face. The
incorrect reasoning went that a change in expression would cue
you that they were about to make a move. People with serious
training in hand-to-hand combat know better. A person's face
may or may not cue you, but their body will always cue you. If
you let yourself stay aware of what a person's body is doing, it
can give you a critical fraction of a second to block or evade a
blow. Barnes looked at me the way a trained fighter looked at an
opponent. All those slight changes, taken as a whole, told me he
was on the point of violence.

My mental impression of him as some kind of caricature evaporated. He didn't look amusing anymore. He looked like someone who could very well take my head off. We were about the same height, but he had thirty or forty pounds on me. Some of that weight looked to be the result of a healthy appetite, but he was broad in the shoulders. His hands were heavy and powerful. I bet he did something demanding in his off time. Maybe he farmed a little, or did some kind of carpentry. Maybe he was just built that way. Whatever the reason, he was probably stronger than I was. In an otherwise even match, even a little extra strength on one side could tip the scale.

On the flip side, I had the advantage of comparative youth and fitness. At least I would have had those advantages under normal circumstances. The adrenaline burst that always accompanied violence would probably let me ignore the pain from my burn, at least for a few minutes, but my lungs were a different story. They were a long way off from a full recovery. Under those conditions, a fair fight that didn't last too long could go either way. If it went on for any length of time, my damaged lungs just wouldn't be able to supply the ridiculous amounts of oxygen a serious fight required. I knew what I was doing, but so did he. If we fought, it wouldn't be over fast. I wasn't in a good mental place to be fighting. Plus, he was armed with more than just fighting know-how. I didn't necessarily believe he'd pull his service weapon on me if he started a fight. That didn't mean he couldn't, or wouldn't, should things go my way.

I slowly raised a hand. "Take it easy. It doesn't need to go that way."

Barnes blinked in surprise. "No, it doesn't, but it will if you don't play me straight right now. I cut you a lot of slack. Let you poke around. Let you kick up hard feelings. Time to come clean."

I yearned to get into my car and drive away. The sheriff wasn't talking tough. He meant it. If I tried to leave without giving him an explanation, he would probably kick my ass. Might even toss me back in jail for whatever reason he could trump up, just to lean on me. He had intuited something bad was going on and that he didn't know what he needed to know to figure it out. So, he turned me loose and let me do my thing. I probably owed him something for that.

"In simplest terms," I said, "this place is cursed."

Barnes didn't move or speak, but the way he didn't move or speak told me that answer wasn't good enough. I ground my teeth.

"There's something trapped in, or possibly under, that building," I said, pointing at the school. "There isn't one damn thing I can do about it, either. Maybe, somewhere else, with something less potent, I could. But I can't do anything here. I want to. I just can't. I'm not good enough."

"So what happens when you're gone?"

I looked away. "Sooner or later, it gets out. Probably sooner, but that'll happen whether I'm here or not."

"And then?"

"People start dying. Maybe not immediately, but they'll all die in the end. It'll use their deaths to give itself more power."

Barnes narrowed his eyes. "Why?"

"Blood sacrifice, sheriff. It's how you make a god."

I was only guessing at that last part, but it was an educated guess. Demons could be terribly powerful when compared to a human practitioner, but not next to the old powers. A few thousand deaths wouldn't give a demon enough power to join the Roman Pantheon, but it'd be enough to make a good start.

Barnes very calmly drew his weapon and aimed it at me. "Turn around, put your hands on the car, and spread your legs."

"Sheriff, this is…" I stopped talking as he clicked the safety off.

"Now," he said.

I did as I was told. He cuffed me and shoved me into the back of his cruiser. As he pulled away from the school, I gave him a dirty look in the rearview.

"Do you mind telling me what I'm being taken in for?"

Barnes gave me a flat look in the mirror. "For not having a good-enough answer."

"I told you the freaking truth," I objected.

He looked away. "I know. I know your type, though, Hartworth."

"Meaning?"

"Meaning that you're going to sit in that cell until one of two things happens."

"What things?"

"You die with the rest of us, or you come up with something to save your own ass."

Damn, I thought. *He really did know my type.* In most circumstances, he'd even be right that I'd come up with something. Only, there wasn't anything I could do to stop what was coming. No one could.

"You're murdering me," I said. "You know that, don't you?"

He looked at me again and I saw it in his eyes. He knew. He knew it and he didn't care.

"Doesn't sound like I'll have to live with it very long," he answered.

God, I hated people with commitment sometimes.

Chapter 35

"SHERIFF," I SAID, even as he closed the cell door on me, "this is pointless. I *can't* do anything."

"I don't believe that. I think you just need some time to think about it."

Patty had stared in utter shock when Barnes hauled me into the station and all but threw me into the cell. She gave me a questioning look. I rolled my eyes and shrugged. I mouthed the word *conspiracy* in her direction. She narrowed her eyes at me and then turned the same look on Barnes. He managed to look a little uncomfortable when she walked over to him.

"Jeremy, what the hell are you doing?"

"What I need to do, to protect the town."

"How does locking him up protect the town?"

"He knows what's happening here. I think he knows how to stop it. I'm providing him," the sheriff looked at me, "an incentive to do it."

I seized the bars of the cell in my hands and gave him a dirty look. "Fine, you want to know how to stop it, I'll tell you the only way I know. Evacuate this town and never, ever come back. That's it. That is the only," I rattled the bars, "God damned," I rattled them again, "way."

Barnes wasn't impressed by my impotent display. "I think you can do better."

Patty looked torn, her eyes moving between me, the guy who technically hadn't done anything, and her boss. It was a hell of an ethical pickle for her. If she raised too much of a stink, Barnes could probably just fire her. On the other hand, she was technically aiding and abetting him in a crime if she let him keep me in that cell without charging me with something. She wore the same expression I'd seen on people who got a mouthful of something that didn't agree with them.

"You can't just keep him in that cell until he talks," she said. "You either have to charge him or I'm letting him out. He hasn't committed any crimes that I know about. He isn't obstructing an investigation, unless you opened one I don't know about. Have you?"

"No, but the law says I can hold him for forty-eight hours," said Barnes.

"Not without a reason. Is he a suspect in a crime?"

"He has knowledge of a crime that's going to happen."

"What crime?"

"Mass murder."

Patty blinked and shot me a look. She shook her head. "Carried out by whom, exactly?"

Barnes shrugged.

"This wouldn't be a demon or some other supernatural cause, would it?"

Barnes said nothing.

"Did he use the words 'mass murder'?"

Barnes continued saying nothing. Patty sighed, gave me another look that said, "I will beat you to death for this," and picked up a key. She walked toward the cell.

"Damn it, Patty, he knows something!"

She stopped with the key a bare inch from the lock. She closed her eyes, inserted the key, and turned it. She looked over her shoulder at the sheriff and it seemed to age her.

"I know he does, or thinks he does. You think he does, too. But it's nothing that any district attorney would believe. Any lawyer with a cup of coffee in them could have Hartworth out of here in two seconds. It'd be a disaster for you."

She swung open the cell door. I looked at Barnes. He was staring at me. The desperation in his features was something truly ugly. He knew something. I'd bet he'd known something for years. He couldn't ever put his finger on it, or maybe he had put his finger on it. That fit better. He'd figured out that something otherworldly was at work and that he didn't have the knowledge or resources to deal with it. He thought I could. He was ready to torpedo his career, his reputation, maybe even his freedom, if it meant he could stop it somehow. I felt for the man. I couldn't say I wouldn't have done the same thing in his position. Well, okay, I could have said that, but most people couldn't have said it. I'd have helped him if I knew how. I stepped out of the cell.

"You'll have to live with this, Hartworth," said Barnes.

I shuddered. "Sheriff, I swear to God, if I could do anything to stop what's coming, I'd do it."

"Then help me, damn it!"

I looked away. "I honestly can't. I don't, I just don't have the power. What's coming is," I tried to think of something appropriate. "What's coming is *Biblical* in proportions. I'd be less than nothing in its way."

"Then who does have the power? You must know someone, somewhere, who can help."

I shook my head. "You think I didn't think of that? It isn't an option."

"Why not?" He growled at me.

"Because, believe it or not, right now there are actually worse things happening in the world than this. I'm sorry, sheriff, there isn't anything to do or anyone to call. It's just a matter of when it happens, not if it happens."

Patty had stood there in silence listening to us and she finally broke in. "Would either of you care to explain to me what you think is going to happen."

Barnes shook his head and walked over to a window. He looked smaller to me, as if the lack of a solution had deprived him of something that had once given him extra mass. I couldn't give him what he wanted or needed, but I wanted to give him something.

"If you have anyone here that you love, sheriff, people you truly care about, I think there's still time to get them clear. Convince them to leave. It's all that you can do."

He didn't turn or even speak, just kept staring out the window. If willpower alone could have averted the impending disaster, I'd have given him good odds. I'd have even given *me* good odds if pure will could get the job done, but will alone wasn't enough. Patty put a hand on my shoulder.

"Come on, Hartworth, I'll give you a lift to your car."

I nodded and followed Patty to the door. I glanced over my shoulder at the sheriff and thought he cut a striking figure silhouetted in the window. It'd make a good campaign poster, I mused, the thought both accurate and irrational. As Patty drove me back to the school, my mind skittering away from my haunting quasi-memories of the building's interior, she was very quiet for a few minutes.

"You said you can't do anything," she said.

I glance at her. "I did."

"Is that true?"

That was a tricky question. As far as I knew, it was true. It was objectively possible that there was some action I could take that might avert disaster, but I didn't know what it was. The Twins were quite certain there wasn't anything I could do to derail the hell train on a collision course with the town.

"Yes, it's true."

"But you had to think about it."

"It's not a simple question."

"What isn't simple about it?"

I snorted. "I don't know everything, for starters. Do you know if you can bench press three hundred and fifty pounds?"

"Of course I can't."

"Okay, but how do you know? Have you ever tried under extreme conditions? Have you ever tried even under regular conditions?"

She hesitated. "Well no, but that's different."

"It isn't different. You think you can't, because people with more information would probably tell you that you can't. As far as you know you can't, but you don't actually know, absolutely, that you can't do it."

She got it. "You're pretty sure you can't do anything. People you think would know told you that you can't. You believe them, but it doesn't mean that there isn't a theoretical way for you do something."

"Bingo."

"Is there a way for you to find out?"

"Well," I thought about it, "shit, maybe if I had twenty years. It's not like anyone is running a deep magic lending library I can go to to do the research."

She blinked a few times. "Deep magic?"

"High level, high-intensity magic."

She gave me a blank stare. I thought for a minute, looking for an analogy that might work.

"Okay," I said. "How good of a shot are you?"

"I'm pretty good."

"So, somewhere along the line, someone taught you how to shoot. How to stand and hold the gun? How to aim? When to pull the trigger? All that stuff, right?"

"Well, yeah, sure. Why?"

"Once you knew all that stuff, were you a good shot?"

"Oh, hell no. I spent years practicing on the range. Still do."

"Now, do you still think about all those things when you shoot? How to stand, hold the gun, aim, and so on?"

She thought for a minute. "I guess I don't give it a lot of conscious thought. It's all ingrained now."

"Okay, but you're still improved. You're still learning. Your insight into how to shoot well gets better over time, yes?"

"Yes, I guess that's true."

"You might think of that as deep shooting. You've gotten to the point where your intuition is becoming more important to improving your shooting than any specific training.

"When it comes to magic, anyone with a bit of talent can learn how to stand, hold the gun, and pull the trigger. I've got that part down, and I've more or less gotten to the point where I don't have to think about it every time I want to do something. Basically, I've achieved competence. Deep magic is the stuff that only people who are absolute masters can even grasp. I might get there if I live another thirty or forty years. What's happening here is the kind of thing that only a few of those masters would have the vaguest idea how to deal with. An even fewer of them would have the power to deal with."

Patty thought in silence for a moment. "So, what you're saying is that you're the kind of guy who can hit a target at thirty feet, pretty consistently, as long as things don't get too distracting and you're using your favorite handgun."

"Yeah, that's probably accurate."

"And you're saying that what we need here is the sniper who can make a headshot from a mile out, in high winds, while there are bombs exploding nearby."

I frowned. "I don't actually know that much about guns. I assume that's one of those very difficult things that only a couple dozen people on the planet can do?"

"Probably more than that, but yes, that's the idea."

"Then yes, that's who I'm saying you need here."

She raised an eyebrow. "Those are the people you told the sheriff aren't available. Really? There's isn't one anywhere?"

"It's a tiny group. And no, there isn't one."

Patty shook her head. "I don't know how you got the sheriff to buy into this."

I looked out the window and didn't say anything. I felt her eyes on my head.

"What?" I asked.

"You didn't, did you? Get him to buy into this?"

"I told him less about all of this than I told you."

"Then he," she mulled it for a second. "He already believed it. That's why he let you run around town without interfering." She took it to the next step. "Jesus, that's why he let you go in the first place. He was hoping you'd get involved."

"I don't know about that last part, but I think the rest is true."

"But it's crazy. All of it. You're basically harmless crazy, but Jeremy? He's never been one to buy into mumbo-jumbo."

I gave her a look that said, *we've had this conversation before.* She held up a hand in acknowledgement.

"Well, now what?" she asked.

"Nothing," I said. "I leave town. Try to get Paul to take Abby and go. It's the only thing that will even kind of protect her at this point."

"What if he won't leave?"

I turned my head even more toward the window. "Then, Abby dies."

Chapter 36

PATTY DIDN'T SAY ANOTHER WORD ON THE RIDE. I couldn't tell if I'd disappointed her or she didn't know what to say, but she just dropped me off at my car and drove away. I felt lousy. The sheriff was interpreting it as me leaving them in the lurch and it was hard to blame him for that. I knew it looked that way from the outside. I tried to shrug off my guilt as I drove to the cabin. Once I was there, I pretended that Lil wasn't giving me reproachful looks as I packed my things into a little nylon bag. I tried to convince myself it didn't bother me that a bunch of innocent people were going to bite it. I reassured myself that I couldn't help them as I put the hard case next to the nylon bag on the bed.

"There's nothing I can do," I said to Lil.

She blinked at me, turned her back, and curled up.

"I can't help them," I said to the motionless gray form.

Lil said nothing. She didn't look at me. I sat on the bed and did my best not to count the minutes. Several million years later, there was a knock on the door. I went over and let Helena into the cabin. She took two steps in, saw my meager belongings on the bed, and stopped. She turned to look at me.

"What's this?" She asked, waving a hand at the bed.

"We need to leave."

"Just like that."

"Yes, just like that. We need to try to get Paul to take Abby the hell away from here. Even if we can't, though, we need to leave. We can't help them. We can't help anyone who lives here."

Helena gave a derisive sniff and toss of her head. "You're such a drama queen sometimes. I'm sure we can do something."

I grabbed her arm, hard, and almost screamed. "It's Midnight Ground, Helena! We can't stop this. We can't beat it. We can't even fight it. This was over before it started. And we need to go!"

Helena's mouth opened and closed a few times, but no sound came out. Her eyes were huge in the dim light of the cabin. We stood like that until she gave her head a firm shake.

"You're hurting my arm."

I looked down at my hand around Helena's arm. It was shaking and the knuckles were white. I made myself let go. She took a few more steps into the cabin and rubbed at her arm. I tried to get a grip on my terror, on the overwhelming impulse to go, and forced my arm to close the door. Helena pushed her hands into her pockets and studied the floor.

"Midnight Ground," she said, voice flat. "How sure are you about that?"

"I'm certain."

"How?"

It was my turn to study the floor. "I went to the school."

"What? I thought you didn't…" she blinked. "You chauvinistic son of a bitch. You always planned to go in there. You just didn't want me to go in there with you."

"It's a little more complicated than that," I objected.

"Do tell," she said, crossing her arms.

"It was just a theory. If I was wrong, there was no point wasting your time."

"And if you were right?"

"Then taking you in there would have been," my mind flashed on the sense of wading through rotted meat, "unconscionable. It was," I swallowed a surge of bile, "everything I could do to walk through the place. I'm not exactly the sensitive type and it was God awful. For you, it'd have been like taking a swan dive into a pit of fire."

"So you decided for me," she said, the anger almost visible around her. "You didn't have the right."

I met her eyes. "Maybe not, but I did have the experience to know. Have you ever been on Midnight Ground before?"

She gave me an expression of equal parts annoyance and anger. "No."

"I have."

That caught her off guard. "What? You never told me that."

I shivered. "It's not the kind of thing you want to reminisce about. Do you know Miguel Ortiz?"

"Is he that guy in southern California? Guides people on vision quests and that sort of thing?"

"That's him."

"I've heard of him, but we haven't met. Why?"

"He taught me some stuff a while back," I said. "He took me to a tiny patch of Midnight Ground, deep in the Mojave Desert."

"What possible purpose could that have served?"

"He told me that I should know what real evil feels like, then he pushed me onto it. Made me stay on it for five minutes."

"That's a harsh way to teach."

"The burned hand and all that. It worked. The point is that I didn't make the decision based on nothing."

"I should still kick your chauvinist ass," she said, but it wasn't convincing. "I guess that answered my next question. You know what it is, for sure. It isn't just a guess."

I nodded. "Yeah."

"You're wrong, though. It can be fought. Obviously someone fought it here."

I shook my head. "Fought, maybe, but they didn't win. It was a flawed attempt from the start and the price was way too high."

"Price?"

"They did a bloodline binding. Thirteen people offed themselves to seal the deal. And their descendants have been paying the price ever since. Abby's mother isn't the only soul in that graveyard trapped in a smoke binding. There's got to be a couple hundred of them. Even if I thought it would work, I don't have the stomach for mass suicide. Besides, we don't have the volunteers."

Helena sat on the bed. She looked like she might be sick. "Oh my god. But if the binding worked…"

"It didn't work. That's the thing. The bloodline binding did part of the job. Then there was the church on top of it. Holy ground, or as holy as a church on top of Midnight Ground can be. Together, I think it was enough to keep the evil contained. Once the town made the church into a high school…" I held my hands up.

"They changed its function. They changed its nature. They let it out."

"Exactly. So long as faithful, devoted people kept going there week after week, praying, worshipping, being all religious," I drifted off as the hamster in my head went into overdrive.

"Are you okay?" Helena asked.

"Yeah, I just, son of a bitch. I really hate this town."

"What?"

"Cavanaugh. God-damn E.J. Cavanaugh told me what was happening."

"I have no idea what you're on about."

"These dreams I've been having. I thought they were just random. Talking about mystery schools and economics. Dollars to donuts, it was E.J. Cavanaugh reaching out from his nice, safe little tomb to send a message."

Helena gave me a long-suffering look. "Could you at least try to make a little more sense?"

"Sorry," I said. "I've been having these dreams. It's always this little guy giving a lecture about mystery schools. What they are, why they fail, that sort of thing."

"So?"

"So, the whole damn congregation was part of a mystery school. Everyone who originally moved here was probably part of it, or the vast majority of them. I'd bet it was at least thirteen families of devotees. People committed enough to sacrifice themselves and their loved ones in the name of the cause. I bet they came here because of the Midnight Ground."

Helena lifted an eyebrow. "If that's true, what happened?"

"The money ran out or Cavanaugh's kid left with it. Same end result."

"No more money for upkeep and the church gets donated. Then, fast-forward fifty or sixty years and Abby gets a one way ticket to cancer," finished Helena.

"Honestly, I don't know that the binding ever really worked. I think all it ever did was limit what the demon could do."

"Demon?"

"Demon, spirit of the ground, there's some kind of consciousness that lives there. Demon is the easiest description."

"And your friends said it would take a fourth-order demon or higher to create one of those smoke bindings?"

"Yeah," I said.

Helena sat in silence for a minute. "You're right. There's nothing we can do here, not by ourselves. Maybe, if we had some help."

She looked at me with expectation.

"What?" I demanded.

"I hear the stories about you. You must know someone who owes you a favor or two."

"For something this big? Midnight Ground? Come on, nobody in their right mind would take that on."

"Are you saying all the people you know are in their right minds?"

I opened my mouth and said, "Okay, that's a fair point. Still, I don't know anyone crazy enough for this. Do *you* know anyone that would make a run at Midnight Ground?"

She shook her head. "If anyone else had asked me that, I might have said you."

"Thanks, I think."

She gave me a pained smile. "Will getting Abby away really help?"

"I don't know. I mean, yeah, I think that would help some. It'll make it harder for the demon to get at her, but it's a stopgap, at best. Sooner or later, that damn thing will kill her. Getting her out just buys her some time. Might be enough time for her to go to college, maybe have a family. "

"Like her parents?"

I didn't meet Helena's eyes. "Yeah."

Something clicked in Helena's mind. "Oh my god. Oh no."

"What?"

"Don't you see what it did by giving her cancer?"

"It's evil. I think we already established that. Demons do evil things to people."

"No, that's not what I mean. I'm talking about the chemo."

"What about the chemo?"

"It makes you sterile. She can't have kids of her own. Not biological children at any rate."

"So, she'll adopt. Lots of people do it. What's the big deal about biological—" I finally saw what Helena was getting at. "No kids means…"

"No bloodline to pass the binding along," she said. "Even if it never does another thing to her, it's already won. It just needs to wait or move on to someone else."

It took me a minute to realize something. "That's awful, and unbelievably evil, but it's not our problem."

"Adrian!"

"It's not! I feel for her. I swear that I do, but we can't help her with that."

I watched Helena grapple with that reality for about the same length of time that I did, before she bowed her head a little. It was cold, that realization, but inevitable. Doctors burned that particular bridge long before we landed on the scene.

"Look," I said, "we can keep debating the details, but taking Abby out of here is the one course of action open to us. It's all we can actually do for her."

I saw the frustration in Helena. She was a healer and Abby was in pain. The knowledge, the certainty, that she couldn't do anything had to eat at her. It ate at me. Even as a middling practitioner, I was still a wielder of significant forces. Wielding power is tricky business. It can make you believe that, push comes to shove, you have the ability to act. It lets you believe that you can alter circumstances to your favor. The damnable truth was that you could a lot of the time, but not always.

Helena's experience and knowledge dwarfed mine. It had to make it even harder for her to escape the same trap, because she'd be able to act even more often than I could. Only, there was nothing for her to do. Given some time, she might be able to improve Abby's health, though I expected that sterility thing was permanent. In the long run, it was just as much of a stopgap as my strategy. Helena wouldn't be fighting an illness, but the very will of something far older and more powerful and simply more terrible than any lone healer could overcome. I knew it, and so did she.

"I don't think your emotional blackmail strategy is going to work on Paul," said Helena.

"Why not?"

"I just have an intuition about it. You might be able to make it work if you had a couple of months to apply reason and gentle pressure. Try straight-up emotional warfare and I think he'll dig his heels in. He's formidable, in his own way."

"What makes you say that?"

I actually agreed with her assessment of his formidableness, but I was curious why she thought so.

"For starters, he's still alive and sane. He's been in proximity to potent dark magic for years. It's taken a toll, no doubt, but there's stainless steel in that man's soul."

I nodded. That sounded about right. "So what do you suggest?"

"I think we need to come clean with him, about all of it."

"You *can't* be serious."

"I don't think he'll leave if he doesn't understand the scope of the danger to Abby."

"Except he'll think we're insane. Hence my not explaining it to him already."

She shrugged. "Then we'll have to convince him."

"How do you propose we do that?"

"Show him something impossible to ignore."

"Show him magic, you mean? Just put it right out there in front of him?"

"Yes."

I shook my head. "Do I need to remind you of all the reasons why that's a terrible idea? Setting aside the whole secrecy for survival thing, he's not a spring chicken. It could give him a heart attack or an aneurysm."

Helena seemed to weigh that one for a little while. "I don't think it will. And unless you propose to kidnap Abby, I don't see an alternative with a better chance at success."

I ran a hand through my hair to buy myself a second to think. "You're going to tell him whether I agree or not, aren't you?"

"You really are brighter than people think you are," she said.

I hated exactly everything about Helena's plan. Even if we didn't kill Paul with pure shock, that didn't guarantee he'd get on board. The more likely result was that he'd tell us to get out and never come back. It's what any rational, non-magical person would do in that scenario. If he did make the leap to accepting that Helena and I could do magic, it was a much longer step to accepting curses and demons. I hated the plan because I was certain it was doomed to near-certain failure. I really hated the plan because I didn't have anything better.

"Damn it," I muttered. "I guess it'll be more convincing coming from both of us. Do you want to do the parlor tricks or should I?"

"You're better with special effects," said Helena. "Most of what I do happens inside people, not out in the world."

"Fine, I'll do it. Let's go."

She shook her head. "It's getting late and they're releasing Abby in the morning. We'll go talk to them afterwards. It'll be easier if we don't do this in a hospital anyway."

I ground my teeth in frustration. A lot of anger and even more fear were pushing me to do things as fast as possible. We needed to get clear. She was right, though. I was pretty sure the volcano of evil under the school, AKA Mount St. Atrocity, wasn't going to blow its top in the next eighteen hours. The conversation could wait until the next day. I nodded. Helena stood, rubbed at the arm I had grabbed, and went over to the door.

"Get some sleep," she said. "You look like you just ran a marathon."

Chapter 37

AFTER HELENA LEFT, I sat down on the bed and contemplated sleep. I wanted to sleep. God knew, I needed the sleep, but the idea frightened me. I could protect myself from outside influence, for the most part. I was stuck dealing with whatever was already inside my head. I'd exposed myself to some of the purest, most distilled evil on the face of the damn planet earlier that day. It had played merry hell with me and my memory of the experience was full of gaps. I didn't doubt, not for one second, that those gaps were filled with terrors that my conscious mind repressed automatically, violently, and for my own protection.

My subconscious either held a better opinion of my ability to withstand unbridled horror or it just wasn't equipped to make those kinds of decisions. If I let something unspeakable past the gates, my subconscious regurgitated it into my dreams. The lesson I never learned was to avoid allowing mind-searing awfulness to get inside my head in the first place. Maybe the nightmares were a drawer-cleaning exercise for my brain, but I believed they were my subconscious punishing me for dumbass behavior.

The idea of returning to the halls and rooms of the school in a nightmare left me in a cold sweat. My lucid dreaming skills were too rudimentary to escape a nightmare at will. I needed some activity to calm and center my mind. I looked at my packed bags. I hadn't planned on staying another day, so I hadn't set up any protections. That would give me something to do that demanded my full attention. I opened the hard case and removed the blessed chalk I'd used in Abby's hospital room. The blessed chalk wasn't a requirement. I could have used any writing implement to do what I planned to do, but chalk was easier to clean up.

I pulled the bed away from the wall until there was enough room for me to walk a full circuit around it. Someone already tried to put me in a psychic headlock. No need to give them a second opportunity while I was asleep and even more vulnerable. I considered the best approach to defense. There were always multiple solutions to stopping magical attacks. It came down to style and preferred consequences. A better person would have thrown up a defensive ring and called it a day. I'm not a better person.

The essential principles of magic are dirt-stupid simple. Everybody knows them already, even if they don't realize it. There are four elements: earth, air, fire, and water. Those were the building blocks of all magic. I'd heard it described other ways, or with other names, and some systems insisted there were actually five or even six elements. Spirit was a popular fifth element. Some called it divinity or holy light or about any other term you can apply to the transcendent. The sixth element, far less often spoken of and used, was darkness. I wasn't sure where I came down on that one.

Human nature was flawed, seemingly by design, to include temptation toward evil. Starting from that fact, it followed that practitioners *could* access darkness as a component of magic. Less clear to me was why anyone *would* access it. That kind of darkness corrupts what it touches. If you wanted to protect yourself from evil, using darkness was counterintuitive. Then again, maybe I lacked sufficient understanding of the high-level theory to properly apply darkness as a component in my own magic. Lacking that knowledge, and being on questionable terms with the holy, I stuck with the basics. Four elements got it done for countless generations of practitioners. I saw no reason to get "creative."

Methods for accessing the power in those elements were as plentiful as wheat. Everyone had a favorite, and I'd tried dozens of them over the years. I'd settled on a hodgepodge system of my own design that used combinations of runes to stand in for what would otherwise have been primitive pictograms. It was a bit like writing sentences to represent my intentions. I'd entertained the idea of just writing in English. It ought to work, in theory, but I never thought to try it when the stakes were low. Writing with runes was slow and, frankly, childlike when compared to Helena. She didn't need stand-in symbols and props. She accessed those powers directly.

The very idea made me shudder. I wouldn't trust myself with that kind of power at my fingertips. I barely trusted Helena with it. My distrust also explained why I couldn't use magic the way Helena used it. Magic depended on your state of mind. As long as I didn't believe I could wield power that way, or didn't trust that I could do so wisely, I never would. In twenty odd years of practice, I'd picked up a handful of things that I could do directly. They were flashy as hell, pretty to look at, and about as dangerous as cotton balls. That was how little I trusted myself with power. For the real stuff, I had to fall back on the slow and steady method. I drew runes.

It took me about forty-five minutes to finish a circle of runes around the bed. There was heavy emphasis on fire and water, and only the tiniest bit of earth and a middling amount of air to provide the necessary counterbalance in the magic. Earth magic did some impressive stuff, but it made me nervous. Get it wrong and you could collapse the building you were standing in or trigger an earthquake. Any of the elements could do catastrophic damage if used improperly, but I'd been through a few earthquakes in California. I'd seen the destruction they could cause. Thanks, but no thanks.

I used earth magic the way most people did, as a way to anchor the magic to the mortal coil. I wanted to keep the offensive elements of the magic strictly physical. Let your magic spill over beyond the edges of the mortal world and it could attract the attention of some nasty things. Let violent, destruction magic spill over and it could lead to those nasty things looking to have a quiet chat with you in some dark and terrible corner of creation. Again, thanks, but no thanks.

The water elements would, in essence, drown the bad vibes and intentions of anyone trying to invade my psyche. Okay, it wasn't literal drowning. It wasn't even physical water, but that was the way I conceptualized the protection. I wasn't clear on the exact nature of the interaction between my magic and the negative energy headed my way. I'd asked someone once and they talked for two solid hours. They tossed around terms like entropy, diffusion factors, and flow dynamics. Then they moved on to metaphysical concepts that gave me a splitting headache. I nodded and smiled in my utter incomprehension. Afterwards, I accepted that it worked because of reasons and left it at that.

The fire was there to make sure that anyone who took a pot-shot at me never wanted to try it again. Assuming they survived. Like I said, I'm not a better person. I like peace and calm negotiation as a first-line approach, but, when I've already been sucker punched once, I take off the gloves. In my early days, I'd frequently left out one or more of the elements in my attempts to build magic of one kind or another. The results were often substandard crap. On a few occasions, the results were positively terrifying. Without all four elements interacting and balancing each other, you just couldn't anticipate the outcome. So, I'd included air to keep things in balance. Plus, fire needs air to burn good and hot. I also used it to help direct and contain the flow of fire. No need to burn down a forest when I just wanted to set some jerk on fire.

The sustained concentration and effort did what I hoped it would do. It pushed me over into the land of exhaustion. If I was lucky, I'd skip straight past dreaming and into the black nothingness of the deepest levels of sleep. I grabbed the hard case and slid it back under the bed, dropped the nylon bag on the floor, and collapsed face-down on the bed. Before I drifted off to sleep, I felt the pillow shift. Then a warm fuzzy body curled up against the back of my head. Lil's purr rumbled against my head like a vibration, rather than a sound. It put me under in less than five seconds.

"Ah, Hartworth and Lil. I'm so glad you could rejoin us," said a voice.

I blinked a few times and took in my surroundings. I was back in the auditorium. The small man on the stage gave me a brief nod and turned his attention to the rest of the audience. He looked to be gearing up to give another lecture or maybe to make a student feel stupid. I looked around the auditorium and experienced a flickering double-vision. One moment, every seat was filled, the next there were just the cold, smooth, marble walls of a very small room. Before he could open his mouth, I spoke.

"Enough, Cavanaugh. I know who you are."

Cavanaugh closed his mouth and lowered his head. The illusion he'd crafted vanished. We faced each other from about two feet apart. He met my eyes for a brief moment and looked away. I caught of a flicker of shame that ran bone deep.

"How did you know?" he asked.

"I pieced it together. A church on Midnight Ground. Thirteen suicides right before construction finished on it. The dreams. Even someone as slow as me was bound to figure it out eventually."

"I suppose so. I expected you to interpret the dreams as your undermind trying to convey information."

"Undermind?"

"Oh, yes, you call it something else. Your subconscious, is it?"

"Yeah."

He frowned. "Undermind is more accurate. Subconscious suggests it's subordinate to the waking mind. That is an obviously false, if popular, axiom. I'm rather surprised your companion didn't alert you to the deception."

I glanced at Dream Lil. She watched Cavanaugh with her blood ruby eyes for a moment, and then turned her head toward me. I knew it wasn't actually possible for a cat to shrug, even one the size of a large van, but that was the exact impression she gave me. She lay down on the floor with her legs curled under her and her head up. It put her uninjured ear about on face level with me. Jesus, she was big in the dream world.

"She probably figured as long as I was getting good information, there was no need," I guessed. "I like your bomb shelter. Too bad you couldn't be bothered to make one for everybody."

He shook his head. "I didn't know until very nearly the end of my life. It was too late by then for most of those poor lost souls already trapped in the smoke bindings. I warned the others. I begged them to flee this accursed place before my vanity doomed them as well."

"Did they?"

"Many did. Others stayed. It didn't matter in the long run. I underestimated what we faced. I had no conception of its power. Our order had battled demons, locked them away forever, but what lives in the Midnight Ground is beyond anything we'd ever seen before. So many died for my mistake and it was all for nothing."

"You said it didn't matter in the long run. Why didn't it matter if they scattered?"

"It killed them anyway. Or it called them back. Or it tricked them into coming back. One by one, they all came back. Or their children and grandchildren came back in total ignorance of what waited for them here. You should take the woman and leave. It won't let Abby go. She's the last link."

"And when she's dead?"

He gave me a look like I was pretending to be an ignorant child. "You've been on Midnight Ground before. Twice. I can see it on you. You know what it is. It is hatred, agony, and power. It will do what those things always do. It will rend and destroy anything in its domain."

I needed to ask Cavanaugh something. I knew it. I just didn't know what. There was some piece of things that didn't fit together. Some element in the timeline of events that didn't mesh up.

"It will rend and destroy anything in its domain, you said."

"Yes?"

"Then," I held up a hand for silence, the question congealing in my mind. "Then how did you ever manage to build the church, let alone the town, in the first place?"

Cavanaugh gave me a smile as empty as Death's heart. "How? It let us build. It was biding its time. I expect it planned to wait until the numbers in town had grown sufficiently large to suit its appetite. It just hadn't anticipated the binding. You are familiar with the power of blood bindings?"

"In theory."

"It wasn't prepared for that. It's had better than a century to make up for that error. Once its full power is unleashed, this bomb shelter, as you call it, won't mean anything. I merely forestalled my fate. I had hoped that, perhaps, you might know or stumble onto a solution. From what I have gleaned, the situation has not changed since my day. There are but one, perhaps two, in all of humankind who might overcome the Midnight Ground."

"Three, but yes."

"All otherwise engaged, I assume."

"So it seems."

"It is as though the hand of Providence itself shields this evil from destruction."

I blinked. "Providence? You believe in God? Last I checked, he frowns on suicide."

"We," he started. "No, I believed that death in this cause, even by our own hands, would be viewed as sacrifice, not suicide. Vanity. My vanity damned us all. As I said, you must take the woman and leave this place while you can. Time grows short."

"We are leaving. Helena and I are going to talk to Paul. Try to convince him to take Abby away from here. Then we're going."

Cavanaugh tilted his head at me. "No, not the healer. She has a divine purpose to fulfill. She will survive regardless."

"Then who are you talking about?"

"The dark-haired one. Your lover, I suppose. You call her Marcy."

Chapter 38

ONE SECOND I WAS STARING AT CAVANAUGH in stunned disbelief. The next I was slamming him against the wall. His little round glasses spun across the room as his head smacked against the marble with a dull thunk. I shook him by the tweed lapels.

"What the fuck are you talking about?" He didn't answer immediately. I shook him again, hard. "Answer me, God damn it! What the fuck are you talking about?"

Cavanaugh looked up at me in surprise. He shook his head, grabbed my wrists, and pulled my hands away from his lapels as if I were no stronger than a child.

"Come now, Mr. Hartworth. Violence is hardly becoming of a gentleman, even as dubious a gentleman as you. It is also utterly pointless against me. I don't have a body. What you see before you is merely a façade devised by your own mind to facilitate communication. I am a soul. You can no more cause me physical harm than you can drink the ocean."

Cavanaugh's glasses simply appeared on his nose again, as pristine as the day they were made. He patted me on the shoulder.

"I suppose," he offered, "that I handled that rather badly."

"You said I needed to take Marcy and go. If she's in danger, why doesn't she just leave?"

"Because she can't, as you well know. Unless," Cavanaugh's eyes went rather wide, "you don't understand the nature of your relationship with her."

"What are you talking about?"

Cavanaugh's eyes moved back and forth, like he was speed-reading something. His lips turned down and he squinted at me. He took a deep breath.

"You must understand that I'm not an expert on such matters. Your own lack of knowledge is, in itself, telling. I don't think I can explain it to you."

"The hell you can't," I said.

"Let me append my statement. I don't believe I am permitted to explain it to you. What I can say is that she is, for the time being, connected to you. So long as you remain here, she is compelled to remain nearby. If you remain here, if you die here, she will be subject to the same fate as the rest of us. You must go, for her sake and your own. Once you leave the town limits, you'll be safe."

"If I *can* leave. I tried a couple of times already and got derailed both times. Your handiwork?"

"You give me too much credit. Even in this form and from the comparative safety of my tomb, my actual power is limited. I wasn't powerful that way in life and death has not altered that fact. Now, for God's sake man, get away from here. Take Abby, if her grandfather will allow it, but don't let yourself become a victim of my mistakes."

Cavanaugh put a hand on my chest and pushed. Where he had crashed against the marble walls and stopped, I passed through them. I tumbled through the air, light and dark whirling around me in kaleidoscopic fury. I felt something seize the back of my shirt and haul me back down to hard earth. I hung a good four or five feet off the ground. I craned my neck around and saw Lil. The back of my shirt was in her powerful jaws.

"I don't suppose you know where Marcy is?" I asked.

Lil stood stock-still for a moment. Her damaged ear twitched, one, two, three times. She gathered herself and bounded into the air. Light and dark swirled around me again, but without the nauseating feeling of spinning out of control. Lil landed as gently as a shadow falling on water. She lowered her head until my feet touched down and I could stand on my own. I smiled up at her and rubbed the spot above her nose. She let loose with one of those earth-trembling purrs.

I looked around to get my bearings and found myself, once again, in pure whiteness. It was broken only by the form of a golden cage. Marcy was inside the cage, seated at a table and playing chess with someone.

"What the hell?" I said.

I started walking toward the cage, anger building inside of me at the sight of Marcy trapped that way. I broke into a jog. I didn't have a plan, just a goal. Get her out of that cage.

"Marcy!"

Her head whipped toward me. Something like panic swept across her face.

"Adrian, no! Don't touch the bars!"

I skidded to a halt and nearly fell into the bars. I only avoided it by falling backwards, painfully, onto my ass. Marcy sagged down into the chair.

"Ow," I grumbled. "Care to explain?"

"The bars are there for my protection. The angel brought me here," she said, then gave me a quizzical look. "How did you find me?"

I hiked a finger over my shoulder. "She brought me."

The person across from Marcy bolted out his chair. "Mother of God, what is that?"

I turned my head and peered at the man. He was young, lean, and bearded. He looked vaguely familiar, but I couldn't place him.

"That's Lil," I said and stood up.

"Adrian," whispered Marcy. "She's— That's—do you know who she is?"

"Um," I said. "Lil?"

"She's—" started Marcy.

Lil made a noise so low that it barely registered in my ears, but I felt it behind my eyes. That noise frightened me more than anything I'd ever heard before. I looked over my shoulder at the enormous, black, feline shape. Lil's gaze was fixed on Marcy. The message was clear. *Keep your mouth shut, or I'll shut it for you.*

"Alright," said Marcy in quiet voice. "Your secret to tell, if you wish."

I turned my eyes back to Marcy.

She shrugged at me. "We all play by some set of rules. Be careful, Adrian. She's powerful and dangerous."

I glanced back at Lil to see how this information would be met. The enormous figure sat on her haunches and began to lick a paw. God, I didn't even understand female cats. No wonder I was such a disaster with human women. I rubbed at my forehead.

"She adopted me. Honestly, the whole thing is sort of complicated. I'm still trying to figure out the details. I guess that doesn't matter now. Are you safe here?"

Marcy averted her eyes. "Yes."

Dammit, I thought. "But?"

"It won't protect me if the demon breaks free."

"You mean, as long as I'm in town."

"What makes you say that?" She asked, all cautious hesitance.

"Cavanaugh let it slip. Something about you being connected to me. You can't get clear if I stick around?"

She sighed. "Yes, but that doesn't matter. Abby is what matters. You have to help her or she's as good as dead."

"I can't help her. I can help you. I can leave."

Marcy stood with great care and purpose before she fixed me with the hardest look I'd ever seen on her face.

"I swear to God, abandon that girl in my name and you will never see me again."

She meant it.

"Marcy, I don't know what else to do. I can't beat this thing in a fight. I can't break her connection to this awful town. I'm not even sure I can get Abby away from here short of kidnapping her, and I'm pretty damn sure that won't end well for anyone. What else can I do that helps anyone, except leave?"

Her expression softened a little. "You'll think of something."

I hung my head. "I'm pretty sure I won't. I haven't so far and according to Everett Jackass Cavanaugh, this is all coming down very soon. I'm out of my league here."

"You'll think of something," said Marcy with an utter confidence that I knew had no basis in fact.

"Sure," I said. "Yeah. I'll think of something."

Marcy tipped her head to one side and seemed to listen to something. She gave me a little smile. "I love you, you know."

"I love you, too."

The bearded man looked back and forth between us. "Will someone please explain to me what on God's green earth is going on? This isn't what I expected at all."

Marcy laughed a little. "Things are a bit complex at the moment, but I expect everything will get sorted out in short order. He'll be heading back soon," she said, tipping her head at me. "This is probably your last chance to send a message."

The bearded man gave me a long look. "Tell her to be braver than me."

"Tell who?" I asked.

The man just said, "You'll know."

The noise of a tolling bell crashed around us. Marcy's head whipped back and forth, trying to identify where the sound came from or why it happened.

"What was that?" The bearded man asked.

"Heh. That was the sound of someone having a bad day," I answered with a grin. "A really bad day."

Marcy quirked an eyebrow at me. "Have you done something wicked, dear?"

"Of course not. I just set a trap that will do something awful and vengeful to anyone trying to do me harm. I can't help it if people wander around setting off traps."

"The bell?"

"It's my internal cue. Time to go, I guess."

Lil padded up next me, impossibly silent on her huge feet, and gave my shoulder a light bump. I lurched sideways a few steps and it took an effort not to fall down. Marcy watched me through the cage bars, her face ageless and sad.

"Don't worry about me," she said. "Help the girl."

I nodded, but didn't say anything. She'd have heard the lie in my voice. If it came down to a choice between saving Marcy or damning her through some impotent attempt to save Abby, I was pretty sure I'd save Marcy. Maybe it wasn't a noble choice, but neither was sacrificing an innocent while you do something knowingly stupid to try to save another innocent. If that meant a lifetime of silence, I'd learn to live with it. I lived with worse.

"You'll remember to tell her?" asked the man.

I looked at him again, trying to see the face behind the beard, but it was too thick. "Yes, I'll remember."

"Appreciate it," he said.

I wanted to procrastinate and keep talking to Marcy, but Lil hovered impatiently. There was something, or someone, that needed attention back in the real world. Marcy and I traded a brief smile and then I put my hand on Lil's side.

My eyes opened and I experienced the inevitable moment of confusion as the subconscious cedes control to the conscious. There was always a second or two when the handoff was going on where it felt like nothing was behind the wheel. That sensation unnerved me. My conscious mind locked down control and started noting sensory input. The blanket was rough against my hands. It was too warm in the cabin. I forgot to turn the air conditioning on before I dropped off the night before. I felt groggier than I should have. Maybe those odd meetings in the dreamspace didn't count as REM sleep. Oh, I also heard the soothing sounds of a fire crackling and the screams of someone who tried to take a cheap shot at me. There were worse ways to start the day.

Chapter 39

I ROLLED OFF THE BED and glanced at the runes on the floor. The pure white chalk had turned a tan color that I associated with pancakes. That was enough to give me pause. A color change like that meant the protective magic I set up came under serious strain. No small-time dabbler could have lobbed an attack that serious. Walking out the door could be risky. Then again, most people lost touch with concentration while they were on fire. I decided it was probably a low-risk move and walked outside.

The smell of burned synthetic material hit me first, harsh and acidic, and then the sulfur stink of burned hair. Beneath all of that, I caught a faintly sweet smell of charred skin. I did my best to ignore the smell as I looked at the figure rolling around on the ground, screaming and trying to extinguish the last of the flames. Parts of his t-shirt were melted and looked to be fused to his chest and back. His left arm was charred black from the back of his hand to where the shirt still bubbled near his shoulder. He'd probably thrown that arm in the way to protect his face. Half the hair on his head was burned off to the scalp, which was blistered in half a dozen places. He was still screaming, batting at the liquefied material of his shirt with his right hand.

Between the burns and the thrashing, it took me a little while to figure out who I was looking at. I scowled down at the figure when I recognized the man. It didn't make any sense, though. He didn't have any power of his own or, if he did, certainly not enough to account for the chalk inside. If he had that much juice, I'd have sensed it. Maybe not during the fight, there was a lot going on, but definitely when he'd confronted me at Connor's. I'd been calm then, more than calm enough to sense any serious power around the guy.

"Hello, Tucker," I said in a casual, conversational tone. "That looks painful."

He screamed and rolled some more. As much as I loathed the idea, I was going to have to help him if I wanted to get any kind of information. I went back inside, got out the chalk, and scrawled a much simpler set of runes on the floor. It only took me a minute or two. It probably seemed longer to Tucker, but you just can't rush magic. There was a snapping sound outside and brief blast of arctic-level cold came through the door for a second. Tucker didn't stop screaming immediately, but it tapered off. I went back to the door and leaned against the frame. Tucker lay sprawled on the ground. A thin layer of ice coated the man. I noticed it was melting fast in the heat. What a pity. Tucker whimpered and twitched.

"Tucker," I said and snapped my fingers a few times. "Tucker!"

He lifted his head a little and gazed through a haze of pain in my general direction. His eyes came into focus and I understood what had happened. Acidic, alien anger rippled out from him. I shook my head. Tucker wanted his vengeance and apparently didn't care about the price of getting it. He traded away a lot to give the thing inside him a place to stay. It had probably burned out a big part of his free will, huge chunks of his memories and personality, and certainly a part of his soul. Most human beings were only designed to carry one consciousness, one life essence. To let something in, you had to sacrifice parts of that consciousness and life essence. I'd underestimated Tucker's hate.

"You did something stupid, Tucker, but it's not too late to come back from it."

"You have failed," said something with Tucker's voice.

"I'm not talking to you, squatter. I'm talking to the person. Tucker, can you hear me?"

I gave it a full thirty count before Tucker, or what was left of the real Tucker, finally surfaced. "Kill you. Son of bitch. Burned me."

"Yeah, but I haven't damned you. If you don't get that thing out of you, though, you will be damned. You won't go to Heaven or Hell. You won't be reborn. You'll just drift on the edge of life, forever."

"Lying," said the real Tucker. "Kill you."

"Yes, yes, we've covered that. Tucker, I'll help you get rid of it, but you have to want it."

Tucker fell silent and the acidic anger of the demon inside him blanketed the area. I'd sort of expected it to go that way. It almost always did when someone invited a demon inside. Still, Tucker was technically human and I'd had to try. The demon pushed Tucker's charred body to its feet. Tucker was probably screaming in agony somewhere inside. It snarled at me. It was a grotesque, animal sound that human vocal cords should never have been able to produce.

"You have failed, conjurer."

Then the demon did something I hadn't expected. It ran straight at me. Well, ran probably isn't the word. It blurred in my direction, and I felt it slam Tucker's shoulder into my chest. As I flew back into the cabin, legs just missing the bed, in the half-second before the pain slammed home, I wondered how many ribs had just been cracked. Then I hit the far wall. There was a burst of red and white in my eyes and the burn on my back roared in agony. I don't remember crashing to the floor. I must have, gravity being an unrepentant smack-daddy and all, but it was lost in the pain.

When I came to, after the initial shock of not finding myself dead, I tried to look around. Moving my head sent electric shocks sparking over my nervous system. I froze. What if that damn thing broke my neck? The immediate fear of that passed when pain signals from my extremities reached my battered brain. Whiplash was the more likely culprit. I heard steps and forced myself to look toward the door. The bed obscured most of what was on the other side, but I saw a singed pant leg. I had to find a way to defend myself. There was no time for magic and I was in too much pain to put up more than a token fight. I saw the hard case under the bed. I stretched my hand out for it. Tucker took another step into the cabin. My fingers touched the smooth plastic of the case and slid off. The handle was on the other side.

"Too late for you, conjurer. Too late by far," said the thing inside Tucker.

Lil materialized from one of the shadows beneath the bed and walked over to sniff at the hand I had on the hard case. She looked back at me, her eyes giving off a dim, green luminescence. She looked from my face, to my hand, then to Tucker's legs.

"Go," I whispered. "Get out of here."

Lil seemed to find that advice as unimpressive as most of my behaviors. She walked out from beneath the bed and sat down in front of Tucker's boots. I could smell the char, the chemical stink of the burned shirt, and the uniquely awful scent of burned hair. It was harder to hold down the vomit with my body screaming and my head ringing. I stared at the cat, horrified at her behavior. She might be powerful and dangerous in the world of spirit and dreams, but in the material world she was just a cat. I expected that a boot or a gun or a car would kill her as easily as any other cat.

"Lil, no," I croaked.

"A pet, conjurer," said the demon inside Tucker, its voice gleeful. "I'll kill the tiny beast first, so you can watch."

I watched the demon draw back one of Tucker's booted feet and it blurred toward the cat.

"No!" I screamed.

Lil didn't move. She didn't flinch. She just let out a tiny little hiss. Invisible force crashed into Tucker and flung him bodily from the cabin. There was a sound like a wet canvas bag hitting something outside and then there was silence. Lil stood, stretched, yawned, and then meandered back toward me.

She patted at my cheek with a paw. "Mrew."

"Yeah, I'm okay. Remind me not to piss you off too much."

Lil sat and watched me with her always inscrutable kitty-cat expression until I started acting like I meant to stand up. At that point, she jumped up onto the bed and watched in apparent interest. It hurt a lot and took a couple tries, but I managed to get to my feet. I stumbled over to the door and looked out. I saw where Tucker had hit a huge old tree. There was a wet smear on it, but no body to be seen.

"Damn," I muttered.

I didn't necessarily wish Tucker dead, but it would have uncomplicated things. I had the feeling that, as long as blood was flowing in Tucker's body, the demon could make that body do just about anything it wanted. That definitely wasn't good for me. It probably wasn't good for Paul or Abby either. In fact, dread danced inside me as the implications of the demon's words hit me. It told me I had failed. I lurched to the nightstand and grabbed my phone. It was almost noon. Abby was supposed to get released in the morning. If she'd gotten turned loose first thing, she was clear of the protection the room provided. She was in the open.

I fumbled at the phone, trying to dial Helena. My hands shook so much from the pain and the fear that it took me four tries. It was only later that I remembered I could have simply dialed her from my recent calls list. Pain and fear were always the enemies of rational thought. I listened in agonized impatience as the ringing went unanswered on the other end. There was a telltale click and I got transferred to voicemail. I hung up and redialed, manually, and waited again as the phone rang. I was shunted to voicemail, again. The case of the phone creaked and made a little pop as my hand tightened around it.

I glared down at the phone and tried Paul's number. I tried that number three times. Same results. The dread inside me evolved into full-blown fear that aimed for stratospheric heights. What if they were hurt? What if they were dead? My mind shrank back from anything even remotely connected to that idea. Whatever was going on, I needed to get to them. Where were they? Not the hospital, I reasoned. If something happened there, they'd have called the sheriff. Barnes might not love me very much, but Patty would have given me a call out of courtesy. Odds were good that Helena would have shown up in the morning to be helpful while they checked Abby out. She'd have engaged Abby and Paul in chit-chat to make the process less aggravating.

Paul would have invited her to come get a look at the new place. I knew that's what he would have done because it's what I would have done. Helena had been kind to Abby and he'd have wanted to repay that kindness in some way. Extending her hospitality wasn't much, but it was something he could do. They would have gone back to the cottage and then, I blanked. What had happened? Almost noon, I thought. More than enough time for Tucker to do something there and come back for me when I didn't show up.

I grabbed my keys off the nightstand. I needed to get there. I got all of two steps before I realized that might have been the plan. Provoke me into action before I was ready. *Think it through*, I demanded of myself. My brain was still trying to get its bearings. My body was reporting pain from everywhere. *Don't rush headlong into anything*, said the voice of cold reason.

I forced myself to put the keys in my pocket and put a hand on the wall.

"Take a minute," I said out loud. "Just take a minute."

Chapter 40

I BEAT DOWN THE IMPULSE to race to Paul and Abby's new cottage. I lashed mercilessly at my psyche to process information and not just react to it. They didn't answer their phones. That meant, if Tucker didn't just murder them because he could, they'd been incapacitated. Maybe they were only restrained, but maybe they were hurt. If they were hurt, they'd need more help than I could give. Based on the pain in my chest, it was possible that I needed medical attention. I didn't think any of my ribs were outright broken, but I'd have bet at least a few were cracked. It hurt to breathe. That was a problem I didn't need on top of my already diminished lung capacity. Fear threatened to overwhelm reason. Images of Helena, Paul and Abby with broken necks, or bleeding out, kept crawling out of the darkest reaches of my imagination.

"Think, damn it. You've got time to think."

The word time set off an intuition. I did have time. Abby wasn't dead, yet, because I was still breathing. The inhabitant of the Midnight Ground wouldn't have sent its errand boy if it were free. That walking nightmare would have shown up personally to subject me to every excruciating thing it ever dreamed up. It might have Abby, and *that* thought was enough to make my stomach do ugly things, but she was alive. It probably wasn't keeping her around for any kind of sociopathic torture or mind games. From the very beginning, the demon of the Midnight Ground had acted with cold, systematic ruthlessness. It spent better than a century murdering its way through the ranks of Cavanaugh's mystery school and their descendants. In all likelihood, it had her. Yet, it hadn't finished the job. Why hadn't it finished the job?

Maybe, I thought, *it hadn't because it couldn't*. At least, it couldn't finish the job immediately. It wouldn't take her if it didn't plan to kill her. What prevented it from just offing Abby at its leisure? After all, it had managed to kill people a hell of a lot farther away than down the street. It had to be something about her, specifically, that kept it at bay. She was the last one. Cavanaugh said as much himself.

"The last one," I muttered out loud.

My intuition screamed at me that I was on the right track. *Okay, self*, I asked, *what makes Abby special*? She's an immensely powerful psychic. She's spent her life in a house that shielded her. *No*, I thought, and scratched that from the list. That had to have been true of other people the demon had gotten to before now. I came up blank. That was it. She was an immensely powerful psychic. Powerful enough, in fact, to have managed to fend off at least some of what was coming at her, but that wasn't enough. The last one, I thought again.

"Holy shit! She's the last one."

My battered brain finally coughed up the answer. It all went back to the basic principles of magic. Things have to be in balance or it doesn't work right. The power of the bloodline binding had been spread over thirteen families. At first, that power would have been negligible in any given person. Start offing everyone who carries it, though, and that power doesn't just go away. It redistributes itself to the rest of the people. At that moment, wherever she was, Abby was holding the full power of that binding inside of her. That was why the messenger-boy demon had set the house on fire. I'd have bet that its boss *couldn't* come at Abby directly. In fact, almost everything it had sent at her over the years had probably missed the mark. Either the binding just slapped it down or diverted it somewhere.

If that were true, though, then why was she sick? I flashed back to the feeling that Abby both was and wasn't under attack. I thought back to the graveyard. I hadn't been paying much attention to it at the time, but there was no smoke binding over Abby's father's grave. His family wasn't part of the binding. They were just people and...

"And people get cancer," I told the wall.

It had gotten smart. It had stopped trying to get at Abby through direct action. It took its shot at the part of her that was her father. That was the part that all her psychic power was protecting. The part not automatically defended by the binding. Try to hit her with a bolt of lightning, the binding diverted it. Get some cells coded with her father's genetic material to misbehave, the binding probably didn't react. It wasn't overt enough. Cells reproduce and why worry if some are reproducing faster. I shook my head. It still didn't all add up. Once Tucker turned to the dark side, he should have been able to slit Abby's throat without a problem. Unless the binding read the house guest in Tucker's body as a mere extension of what lived in the Midnight Ground. That had to be it.

Tucker the human being might have murdered *me* in my sleep, but he probably wasn't wired to murder a teenage girl. The thing inside him would have had to take control and the blood binding wouldn't allow for it. So Tucker the sock puppet couldn't do it. The thing living in the Midnight Ground couldn't do it. I blinked a few times. No, it would have to be able to do it or there wouldn't be any point in taking Abby. So it just can't do it, yet, but soon. What would need to change? I reached up and rubbed my eyes. They ached from combination of the impact and the light coming through the window.

"Light," I said, realization dawning. "It's waiting for darkness, when it'll be at its strongest. Strong enough to overcome the full force of the binding."

It might not try to kill her as soon as the sun went down, but I doubted it would wait very long. I did some guessing. I probably had seven hours, give or take, until nightfall. It wasn't a lot of time, but it might be time enough to get Abby clear. At least I didn't need to figure out where they were holding her. The trick was going to be convincing myself that I had the nerve to go back into the school. Still, I had precious time to work with and that meant I could get help. I dialed the person I was sure would help, especially since I had a real live human culprit she could handcuff.

That thought made me smile, which lasted about as long as it took for Patty's phone to go to voicemail. I tried again and got her voicemail a second time. I started shaking my head in a reflexive negation of reality.

"No. No. No, this is not happening," I said.

I started to dial 911 and stopped myself from hitting the 1 a second time. I had a working theory, but I had no facts. I didn't know that Paul and Helena were hurt or in distress. I didn't see

Abby get abducted. No one was going to get dispatched based on my instincts. I stood there in indecision, haunted again by the images of everyone I knew dead or dying. I hated the thought of leaving Helena and Paul without immediate aid, but I had to get Patty or the sheriff involved as soon as humanly possible. I called myself ten kinds of stupid for not getting the man's card. The sheriff's office was going to have to be my first stop.

I knew the drive was only about fifteen minutes. I kept reminding myself of that for every subjective hour that crawled by on the drive. I probably could have done seventy the whole way, but I was certain that such behavior would inevitably lead to me either getting into a car accident or killing some innocent bystander. I was desperate, but not quite desperate enough to create collateral damage in a mad bid to get to the sheriff's office five seconds sooner. After all, something exactly like that, only more senseless, was exactly what had set me off on the mad journey that was my adult life. *I had time*, I reminded myself. I could spare the fifteen minutes to collect Patty or the sheriff. Just because it didn't feel that way didn't make it less true. I parked in front of the sheriff's office in a more or less legal fashion. I was mostly between the lines. I got out and headed for the front door when a man said my name.

"Mr. Hartworth?"

I stopped short and turned. A pear-shaped man with a big soda in his hand gave me a perplexed smile. I dug deep.

"Mr. Brubaker," I said. "Nice to see you again."

"I heard you were still knocking around in town."

"Yeah," I said, feigning normalcy. "You know how it is when you travel. I got sidetracked. I'll probably be gone by tomorrow."

Gone. Dead. Basically the same, I decided.

"Oh yeah, I lost a week in Virginia Beach that way once. The car treating you okay?"

Impatience flared inside me like thermite fire, but I kept things as casual as I could.

"Oh yeah. Still running fine. I've got no complaints."

Eddie Brubaker gave the car a wistful look and I heard him say something under his breath. "Lot of fun in that car."

I gave him a little tip of the head. "I don't mean to rush off, but there was something I needed to talk to Patty about. Follow up."

"Right," said Eddie. "The bar fight. Nasty business. I won't keep you."

He gave me a wave, which seemed utterly ridiculous from a distance of three feet away, and then yelled down the street.

"Tim!"

I watched as he hurried down the street toward a pale teenager that seemed familiar. It took me a good five seconds to place him as the door greeter at Connor's. He looked even more tired than he had at the store, but he'd probably been going into that damnable school on a regular basis. That'd be enough to exhaust anyone. Tim gave the math teacher a weary look and then forced a smile. I watched them talk for a moment, imagining a conversation about late homework. Then, urgency reasserted itself. I went into the building and took the first two steps up to the second floor in a big, hurried lunge. My aching body howled in agony and told me to stop doing stupid things. I took the rest of the stairs at a more sedate pace that befitted my walking wounded status. I reached the landing and stopped short outside the door. A life filled with trouble gave me reliable instincts about the emotional tenor of a place. There was something very wrong inside the office.

I braced myself mentally and pushed open the door, fully expecting something to either jump out at me with a machete or for someone to open fire. Neither thing happened. I looked around. Patty was sitting at her desk with her hands clasped together. She wasn't crying as I came through the door, but it looked like she'd done a bit of it in the last hour or so. She looked haunted. I stared at her for a long time, stunned at the sight. I tried to imagine what could be terrible enough to set a woman that strong to tears and came up empty. I gathered what little calm I had left and stepped into the office. I closed the door behind me. Patty looked up and registered that another human being was in the room. I don't think she knew who I was at first. That was bad. I needed help, and she looked like she was verging on catatonia.

"Patty," I said. "Are you alright?"

She looked away and then back at me. She nodded down at her desk. "He left this for you."

"He who? Left what?"

Patty's gaze went through me, as though I were a ghost. I clenched my teeth and walked over to her desk. There was a folded sheet of printer paper sitting on the desk. In tiny block letters, I saw my name written on it. I picked up the sheet of paper and unfolded it.

I can't help them either.

Barnes

I blinked down at the paper for a second. "I don't understand."

Patty looked up at me, her face pale and drawn in profound pain. That sense of solidity and total focus in the present that always surrounded her was gone. She felt ephemeral. I worried that any loud noise would scatter her like dandelion fluff. She pulled her hands apart and something dropped onto the desk. Whatever it was, it fell face-down. All I saw was a rectangular patch of black leather. I noted that Patty's hands remained curled like arthritic claws. I wondered how long she'd been holding the thing.

She didn't move to turn the object over, just stared through me with that expression of pain. I reached out and flipped the object over. It was a six-pointed star enclosed in a ring, made of a pale, silvery metal. Dry, brown splotches marred the metal surface. The word *Sheriff* was stamped into the metal. I yanked my hand back when I figured out what I was looking at. The badge was splattered in blood.

Chapter 41

THAT SUDDEN MOTION OF MY HAND sent ripples of pain across my back, up my neck and across my skull. Things got hazy around the edges as I inched very near to the limits of my tolerance. The pain was so severe that it obliterated anything like coherent thought. Eventually, a thought broke through the surface of that dark lake of agony. The pain wasn't the problem. The accumulation of injuries was the problem. The human body was a remarkable healing machine, capable of fixing a mind-boggling number of injuries. It just needed time, which I'd denied my body. Add new injuries before old injuries were fully healed, and the pain built up at interest rates that would make credit card company executives blush in shame. I gave the pain a minute to recede.

I gestured at the badge and started to ask if someone killed the sheriff before I remembered the paper clutched in one of my hands. *I can't help them either*, it said. I looked from the badge to the note in my hand. I did the math and the answer was obvious, if horrible and beyond sad. I skipped past the first, awkward sentences of the conversation. I didn't see any need to make Patty say out loud what I already knew. It wouldn't make it more real than the blood-splattered badge. Barnes killed himself. So often, the why of any given suicide went down as something of a locked-box mystery, only the locked box was the inaccessible mind of the victim. I'd much rather have been confronted with the haunting questions, but I knew the miserable answer to why already. It was despair and helplessness.

Barnes was faced with a situation he could not alter. The mass death of the people he swore to protect was the only apparent outcome. Why wouldn't he think that? I'd told him so, repeatedly. He couldn't stop it or even mitigate the damage. He couldn't evacuate the town because there was no tangible threat. There was no federal authority he could appeal to for help. All he got was me. I felt a swell of shame. The man had needed hope. He needed a life preserver in a storm he didn't comprehend. I threw him a barbell weighted with the inevitability of failure. I thought it went deeper than that, though. If everything did go to hell and a bunch of people died on his watch, Barnes did not want to have to live with it afterwards. I couldn't blame him for that. My plan had been to run like hell.

I looked at Patty. "When?"

She spoke in flat, mechanical tones. "Early this morning. He called me. Told me he thought I'd be a good sheriff. He said goodbye. I knew something was wrong. I told him not to do anything until I got there. I tried to keep him on the line, but he hung up. I called him again and again, but he never picked up. I drove as fast as I could, but when I got there," her voice failed for a moment, then picked up in the same monotone. "He did it before I could get there. He was in his uniform. He used his service pistol. He left the badge on a table with a note for me. It said, 'This is yours now.' Like that mattered somehow."

I was acutely aware of the clock ticking on the wall. Six-and-a-half hours sounded like a long time to most people. Most people were stupid about a lot of things. I knew just how fast six hours could evaporate and I felt it happening, second by precious second. *Tick-tock*, and maybe Helena finished bleeding out. *Tick-tock* and maybe Abby was screaming in a dark room somewhere. *Tick-tock*. All those maybes, but the only thing I knew for sure was that a person I liked, someone I respected, was bleeding to death emotionally right in front of me. I hated Barnes a little for what it did to Patty, no matter how understandable his decision was in other respects.

I looked around and pulled a chair over to sit facing Patty across her desk. I thought she was probably using the desk as a kind of mental shield. It was normalcy. It was a symbol of her professionalism. As long as she sat behind it, she could put on her deputy face and do her best to ignore what she was feeling. I had no idea what to say to her. Give me a supernatural crisis and I can either figure out what to do or when to cut out. Give me an emotional crisis and I'm as useless as the next man, which means pretty damned useless.

"You couldn't have stopped him," I said after a while.

"You don't know that," she said, her voice going flatter and even more mechanical.

"I read somewhere that there are two kinds of suicide attempts. One kind is the cry for help. Those are the ones where people do something knowing they'll be found or making sure someone has time to get to them," I said, positive Patty knew these facts better than I did. "The other kind is when there's nothing anyone can do, unless you happen to walk into the situation right as it's going down. Those people don't want help or take half measures. Sheriff Barnes didn't take half measures."

I looked at the blood splattered badge. I was struck by how small and how flimsy it looked. It was hard to believe that anything so small conferred so much power. That little piece of metal allowed men like Barnes to detain, to question, to investigate, and even to use lethal force against fellow citizens. Yet, as it sat on the desk, I thought that it wouldn't take much more than some pliers to mangle it beyond recognition. Then, I was struck by how something even smaller took all that apparent power, along with everything else, away from Barnes. We were so fragile compared with the forces we could bring to bear on each other or ourselves. I wondered how anyone ever managed to survive into adulthood, let alone managed to die of old age.

Patty sat there, said nothing, and I bit back impatience. Tick-tock. Tick-tock. *Repent Harlequin*, thundered the voice of wild inappropriateness in the back of my head. I felt another stab of shame, followed by a deeper stab of guilt. I knew that I hadn't killed the sheriff. He must have been on the verge for a while, but I couldn't help but wonder what role I played in his tragedy. I accepted that he might not have done it without my involvement, but I also acknowledged that he might have done it anyway. To call the human heart hideously complicated underestimated the truth by orders of magnitude, and I'd probably never know for sure where my influence fit into his decision. If I survived the next few hours, I expected my conscience to spend a lot of time poking at that uncertainty.

"Maybe so," said Patty, snapping me out of my dark thoughts.

Her expression remained unchanged, but her hands relaxed away from the rigid claws and she let them rest on the desktop. That was progress, but it was happening too slowly. I needed to move before it was too late.

"So, now what?" I asked.

Barely contained rage contorted Patty's face. "Now what? Now I bury my friend, you self-involved son of a bitch!"

I let her words pass through me without feeling one way or the other about them. I was a convenient target for a tremendous amount of psychic and emotional pain. Besides, rage beat catatonia any day. I needed her feeling and thinking, not staring blankly at walls while the world came to an end.

I gave her a calm look. "I meant what happens now with the sheriff's office?"

She averted her face, but I saw her awkward embarrassment.

"Oh," she said, her voice quiet. "I'm the acting sheriff for now. At least that's what they tell me."

"They?"

"The mayor and town council. They're trying to keep it quiet, at least for today."

I nodded, and then gave the badge on the desk a pointed look. Patty's hands closed into fists and she shook her head in a couple spasmodic jerks.

"I just can't," she whispered. "It's his badge. It wasn't supposed to be like this."

I reached out and picked up the bloodied badge. A second examination told me about as much as my first brief look had told me. It was just a badge. The metal looked a little worn around the edges, smoothed by years of handling, but still serviceable. I stood slowly. It wasn't because of the pain. It was the murderous look that Patty gave me. I held up a hand to put off her anger. I took the badge to the little bathroom and turned on the hot water. A balled up paper towel would serve well enough as a wash cloth. I removed the badge from the leather case and wiped the blood from it with care and reverence.

It was just metal, but it was also a symbol of power and authority. Practitioners who got into the habit of treating symbols with a cavalier attitude rarely understood their folly until right before it killed them. Looked at one way, the badge was just a mass-produced hunk of metal. Looked at another way, that six-pointed star in a circle was indistinguishable from the Seal of Solomon. In my circles, treating that symbol without care and reverence was wholesale stupidity. I dropped the bloodied paper towels into the trash. I wasn't normally so careless with blood, but it couldn't hurt Barnes anymore. I took a couple minutes to do one more thing to the badge before I went back out to the office proper. I set the badge on the desk in front of Patty. She looked from it to me.

"Like the man said, that's yours now, and we'll need a sheriff today," I said.

Those words reached her in a way nothing else did. She blinked and some of that lost solidity seeped back into her. "What? What are you talking about?"

"It's happening today. Unless I miss my guess, all hell will break loose right after sunset."

"This more of your conspiracy stuff?"

She tried to make it sound like a mocking joke, but it came out sounding grim and final. A self-flagellating part of me said that I was a complete bastard for what I was doing. It was true. I was using Patty's sense of duty to yank her out of her mourning. Another part of me noted that I was just doing what I promised to do, which did nothing to alleviate the feeling of right bastardness in my heart.

"Yeah, but that's not why I came here. You made me promise to tell you if I found a person. I did."

She sat statue still for a five count, before she planted her hands on the desk and rose. I saw the effort it took for her to push her pain and grief aside, but she did it. Tough lady.

"Who?" She asked.

"Tucker Smith."

She gave me an annoyed look. "If you're trying to settle some score, Hartworth, it won't go well for you."

"He attacked me this morning. Told me I was already too late to stop what's happening."

"He attacked you? What happened?"

Then she looked hard at me. It was coldly evaluative.

I shook my head. "I didn't kill him."

"What did you do?"

I shrugged, "I might have set him a little bit on fire."

Her mouth hung open for a second before she said, "You did *what*?"

"I set him on fire, but that's not the point. I tried calling Paul after Tucker—well, took his leave. I couldn't reach him. Or Helena."

Patty frowned. "Helena? Oh, that woman who's been around. Pretty, looks like she could run a marathon?"

"That's her."

"Friend of yours?"

I hemmed and hawed for a second. "She's, sure, we'll say friend. She's not an enemy, anyway."

"You think he went after them?"

"I think he took Abby and they got in the way."

"Why would Tucker take Abby?"

I gritted my teeth. "Because he's not really Tucker anymore. Not in any meaningful way, at any rate. He's been possessed."

"Hartworth," said Patty, frustration in her voice.

Tick-tock. Tick-tock. More time bled away. My overtaxed patience splintered.

"If I'm right, it doesn't matter why he did it! He's already hurt or killed two people and kidnapped a teenage girl."

Chapter 42

MAYBE IT WAS MY WORDS or the ragged edge of fury in my voice, but Patty jerked and I saw the reality of the situation drive home for her. It all crossed her face in a second or two. First there was shock, then the truth that it didn't matter if I was crazy because people could be in real danger. She had a responsibility to act if people were in danger. She stowed her disbelief and walked over to a cabinet. She unlocked it and pulled out a black, pump-action shotgun. She fed rounds into it faster than I could believe. She checked the safety and set the shotgun onto the desk. Then she reached back into the cabinet, drew something out, and threw it at me. I caught it on reflex and then held it out.

"A bulletproof vest?"

"Put it on, under your shirt," she ordered.

I stood there doing nothing. "Huh?"

"Shirt off," she said, glaring at me.

I did as I was told and took my shirt off. I fumbled with the straps on the vest and felt stupid. I could set a man on fire with nothing but some chalk, but a basic piece of police equipment was beyond me.

"Oh for God's sake," said Patty.

She came over and snatched the vest from my hands. She bustled around me and then stopped. I felt a gentle prod on my back and winced.

"Are these new bruises?" She asked.

"Tucker's work," I grumbled.

A few seconds later, she had the vest wrapped around my torso. Somewhere along the line I realized she didn't have her shirt on either, just a utilitarian bra. The sight was so unexpected that I froze. I'm not one of those sex obsessed guys who loses all rational thought at the mere thought or sight of breasts. I'd seen plenty along the way, but I'd never associated putting on tactical gear with boobs either. It didn't help that I'd been thinking of Patty all along in terms of her position. She was gender *cop*, not gender *woman*. Also, inevitable back pain aside, Patty hadn't been lying. Her bosoms *could* stun a man into submission, and I was a hell of a lot closer than thirty paces.

It hit me that I was staring, openly, blatantly, shamelessly staring, and had been for a good ten seconds. I jerked my eyes toward her face. I expected annoyance or possibly anger, but she looked amused and maybe a touch pleased, too. Women confounded me. It took me a few more moments to realize something else. She'd just stood there the whole time and let me leer at her like a teenage boy. What was that about? I tried to think of something to say other than a lame-ass apology that I wasn't entirely sure was appropriate.

"I did warn you," she said.

"So you did."

I picked up my shirt and put it back on, while Patty slid into a vest that had to have been custom made for her. I focused on my shirt buttons while she got her uniform shirt back on. I looked up when she grabbed the shotgun off her desk. All the playfulness was gone, replaced by an almost frightening non-expression.

"Let's go," she said.

She walked toward the door. I walked to her desk.

"You forgot something," I said with all the compassion I could muster.

She stopped, but didn't turn around. She hadn't forgotten. Symbols have power and the sheriff's badge had particular meaning to her. Taking up the symbol meant taking responsibility for that power. At some level, she knew that and wasn't ready to take the step. I couldn't afford to wait for her to be ready. I picked the badge up and took it over to her. I held it out. Her non-expression started to crack around the edges, pain and fear creeping into it by degrees. That was when I realized who the man I'd seen with Marcy had been. With decades of age and cares stripped away, it was no wonder I hadn't recognized poor, dead Barnes. He'd given me a message for Patty, but the message and the story behind it would likely shatter her self-control. I gave her the part that mattered.

"Be brave. It's what he would have wanted."

She closed her eyes, took a deep breath, and nodded.

"Alright," she said, handing me the shotgun to hold.

She unpinned the deputy's badge from her shirt and put it in a pocket. She took the Sheriff's badge from my outstretched hand. I watched for about three seconds as she tried to pin it on, her hands trembling. That was no good.

"Here," I said, handing her back the shotgun.

I took the badge from her fingers and pinned it to her shirt. I didn't make a big show of it, just slid the pin through the material and closed the clasp. I made sure it was straight and then opened the door. Patty bowed her head for a moment. When she looked up, the non-expression was back in place. She marched down the stairs and out the front door to protect the citizens. That was when Patty became the sheriff.

I insisted on driving my own car. There was too much to do and I'd burned a lot of time at the police station. I'd need to split off on my own at some point, and I didn't want to get stuck without transport. I followed her to Paul and Abby's cottage. She pulled off the road before we got close enough to see the cottage and got out. I followed suit. She squinted up the road before looking my way.

"Stay here for a minute," she said.

"Why?"

She shot me a dark look. "Because I damn well told you to do it."

I wondered what got her riled in such a hurry. I tried to see it from her position and then it made a lot of sense. We were on her professional turf, walking into what could be a volatile or lethal situation. I knew nothing about how law enforcement handled those situations, or how to avoid contaminating a crime scene, or how to subdue a person without flagrantly violating their rights. For that matter, I didn't even really know what constituted someone's civil rights. My question wasn't just stupid or a waste of time. It suggested that I questioned her competence.

"Right. Sorry," I said. "I get it. Idiot civilian stays where he's less likely to get shot in the head. Professional law enforcement officer goes to check things out."

My moment of insight must have earned me a brownie point or two, because she flashed me a little smile. She disappeared for about five minutes. She looked grim when she reappeared. My stomach lurched.

"What did you see?"

"Nothing I like. The front door is hanging open, and I didn't see any movement inside."

"Shit," I said, straining uselessly to see through the shrubs and trees.

"You said you don't know much about guns. What do you know?"

I frowned. I suspected brutal honesty was the way to go. "I know enough not to shoot myself or someone else by accident, but I'm no kind of marksman. I haven't so much as fired a gun in years."

"Handguns?"

"Yeah," I said. "Mostly nine-millimeter. Couple of forty-fives way back in the day."

Patty nodded and popped the trunk. She dug around for a minute before she came up with a compact semi-automatic handgun. She checked the chamber and the safety, slid in a magazine, chambered a round, rechecked the safety, and then offered me the weapon. I didn't take it.

"Take the gun, Hartworth," she ordered.

I reached out and took it from her. I checked the safety, too. I hefted the gun and was a little surprised by the weight. Handguns were always heavier than I expected. I remembered to hold the gun by the side of my leg, finger off the trigger. You can't accidentally shoot yourself if you don't keep your finger on the trigger. Patty looked me up and down. Then she reached into her pocket and pulled out the deputy's badge. She grabbed my shirt and started pinning the badge to it.

"What the hell are you doing?" I demanded. "You can't just make me a deputy. I don't know anything about being a cop."

"I'm not making you a deputy," she said, swatting my hand away from the badge, "but you look like you could be one. If there is someone waiting up there, I'd rather they think there are two armed cops approaching, than one cop and whatever you actually are."

"Oh," I said. "In that case, bravo for deviousness."

She dug around inside the car for a minute and came up with a pair of sunglasses. "Put these on. They'll make you a little less recognizable. Normally, we'd come in from two sides. Since you don't have any legal authority to shoot someone, though, I want you to stick to my back. Keep the gun pointed down or straight up. Do not shoot unless you are in imminent danger. If you are in that kind of danger, shoot first. We'll deal with questions later. It's a nine-millimeter, so you know what to expect from it. You've got one in the chamber and nine in the magazine. Unless the other person is all jacked-up on drugs, a round from that should be enough to kill them, or cause them enough pain to stop."

I thought about the way the demon in Tucker shrugged off the pain of those burns. The shotgun in Patty's hands started looking very desirable.

"Basically, keep the safety on and my mouth shut. Don't do anything to anyone unless there is no other choice."

She nodded. "Yes."

"Well then, I'm your huckleberry."

"Jesus, Hartworth, do you even know what that means?"

"It means I'm the person you're looking for. I like to read, remember?"

"Let's go, huckleberry."

The approach to the cottage was tense. There was a fair amount of cover along the road, but the place was surrounded by lawn on all four sides. It looked great from a customer perspective a few days earlier. It looked like a tactical nightmare when you thought there could be someone inside with a hunting rifle. In the end, there was no choice but to cover the distance as fast as we could manage in odd, three-step bursts. Every third step we changed direction, took three steps, changed direction again, and took three more steps. Patty said it made it harder to shoot you. I believed her. Or, she said it to make me feel better, and I chose to believe her. Either way, it felt like an eternity, every step like something out of a slow motion sequence in a movie, only with terror. Lots and lots of terror rolled through me as we moved across that lawn.

I'd been a pretend cop for all of about five minutes and had a whole new appreciation for how scary their jobs really were. I'd always thought a lot of cops did things they shouldn't. Still, the kind of terror I felt coursing through me right then made it easier to see how some rookie could overreact. I made sure my finger stayed well-clear of the trigger. Patty announced herself as a police officer, got no response, but also didn't get shot at, thank

God, and went through the front door first. She veered right. I went in behind her and turned to watch the other side of the room. A few seconds went by and then I heard Patty.

"Hartworth, get your ass in here."

Her voice was low, tight, and harsh. I turned and moved toward her, that same terror-driven slow-motion feeling coming over me. I stopped when I saw two forms on the floor. One was Paul. The other was Helena. They were both covered in blood.

Chapter 43

I'VE CONFRONTED MORE THAN MY FAIR SHARE of violence over the years. I've seen people get killed because they tried to double cross the wrong thing. Often, they were operating in blind ignorance of who or what they were crossing, which just proves the value of the advice to know thine enemy. I've seen random street violence and, once or twice, the not at all random violence of organized military and paramilitary operations. In all honesty, I've doled out an above-the-mean amount of physical and magical brutality. For the most part, it happens fast and with a minimum of rational thought. I generally did my best to get the hell away from it as fast as I could afterwards. I'd been operating under the assumption that I was more or less inured to the impact of violence.

As I stood there and looked down at Helena and Paul, I discovered how very wrong I was about that. It was different when you actually knew and cared about the people on the receiving end. Not that watching strangers die was easy, that should never be easy, but you could distance yourself from it. Giving a crap about the victims turned off most of my higher brain functions, while my emotions swirled in a cyclonic madness that blended pain, grief, and disbelief into a chest-constricting band. I couldn't breathe and I couldn't think, but I could hate. Unspeakable, uncontrollable hatred burned across my psyche and ignited my nervous system. It was for the best that we didn't find someone standing over them. I'd have executed that person on the spot. Echoes from somewhere started to bleed into my maelstrom.

"Goddammit Hartworth, check their pulses!"

Pulses? Dead bodies didn't have pulses, said some factoid obsessed part of my mind. It took a moment or two for the implication to reach me inside the emotional storm. My subconscious got the message first and, by the time my conscious caught up, I was kneeling on the floor by Helena. They couldn't be alive, could they? There was so much blood. I pressed two fingers to the side of Helena's neck. I waited, breath held, and then the breath exploded out of me as I felt the thump-thump of a pulse against my fingertips. The thump-thump repeated itself several times, steady and reliable. I turned to Paul and did the same thing, fingers pressed beneath his collar. As I waited, I realized that the old man was clutching a poker in his hand. It had blood on the end. He hadn't gone down gently. I felt his pulse and heaved a sigh of pure relief.

"They're both alive," I said, fighting off an urge to weep uncontrollably and simultaneously howl in a triumph. "I think Helena's just unconscious. Paul needs an ambulance, right now. His pulse is irregular and, shit, thready. That's the word."

"Stay with them. I need to check the rest of the house."

"They need help!"

"It won't do them any good if we all get killed by someone hiding in here," she said, calm, certain, and damnably right.

I ground my teeth in frustration, but nodded. Concern was overwhelming common sense, which was a good way to get dead. I experienced an odd moment of clarity. My reaction was exactly why civilians weren't needed or wanted at crime scenes until after police swept the area. I was no stranger to violence, but I hadn't been trained to think through the visceral, emotional response. I would have ignored the obvious danger in a bid to help. It was the intuitive reaction and probably helped along by the fact that I worked by myself most of the time. My experiences were confined to rationally managing risks to myself, not managing risks to a group while under emotional stress. Patty watched me for a second, probably trying to gauge the odds of me doing something stupid, before she moved away.

While Patty secured the rest of the house, opening doors with audible bangs, I hovered by Helena and Paul. I checked their pulses a lot more often than necessary, every few seconds or so. After a minute or two of that, it sank in that they weren't dead. The fear, emotional pain, and adrenaline started to drain away. It left me feeling exhausted and very shaky. I hadn't even done anything strenuous and I wanted to sleep for a month. I tried to focus. They weren't dead, but where had the blood come from? I forced myself to start checking both of them for cuts and gashes. I didn't see any, but I also didn't dare move them.

Patty came back. "The house is clear, as near as I can tell. Unless there's a demon in here somewhere."

I thought she meant it to be funny, but I wasn't in a joking mood. "Pray there isn't."

She went a little pale. "Ambulance is on the way."

Helena came around before the ambulance arrived and was drifting toward coherence by the time the paramedics came through the door. I stayed out of the way while the paramedics did their jobs and hoped like hell they wouldn't demand Helena go to the hospital before I talked to her. Maybe God was paying attention to me right then, or maybe Helena noticed me staring and willing her not to leave. The paramedics might have insisted Helena go, but they were a lot more concerned about Paul's condition. He had a nasty cut across his chest that accounted for some of the blood.

After Patty assured them that she'd see to it Helena saw a doctor sooner than later, the paramedics wheeled Paul out. I waited until I heard the sirens getting quiet before I focused on Helena. She stared down at her bloodied clothes and looked ready to vomit at any second. It wasn't the blood itself that bothered her. I knew she wasn't squeamish that way.

"He took her, didn't he?" I asked.

Helena nodded.

Patty chimed in. "Was it Tucker Smith?"

"I don't know. I'd never seen him before."

I opened my mouth to describe him, but Patty shook her head at me.

"Can you tell me what he looked like?" Patty asked.

Helena thought for a second. "Lean guy with dark hair. Needs a shave. Likes his hunting knife."

Patty jotted down some notes. "Can you tell me what happened? How you ended up here?"

I wanted to scream. I could feel an invisible timer ticking down, and I needed to ask my own questions. I held my tongue, though. Interrupting would waste time no one could afford to lose. I started impatiently tapping a foot and forced myself to be still. Helena pressed gingerly at a swollen lump on her head, winced, and sucked in a breath. She gave Patty a rueful look and gestured at the lump.

"It's pretty hazy right now."

"That's fine. Just tell me what you remember."

"Okay. Well, the hospital was letting Abby check-out this morning. I went to see if they needed any help, but Abby and Paul had checking-out down to a science. Abby asked if I could come and see the new place."

I nodded to myself. Paul probably would have extended the invite, but Abby was going somewhere new. She'd have been uncertain, daunted by the new living situation. Helena was a comparative port of safety and familiarity, no doubt given unofficial status as an aunt. It made sense that the girl would want some kind of support system around her while she assessed her new, temporary home. Helena paused and I could see her concentrating, almost willing her battered brain to dredge up details.

"We were going to stop somewhere and get food, but Abby said she wasn't that hungry. She looked ill, pale, and sweaty, like she was running a fever. So Paul drove her back here, and I followed them."

"You came in your own vehicle?" Patty asked.

"What? Oh, yeah, I drove my rental."

Helena kept looking down at her bloodied clothes. They were distracting her when her mind was already working below par, slowing the process. I caught Patty's eye and held up a finger. She gave me a frown, but nodded.

"Helena," I said, "do you have any clean clothes in your car?"

She blinked at me a few times and said, "I'm not sure. Maybe."

"Keys?"

She squinted at me. "Jacket pocket, I think. By the door."

While Helena did her best to answer Patty's questions, I went out to her rental car and dug around. I didn't find clean clothes, but there was a shirt on the backseat that didn't look or smell too soiled. It had to be better than the bloody thing she was wearing. I took it inside. Helena excused herself to go change, with a warning from Patty not to throw the bloody shirt away. It might be evidence. Patty's shoulders were hunched and her face pinched in apprehension.

"Tucker took that girl. I need to call in some help. State police, maybe the feds. Kidnappings are almost always federal territory."

"No," I said.

"We'll have to organize search parties to—" her eyes went wide. "Did you just say no?"

"I said no."

"Maybe you've forgotten who the deputy is in this room. You don't get to decide this."

"I haven't forgotten anything, Acting Sheriff Michelson. I've played this your way, out of respect for your expertise, and because it was the smart move. But now it's time for you to listen to me. Calling a bunch of people with badges and guns in here won't help Abby. You saw my back. Tucker did that after I set him on fire. He did that *after* all of this."

I swept my hand around the room. Paul and Helena had stood their ground and the living room was in shambles. Furniture was toppled. Books were scattered everywhere and shattered glass made every step a calculated gamble. The blood on the floor was drying into a black pool and looked downright eerie. Patty's face was going a nasty shade of red that let me know a volcano was about to explode in my face. I didn't let her get a word in edgewise.

"He isn't a human being anymore, Patty. No human being could have done all this, taken a terrified girl somewhere, and then come to pick a fight with me. By the way, I basically lost that fight. He's beyond dangerous and he's not the entrée. He's the appetizer. Besides, you don't need a search party. I know where he took her."

Patty had worked herself up for a serious screaming at me. That last derailed the fury train, at least temporarily, with pure shock.

"You know? How the hell can you know?"

"Easy. I know what's giving him his orders and where it is. I also know why it wants her. Tucker took her to it."

"Where?"

"The school."

"The school! Why the hell would Tucker take her there?"

"So his master can kill the girl," said Helena.

"So he's working with someone," said Patty.

Helena spared me a look. "She doesn't want to see it."

I shrugged. "I know."

"You'll have to show her."

"Why me?"

"Because she knows you," said Helena.

Despite Helena not actually saying the word "dumbass," I swore I heard it. I held up a hand to acknowledge her point. "Water, do you think?"

"Probably the safest approach," she agreed.

"Excuse me," said Patty, "but would you mind clueing me in here? Show what to who? And what does any of this have to do with what's happening?"

I sighed, certain of how it would go over, but I said it anyway. "It has everything to do with what's happening. I'm going to show you magic, Patty. The real deal, live, right before your eyes."

"Yeah, sure you will," said Patty.

I ignored her.

"Helena, will you get a glass of—wait, no, scratch that. Patty, will you please get a glass of water. Plain tap water from the sink."

"Why?"

"Please, just humor me for a minute."

"Fine," she said. "Then you'll explain what you're on about?"

"Yes," I said, then added, "and, I'm sorry."

"For what?" She asked.

I shook my head. "You'll understand in a minute."

Chapter 44

"YOU COULD HAVE JUST DRAWN THE WATER FROM THE AIR," said Helena.

"Yeah, but I need her to know it's really water and that it's just water."

"Are you up for this?"

"Does it matter?"

It came out harsher than I meant it to, but that happens when I'm in pain and feeling backed into a corner. Time was slipping through my fingers and I had to do parlor tricks to keep Patty from getting a bunch of people killed with her good intentions. Sometimes, I really do believe it would be easier to just put on a black hat and call it a day. Unfortunately, I couldn't fill out a black hat any more than a white one. I had too much of a moral code for the one, too little for the other. It's a gray old life for me.

"Sorry," I said. "I'm feeling time crunched."

Helena gave me a sympathetic look as Patty came back into the room with a tall glass of water in one hand.

"Okay. I got the glass of water. Now what?"

Helena gave Patty a steady, serious look. "Throw the water at him."

"Is this some kind of joke? If it is, I'll arrest you both."

"It's not a joke. Throw the water at me."

Patty looked at me, shrugged, and flung the water at me. It flew at me in a liquid arc and, with a wholly unnecessary flourish of my hand, stopped in midair. Patty's eyes went very wide. I raised my other hand and threw my arms out to each side. The water split into two portions, coalescing into two small spheres of water that hovered about six inches from the palms of each hand. Like I said, the few things I can do directly are flashy as hell, if not terribly useful. I concentrated and the spheres of water drew out into two snakelike shapes. I sent them spinning around me and, sometimes, through each other. Then I split them into four separate snakes of water, then six, forcing them into ever more convoluted patterns around me. Patty looked torn between wanting to scream and utter fascination.

I sent the snakes of water twirling, spinning, and twining around Helena and Patty. Helena laughed in delight. It was her favorite party trick. Patty stood stock still, as if she was certain that coming into contact with the water would prove lethal. The reality was that she'd just get a little bit wet. The effort of sustaining the magic started to take a toll, so I summoned the water back to me. I gather it into one ball and walked over to Patty.

"Would you mind holding that glass up?" I asked.

She held the glass up in a trembling hand, her face devoid of color. I dumped the water back into the glass and felt a pressure that had been building on the interior of my forehead vanish. I sagged a little. The mental effort cost me more than I expected. I forced myself to stand up straight and plucked the cup from Patty's hand before she started spilling water all over her crime scene. I took a few sips and grimaced.

"God, I hate the taste of chlorine," I said.

Patty kept looking around, like she really wanted to believe that I'd set this whole thing up somehow and that she'd see the wires and mirrors if she looked hard enough. I waited it out and tried to ignore the voice in the back of my head that was screaming about the time.

"Mother of God," said Patty, her eyes finally settling on me. "How did you do that?"

"I told you how before we started. It was magic."

Her mouth worked back and forth, up and down, several times. I expect it went dry on her. What Patty faced wasn't as hard as what Abby had faced, but it was still a mind-twisting experience of the first order. I took a little pity on her.

"Don't take it so hard. In this, you're the civilian. Here's the big takeaway. What I just did was nothing."

"That wasn't nothing! It's impossible. It's—"

"It's a cheap trick. Take it from the guy who just did it. The *thing* inside Tucker can probably do a hundred times as much, now that it's got direct access to the material world. The even bigger *thing* it serves is a thousand times more powerful and dangerous. All that's keeping it from crushing this town and everyone in it is Abby. If it kills her, we all die. If you call in the state troopers and the feds, one of two things happens. They shove me in a room and ask questions until it kills Abby. Then we all die. Two, they ignore me, storm the school, and it kills Abby anyway. Then, we all die."

Patty tried to shake off the shock the way she had with the holy water, but she couldn't. That had been a flash of light that came and went in a blink. It was easy to explain away or ignore. My party trick lasted too long to discount or explain away without a lot of time and serious effort.

"So what then? We leave her there to die?"

"No. I'll go in after her. Try to get her clear before the thing in the school is strong enough to finish the deed."

She stared at me. "So you really could fight it. You could fight it all along and you let Jeremy kill himself!"

Patty made a move for her sidearm. Helena caught her hand before it made contact with the grip.

"No," she said. "He can't fight it."

"But, he just said—I don't understand."

"I'm going in, but not to fight. I don't have any weapons that will kill it. I don't even know if I can hurt it. I might be able to reason with it or trick it."

Helena held up a hand. "I've had a thought about that."

Hope welled up inside of me. "What?"

"Why did it use smoke bindings on the dead?"

I tried to make sense of the change in direction. I tossed my hands up in the air. "Punishment, I assume. It's taking vengeance on them."

"But why? It only needed them dead to break the blood chain. Every action it has taken so far has been methodical, driven toward the end of freeing itself. Expending power to bind their souls after they were dead serves no purpose, unless they pose a threat to it."

I did a lot of very fast thinking, trying to play catch up with Helena's insight. The theory worked. Individually, no single human soul was a threat to it, but it had been killing people for a long time. The souls of hundreds of murdered people were trapped in that graveyard. I had no clue what that translated to in terms of actual power to wield, but it had to be significant. Plus, all those souls had an axe to grind. I nodded.

"Sure, it makes sense, but it doesn't do any good. They're trapped. Free, they might be a viable weapon or a distraction, but they aren't free."

Helena gave me a sober look. "But they could be."

"In theory, yes, if we had the Pope or a bodhisattva handy."

"I can do it," she said. "Your friends already told us how."

I didn't speak for a long time. I didn't dare. When I was certain I could use actual words again, I spoke with as much calm as I could. "Absolutely not. You damn well know that there's a huge difference between knowing how to do something and actually pulling it off. Even The Twins weren't sure if you could do it."

"I can do this," she insisted.

"Even if you can, at what price?"

Helena studied my face for a minute. "She's fifteen years old, Adrian. She's spent most of her time in one hospital or another. Her whole life has been about this nightmare. I couldn't live with not trying. Besides," she said, her expression hard and brittle at the same time, "who are you to lecture me about prices?"

"That's different," I said.

Patty looked at Helena. "Wait, what do you mean? About prices?"

"She doesn't mean anything," I said.

Helena turned her face away. "Adrian knows that if he goes into that school, what's waiting inside will almost certainly kill him."

"And you know that if you attempt to undo those bindings and fail, it'll almost certainly kill you."

I felt the weight of Patty's eyes on me and glanced at her. She looked at me, then at Helena, and I saw some kind of understanding on her face.

"Why?" Patty asked, the incredulity gone from her face.

"Because the magic she wants to try is about as dangerous as building an atomic bomb in your basement. Anything goes wrong, anything at all, and it's harps and halos time," I said.

"That isn't what she means," said Helena.

"It isn't?"

"She wants to know why you'd do this."

I thought for a moment. "For the same reason you shouldn't try to unmake those bindings. When you get right down to it, the world won't suffer if I don't come out of this. It will suffer if you're not in the picture, Helena. It'll suffer if Abby doesn't come out of it. She's filled with all the potential of youth. She's kind. There's not enough of that in the world. There's plenty more like me."

Helena made one of those choked sounds that I knew was someone trying to quell something impossibly painful. There wasn't much I could do about that.

"God, you're stupid," said Patty, rubbing at her eyes. "Okay, let's say I'm willing to entertain this until I realize how insane it all sounds. Can you actually get Abby clear?"

Helena gave Patty a sharp glance. It was understandable. Helena probably expected a protracted argument or the need for a lengthy explanation. I'd laid the groundwork, though, and kept adding to it very nearly every time Patty and I crossed paths. Whether Patty liked it or not, knew it or not, she was primed to accept the supernatural as a real possibility. She'd just needed the evidence put in front of her eyes.

"It's—" I hesitated, "possible that I can get her clear."

She glowered at me. "Can you do it without shutting down these smoke things?"

"I'd say that," I tried to hedge some more.

"No," said Helena. "He can't reasonably expect to get her out without a big-enough distraction."

Patty rubbed at her eyes again before she looked at Helena. "How sure are you that you can do it?"

"I can do it," said Helena, then she looked at me. "And I'm going to do it."

I knew it was a losing battle. She was going to act with or without my help. I tried to think it through, as one part of my brain gibbered the word "time" in an endless loop, and another suggested that I was an idiot for bringing Helena into this mess. I racked my brain for something to improve the odds of success. Barring that, I'd settle for something that minimized the chances of Helena dying in the backlash if she somehow broke the bindings. Sure, Cavanaugh said she'd survive, but I didn't put much stock in anything Cavanaugh said.

Another little part of my mind decided to remind me how this was all E.J. Cavanaugh's fault. Then it suggested how disappointed it was that his current condition prevented me from breaking his nose. I tried to check my anger at the thought of Cavanaugh hiding in his nice, safe, bomb shelter. My mind stuttered there, fixated on the idea, and refused to let go.

"Bomb shelter," I mumbled.

Helena and Patty spoke in unison. "What?"

I looked at Helena. "What you need is a bomb shelter."

With that, a plan took form. It was a terrible plan, with about a one-in-a-million shot of success, but it beat the one-hundred-percent certainty of death I'd faced just moments before. I smiled at Helena and Patty, and then I told them my plan.

Chapter 45

PEOPLE MUCH MORE EXPERIENCED THAN ME in the art of war say that no plan survives contact with the enemy. Since I started with that as a fixed truth, I eschewed any kind of exotic, multi-step plan that required every single thing to go right. I went basic. Then we all went to work. It took a couple hours of my fast-dwindling time to get things set up. By the time we were ready, I was resisting the urge to glance at the nigh-setting sun every half-second or so. The three of us stood outside the gate of the graveyard. Helena looked eerily detached and I had a sense that she was already deep inside the gears of the magic she was going to perform. I handed Patty a sheet of paper. Most of my two hours were spent working on it. She frowned down at the scrawled Enochian letters.

"What does it say?" she asked.

"Think of it as, I don't know, marching orders. I need to make sure that the souls here have a direct path to the school. That paper will do that. Here's the important thing. As soon as Helena says it's done, burn the paper."

"That's it?"

"Trust me," I said, "it's more than enough."

"I don't like this, Hartworth. I should be going in with you. What if Tucker's there?"

"I'm sure he will be. I expect he plans to murder me."

"And you don't think that warrants some backup?"

"Stick with the plan. When Helena's done, burn that and help her into Cavanaugh's tomb. It should shield her from the worst of the backlash."

"Why will Helena need help?"

I tried to think of a way to explain it that would make sense. "The bigger the magic is, the harder it is to do. Think of it like lifting something. You can probably pick up a pencil hundreds of times without getting too tired. Make it a jug of milk, you'll get tired a lot faster. It costs you more."

"So, the thing you did with the water," she shivered a little, "that was like—?"

"For me, that was like bench-pressing two-hundred pounds. I couldn't keep it up for very long."

Patty nodded. "And this thing with the graveyard?"

I rubbed my cheek as I thought about it. "I've never done anything remotely that big. My best guess, it'd be like dead lifting a train car and holding it over your head."

Patty's eyes went very wide. "She can do that?"

"She thinks she can."

"That's not an answer, Hartworth."

"I honestly don't know. She's a lot stronger than I am, but this isn't just a question of raw power. Some kinds of magic require a—" I cast around for the right descriptive. "I guess you'd call it spiritual purity. I don't play with those things because, well, obviously. I can set someone on fire or knock down a building because I know how to manipulate the right forces, but it's just brute force and applied knowledge."

"Really?"

"Yeah, though it takes me forever. Case in point," I said, waving at the paper in her hand.

"I see," she said. "You need a lot of prep time to do these kinds of things. But the water?"

"It really is a cheap trick, and I've had years of practice. Anyway, what Helena is going to be doing is next-level stuff. I can't explain it because I just don't comprehend it. If she can do it at all, and if it doesn't kill her outright," I said through clenched teeth, "it'll take a hellish toll on her. She might not be in any condition to move under her own power when it's done."

"But why is that an issue, if all the bad guys are at the school?"

"Backlash," said Helena, joining the conversation. "In all likelihood, it won't touch you at all, but for Adrian or me, it's bad. When you rupture a magical construct you release its power into the world. Larger and more complex constructs release larger backlashes. If you're conscious and ready for it, you can protect yourself. If you're not conscious or aren't ready for it, it can burn out your mind. Burst blood vessels in your brain. If it's sufficiently large, it can kill you."

I added, "Cavanaugh's tomb is built to withstand exactly those kinds of forces. Get her inside, conscious or not, and she's got a fighting chance. So, someone needs to be on hand to help her."

Patty wasn't happy with it, but she nodded. She was starting to understand how insanely dangerous a game I was playing. I only hoped that I understood it. I glanced at the sky. I was cutting it way too close for comfort.

"Time to go," I said. "Remember, stick to the plan."

I turned to walk to my car. Helena caught my arm and I looked back at her. Her eyes were focused on something in deep space, but I saw raw fear swimming in their depths.

"In case I don't see you again."

She hugged me with fear-strength and it hurt. I hugged her back.

"I'll be okay," I said.

"Jesus, you're an awful liar. Try not to die."

I nodded. "I'll try."

I kept my brave face on while I got into the car. I kept it on while I drove. I kept it on right up until the moment I pulled up in front of that church turned high school. Then it slipped and I was just afraid. No, not afraid. People were afraid of spiders and heights and walking under ladders. That kind of fear was manageable. I experienced a blind, irrational, phobic response. My heart pounded. My hands shook. My legs trembled. I flashed back to my dream of staring up at the school's open doors and seeing the interior engulfed in flames like Satan's own hearth. I ducked my head to cut the line of sight. If I'd been coming at the building cold, that fear might have paralyzed me. I'd been in there before. I knew what to expect.

I started to build walls in my mind, probably very much like the ones Abby had needed to build in her mind. I laid them down, mental brick-by-brick, until they formed a protective shield around my consciousness. Then I built another layer, right behind it, and then another right behind it. By the time I was done, it was a multilayered sphere of will and idea and imagination. The shield wasn't perfect and never could be perfect.

Things would bleed through. The walls could be breached, but it would be enough to see me through for a little while. That's all I needed, a little while. After a little while, it'd all be over for better or worse. On the upside, if things went to hell, I'd be dead. So there was always that to look forward to.

I went around to the back of the car and opened the trunk. The hard case sat there looking plastic and benign. I opened it and stared down at its contents, which were anything but benign. The hard case served a two-fold purpose. It was a measure of last resort and a kind of pre-emptive protection for the world at large. Most magic needed a person, or at least a mind, with innate magical talent to direct and control the forces. I used runes to accomplish that, while Helena had transcended such limitations. Some magic, however, didn't require someone with any active magical talent. It just needed a body.

The things in the hard case were of the latter type. Any fool with enough of a mind to pick them up could use them. That is to say, if they were deeply stupid. Only a few things in the case were even nominally safe. The Eye of Horus was innocuous enough, assuming you didn't point it at the wrong thing. The chalk was actually benign. The mirror pendant I'd given Abby was safe, although I'd made that one myself. There was an old skeleton key that I was pretty sure was safe, though I'd never quite worked up the nerve to test it myself.

The key didn't fit any mortal lock. If you took it to certain places of power, though, it would open a door to one specific destination. My understanding was that it was a pocket dimension inhabited by beings that were not remotely human, but were not predisposed to automatically kill anyone who stumbled into their domain. Play your cards right and they would teach you things, provide you with secret knowledge, and help you to unfold any native power inside you. I didn't know what happened if you played your cards wrong, which was why I'd never tried it. I'd offered it to a few people that I trusted. Every single one had asked me the same question.

"Have you tried it?"

When I said I hadn't, they all turned me down. I guess I was some kind of litmus test. Anything *I* wasn't willing to try was perceived as suicidal. In retrospect, there might be some wisdom in that. My reputation, as I understood it, was that of someone willing to take calculated risks, and even dangerous ones, for the right payoff. I suppose my unwillingness to try the key, based largely on my own uncertainties about my character and politicking skills, gave other people the wrong idea that the key was fundamentally dangerous.

Then there were the things I wasn't sure were dangerous, but had been taken from people and things that were dangerous. They were probably just tools, but every tool functioned as a double-edged sword. After all, a hammer was fabulous for driving nails, but it was also fabulous for caving in someone's skull. It's all about how you use it. There was a small crystal ball that I'd lifted off the catatonic body of Tony Damelus. I leaned toward the opinion that it was dangerous. I'd gotten a nasty vibe from it when I plucked it from his hand. Sanity overruled curiosity and I didn't try to use it.

There was an ivory carving of a something that looked like a mix between a hedgehog and a lion. It hurt my eyes just to look at the stupid thing. I thought I knew what it did, but wasn't sure I could control it. As with the crystal ball, I chose to exercise restraint. There were a handful of other items in the case that fell into the same category. I'd used a few of them, experimentally, and concluded that I didn't understand them well enough to employ them in anything like a danger situation. Magic you did understand could still prove lethal to you if you used it the wrong way. Magic you didn't understand was like a lobbing a live grenade into the situation when your life was on the line.

The rest of the items, the majority of them, in fact, were things I knew were dangerous. I'd either seen them in action, found people who knew, or used them myself, generally in a state of abject desperation. There was a ring inset with a shard of obsidian from an Aztec sacrificial knife. Pierce someone's skin with it and that little beauty ripped their life out of their body and fed it to you. Of course, do it once and you had to keep doing it to stay alive. It could make you immortal, if you had enough victims lined up, but stop feeding it for long enough and it ate your life.

There was a silver pendant crafted to look like a series of concentric circles that would bind someone to your will forever. Pitfall, you had to exert your will over them constantly or they became the equivalent of bloodthirsty zombies, minus the craving for brains. I figured that out the hard way when I distracted the last owner. There were at least a dozen such objects, all horrible in use and consequence. I considered and rejected almost all of them. Granted, I probably wasn't going to survive to see those consequences, but if I did survive, I had no interest in becoming a serial killer or zombie master or any of the other truly miserable fates those objects heralded.

There was one thing in there I could use, if I dared. I stared down at it, nestled in the foam, and I wavered. It was a small kris knife, though probably not made in the usual way or for the usual reasons. Kris knives of legend were reputed to possess extraordinary magical powers, and I knew why. This particular blade was a cage for some kind of malevolent spirit. I didn't know exactly what kind. The demon I took it off wasn't feeling talkative, what with not having a head anymore. The knife was probably strong enough to at least hurt what was inside the school, but I hated to even pick it up. There was no obvious pitfall to using it, which made me quite certain the price was both heavy and spiritual. My theory was that it stained the soul and added tons of karmic debt that I'd have to pay off in another life.

In truth, given the option, I'd have destroyed everything in the hard case. Unfortunately, it's always easier to make a magical object than it is to destroy a magical object. In the case of the knife, it might have even been the wrong choice. It's no small chore to bind a spirit into an object and I'd never known it to happen without compelling reasons. I glanced up at the school, felt the fear it generated skitter along the surface of my mental shield, and picked up the knife. I slid it into my back pocket, where it would be a little less obvious. I closed and locked the hard case. I shut the trunk. Then I walked up the steps, opened the door to the school, and stepped inside.

Chapter 46

I EXPERIENCED ANOTHER ONE of the disjointed spaces in my memory right after I stepped through the door. The first thing I do remember with any semblance of clarity was being on the floor with my hands over my ears. There was noise of such volume that I thought it was going to rip my head apart. Covering my ears did nothing to cut the volume. The noise was inside my head, transported from some netherspace occupied by things that had no business on the material plane. Once I managed to piece together that thought, I was able to adjust my mental shields enough to mute that horrific, all-consuming noise well enough to let me do little things, like breathe, stand, and walk. Despite damping down the volume, I was certain that every second of exposure to that noise did psychic damage that would take years to heal, if ever.

"Doesn't matter," I told myself.

I lurched a few steps. Where would Abby be? Down, I thought. They'd take her as far down as they could go. I stumbled through the halls, my head pounding in time with the psychic noise, and looked for a stairwell. It took longer than I liked to find the stairwell. Every door looked the same, probably because of some bureaucratic ordinance. I stopped on the top landing and leaned against the wall. The noise battered my mind as effectively as a baseball bat to the skull. I felt disoriented and nauseated. The burn on my back started to throb and sent increasingly urgent, painful messages up my spine. I hardened the shell around my consciousness as well as I could, but I was fighting a Niagara Falls-sized torrent of discordant, psychic interference.

I made my legs start taking me down, one lurching step at a time. I stopped at the next landing, more disoriented and feeling even sicker. I let myself vomit all over the floor. To my surprise, it helped a little. The next set of steps left me on the basement level. There was a sensation of spinning that almost toppled me over. I leaned against the wall. My whole body shook and muscles started to spasm at random. Every instinct told me to run away. Whatever was going on down there wasn't meant for human beings. My body started to turn back towards the stairs with no input from me, self-perseveration instincts overtaking my conscious intentions.

It was touch-and-go for a second, with my body trying to leave and my mind determined to move forward. My will won out, by the barest conceivable margin, and I turned back. I stared hard at the door, trying to force the spinning sensation to stop. It didn't stop, but I managed to push it back enough that everything just wobbled along the edges. I banged the door open with my hip and dove through. Flopped through and fell to the floor like a dead fish might be more accurate, but dove through suggests that I intuited the attack and cleverly avoided having my throat slit by Tucker Smith.

The hunting knife swept through the air so fast it whistled. If I'd been less disoriented and stepped through the door, the knife might have decapitated me. As it was, I heard the knife, felt the acidic anger of the demon inside of Tucker, and scrambled away. I managed to get a hand on something firm and dragged myself up to standing. I turned my wavering vision to look at Tucker. He was still dressed in the scorched and melted remnants of his clothes. Where my fire had burned his scalp was a mass of red blisters. Even with my impaired vision, I could see he looked misshapen and hunched. *Lil*, I thought. That was her work. She must have wrecked a fair number of bones, maybe even done some spinal damage, when she flung him against that tree.

"You!" he screamed, bloody spittle spraying from his lips.

He tried to do that same blurring thing he'd done at the cabin, but Tucker's body was just too damaged. The move was still awful in its speed, but slow enough for me to see it coming. I lurched to one side and the knife only managed to open a line of fire on my left arm instead of impaling me. Tucker's overtaxed body slammed into whatever I was leaning on and I heard another bone break. He howled in pain, but his arm was already in motion. I stumbled away, the disorientation too much to let me fight back. The knife ripped against the bulletproof vest and opened the layered fabric. They weren't meant to stop knives, but it probably saved my life, sparing me the indignity of being eviscerated, and limiting the damage to another line of fire across my stomach. I took another drunken step back and the knife opened a deep cut across my thigh. I think I screamed that time, but who could tell in all that mental noise.

My back came up against a wall. Even in that state of disorientation, I knew that I couldn't keep things up. Demon Tucker was just too fast and he wouldn't keep missing. His last swing with the knife, the one that opened up my leg, also gave me an opportunity. The speed of it carried Tucker almost one hundred and eighty degrees. So, I did the only thing I could do. I threw myself at his exposed back. I couldn't maintain the concentration to keep the world from spinning and fight with Demon Tucker, so I closed my eyes.

I felt the inhuman strength that fueled Demon Tucker. At that range, the acidic anger of the demon threatened to scorch the skin off my face. If I was going to do anything, I needed to do it fast. His own swing had left him off-balance and my tackle had carried him to the floor. The knife slid away with a scrape of metal on concrete. In the heat of moments like that, the mind ups its game and boosts the processor speed. Or, in my case, it hits the hamster with a cattle prod and the wheel goes into overdrive. You get the false impression that the world has slowed.

One upside was that the overdrive mode was seemingly immune to the psychic noise and I got a few precious moments to think clearly. I couldn't take Demon Tucker in a fair fight. He was too strong and too fast. What I did have was a momentary leverage advantage. Whatever extra strength and power the demon gave Tucker, it didn't make his body any less vulnerable to damage. I heard the bone break a moment before, which meant I just needed to do something Tucker's body couldn't survive. Once the host body died, the demon had to go back to wherever it came from.

I considered the knife in my back pocket and dismissed it. I didn't dare take the time to pull the knife. In the end, there are only a few surefire ways to kill someone with your bare hands from my position. All that passed through my head in the moments between me crashing into Demon Tucker's back, him hitting the floor, and me landing on top of him. Demon-infested or not, Tucker's body was still human. An impact like that scrambles the nervous system for a second. If I'd left him even that second or two to recover, I would have died right there. I didn't allow him that time.

Tucker Smith didn't enjoy a pretty death. While his body didn't know what the hell was going on, I planted a knee in his back. I reached under his head, seized his jaw, and I jerked his head back to an angle it was never meant to reach. Even with the leverage, it still took all of my strength to break his neck. I heard and felt the crackle and pop as the bones, tendons and ligaments gave way and severed the spinal cord. I let go and his head flopped against the floor with dull thud. I leaned forward, breathing hard. My lungs burned and it felt like I couldn't get enough air into them. I felt a slight movement beneath me and chalked it up to stray chemical messages and misfiring neurons in Tucker's body.

"Kill you," wheezed a voice beneath me.

My blood ran cold. I forced myself to look down. Tucker's eye glared up at me, before it fixated on the knife. The demon was using its inhuman will to squeeze every last ounce of utility out of Tucker's broken body. I heard a telltale metallic scrape. I didn't wait to see if the demon could hurl the knife across the room with its mind. I grabbed Demon Tucker's head and started slamming it against the floor. I didn't stop when blood splattered. I didn't stop when I heard bones break. I stopped when I almost passed out from oxygen deprivation. I crawled off the body and dragged myself away from the corpse. I heard a scream of frustration. Acidic anger washed over me, one last time, and then the demon was gone.

I slumped to the cool floor. I don't know how long I stayed there, my chest heaving and unable to catch my breath. It wasn't that I didn't recognize the passage of time. I knew time passed, but not in any sensible way. It was distorted by all the psychic noise and the presence of a being so immensely powerful that it overcame a blood binding to exert its will across a continent. When the oxygen my lungs could provide finally started to line up with my body's needs, rational thoughts asserted themselves.

Was I too late? No, I decided in a fog. There wouldn't have been anything left to think that question if I were too late. I remembered I was bleeding. Without opening my eyes, I ripped off a piece of my shirt and wadded it up. I pulled my tie off and used it to cinch the makeshift bandage against my leg over the cut Demon Tucker had opened up. I figured he missed the big arteries, since I was still around to feel disoriented and sick. Not to mention all the pain that assaulted me. The injuries, old and new, seemed to have formed a union and were voicing their unhappiness with the working conditions in one voice. That voice worked very hard to sap me of my will to continue. If Tucker was the opening act, I couldn't possible beat the star of that show, that voice assured me. It was over before it started, it said. Just get out of here, it demanded.

It sounded good. It sounded really good. In my experience, the wrong thing almost always sounds like a great course of action when things get hard. After all, the wrong thing generally involved doing the self-interested thing. The wrong thing, in the short term, usually conferred wealth, or power, or survival in some form. I didn't want to die in that awful basement, mere feet from where I'd been forced to murder someone. I didn't have a choice about it. He was going to kill me, but that didn't make me feel great about it. I could go. If I announced my intention to leave to the thing in the basement and asked for safe passage, even at the eleventh hour, it would probably give it.

All I'd have to do was sacrifice a few thousand people and one terrified teenage girl. I mean, sure, I basically promised to help her and she probably still looked up to me a little. Then again, you can't enjoy admiration when you're dead. If I bailed, it'd probably lead to Helena's death. Once she started at the graveyard, which she must have done by then, interrupting her would be as lethal as cyanide. She needed to finish what she started or she wouldn't do anything ever again. I'd have to leave her to manage her own survival. Maybe she would survive, though. Cavanaugh said she would, regardless of what happened to the rest of us. If that was true, then I could walk. I just had to do the wrong thing, and consequences be damned.

I pulled the tie a little tighter around my leg and knotted it in place. I dragged myself around until I felt something solid and used it to pull myself up to standing. I concentrated on keeping the world from spinning and opened my eyes. The same wobble was there, maybe a little worse, but I could see. I straightened up a little more and looked around. I saw the door that led out to the stairs. I looked at that door for the longest ten seconds of my life.

"The wrong thing," I said out loud, testing the words in the air. "Yeah, the wrong thing always looks good."

With that, I turned and started limping deeper into the basement. I just hoped that shock didn't set in before I got there. I'd have hated to deprive the Midnight Ground of a final chance to kill me.

Chapter 47

THE DEEPER I WENT INTO THE BASEMENT, the tougher it got to keep the world from spinning crazily. The nausea grew so intense it felt like a live snake was thrashing in my stomach. Every limping step forward was liquid fire in my nervous system. My arm and stomach throbbed and pulsed in angry coordination with my heartbeat. I tried not to think about how much blood I left on the floor behind me. It didn't matter, because I didn't have any good way to staunch the flow. The fact that I was going to die down there started to take on a concrete reality for me.

It didn't thrill me, but I decided there were worse ways to go out. If I died down there, it meant I got to take a pass on the creeping indignities of old age. The perpetual weakening of muscle and increasing fragility of bone weren't going to be a problem. I wouldn't face the horror of incontinence or some nightmare of a nursing home where the staff abused and robbed the patients. Killed making a run at Midnight Ground and trying to save an entire town? That was the stuff of legend. People would talk about it for decades. There were worse legacies to leave behind. It was a better legacy than I had any right to hope for, based on my life to date.

Even so, I still hoped I wouldn't die. Maybe Helena would do the impossible and free the trapped souls. If she was right that they were a threat, and my marching orders worked, which was not guaranteed, I might get a window of opportunity to get Abby clear. *I* might even get clear if that happened. Of course, that plan hinged on me surviving until Helena was done. I didn't know how much chance there was of that. I'd probably pissed off the spirit of the Midnight Ground something fierce. It might murder me out of hand, simply for inconveniencing it. Unlike Abby, I had no bloodline binding to stave it off. I didn't have the raw magical power to keep it at bay either.

I wasn't the kind of person who lusted after power ninety-nine days out of a hundred. It was just too damned easy to abuse it and, in doing so, turn into something so abhorrent that you couldn't be saved. My sins were many, and some of them very dark, but none so black that I thought I was utterly beyond redemption. There were lines that I had not crossed, and thresholds of evil that I was willing to brush near, but not to pass over. I'd had plenty of opportunity. Most of the things in the hard case were exactly that kind of opportunity. Those talismans and weapons could have given me power, but power that would have left me less than human. Some things just weren't worth it.

I lost concentration and the world spun in crazed circles. I careened into a wall and retched up bile. The sour taste of it made me want to retch again. I closed my eyes and managed to suppress the reflexive gagging. I spat a few times to clear the taste from my mouth and waited for my stomach to settle. I noticed that the corner of my mind that spent most of the day hounding me about time was silent. Or maybe the psychic noise just made it impossible to hear. I wasn't sure whether to find that annoying or a relief. I leaned my head against the wall. The surface was as cool as only earth-backed concrete can be cool.

I focused again, driving back the noise and the spinning with a monumental effort of will. Every action demanded more and more from me. Every movement was agony for my leg. Every breath sent fire across my lacerated stomach. By the time I got to Abby, I doubted I'd have anything left in me to fight with, let alone give a good showing of myself. *At least she won't die alone, thinking that no one even tried to help her*, I thought. That had to count for something in the big picture, didn't it? I pushed off the wall and staggered down the hall, every ounce of my concentration and will focused on staying upright. If I fell, I doubted I'd ever get back to my feet.

After I went another five or ten feet down the hall, the psychic noise went up another notch and I froze in place. It just hurt. It didn't hurt in the intense but localized way the cuts or the burn hurt. It hurt everywhere, through every molecule of my body, through every fiber of my heart, and it hurt straight through the core of my soul. It wasn't a sound. It was pain. It was the residual pain of something so huge, so vast, that the echo of it rendered me barely coherent. It was a sense-memory never meant to be processed by a human consciousness and it threatened to tear me

apart. Then, I heard something even worse. I heard Abby screaming in pain.

Say what you like about the human species. We are a sad,
flawed, selfish species with an almost unlimited ability to lie to
ourselves about the consequences of our choices. We talk a good
game about ethics and morality, but most of us are really just
interested in christening things we don't like as wrong. We pol-
lute our world, mistreat our fellow human beings, and generally
act like miserable assholes for no good reason. But beneath all
that shit, we are hardwired as pack animals. We are built to defend our young with a profound disregard for our own safety or
whether the fight can be won.

Intentional or not, proximity to the echo of that primordial
pain stripped me down to the point where a fixation on reaching
my goal was about the only conscious thought left in my head.
My *undermind*, as Cavanaugh would put it, was doing most of
the heavy lifting. Abby's scream triggered that protective instinct
in me the way it might trigger an instinct in a jungle predator.
Singularity of purpose took over then. Not the single-mindedness
that one associates with a zealot or that odd breed known collec-
tively as geniuses. It was something far deeper and deadlier, a
psychological and emotional state that belonged to the world of
prehistory, where life-and-death struggles were the status quo.

The psychic noise didn't go away; the sensation of the world
spinning didn't let go, so much as they both ceased to matter to
me. Once they ceased to matter, they ceased to plague me. From
that moment on, my conscious was riding shotgun and taking
notes while the undermind took the wheel for a bit. I straightened
up and purposefully limped the last few steps, grabbing the first
heavy thing to come to hand. I shoved through a door, the one
that seemed closest to where the scream came from, and looked
around.

It wasn't a huge room, but it had been emptied. My conscious mind wondered if it had always been empty, but the undermind ignored it. On the far side of the room, Abby was on the
floor, back against the wall. She had her knees pulled up and her
arms covered her head protectively. I snarled at that sight. The
child was in danger. Things needed to be done. Between me and
her, I saw the inky black thing of my nightmares. I was aware of
the power it held, pulsing, writhing power that set my teeth on
edge. That was the problem. That was what threatened the child.

If my conscious mind possessed any influence at that moment, it might have advised a different course of action.

Despite all the things the subconscious does for people, giving them intuitions, sending dreams, sparking ideas, it is not naturally suited to developing strategy. As my conscious mind screamed in impotent warning, my undermind sent me directly at the inky demon, heavy object in hand. It turned and looked at me. I expected it to recoil or express anger or to charge at me. Instead, I got the vaguest sense of annoyance and a sliver of curiosity from it. Then I hit it in the head with what turned out to be a full gallon of interior latex paint.

The sum total effect of this brute-force physical assault was a dented can. The demon's head didn't move as much as a millimeter. I sensed that its annoyance deepened. My conscious mind was still screaming, telling me to get the fuck back from that thing, while my undermind, grand strategist that it was, told my arm to take another swing with the can. The can swung through the air, hit the inky head with a dull *thunk*, and developed a second dent. The top flew off the can at that point and a particularly gloomy shade of gray paint splattered the demon. I caught some of it. Unlike the paint on the demon, the paint on me did not bubble, hiss and then vanish. There was a lone spark of anger from the demon and instantaneous agony turned the world white in front of my eyes.

There was a patchy montage of images and sensations after that. I remember seeing, but not hearing, Abby scream as the demon picked me up and hurled me at the wall. I remember hearing bones crack when I hit. There was a blurry stretch of gray. I saw Abby try to get to me and I got to hear her screaming that time. She wasn't even trying to form words. It was noises of anguish and emotional torment. The kinds of sounds someone makes when they've been pushed beyond some edge of sanity. There was more gray, then Abby was pressed hard against the wall, the demon towering over her. I felt its cold, clear intention to kill her and its impatience for the time to be right. It hurt to see her like that. It also hurt to twitch.

I think everyone likes to believe that when it all falls apart, they'll rise above. They'll be more noble, more self-sacrificing, simply *better* than they are the rest of the time. Maybe I even believed that too, a little bit, but it's easy to think that when things continue trucking along without much in the way of a crisis. I'd met the crisis, done what I could to avert it, and I'd failed. There was no shame in it. You don't win every fight. I don't win every fight, anyway.

Maybe if I'd been smarter than I was, or stronger, I might have pulled out some kind of victory. Maybe if I'd been purer of heart, or simply less afraid of my failings, I could have reached deep and wielded power the way Helena did. I was just me, though, and I was tired. I was cold. I was hurting in ways I'd never imagined possible. As I lay there, blood trickling from my wounds into a pool beneath me, I missed Marcy on a scale that I had not experienced since the night she died. I didn't want to fight anymore. I didn't want to hear Abby's screams of terror and pain. I just wanted to close my eyes and let it all go. So I did. Everything went still, black and quiet.

Chapter 48

"BABY, YOU NEED TO OPEN YOUR EYES," said a voice.

The words were soft, gentle, but I heard the undercurrent of urgency. Not just urgency, there was also fear.

"Adrian, please, you need to open your eyes."

It took effort. It was so hard to open my eyes. I realized that it wasn't just that it was hard. I didn't want to open my eyes. I knew that, if I did, hurt and obligation would follow in its wake. I fought. I failed. Wasn't it enough that I fought? That I had suffered in the final moments? Why wasn't that enough? A cynical portion of me that I think of as Mr. Self-Hatred answered the question. *When is it ever enough?* I pushed open my eyes, fighting overwhelming fatigue and the desire to keep them closed. Marcy crouched over me. I looked around the room.

I saw the inky black figure of the demon towering over Abby. Unbidden, a memory rose up of Tucker Smith on the floor, his head beaten to a bloody mass. I pushed the memory away as hard as I could. I kept looking around. I saw the unbridled fear on Abby's face and her body locked into some kind of stasis. Nothing in the room moved. No breath, no screams, no mind-blistering noise from the netherspaces. Nothing at all. I looked back at Marcy.

"What's happening?" I asked.

"You're dying," she said, then frowned. "No, you're choosing to die. It's not quite the same."

"I lost. It won. Dying is what happens next."

Marcy shook her head. "No. It's what you decided happens next. You can't make this choice."

I started to close my eyes.

Marcy slapped me across the face. "Stop it!"

Anger flared somewhere deep inside me. "What the hell, Marcy?"

"I knew you were no saint, but I never realized how god-damned selfish you were."

Disbelief washed through me. "Selfish?"

Marcy swept her arm around the room. "This fight isn't over yet! If you decide to quit now and die, that girl will die. Then anyone left in the building. Then everyone in the town. You will be damned for that choice. You will burn for it!"

I let out a bitter snarl. "God would condemn me for that?"

She closed her eyes. "No, you will. You'll do it to yourself. You'll do it because you'll know what I know. You had strength and power left in you. You'll know you could have bought Abby a few more seconds or minutes. Maybe you could even buy her enough time for help to arrive. It will haunt you. You'll carry that guilt into your next life. You'll punish yourself for it. It's who you are."

I wanted to scream at her to leave me alone. I wanted her to be wrong. I wanted to rest. Except, I knew she was right. I hadn't played the game to the end. I'd quit at the final hand, without laying all my cards down. I might still fail. Hell, I probably would still fail, but that was a failure I could live or, perhaps, die with, and keep a clear conscience.

"I miss you," I whispered. "I miss you so much it's like being on fire."

She smiled and leaned down to me. She kissed me on the lips. It conveyed so much that, in hindsight, I knew it had been more than a kiss. It had been some kind of psychic transference. There was nothing like a thought in it, just a wellspring of love, soothing feelings, and, in some way, she shined a spotlight on the strength that I had left. It was more than I thought was there, or maybe it was there because she believed it was there. She drew back, her hair brushing my face, and smiled again. The truth in Cavanaugh's words became apparent. I did *not* understand the nature of my and Marcy's relationship. She should not have been able to do what she just did. It wasn't unlikely or improbable or odd. It was, end of statement, impossible for a spirit to reach out and touch the living that way.

"You'll see me again, soon enough. Now go and help her."

My eyes snapped open and the room was in motion again. The cacophony of netherworld noise crashed down on my mind and I shoved it away with a mental effort. I heard Abby vacillate between screams and whimpers. That same paternal instinct that had kept me in the town, led me to risk angelic script, brought me to the very doorstep of the inky black nightmare, exploded into blinding white fury. I rolled onto to my stomach. I did my best to ignore the puddle of my own blood that squelched beneath my hand and the unpleasant grating sound of my ribs. Oh, and blinding flashes of pain, let's not forgot those. I pushed myself up to my feet, but even the fury roiling in me couldn't wholly overcome blood loss and my injuries. I swayed and staggered a little, but managed to stay up.

"Hey," I said. "I'm not done with you yet, prick."

The inky form whirled toward me and I could sense its shock. It had thought I was dead. It was probably right. I had a suspicion that maybe I had been dead, at least for a second or two. That didn't matter, though. I was alive and Abby was alive. Abby's head swung toward me, her face shocked and suffused with sudden hope. God, I wanted to deliver on that hope. I thought about smiling at her, but I could taste the blood in my mouth. It'd probably just scare her even more. I settled for giving her a little nod.

"Hang in there, kid," I said.

Maybe I couldn't save her, but I could still buy her some time. I slid a hand around to my back pocket and wrapped bloodied fingers around the handle of the kris knife. Mere contact with it made my skin crawl. Like so much else, using the knife was a calculated risk. I didn't think I could kill the demon with it. I smiled. It'd be enough for me just to hurt it. The inky figure came at me with impossible speed. Demon Tucker had blurred, but was visible. The inky thing moved so fast that I couldn't distinguish it. I heard the impact of my body against the wall a moment before the pain slammed home. The demon had its left hand wrapped hard around my throat and the pressure grew steadily. The blood pounded in my skull as my brain fought a losing battle for oxygen.

I waited for the demon to start gloating or to toss off a comment about how it was going to kill me for certain this time, but it didn't. Maybe it missed that day of bad guy training. Maybe it was just smart enough not to bother. I slid the knife out of its sheath and slammed it into the demon's chest. It screamed in pain and bounced my head off the wall. I lost time there. When I managed to focus my eyes, the demon had yanked the knife free and tossed it aside. My vision was closing in around the edges, going dark and tunnel-like.

"You wish to trade pain, mortal," it said, finally engaging. "Then let us trade pain."

It drew its right hand back and slammed it into my chest. I think its goal was to plunge its inky claws into my sternum, but that's not quite what happened. Its fingertips sank all of a quarter inch into my skin, which hurt so much that I couldn't even scream. Imagine being stabbed with red hot metal, getting stung by a thousand wasps, breaking every rib at the same time, having dull razor blades scraped across every inch of your skin, slamming your hand in a car door, and having a mad dentist go to work on your teeth without giving you Novocain. Multiply that by a factor of about fifty million or so and that might, sort of, approach what it felt like to have those black talons sunk a quarter-inch into my chest. If it had managed to sink them any deeper than that, I expect the pain would have killed me on the spot.

Instead, I felt a blossom of cold on my chest exactly where one of the tattoos was located. Silver-blue light erupted from beneath my shirt. The demon screamed, let go of my throat, and yanked its hand back from my chest. Silver-blue fire engulfed the demon's hand and, I couldn't believe my eyes, simply ate the appendage as if it had been dipped in acid. The fire started crawling up the arm and the demon's shrieks rose in pitch until I could no longer physically hear them, but the sound cut across my skull like a smoldering blade.

In its position, I don't know that I could have done what the demon did, even if I had the strength. It seized its right arm at the bicep with its left hand and, with a wet, popping sound that was sure to haunt my dreams for ages, ripped the limb off and tossed it to the floor. Within moments, the limb was burned into nothing but memory. The demon turned its eyeless gaze on me, as anger and fear and disbelief washed over my psyche.

I flashed onto the image of a woman with raven-black hair, cold eyes, and a warm smile. Her face was my only memory from the night I'd been scarred and tattooed. I didn't know her, but she knew me. Her eyes fixed on mine and, for a moment, it felt like my entire being was pushed aside and someone else used my eyes. The sensation faded, but I saw her throw her head back and laugh. It was a terrible thing, her laugh. I realized that laugh was echoing through the room and the demon recoiled from it, fell to the floor, and used its one arm to drag itself away from me, or the laugh, or both.

A basic rule of engagement, whether you've taken a captive or are trying to retrieve one, is to keep track of said captive. The inky demon was fixated on me, and I was in such a state of stupefied disbelief, that nobody paid attention to Abby. Abby, on the other hand, had paid very close attention to where the knife went. Maybe it was when the demon was hurting me, or maybe it was when the tattoo set fire to the demon, but Abby had grabbed the awful blade. Needless to say, there was a lot of shock in the room when she flung herself at the demon.

Abby didn't have much in the way of form. She had, however, spent the day being terrorized by that thing. She made up for inexperience with hateful enthusiasm. I was a little bit proud. She stabbed it repeatedly, eliciting mind-piercing screams from the monster. Unfortunately, she had no way to know the knife just wasn't powerful enough to kill it. She hurt it plenty, but the demon managed to get around the binding enough to toss her, knife still clutched in hand, about six feet. She didn't hit the wall or land as hard as I did, but it clearly hurt her.

"Abby," I croaked. It hurt to talk. "Come over here."

The demon's fury was palpable, almost crippling in its intensity. Things hadn't gone its way. Now Abby was armed with something that could hurt it, and semi-protected by the binding. It had taken a shot at me and paid for it with an arm. It couldn't know that I had no clue how that happened or how to make it happen again. Abby looked at me with pain-befuddled eyes, and I could see she didn't understand.

"Abby," I croaked with all the authority I could muster. "Come here."

She struggled to her feet and made her way toward me. If all of that had happened a minute sooner, we might have gotten away clean. The inky demon's fury changed to something vaguely smug. There was that same, impossible, space-ignoring speed and the demon ripped the knife out of Abby's hand. I watched in horror and with no tricks left in my bag as the demon hefted the knife and prepared to kill Abby.

The truth hit me. Night had fallen. I stumbled toward them, knowing I'd never cover the distance in time. I think I screamed.

Chapter 49

SOMETHING A BLINDING, IRIDESCENT WHITE exploded to life between Abby and the knife. The demon howled in frustration and slashed with no effect at the white light. More of the lights exploded into life around the room, leaving me all but blind with purple splotches in my eyes. Their arrival also lifted that nausea-inducing, world-spinning echo of pain from my mind. The exit of that pressure was such sweet relief that the physical pain I was in seemed almost negligible, but I knew that couldn't last. I staggered toward Abby and came up against a solid barrier. Whatever the lights were, they were making sure nothing could get at Abby. That also meant that Abby was stuck.

My overtaxed brain finally made the connection. Helena had done it. These were the souls that the demon had trapped. It wasn't working out the way I expected. They were inhibiting the demon, but not attacking it. I'd just assumed they would, or would at least act to let me get Abby out, but neither of those things was happening.

"Let me get to her, dammit," I screamed at the blinding lights.

They ignored me. I tried to figure out why. Why weren't they attacking the stupid demon? After all this time, they should want some epic-level vengeance on that thing. If they weren't taking it, it meant they probably couldn't do more than what they were already doing. They could keep it off Abby, but if they lightened up that interference, it would probably get at her. They needed a channel, I realized, just as that demon needed Tucker to work its power in the world. I almost yelled for them to use me, but I stopped myself. I wasn't sure if they could use me. Whatever magic in the tattoos had lashed out at the demon with such fiery results might also harm the souls. That only left one other choice.

"Abby!" I screamed. "Let them in! Take down your walls and let them in!"

Aside from my own prayer that I hadn't just advised Abby to participate in lobotomizing herself, the next few moments were hard to comprehend. One second there were hundreds of those iridescent lights crowding into the room; the next, everything went black. Everything didn't really go black. There were still lights on in the room, but the illumination shift was simply too monumental and fast for my eyes to adapt. I didn't see much of anything except lots of purple blotches for about ten seconds. By the time my vision started to come back in, Abby was standing in perfect stillness, head down. The inky demon was standing just as still. The big difference was that I could feel the uncertainty in the demon. I couldn't feel anything from Abby. I guess the demon decided to try its luck while the trying was good. It leapt forward, swinging the knife toward Abby's throat.

"No," said Abby, with a negligible twitch of her head.

I realized that the voice I heard wasn't really Abby's. It came from Abby's general vicinity and probably from her lips, but it wasn't Abby. At least, it wasn't the Abby I had played cards with or helped get clear of a fire. The first clue I had was the way that lone syllable felt like a gong resounding in my chest. The second way I knew was that the knife was ripped from the demon's hand, taking several inky fingers off on the way. It flew across the room and hovered in front of me until I took it. When Abby finally looked up at the demon, her eyes were that same blinding, iridescent white that the lights had been. Her skin was luminous and the demon fell back from her. She advanced on it, with measured steps.

"Sad little remnant," she said.

With every resounding syllable, fragments of the demon flew outward from it and evaporated into nothing. I stared in disbelief. My best shot, apparently arranged by someone I couldn't remember, had cost it an arm. Abby's mere spoken word was dismantling the thing. That was power of a kind that made me want to run away in blank terror. Instead, I stood rooted to the spot in mute, horrified fascination.

"Millions of years, wasted in pointless hate," she said, still advancing, as more pieces of the demon flew off. "Trapped here, you imagined, by the vindictiveness of your God."

Pieces flew away from the demon even when she wasn't speaking, as if the thing could no longer hold itself together. The power of her words and her presence was starting to make me feel drunk. Was it some kind of contact high? Was proximity to things that powerful just plain dangerous for mortals? Jesus, what was it doing to Abby's mind? Had I killed her?

"Had you but thought for a moment, you would have realized the truth. You could have left here any time."

"Lies!" the increasingly insubstantial demon howled.

"No. It was not your God who bound you here, but your hate. If you had abandoned hate, you could have gone home. Now, you will simply *cease*."

With that, Abby reached out and pressed her index finger against the demon's chest. There was a sense of compression, as if all the air in the room were drawn in by huge lungs. The demon shuddered and then exploded. Pieces of it went everywhere, some evaporating immediately, others traveling inches or feet, and one passed directly through me. There was a flash of knowledge. I saw the huge statue Lil had shown me and understood that it had not been a metaphor. It was a literal truth. That statue had existed, had been alive in some way that I'd never grasp. It came to blows with whatever god it worshipped, for reasons I'd also never grasp. The statue lost that argument.

How powerful, how nigh omnipotent must that statue have been for fragmentary ghosts of its existence to prove so unbelievably powerful? More troubling still, how much more powerful was the thing that destroyed it? I shuddered at the thought, and found myself rather grateful that I understood less about the universe than I thought I did. I looked up to see Abby staring at me with the iridescent white eyes. It was scary as hell. She held her hands out to both sides, fingers spread like fans and the light expanded out from her eyes.

I experienced another hazy gray spot, not from pain, but simple sensory overload. When the gray cleared out, I saw Abby slumped to the floor. I tried to run to her, but my leg threatened to give out and I went dizzy with pain and fatigue. I limped to her, lowered myself into an unsteady crouch, and turned her head. She blinked up at me with unfocused eyes. Her head lolled from side to side.

"Abby, can you hear me?"

She blinked a few more times, eyes still bleary. *Jesus*, I thought, *it fried her*. Her eyes snapped into focus. She grabbed my arm hard.

"They asked me to say, thank you," she went a little out of focus, then zeroed in on me again. "They said you need to get to the cemetery."

Fear washed over me. "Helena."

If I was a real tough guy, or some kind of movie hero, I'd have carried Abby out of that building. Since I wasn't those things, I needed her to help me limp my sorry, bleeding ass up those stairs and out to the car. I was very tempted to tell her to drive, but thought better of it. She'd probably never driven anything more complicated than a bumper car. Or a horse, I reminded myself. Abby huddled in the passenger seat and shivered. I hadn't expected to survive, let alone get her out, so I didn't have any of things I'd normally bring to a violent scene. Things like first aid gear, food, or blankets. I turned up the heat as we drove, though it didn't seem to help much with her shivering. I felt cold too, but that was probably blood loss. That thought triggered something in the back of my head, a vague nagging.

Every mile or so, Abby whipped her head around until she saw me. That seemed odd to me, until I realized she was probably dozing off. Sleep, I thought. I could sleep. I was so tired. I remembered that I needed to get to the cemetery. Helena and Patty were there. They might be hurt. I managed not to crash the car on the way to the cemetery. Once we were there, I just sat in the car, staring out at the graves through the cast iron gate.

"Cemetery," I said.

"What?" Abby screamed, jerking awake.

I blinked and tried to arrange my thoughts. "Why are we here?"

Abby squinted at me, frowning hard, like she was struggling to remember something. "They, the others, they said you needed to come here. Is someone here?"

It came back. "Helena!"

I got out of the car and stumbled toward the gate. I ran into it, jerked it open and staggered in the general direction of Cavanaugh's tomb. The door was open and I saw a light moving around inside. I tripped up the steps and stared around the empty space, wild eyed and barely sane. I saw Helena on the ground.

Patty was kneeling next to her, finger against the side of Helena's throat.

"Is she alive?" I demanded.

"Yes," said Patty. "Abby?"

"In the car," I mumbled.

'Oh thank god! I think Helena needs to get to the hospital. Does she have anyone we should call?"

"Yeah," I said, my voice tinny to my own ears. "Her girl-friend, Laurie."

"Okay. I'll see to it. I have to say, Hartworth—" she said, swinging the flashlight onto me.

A voice from a long way away said something like, "God damn it, Hartworth!"

I felt a sensation like falling, only I didn't land on the marble floor. I landed on the beach. I lay with my face in the warm sand and tried to figure out what happened.

"So you saved the girl."

I pushed myself up and brushed some of the fine grain of sand off my face. A barefoot man of indeterminate race stood there in white slacks and a white shirt. I glanced around, not sure what to make of the scene. I nodded to him.

"I guess I did. Sort of. Abby and Helena did all the heavy lifting. I was just the distraction."

The man shot me a curious look, as though he didn't quite believe what he heard.

"What?" I demanded.

"It's a remarkably narrow view of events. You facilitated everything. You determined the nature of the threat. You secured the knowledge regarding the smoke bindings. You drew someone who possessed the ability to release them. You eliminated the minor demon. You even told the child how to use the weapon you provided. Perhaps it was you who did the heavy lifting, and they merely enacted your will to save her."

I stared up the man with absolutely nothing to say. I guess it happened to everyone sooner or later. Finally, I shrugged. "So, why am I here?"

The man shot me another curious look. "You seek answers to universal questions?"

"Definitely not. I just got an answer to a question I didn't know I had and it scares the hell out of me. I meant why here, in this place, where we are right now?"

"Ah. So I could meet you again under less dire circumstances. Also, because she asked me for it," he said, pointing down the beach.

I looked past him and saw Marcy walking toward us. What he said sank in. "Wait, when did we meet before?"

The man smiled at me and vanished. Words echoed from nowhere.

"Work on your grammar."

"Holy shit," I said to no one in particular.

Marcy walked up and sat beside me. We held hands for a long time. After a while, a question surfaced from the recesses of my mind.

"So, Cavanaugh told me I didn't understand the nature of this relationship. You shouldn't have been able to—" I frowned, "touch my consciousness the way you did."

"Plenty of mysteries in the world," she said. Her tone was cheerfully cryptic.

"I'm serious," I insisted. "What don't I know?"

She looked at me and started to speak, but stopped. She shook her head. "I can't."

"It's one of *those* things, isn't it?"

"Yes," she said.

My *life* had just moved into the category of things that the dead know but can't communicate. Lovely. I was quite certain no good could come of that.

Chapter 50

I DID NOT WAKE UP DEAD. I wished I had, but the doctors assured me that I was, indeed, going to make it. One doctor cheerfully told me that it took stitches in the high double-digits to put me back together. Another gravely warned me that that I had eight cracked ribs and, in combination with my still-recovering lungs, breathing was going to be a chore for some time. Most of my first day or two was spent in a chemical-induced, euphoric haze. I'd have to be careful not to get too used to that feeling. That haze did account for why I had no idea how Lil appeared on my hospital bed. I never got a clear explanation as to why the nurses didn't demand she be removed. Self-preservation instinct, I expect.

On the third or fourth day, Laurie came storming into my hospital room. She was a little heavier than I remembered, a little more careworn, and there were bags under her eyes in an ugly shade of blue. Other than that, she looked like the same woman I'd met in Chicago years ago. She was tall for a woman, with long chestnut hair, and spooky dark eyes. She'd disliked me on sight, for reasons she never bothered to articulate. I'd expected some kind of scene from her, but I hadn't expected it while I was in the middle of getting my bandages changed.

"I warned you, you bastard," she said, yanking back the curtain.

She stopped in her tracks and stared at me. It wasn't a pretty sight. Between Demon Tucker and his inky master, I was more bruise than man and the bruises were held together with stitches. I'd gotten a lot more banged up than I first thought. There were cuts all over my arms, some on my face, and I doubted my ribs would ever stop hurting. I'd broken a finger somewhere along the way. I supposed it was an indication of how badly I was hurt that I hadn't even registered those injuries at the time. Laurie's hand dropped from the curtain and the nurse gave her a baleful glare. Lil made an unfriendly noise from the chair she was curled up in. Laurie looked at the cat and went a ghostly shade of pale.

"Ma'am, you'll have to wait until I'm done here," said the nurse.

"It's alright," I said. "She's an old friend."

Laurie shook her head a little and her cold fury thawed a lot. "I was going to snap your neck, but, but my god, what happened to you? It looks like you got hit by a truck."

"Felt like that too. It's a long story. We should be done here in—" I looked at the nurse, "twenty minutes, do you think?"

The nurse gave Laurie another poisonous stare. "I expect so."

Half an hour later, I was sitting uncomfortably in Helena's room. Laurie was holding Helena's hand while the monitors gave off steady beeps and tweets and sounded generally non-alarming. I'd tuned out for a second and made myself pay attention.

"They say it's not a coma," said Laurie. Her voice shook a little. "They say it's like she's stuck in some kind of really deep REM sleep."

"They can't wake her up?"

"They're afraid to try. They said they could give her stimulants to try to snap her out of it, but since they don't know what's causing this, they don't want to rush into anything. They've run about a million scans of her head, and they keep testing her blood for increasingly exotic viruses and parasites. Things she could only have gotten if she was nude diving in Indonesia while simultaneously having sex with a South American pig; that kind of rare. I keep telling them she hasn't even been out of the country in the last year."

She went on like that for a while, dumping days of pent-up grief and frustrations on me because I was there and, in her mind, responsible for Helena's condition. I wasn't sure I disagreed. After a while, she wound down and asked the hard question again.

"What happened?"

"I need coffee for this," I said. "Would you mind?"

"Of course I mind, you asshole."

I didn't rise to the bait. I started to push myself up out of the chair. I needed caffeine. If she wasn't getting coffee, it was up to me. She apparently replayed the last few seconds of the conversation and looked over at me, struggling to stand up. Her face went a little pink and then a little pale.

"Sit down," she said. "I'll get the coffee. It's just, it's really hard not to hate you."

"You know," I said, in a bout of suicidal bravery, "I never did you a wrong turn. Why the hell do you hate me so much?"

"Other than this?" She said, waving her free hand at Helena's still form.

"Yes, other than that. You never liked me. I have no idea why."

She fixed her spooky dark eyes on me, and I felt like a bit like a teenager about to be taken to task for something. The muscles in her jaw worked a few times.

"I don't know," she admitted. "I honestly don't know. From the second I saw you, I just wanted to throttle the life out of you. You're trouble. When you aren't busy being trouble, you're busy getting into it. You've left a lot of bodies in your wake."

"That isn't fair," I said.

She held up a hand. "I know you didn't kill most of them. I know you do your best to avoid those kinds of situations, but they're still dead and there you sit. Battered and bruised, I'll grant you, but alive. So tell me, why is it that you're there, alive, conscious to have this conversation, and Helena is lost somewhere. Does that seem right to you? Does that seem fair? What have you ever done to deserve to live more than her?"

"Not a damn thing that I know of," I said. "But before you get too far down this it's-all-Adrian's-fault line of thinking, you should get that coffee and listen to a story."

Laurie got us coffee and she listened to the story. I didn't tell her everything because I didn't have the stamina for that, but I told her enough to get an accurate picture. It still took a while. She listened without comment until I wound down.

"And then you burst into my hospital room to brain me with extreme prejudice," I finished, a little hoarse from talking for so long.

She was very quiet. "The whole town?"

"Yeah," I said. "Helena didn't do this for me. She did it because a whole lot of people were going to die. She did it because the murder of a fifteen-year-old girl was going to trigger the whole thing. She decided that trying to help those people was more important than her life," I said. "And she did it over my objections."

Laurie gave me a disbelieving look. "You didn't mention that."

"It's a long story. I edited some to keep it manageable. Hate me because reasons, if you must, but stop acting like I'm a havoc engine that gets people killed."

I said that last with enough conviction that someone else might even believe it, even if I wasn't precisely convinced. I rubbed at an aching spot on the back of my head, winced, and carried on. "I don't engineer situations to get people hurt. I'm sorry that Helena is in this condition. I'm not sorry that girl and everyone else in this town is alive. Helena wouldn't be sorry, either."

Laurie looked down at Helena's still form. "No, she wouldn't be sorry."

"Mind if I ask you something?"

One of her shoulders twitched a little, so I took it as permission.

"You must have sensed that she was in danger. Frankly, I half-expected you to come charging in here days ago to drag Helena away. Why didn't you?"

Laurie's face was carved bitterness. "She wouldn't tell me where she was going, because it was you."

She didn't elaborate, so I limped away, because limping is the best you can do with dozens of stitches holding your leg together. As I did, I thought I heard Laurie say something under her breath.

"It's always you."

I almost turned back, but thought better of it. I left her there to think whatever she wanted to think.

Abby was a daily presence, bringing food, games, or just being around to break up the monotony of the day. Lil took up semi-permanent residence in Abby's lap, implicitly declaring Abby one of the special people. She didn't talk about what happened. I didn't press her. Some things need to settle for a while. Paul stopped in one afternoon and sat by my bed. He was in regular clothes, but he still had the hospital vibe around him.

"Patty says you wound up like this saving my girl, again," commented Paul.

I shrugged. "It was a crazy day. Lots of people helped her."

He looked down at the floor. "Nobody else had to kill a man to help her, though."

I thought about telling Paul the truth right then and there, but the old man wouldn't believe it. He was a good man. He loved his granddaughter enough to attack a man half his age with a fireplace poker. I just knew that his mind wasn't flexible in the right ways. I frowned and nodded. There might still be a way to ease his mind.

"He'd lost his mind," I said. "Complete gibbering insanity. He didn't give me any other options."

Paul considered this for a moment and his back straightened a little. He looked at me again. "It was a hell of a thing you did for us. If you ever need anything, and I mean anything, you say the word."

"Just keep taking care of Abby. She's a good kid and that's all because of you. Between us," I said conspiratorially, "I think her life will get a lot easier from here on in."

He raised a bushy eyebrow at me. "You know something I don't know?"

"Call it an intuition."

Paul gave me a little smile, then frowned. "Helena still hasn't woken up from that coma thing they insist isn't a coma. They have any notion when she'll come out of it?"

I loved Paul for saying "when," and not "if."

"No. I'm pretty sure they've abandoned all currently known medicine and are scouring science fiction novels for ideas."

"She'll probably come out of it on her own," Paul suggested, trying to sound optimistic.

"Probably so," I agreed.

Or, I thought, *maybe someone will help her along.*

I'd explained to Abby what I thought had happened to Helena. My theory was that she'd managed to avoid the worst of the backlash, but the raw strain of undoing that many bindings taxed her beyond her limits. Her mind acted in self-defense and dropped Helena into a sleep state to give her time to recover. Only, the sleep state was so deep that Helena couldn't find her way back to the waking world.

"I think you can help her," I told Abby.

The girl looked green around the gills. "I don't—I want to help. I do! I don't really understand how it works yet. I don't want to do something wrong and make her worse."

The kid looked miserable. I felt for her. "Abby, I won't try to make you do it. If you don't think you should, then that's the end of the story. But, I don't think you'll hurt her. You aren't trying to rewire her brain or make her think anything she doesn't already think. You'd be more like a lighthouse."

"A lighthouse?"

"Yeah, lighthouses let ships know where the coast is, so they don't crash. In this case, though, you'd be helping Helena get close enough to shore to find it on her own. I think she's just too far out to sea right now."

"You really think I won't hurt her?"

"As long as you don't change anything around in there, no, I don't think you will."

Abby proved to be a hell of a lot smarter than I was at fifteen. She thought about it for two days before she decided.

"I'll try," she said. "But I want you to be there. She knows you. She trusts you."

I doubted that last part. It seemed a lot more plausible that Abby wanted me there because *she* trusted me, rather than Helena trusting me. Still, if it got the job done, I'd stand in the corner. "Okay."

What I hadn't accounted for was Laurie. She had some rather pointed thoughts on that matter.

"Absolutely not," she said, glaring at me.

"Why not?"

Laurie stabbed a finger at Helena's still form. "Because every time Helena gets involved in some plan of yours, something like this happens!"

"I'm trying to make it right."

"Make it right? You want me to let some *child* go digging around inside Helena's head. Use your brain, Hartworth. That's never going to happen."

"That *child* has endured more pain and suffering than you, me, and Helena combined. That *child* vaporized a demon that tossed me around like a rag doll. That *child*..."

Somewhere along the way, Laurie and I had both forgotten Abby was standing there. We both remembered rather abruptly when she cut us off.

"Stop it!"

The words resonated inside my head. If I hadn't been on painkillers already, I'd probably have needed some after that. Laurie put a hand over her eyes like she'd gotten punched in the face. Abby fixed her gaze on Laurie. There was an audible hum in the air as something passed between the two. Laurie's hand dropped from her eyes, and she stared at Abby in something between shock and dismay. I have no idea what knowledge or imagery Abby transmitted in that moment, but it put a stop to all the objections.

From my perspective, it took Abby about fifteen minutes before Helena's eyes fluttered open. Based on what the two of them told me later, it was a subjective three-year journey. The mind is a strange place.

It took a while, but the doctors eventually conceded that they had no legitimate medical reason to hold Helena, other than not understanding why she fell into her not-coma or why she came out of it. Abby, Paul, and I went with her to the hospital lobby. There was a lot of hugging and a few tears shed, but it was agreed that Abby would visit with Helena and Laurie over the summer. I considered that a good thing for everyone concerned. I stepped outside with Helena while Laurie fetched the rental car they would take to the nearest airport. She didn't say anything for a minute, but leaned against my arm.

"You always did have a flair for the dramatic," she said. "Thanks for not dying."

I smiled. "Thanks for waking up."

Helena turned and gave my face a searching look before she hugged me. She was mindful of my cracked ribs, for which I was very grateful. She patted my cheek.

"I don't know what you said to her, but I think Laurie hates you even more than she did. So, don't call." She glanced through the window at Abby. "Unless you need to."

"I won't."

I waved as Helena and Laurie drove off. Once the doctors were sure that my injuries were just painful, rather than inclined to give me a lethal infection, they let me check out. I limped out the front door of the hospital, Lil cradled in one arm, and climbed into Patty's cruiser.

"You leaving us?" she asked, as she reached over and scratched Lil's ears.

"Are you kidding me? I need to get out of here before this place kills me."

She snorted. "You're such a crybaby, Hartworth. You've only had two near-death experiences here."

"I'm a weak, tender creature. Easily spooked."

"Fair enough. So, before you ride off into the sunset, mind if I ask you something?"

"Shoot."

"What did you do to my badge?"

I blinked in confusion. For about five seconds, I had no earthly idea what she was talking about. In my defense, a lot happened that day. It finally came back to me.

"Oh, that. I just made it what it already wanted to be."

"Which is?"

"A defensive symbol. I just upped the juice with a basic mirror spell. How did you know?"

She shrugged. "Magic."

I laughed. "Well played."

"At the graveyard, right after Helena said she was done, the badge glowed bright blue for a few seconds. I didn't feel anything, but I thought I'd ask."

"Think of it as adding a few extra layers of Kevlar to your bulletproof vest."

"Kevlar?"

"I read up."

She snorted. "Sure, *now* you read up. After you ogle my breasts."

"I knew that was going to bite me in the ass."

"Do you want to know what color my bra is today?"

"No."

"Liar," said Patty. "It's black."

"You're enjoying this aren't you?"

"It's lacy, too."

"Should I ask to see it?"

She frowned at me. "Ribs healed up yet?"

Gears crashed to a halt in my head. "Um, still mending."

"Too bad for you. Ask me next time."

Women confound me.

Chapter 51

I TOOK MY TIME DRIVING TO SEATTLE. There was no rush, no crisis, just time to kill. So, I killed time on my way. I stopped more often than I needed to stop. I wandered the occasional roadside attraction. I ate fruits and vegetables from stands along the side of the road. I fed Lil things that I probably shouldn't have, like bits of fast food hamburgers. She didn't mind at all.

I spent a lot of time considering Jeremy Barnes and his suicide. I'd been so rushed and afraid at the time that the wrongness of it didn't strike me until later. He and I were cut from similar cloth, even if his was a better quality of cloth. It wasn't that there was no circumstance that would make someone like me commit suicide, but I'd started doubting that putting a bullet in his own head was the way the sheriff would have chosen. If all hope was lost, he was the kind of guy to make a last stand. I wondered if Demon Tucker had gotten into Barnes' head, the same way he'd tried to get into mine. Lil's intervention and decades of experience were all that saved me. Barnes hadn't had the benefit of either of those things. I supposed I'd never know for sure.

I also thought about Paul and Abby. I'd stopped by before I left to see the work being done on their house. The insurance company had been inclined to declare the house a loss, but Paul pressed his case and they relented. There was something affirming about the buzz of activity around the house. The smell of fresh-cut lumber and the aggravated bellow of the construction crew supervisor suggested normalcy to me.

Abby came over to hug me. She held on a long time. I suspected she knew that it would be some time before she saw me again—if, that was, she ever did. She looked healthy, the weight going back on faster than I could have imagined, but she also looked haunted. It was to be expected. She'd seen things no one her age, or any age for that matter, should see. She channeled the collective will and power of hundreds of souls. It would leave a mark, probably for life.

"Grandpa says we'll get to move back in soon," said Abby.

"That's good. Are you excited?"

"I guess. It's hard to know what to think. I can—" she struggled for a second, "*feel* the house. I know it wants to protect me."

"Homes are like that," I said. "How are you doing with the other part?"

She looked down and away, her lower lip caught between her teeth. "Okay, I guess. It's hard sometimes, to keep it all out. Sometimes, it's hard not to peek. I think I want to know what people really think. Then, I wonder if I really want to know."

I nodded. "It's a tough line to tread. In my experience, though, it's easier not to know."

"It is?"

"Just because someone happens to think something, that doesn't mean it's what they believe in their hearts. We all think things and regret them, or change our minds later. We have impulses we don't act on, because they're wrong or rude. What matters is how people choose to act."

"Like choosing not to look?"

"For example."

"Are you ever going to come back here?"

There it was, the big question. I wanted to tell her the comforting lie, but it would have been wrong to do that on so many levels. I shrugged and tried to come up with something that at least resembled the truth.

"Honestly, I don't know. Probably not, at least, not unless you're in some kind of trouble."

"Why not?"

I checked a frustrated sigh. "I don't stay anywhere long. I'm not a nice person, all things considered. I've made enemies. If I stayed or came back very often, it'd make you a target. I won't put you in that kind of danger. You have enough challenges already, without adding my troubles."

Abby looked up at me, her brow furrowed in a way that made her seem decades older. *Marked*, I thought. *She's been marked.*

"That's not true," said Abby, with a quiet certainty that unnerved me. "The part about enemies and putting me in danger is, but not the other part. I don't remember everything about what happened at the school, especially at the end, but I remember one part. I saw you," she frowned. "No, I saw *into* you, I guess. You were ready to die to give me a chance to live."

I looked away at that. It was true enough, but made me sound nobler than I was. "It's more complicated than that."

She giggled. "No it isn't. Maybe you think it is, but it isn't. You did what you did because you cared."

She hugged me again. I hugged her back. She looked up at me, her eyes huge, and the scary grownup knowledge gone. She was just a kid right then.

"Will you at least come back at Christmas? It's just me and grandpa..." She trailed off when she saw the look on my face. "If you don't want to, it's cool. I get it."

Grown women have nothing on teenage girls for twisting the knife. What made it worse was that Abby was doing it in the least malicious and wholly unintentional way possible. She was trying to give me an out, without showing how much it would wound her if I didn't come through. I wondered how in the hell fathers exerted any kind of discipline on their daughters. No wonder moms got stuck with those duties. I'm not too proud to admit that I folded like a bad hand at a poker table.

"I think I can see my way to being here at Christmas. If your grandfather says it's okay."

"Really?"

"Yeah, really."

She turned and bolted toward the house at just short of the speed of sound. I heard her yelling, "Grandpa!"

I blinked after the teenage blur and snorted. I couldn't remember the last time something excited me that much. She came back out the front door, all but dragging Paul behind her. He saw me standing there and smiled. With the threat to Abby gone and the house being rebuilt, a mountain of fear and tension had lifted off the man. He still looked like a man in his sixties, but the kind of man who would stay vigorous and attentive to his grand-daughter well into his eighties.

"Adrian," said Paul, extending his hand to me. "Good to see you, son."

I took his hand. "Good to see you."

Abby looked back and forth between us. She bounced on her toes and then noticed she was bouncing. I saw her make a conscious effort to stop. As soon as she stopped concentrating on it, though, she was bouncing again.

"Didn't hear you pull in, what with all the noise inside," said Paul.

"Not a problem. The repairs going well?"

"Oh yes, even if the contractor keeps telling me it would be easier and cheaper to just tear the old girl down and start fresh."

I nodded. "So long as the work gets done, right?"

"Exactly," said Paul.

He was pretending not to notice Abby's impatience, but the sparkle in his eyes gave it away. He played it out like a pro, though.

"You going to be able to replace the antiques?" I asked.

"I expect I could, if it came right down to it. Might be time to try some new things. Been a while since I had the—" I saw him mentally cross off the word *time*, "interest to devote to decorating."

Abby's patience ran dry and she overflowed like a geyser, words tumbling out in a barely coherent amalgamation. "Grandpa, canMr.HartworthcomeforChristmas?"

I checked a smile before it could form. Paul, an old hand at parenting, gave the girl an appraising look. He appeared to ponder the question and dragged it out. It was almost mean.

"I don't know, Abby," he said. "Mr. Hartworth strikes me as a busy man. Doesn't seem right to pull him away from his life that way."

"He said he'd come, if you said it was okay!"

"Oh, well then, that's an entirely different story," he said, and gave me a wink Abby couldn't see. "I'm sure we can find another spot at the table come Christmas."

"Thank you, Grandpa!"

She threw her arms around the old man and the air actually whooshed out of him. He gave the girl an awkward, airless hug.

"Of course, you're welcome here at Christmas or any other time you'd care to stop by," he said to me.

I nodded. "Much appreciated. Christmas it is."

With nothing but time on my hands in the hospital, I'd dipped into the money the Twins had paid me to have the car I drove into town fixed. I'd also gotten every repair the Neon needed taken care of. Before I left, I gave Paul an envelope with the title and keys to the Neon. I told him I thought it'd make a good sixteenth birthday present for Abby.

I'd noticed somewhere on the way to Seattle that I was looking forward to going back to see them. I was planning gifts and mapping a strategy to ensure I wasn't occupied when the yuletide season rolled around. It comforted me to know I had somewhere to be at year's end. It gave me a reason to keep going.

I surreptitiously checked on my sister and her family. I decided they were doing well for themselves. Their house was in Laurelhurst, one of Seattle's more expensive neighborhoods, and they'd upgraded their minivan to a Lexus hybrid SUV. They all looked healthy and happy, in the distracted way that active, over-scheduled families always did to me. Maybe I was projecting, but I didn't think that was the case.

I followed the tug of a very old tracking spell north through the city, mostly sticking to Interstate 5. It drew me to the much less ritzy neighborhood of Lynnwood. The man I'd bound the tracking spell to had moved several times over the years, trying to avoid me and the reminder of past sins. I wasn't about to let that happen. I parked across the street from his house, a two-story affair with a front porch. It was modest, but tended. I watched a brunette woman with a liberal smattering of gray hair harangue a pair of teenage boys into a car. They drove away. I got out of my car, Lil in one arm, and eyed the house. In the past, I'd always stood across the street and let him see me. There was no talking, just the reminder that I could *always* find him. I felt different, though, as I looked at the house. I was angrier in some indefinite way. I crossed the street and checked the name on the mailbox. Then I climbed the steps and leaned next to the door. Lil jumped down and took up residence on the porch railing. About ten minutes later, Jack Reed came out the door.

His hair was completely gray and he leaned on a cane. He'd needed it for fifteen years. He was thinner than I remembered from a few years back. I wondered if he was working out or if he'd been sick. He wasn't looking around, just going about his daily routine. He locked the front door and turned toward the steps. He noticed Lil and gave her a bemused smile.

"Hey there, kitty," said Reed, taking a slow step and reaching out a hand toward her.

Lil directed one of her opaque kitty-cat expressions at him, but I could feel the utter malice radiating off her. Reed froze in place. I took the opportunity and cleared my throat. Reed whirled toward me. His bad leg didn't support the move well and he tipped to one side. He saw me and went ashen, raising a hand as if to ward off a blow. He tried to step back with a wordless noise of fear and went down in a heap. Reed started crawling backwards and slipped onto the steps. He kept moving down the steps, almost crab-walking, in an attempt to put some space between us. I took deliberate steps toward him, closing the distance until I towered over him. I frowned down at him. He whimpered and his bladder let go. We hadn't been this physically close since I crippled him.

"It's been a while, Jack. We should talk."

—THE END—

Adrian Hartworth will return, in

FAVORS GIVEN

Coming Summer 2019

Also by Eric Dontigney

The *Samuel Branch* Series
Falls
Turns
Rises

Contingency Jones: The Complete Season One

ERIC DONTIGNEY is the author of the *Samuel Branch* urban fantasy series, numerous short stories, and the short story collection, *Contingency Jones: The Complete Season One*. Raised in Western New York, he currently resides near Dayton, Ohio. You can find him haunting obscure sections of libraries, in Chinese restaurants, or occasionally online at ericdontigney.com.